The Young Castellan

A Tale of the English Civil War

by

George Manville Fenn

Double 9
BOOKS

The Young Castellan
A Tale of the English Civil War
by George Manville Fenn

Copyright © 2023

All Rights reserved.

ISBN: 978-93-60469-82-5

Published by

DOUBLE 9 BOOKS

2/13-B, Ansari Road
Daryaganj, New Delhi – 110002
info@double9books.com
www.double9books.com
Tel. 011-40042856

This book is under public domain

ABOUT THE AUTHOR

George Manville Fenn was a very productive author of novels, a writer, an editor, and an educator from England. He was born on January 3, 1831, in Pimlico, London. He mostly learned on his own; he taught himself Italian, French, and German. During the years 1851–1854, he went to Battersea Training College for Teachers and then became the head of a state school in Alford, Lincolnshire. In the early 1850s, Fenn started to write short stories and pieces for newspapers and magazines. The Old Forest Ranger, his first book, came out in 1856. Afterward, he wrote more than 100 books, many of them for teenagers and young adults. He was one of the most famous writers of his time, and his books were well-liked and read by many people. He also worked as a reporter and writer for Fenn. Among the newspapers and magazines, he worked for was The Boy's Own Paper, which he ran from 1866 to 1874. He worked hard to make children's books better and was a strong supporter of education and reading. The Englishman Fenn passed away on August 26, 1909, in Isleworth.

CONTENTS

Chapter One
In the Old Armoury

"See these here spots o' red rust, Master Roy?"

"I should be blind as poor old Jenkin if I couldn't, Ben."

"Ay, that you would, sir. Poor old Jenk, close upon ninety he be; and that's another thing."

"What do you mean?" said the boy addressed.

"What do I mean, sir? Why, I mean as that's another thing as shows as old England's wore out, and rustin' and moulderin' away."

"Is this Dutch or English, Ben?" said the manly-looking boy, who had just arrived at the age when dark lads get teased about not having properly washed the sides of their faces and their upper lips, which begin to show traces of something "coming up." "I don't understand."

"English, sir," said the weather-beaten speaker, a decidedly ugly man of about sixty, grizzly of hair and beard, deeply-lined of countenance, and with a peculiar cicatrice extending from the upper part of his left cheek-bone diagonally down to the right corner of his lips, and making in its passage a deep notch across his nose. "English, sir; good old honest English."

"You're always grumbling, Ben, and you won't get the rust off that morion with that."

"That I shan't, sir; and if I uses elber grease and sand, it'll only come again. But it's all a sign of poor old England rustin' and moulderin' away. The idea! And at a place like this. Old Jenk, as watch at the gate tower, and not got eyes enough to see across the moat, and even that's getting full o' mud!"

"Well, you wouldn't have father turn the poor old man away because he's blind and worn-out."

"Not I, sir," said the man, moistening a piece of flannel with oil, dipping it into some fine white sand, and then proceeding to scrub away at the rust spots upon the old helmet, which he now held between his knees; while several figures in armour, ranged down one side of the low, dark room in which the work was being carried on, seemed to be looking on and waiting to have their rust removed in turn.

"Then what do you mean?" said the boy.

"I mean, Master Roy, as it's a pity to see the old towers going down hill as they are."

"But they're not," cried the boy.

"Not, sir? Well, if you'll excuse me for saying as you're wrong, I'll say it. Where's your garrison? where's your horses? and where's your guns, and powder, and shot, and stores?"

"Fudge, then! We don't want any garrison nowadays, and as for horses, why, it was a sin to keep 'em in those old underground stables that used to be their lodging. Any one would think you expected to have some one come and lay siege to the place."

"More unlikely things than that, Master Roy. We live in strange times, and the king may get the worst of it any day."

"Oh, you old croaker!" cried Roy. "I believe you'd like to have a lot more men in the place, and mount guard, and go on drilling and practising with the big guns."

"Ay, sir, I should; and with a place like this, it's what ought to be done."

"Well, it wouldn't be bad fun, Ben," said the boy, thoughtfully.

"Fun, sir? Don't you get calling serious work like that fun.—But look ye there. Soon chevy these spots off, don't I?"

"Yes, it's getting nice and bright," said Roy, gazing down at the steel headpiece.

"And it's going to get brighter and better before I've done. I'm going to let Sir Granby see when he comes back that I haven't neglected nothing. I'm a-going to polish up all on 'em in turn, beginning with old Sir Murray Royland. Let me see: he was your greatest grandfather, wasn't he?"

"Yes, he lived in 1480," said the boy, as the old man rose, set down the morion, and followed him to where the farthest suit of mail stood against the wall. "I say, Ben, this must have been very heavy to wear."

"Ay, sir, tidy; but, my word, it was fine for a gentleman in those days to mount his horse, shining in the sun, and looking as noble as a man could look. He's a bit spotty, though, it's been so damp. But I'll begin with Sir Murray and go right down 'em all, doing the steeliest ones first, and getting by degrees to the last on 'em as is only steel half-way down, and the rest being boots. Ah! it's a dolesome change from Sir Murray to Sir Brian yonder at the end, and worse still, to your father, as wouldn't put nothing on but a breast-piece and back-piece and a steel cap."

"Why, it's best," said the boy; "steel armour isn't wanted so much now they've got cannon and guns."

"Ay, that's a sad come-down too, sir. Why, even when I was out under your grandfather, things were better and fighting fairer. People tried to see who was best man then with their swords. Now men goes to hide behind hedges and haystacks, to try and shoot you like they would a hare."

"Why, they did the same sort of thing with their bows and arrows, Ben, and their cross-bows and bolts."

"Well, maybe, sir; but that was a clean kind o' fighting, and none of your sulphur and brimstone, and charcoal and smoke."

"I say, Ben, it'll take you some time to get things straight. Mean to polish up the old swords and spears, too?"

"Every man jack of 'em, sir. I mean to have this armoury so as your father, when he comes back from scattering all that rabble, will look round and give me a bit of encouragement."

"Ha, ha!" laughed the boy; "so that's what makes you so industrious."

"Nay it aren't, sir," said the man, with a reproachful shake of his head. "I didn't mean money, Master Roy, but good words, and a sort o' disposition to make the towers what they should be again. He's a fine soldier is your father, and I hear as the king puts a lot o' trust in him; but it always seems to me as he thinks more about farming when he's down here than he does about keeping up the old place as a good cavalier should."

"Don't you talk a lot of nonsense," said Roy, hotly; "if my father likes to live here as country gentlemen do, and enjoy sport and gardening and farming, who has a better right to, I should like to know?"

"Oh, nobody, sir, nobody," said the man, scouring away at the rusted steel.

"And besides, times are altered. When this castle was built, gentlemen used to have to protect themselves, and kept their retainers to fight for them. Now there's a regular army, and the king does all that."

That patch of rust must have been a little lighter on, for the man uttered a low grunt of satisfaction.

"It would be absurd to make the towers just as they used to be, and shut out the light and cover the narrow slits with iron bars."

"Maybe, Master Roy; but Sir Granby might have the moat cleared of mud, and kept quite full."

"What! I just hope it won't be touched. Why, that would mean draining it, and then what would become of my carp and tench?"

"Ketch 'em and put 'em in tubs, sir, and put some little uns back."

"Yes, and then it would take years for them to grow, and all the beautiful white and yellow water-lilies would be destroyed."

"Yes; but see what a lot of fine, fat eels we should get, sir. There's some thumpers there. I caught a four-pounder on a night-line last week."

"Ah, you did, did you?" cried the lad; "then don't you do it again without asking for leave."

"All right, sir, I won't; but you don't grudge an old servant like me one eel?"

"Of course I don't, Ben," said the lad, importantly; "but the moat is mine. Father gave it to me as my own special fishing-place before he went away, and I don't allow any one to fish there without my leave."

"I'll remember, sir," said the man, beginning to whistle softly.

"I don't grudge you a *few* eels, Ben, and you shall have plenty; but next time you want to fish, you ask."

"Yes, sir, I will."

"And what you say is all nonsense: the place is beautiful as it is. Why, I believe if you could do as you liked, you'd turn my mother's pleasaunce and the kitchen-garden into drill-grounds."

"That I would, sir," said the man, flushing up. "The idea of a beautiful square of ground, where the men might be drilled, and practise with sword and gun, being used to grow cabbages in. Er! it's horrid!"

Roy laughed.

"You're a rum fellow, Ben," he cried. "I believe you think that people were meant to do nothing else but fight and kill one another."

"Deal better than spending all their time over books, sir," said the man; "and you take my advice. You said something to me about being a statesman some day, and serving the king that way. Now, I s'pose I don't know exactly what a statesman is, but I expect it's something o' the same sort o' thing as Master Pawson is, and—You won't go and tell him what I says, sir?"

"Do you want me to kick you, Ben?" said the boy, indignantly.

"Oh, I don't know, sir," said the man, with a good-humoured smile lighting up his rugged features; "can, if you like. Wouldn't be the first time by many a hundred."

"What! When did I kick you?"

"Lots o' times when you was a little un, and I wouldn't let you drown yourself in the moat, or break your neck walking along the worsest parts o' the ramparts, or get yourself trod upon by the horses. Why, I've known you kick, and squeal, and fight, and punch me as hard as ever you could."

"And did it hurt you, Ben?"

"Hurt me, sir? Not it. I liked it. Showed you was made o' good stuff, same good breed as your father; and I used to say to myself, 'That young cub'll turn out as fine a soldier as his father some day, and I shall have the job o' training him.' But deary me, deary me, old England's a-wasting all away! You aren't got the sperrit you had, my lad; and instead o' coming to me cheery-like, and saying, 'Now, Ben, get out the swords and let's have a good fence, or a bit o' back-sword or broad-sword-play, or a turn with the singlestick or staves,' you're always a-sticking your nose into musty old parchments, or dusty books, along o' Master Palgrave Pawson. Brrr!"

The latter was a low growl, following a loud smack given to the side of the helmet, after which, as the lad stood fretting and fuming, the old servant scrubbed away at the steel furiously.

"It isn't true, Ben," the boy cried at last, indignantly; "and perhaps I'm going to be a soldier after all, especially if this trouble goes on."

"Tchaw! trouble goes on!" said the man, changing the steel headpiece for a cuirass. "There won't be no trouble. First time your father gets a sight of the mob of tailors, and shoemakers, and tinkers, with an old patch-work counterpane atop of a clothes-prop for their flag, he'll ride along the front of his ridgement of cavaliers, and he'll shout to 'em in that big voice of his as I've followed many's the time; and 'Don't draw, gentlemen,' he'll say; 'ride the scum down, and make the rest run;' and then they'll all roar with laughing loud enough to drown the trumpet charge. My word, I'd a gi'n something to ha' been there to see the rebels fly like dead leaves before a wind in November. But it were a mean and a cruel thing, Master Roy. Look at that arm, look at these legs! I'm a better and a stronger man than ever I was, and could sit any horse they'd put me on. But to leave an old soldier, as had followed him as I have, at home here to rust like the rest o' things, when there was a chance for a bit o' fun, it went right to my 'art, sir, and it seemed to me as if it warn't the master as I used to sit with in the ranks."

The old fellow was bending now over the breastplate and rubbing hard, while as Roy listened to his excited words, wondering at the way in which he seemed to resent what he looked upon as a slight, something dropped upon the polished steel with a pat, and spread out; and Roy thought to himself that if that drop of hot salt water stayed there, it would make a deeper rust spot than anything.

But it did not stay, for the man hastily rubbed it away, and began with a rough show of indifference to hum over an old Devon song, something about "A morn in May, to hear birds whistle and see lambkins play."

But he ceased as the boy laid a hand upon his shoulder, and bent over the breastplate and rubbed at it very slowly, listening intently the while.

"Don't you get thinking that, Ben Martlet," said the boy, gently; "father wanted to take you, and he said you were not too old."

"Nay, nay, nay, sir; don't you get trying to ile me over. I know."

"But you don't know," said the boy, hotly; "he said he should take you, but my mother asked him not to."

"Ay, she would, sir. She won't let you be a soldier, and she comes over your father as I was too old and helpless to be any good."

"You're a stupid, pig-headed, old chump," cried Roy, angrily.

"Yes, sir; that's it; now you're at me too. Rusty, and worn-out, and good for nothing; but it'll soon be over. I used to think it must be very horrid to have to die, but I know better now, and I shan't be sorry when my turn comes."

"Will—you—listen to—what—I have—to say?" cried the boy.

"Oh, ay, sir, I'll listen. You're my master, now Sir Granby's away, and nobody shan't say as Ben Martlet didn't do his dooty as a soldier to the end, even if he is set to dig in a garden as was once a castle court-yard."

"Oh, you obstinate old mule!" cried Roy, gripping the man's shoulders, as he stood behind him, sawing him to and fro, and driving his knee softly into the broad strong back. "Will you listen?"

"Yes, sir, I'll listen; but that's only your knee. Kick the old worn-out mule with your boot-toe, and—"

"I've a good mind to," cried Roy. "Now listen: my mother begged of father to leave you here."

"Oh, ay, of course."

"Quiet!" roared Roy, "or I will really kick—hard; because she said she would feel safer, and that, if any trouble did arise with some of the men, Martlet would put it down at once, and everything would go right."

The cuirass went down on the dark oaken boards with a loud clang, and the old soldier sprang to his feet panting heavily.

"Her ladyship said that?" he cried.

"Yes."

"Say it again, sir; say it again!" he cried, in a husky voice.

Roy repeated the words.

"Yes, yes, sir; and what—what did Sir Granby say to that?"

"Said he was very sorry and very glad."

"What?"

"Sorry to leave you, because it didn't seem natural to go back to the regiment without his right-hand man."

"Right-hand man?"

"Yes; but he was glad my mother felt so about you, for he could go away more contented now, and satisfied that all would be right. For though—ahem!—he had the fullest confidence in me, I was too young to have the management of men."

"Wrong, wrong, sir—wrong. On'y want a bit o' training, and you'd make as good a captain as ever stepped.—Then it was her ladyship's doing, and she said all that?"

"Yes."

"God bless her! my dear mistress. Here, don't you take no notice o' this here," cried the rough fellow, changing his tone, and undisguisedly wiping the salt tears from his face. "I don't work so much as I ought, sir, and this here's only what you calls presperashum, sir, as collects, and will come out somewheres. And so her ladyship says that, did her?"

"Yes, Ben."

"Then why haven't I knowed this afore? Here's three months gone by since the master went to take command of his ridgement, and I see him off. Ay, I did send him off looking fine, and here have I been eating my heart out ever since. Why didn't you tell me?"

"Oh, I don't know. Yes, I do. Of course, I wasn't going to tattle about what my father and mother said, but when I heard you talk as you did, and seem so cut up and unjust, why, I did."

"Here, let me have it, my lad! Kick away! Jump on me for an old fool. Why, I'm as blind as old Jenk. Worse.—She'd feel safer if there was any trouble. Bless her! Oh, what an old fool I've been. No wonder I've got so weak and thin."

"Ha, ha, ha!"

"What are you laughing at, sir?"

"You weak and thin! Why, you're as strong as a horse."

"Well, I am, Master Roy," said the man, with a grim smile of pride. "But I have got a bit thin, sir."

"Not a bit thinner."

"Well, I aren't enjoyed my vittles since the master went, sir. You can't contradick that."

"No, and don't want to; but you did eat a four or five pound eel that you'd no right to catch."

"That I didn't, sir. I give it to poor old Jenk to make a pie. I never tasted it."

"Then you may catch as many as you like, Ben, without asking."

"Thank you, sir; but I don't want to go eeling now. Here, let's have all this fighting-tackle so as you can see your face in it. But I say, my lad, do 'ee, now do 'ee, alter your mind; leave being statesman to them soft, smooth kind o' fellows like Master Pawson."

"I don't see why one couldn't be a statesman and a soldier too," said the boy.

"I don't know nothing about that sort, sir; but I do know how to handle a sword or to load a gun. I do say, though, as you're going wrong instead of right."

"How?"

"How, sir? Just look at your hands."

"Well, what's the matter with them?" said the boy, holding them out.

Ben Martlet uttered a low, chuckling laugh.

"I'll tell you, sir. S'pose any one's badly, and the doctor comes; what does he do first?"

"Feels his pulse."

"What else?"

"Looks at his tongue."

"That's it, my lad; and he knows directly from his tongue what's the matter with him. Now, you see, Master Roy, I aren't a doctor."

"Not you, Ben; doctors cure people; soldiers kill 'em."

"Not always, Master Roy," said the old fellow, whose face during the last few minutes had lit up till he seemed in the highest of glee. "Aren't it sometimes t'other way on? But look here: doctors look at people's tongues to see whether they wants to be physicked, or to have their arms or legs cut off. I don't. I looks at a man's hand to see what's the matter with him, and if I see as he's got a soft, white hand like a gal's, I know directly he's got no muscles in his arms, no spring in his back, and no legs to nip a horse's ribs or to march fifty mile in a day. Now, just look at yours."

"Oh, I can't help what my hands are like," said the boy, impatiently.

"Oh, yes, you can, sir. You've been a-neglecting of 'em, sir, horrible; so just you come to me a little more and let me harden you up a bit. If you've got to be a statesman, you won't be none the worse for being able to fight, and ride, and run. Now, will you? and—There's some one a-calling you, my lad."

"Yes, coming!" cried Roy; and he hurried out of the armoury into a long, dark passage, at the end of which a window full of stained glass admitted the sunbeams in a golden, scarlet, blue, and orange sheaf of rays which lit up the tall, stately figure of a lady, to whom the boy ran with a cry of—

"Yes, mother!"

Chapter Two
Roy's Mother and Tutor

"I had missed you, Roy," said the lady, smiling proudly on the boy; and he looked with eyes full of pride at the beautiful woman, who now rested her arm upon his shoulder and walked by his side into the more homelike part of the old fortalice, whose grim interior had been transformed by wainscoting, hangings, carpets, stained glass, and massive oak furniture into the handsome mansion of the middle of the seventeenth century.

They passed down a broad staircase into a noble hall, and from thence into a library whose broad, low, mullioned stone window opened into what had been the inner court of the castle, whose ramparts and flanking corner towers were still there; but the echoing stones that had once paved it had given place to verdant lawn, trim flower-beds ablaze with bloom, quaintly-cut shrubs, and creepers which beautified the walls once so bare and grim.

"I want to talk to you, Roy," said Lady Royland, sinking into a great formal chair. "Bring your stool and sit down."

"Got too big for the stool, mother," said the boy; "I can't double up my legs close enough. I'll sit here."

He threw himself upon the thick carpet at her feet, and rested his arms upon her lap.

"Want to talk to me? I'd rather hear you read."

"Not now, my dear."

"Why, what's the matter, mother?" said the boy, anxiously. "You're as white as can be. Got one of your headaches?"

"No, my boy,—at least, my head does ache. But it is my heart, Roy,— my heart."

"Then you've heard bad news," cried the boy. "Oh, mother, tell me; what is it? Not about father?"

"No, no; Heaven forbid, my dear," cried Lady Royland, wildly. "It is the absence of news that troubles me so."

"I ought to say us," said Roy, angrily; "but I'm so selfish and thoughtless."

"Don't think that, my boy. You are very young yet, but I do wish you would give more thought to your studies with Master Pawson."

The boy frowned.

"I wish you'd let me read with you, mother," he said. "I understand everything then, and I don't forget it; but when that old—"

"Master Palgrave Pawson," said Lady Royland, reprovingly, but with a smile.

"Oh, well, Master Palgrave Pawson. P.P., P.P. What a mouthful it seems to be!"

"Roy!"

"I've tried, mother; but I do get on so badly with him. I can't help it; I don't like him, and he doesn't like me, and it will always be the same."

"But why? Why do you not like him?"

"Because—because—well, he always smiles at me so."

"That does not seem as if he disliked you. Rather the reverse."

"He's so smooth and oily."

"It is only his manner, my dear. He seems to be very sincere, and to have your welfare at heart."

"Yes, that's it, mother; he won't let me alone."

"But he is your tutor, my dear. You know perfectly well that he came to be your father's secretary and your tutor combined."

"Yes, I know, mother," said the boy, impatiently; "but somehow he doesn't seem to teach me."

"But he is very studious, and tries hard."

"Yes, I know. But he seems to think I'm about seven instead of nearly seventeen, and talks to me as if I were a very little boy, and—and—and we don't get on."

"This sounds very sad, Roy, and I cannot bear to have a fresh trouble now. Your studies are so important to us."

Roy reached up to get his arms round his mother's neck, drew her head down, and kissed her lovingly.

"And she shan't have any more trouble," he cried. "I'll get wonderfully fond of old Paw."

"Roy!"

"Master Palgrave Pawson, then; and I'll work at my lessons and classics like a slave. But you will read with me, too, mother?"

"As much as you like, my son. Thank you. That has taken away part of my load."

"I wish I could take away the rest; but I know you're fidgeting because father hasn't written, and think that something has happened to him. But don't you get fancying that, because there can't be anything. They've only gone after a mob of shoemakers and tailors with a counterpane for flag, and father will scatter them all like dead leaves."

"Roy! My boy, these are not your words?"

"No, mother; old Ben Martlet said something of that kind to me this morning."

"Does he not know, then, how serious it is?"

"Serious? What do you mean by serious?"

Lady Royland drew a deep breath, and laid her hand upon her side as if in pain.

"Why, mother," repeated the boy, "what do you mean by serious?"

"This trouble—this rising, my dear. We have had no news, but Master Pawson has had letters from London, and he tells me that what was supposed to be a little petty discontent has grown into a serious revolution."

Roy gazed in his mother's troubled face as if he did not quite comprehend the full extent of her words.

"Well, and if it has, mother, what then?"

"What then, my boy?"

"Yes. You've nothing to fidget about. Father is there with his men, and he'll soon put a stop to it all. You know how stern he can be when people misbehave."

"My dear Roy, this, I am afraid, is going to be no little trouble that your father can put down with his men. Master Pawson tells me that there is every prospect of its being a civil war."

"What! Englishmen fighting against Englishmen?"

"Yes; a terrible fratricidal war."

"But who has quarrelled, mother? Oh, the king will soon stop it."

"Roy, my boy, we have kept you so shut up here in this retired place for home study, instead of parting with you to send you to one of the great schools, that in some things you are as ignorant as I."

"Oh, mother!" cried the boy, laughing. "You ignorant! I only wish I were half as learned and clever. Why, father said—"

"Yes, yes, dear; but that is only book-learning. We have been so happy here that the jarring troubles of politics and the court have not reached our ears; and I, for one, never gave them a thought till, after all these years of peacefulness, your father found himself compelled to obey the call of duty, and left us. We both thought that it was only for a week or two, and then the disturbance would be at an end; but every letter he has sent me has contained worse news, till now it is nearly a month since I have heard from him."

"Then it is because he is putting down the rioters," said Roy, quickly.

"Rioters, my boy! Rebels you should say, for I fear that a great attempt is to be made to overthrow the monarchy. Master Pawson's informants assure him that this is the case, and before long, he says, there must be an encounter between the Royal and the Parliamentary troops."

"Is Master Pawson right, mother? Royal troops—Parliamentary troops? Why, they're all the same."

"No, Roy; there is a division—a great division, I fear, and discontented people are taking the side against the king."

"Then I'm sorry for them," said the boy, flushing. "They'll get a most terrible beating, these discontented folks."

"Let us hope so, my boy, so that there may be an end to this terrible anxiety. To those who have friends whom they love in the army, a foreign war is dreadful enough; but when I think of the possibility of a war here at home, with Englishmen striving against Englishmen, I shudder, and my heart seems to sink."

"Look here," cried the boy, as he rose and stood with his hand resting upon his mother's shoulder, "you've been fidgeting and fancying all sorts of things, because you haven't heard from father."

"Yes, yes," said Lady Royland, faintly.

"Then you mustn't, mother. 'Tis as I say; he is too busy to write, or else he hasn't found it easy to send you a letter. I'll take the pony and ride over to Sidecombe and see when the Exeter wagon comes in. There are sure to be letters for you, and even if there are not, it will make you more easy for me to have been to see, and I can bring you back what news there is. I'll go at once."

Lady Royland took hold of her son's hand and held it fast.

"No," she said, making an effort to be firm. "We will wait another day. I have been fidgeting, dear, as you say, and it has made me nervous and low-spirited; but I'm better now for talking to you, my boy, and letting you share my trouble. I dare say I have been exaggerating."

"But I should like to ride over, mother."

"You shall go to-morrow, Roy; but even then I shall be loath to let you. There, you see I am quite cheerful again. You are perfectly right; your father is perhaps away with his men, and he may have sent, and the letter has miscarried in these troublous times."

"I shouldn't like to be the man who took it, if it has miscarried," said the boy, laughing.

"Poor fellow! it may have been an accident. There, go to Master Pawson now; and Roy, my dear, don't talk about our trouble to any one for the present."

"Not to old Pawson?"

"Master Pawson."

"Not to Master Pawson?" said Roy, smiling.

"Not unless he speaks to you about it; then, of course, you can."

"But he won't, mother. He only talks to me about the Greek and Latin poets and about music. I say, you don't want to see me squeezing a big fiddle between my knees and sawing at it with a bow as if I wanted to cut all the strings, do you, mother?"

"My dear boy, not unless you wished to learn the violoncello."

"Well, I don't," said Roy, pettishly; "but old Master Pawson is always bringing his out of its great green-baize bag and talking to me about it. He says that he will instruct me, and he is sure that my father would have one sent to me from London if I asked him. Just as if there are not noises enough in the west tower now without two of us sawing together. *Thrrum, thrrum, throomp, throomp, throomp!*"

Roy struck an attitude as if playing, running his left hand up and down imaginary strings while he scraped with his right, and produced no bad imitation of the vibrating strings with his mouth.

"I should not dislike for you to play some instrument to accompany my clavichord, Roy," said Lady Royland, smiling at the boy's antics.

"Very well, then; I'll learn the trumpet," cried the lad. "I'm off now to learn—not music."

"One moment, Roy, my dear," said Lady Royland, earnestly. "Don't let your high spirits get the better of your discretion."

"Of course not, mother."

"You do not understand me, my dear. I am speaking very seriously now. I mean, do not let Master Pawson think that you ridicule his love of music. It would be very weak and foolish, and lower you in his eyes."

"Oh, I'll mind, mother."

"Recollect that he is a scholar and a gentleman, and in your father's confidence."

Roy nodded, and his lips parted as if to speak, but he closed them again.

"What were you going to say, Roy?"

"Oh, nothing, mother."

"Nothing?"

"Well, only—that—I was going to say, do you like Master Pawson?"

"As your tutor and your father's secretary, yes. He is a very clever man, I know."

"Yes, he's a very clever man," said Roy, as, after kissing his mother affectionately, he went off towards the west tower, which had been specially fitted up as study and bedchamber for the gentleman who had come straight from Oxford to reside at Sir Granby Royland's seat a couple of years before this time. "Yes, he's a very clever man," said Roy to himself; "but I thought I shouldn't like him the first day he came, and I've gone on thinking so ever since. I don't know why, but—Oh, yes, I do," cried the boy, screwing up his face with a look of disgust: "it's because, as he says, I've no soul for music."

For just at that moment a peculiar long-drawn wailing sound came from the open window of the west tower, and a dog lying curled up on the grass in the sun sprang up and began to bark, finishing off with a long, low howl, as it stretched out its neck towards the open window.

"Poor old Nibbs! he has no soul for it, either," said the boy to himself, as his face lit up with a mirthful expression. "It woke him up, and he thought it was cats. Wonder what tune that is? He won't want me to interrupt him now. Better see, though, and speak to him first, and then I'll go and see old Ben polish the armour."

Chapter Three
Coming Events cast their Shadows before

The wail on one string went on, and naturally sounded louder as Roy Royland opened a door to stand gazing in at the quaint octagonal room, lit by windows splayed to admit more light to the snug quarters hung with old tapestry, and made cosy with thick carpet and easy-chair, and intellectual with dwarf book-cases filled with choice works. These had overflowed upon the floor, others being piled upon the tops of chairs and stacked in corners wherever room could be found, while some were even ranged upon the narrow steps of the corkscrew stone staircase which led to the floor above, occupied by Master Palgrave Pawson for a bedchamber, the staircase being continued up to the leads, where it ended in a tiny turret.

"I wonder what father will say, my fine fellow, when he finds what a lot of his books you've brought up out of the library," said Roy to himself, as he stood watching the plump, smooth-faced youngish man, who, with an oblong music-book open before him on the table, was seated upon a stool, with a 'cello between his legs, gravely sawing away at the strings, and frowning severely whenever, through bad stopping with his fingers — and that was pretty often — he produced notes "out of tune and harsh." The musician was dressed, according to the fashion of the day, in dark velvet with a lace collar, and wore his hair long, so that it inconvenienced him; the oily curls, hanging down on either side of his fat face like the valance over an old-fashioned four-post bedstead, swaying to and fro with the motion of the man's body, and needing, from time to time, a vigorous shake to force them back when they encroached too far forward and interfered with his view of the music.

The slow, solemn, dirge-like air went on, but the player did not turn his head, playing away with grave importance, and giving himself a gentle inclination now and then to make up for the sharp twitches caused by the tickling hair.

"You saw me," said Roy, speaking to himself, but at the musician, "for one of your eyes turned this way; but you won't speak till you've got to the end of that bit of noise. Oh, how I should like to shear off those long greasy curls! They make you look worse even than you do when they're all twisted up in pieces of paper. It doesn't suit your round, fat face. You don't look a bit like a cavalier, Master P.P.; but I suppose you're a very good sort of fellow, or else father would not have had you here."

Just then the music ended with an awkwardly performed run up an octave and four scrapes across the first and second strings.

"Come in, boy," said the player, taking up a piece of resin to apply to the hair of the bow, "and shut the door."

He spoke in a highly-pitched girlish voice, which somehow always tickled Roy and made him inclined to laugh, and the desire increased upon this occasion as he said, solemnly—

"Saraband."

"Oh! Who's she?" said the boy, wonderingly.

The secretary threw his head back, shaking his curls over his broad turn-down collar, and smiled pityingly.

"Ah," he said, "now this is another proof of your folly, Roy, in preferring the society of the servants to that of the noble works with which your father has stored his library. What ignorance! A saraband is a piece of dance music, Italian in origin; and that was a very beautiful composition."

"Dance?" cried the boy. "People couldn't dance to a tune like that. I thought it was an old dirge."

"Want of taste and appreciation, boy. But I see you would prefer something light and sparkling. I will—sit down—play you a coranto."

It was on Roy's lips to say, "Oh, please don't," but he contented himself with crossing the room, lifting some books off an oaken window-seat, his tutor watching him keenly the while, and putting them on the floor; while, with his head still thrown back on one side, Master Palgrave Pawson slowly turned over the leaves of his music-book with the point of his bow.

Roy seated himself, with a sigh, after a glance down through the open window at the glistening moat dotted with the great silver blossoms and dark flat leaves of the water-lilies, seeing even from there the shadowy forms of the great fish which glided slowly among the slimy stalks.

"Ready?" said the musician, giving his hand a flourish.

"Yes, sir," said Roy, aloud; and then to himself, "Oh, what an awful fib." Then he wrinkled up his brows dismally, and began to think of old Ben polishing the armour and swords; but the next moment his face smoothed out stiffly, and he grew red in his efforts to keep from laughing aloud, for Master Pawson commenced jerking and snatching from the strings a remarkable series of notes, which followed one another in a jigging kind of fairly rapid sequence, running up and down the gamut and in and out, as if the notes of the composer had suddenly become animated, and, like some kind of tiny, big-headed, long-tailed goblins, were chasing one another in and out of the five lines of the stave, leaping from bar to bar, never stopping for a rest, making fun of the flats and sharps, and finally pausing, breathless and tired, as the player now finally laid down the bow, took out a fine laced handkerchief, and began to wipe his fingers and mop his brow.

"There," he said, smiling; "you like that bright, sparkling composition better?"

"No," said Roy, decisively; "no, I don't think I do."

"I am glad of it; very glad of it. I was afraid that you preferred the light and trivial coranto to the graceful saraband."

"But, I say. Master Pawson, the Italians surely don't dance to such music as that?"

"I have never been in Italy, my dear pupil, but I believe they do. Going?"

Roy had risen from his chair.

"Yes, sir; I thought, as you were practising, you would not want me to stop and read to-day, and you are writing a letter, too."

"Letter?" said the secretary, hurriedly reaching towards an open sheet upon the table and turning it over with the point of his bow. "Oh, that? Yes, some notes—some notes. Well, it is a fine day, and exercise is good, and perhaps I shall run through a few more compositions. So you can go, and we will study a little in the evening, for we must not neglect our work, Roy, my dear pupil; we must not neglect our work."

"No, sir. Thank you, sir," said the boy; and, for fear of a change of decision, he hurried from the room and made his way out upon the old ramparts, to begin walking leisurely round the enclosed garden, and looking outward from the eminence upon which the castle was built across the moat at the foot, and away over the sunny forest towards the village and little church, whose spire rose about two miles away.

"I wish he wouldn't always call me 'my dear pupil,' and smile at me as if he looked down from ever so high up. I don't know how it is, but I always feel as if I don't like him. I suppose it's because he's so plump and smooth.

"Seems hard," mused the boy, seating himself in one of the crenellations of the rampart, and thinking deeply, "that he should get letters with news from London, and poor mother not have a line. That was a letter on the table, though he pretended it was not, for I could see it began like one. I didn't want to read it. Perhaps he was ashamed of being always writing letters. Don't matter to me. Afraid, perhaps, that he'll be told that he ought to attend more to teaching me. Wish he'd be always writing letters. I can learn twice as much reading with mother."

It was very beautiful in that sunny niche in the mouldering stones close to the tower farthest away from that occupied by the secretary, and a spot much favoured by the boy, for from there he could look right over the square gate-way with its flanking towers, and the drawbridge which was never drawn, and the portcullis which was never lowered.

"Can't hear him playing here," thought Roy that day; and he congratulated himself upon the fact, without pausing to think that the distance was so short that the notes should have been audible.

Roy had been successful in getting off his reading with the tutor, but he was very undecided what to do next, for there were so many things to tempt him, and his mind kept on running in different directions. One minute he was dwelling on his mother's troubles and the want of news from his father, and from this it was a natural transition to thinking of how grand it would be if he could prevail upon her to let him go up to that far-away mysterious city, which it took days to reach on horseback, and then he could take her letter and find where his father was lying with his regiment, and see the army,—maybe see the king and queen, and perhaps his father might let him stay there,—at all events for a time.

Then he was off to thinking about the great moat, for twice over a splash rose to his ears, and he could see the rings of water which spread out and made the lily-leaves rise and fall.

"That was the big tench," he said to himself. "Must catch that fellow some day. He must weigh six or seven pounds. It ought to be a good time now. Want a strong line, though, and a big hook, for he'd run in and out among the lily-stems and break mine. Now, if I knew where father was, I could write and ask him to buy me one and send it down by his next letter. No: he wouldn't want to be bothered to buy me fishing-lines when he's with his regiment. I know," he said to himself, after a pause; "old Ben has got the one he caught the big eel with. I'll make him lend me that. Poor old Ben! who'd ever have thought that he could cry. For it was crying just as a little boy would. Seems funny, because he has been a brave soldier, and saved father's life once. Shouldn't have thought a man like that could cry."

Roy began to whistle softly, and then picked up a little cushion-like patch of velvety green moss and pitched it down towards a jackdaw that was sitting on a projecting stone just below a hole, watching him intently, first with one eye and then with the other, as if puzzled to know what he was doing so near to his private residence, where his wife was sitting upon a late batch of eggs, an accident connected with rats having happened to the first.

It did not occur to the bird that it was quite impossible for its nesting-place to be reached without a swing down from above by a rope; but, being still puzzled, it tried to sharpen its intellectual faculties by standing on one leg and scratching its grey poll with the claws of the other, a feat which made it unsteady and nearly topple over towards the deep moat below.

"*Tah!*" it cried, in resentment of the insult when the little green moss cushion was thrown; and, as the bird sailed away, Roy rose and walked slowly along the rampart, through the corner tower, and then on towards the front, where that over the outer gate-way stood tall, massive, and square. Here the boy left the rampart, entered through a low arched door, and stood in the great chamber over the main gate-way, where the rusty chains were wound round the two capstans, held fast now by their checks, and suspending the huge grated portcullis, with its spikes high enough to be clear of a coachman driving a carriage.

"Wonder whether we could let that down?" thought Roy.

He had often had the same thought, but it came very strongly now, and he began to calculate how many men it would take to lower the portcullis, and whether he, Ben, and a couple more could manage it.

"Looks as if everything must be set fast with rust," he thought, and he was about to turn and descend; but as he reached the corner where the spiral steps led down, he stood where they also led up to another chamber in the massive stone-work, and again higher to the leads.

The result was that in his idle mood Roy began to ascend, to find half-way up, by the slit which gave light, that the jackdaws had been busy there too, coming in and out by the loop-hole, and building a nest which was supported upon a scaffolding of sticks which curved up from the stone step on which it rested, and from that to the splay and sill by the loop-hole.

"Only an old one," said the boy to himself, and he brought the great edifice down with a sharp kick or two, thinking that it must be about a year since any one had come up that way.

"What a lot of the old place seems no use!" he said to himself, as, with the dry sticks crackling beneath his feet, he climbed up the dark stairway and entered the next chamber through its low arched door.

"Why, what a jolly private room this would make!" he said to himself; "only wants a casement in and some furniture. I'll ask father to let me have it for my play—I mean study; no, I don't—I mean odds and ends place."

He paused—after glancing out at the beautiful view over the woodland country dotted with meadow-like pastures in which the ruddy cattle of the county grazed—by the open fireplace with the arms of the Roylands cut in stone beneath the narrow shelf, and the sight of this opening, with the narrow, well-made chimney and some projecting stone blocks from the fire-back, set him thinking.

"Fight differently now," he said, as he recalled the object of the furnace before him, and how he had heard or read that it was used on purpose to melt lead ready for pouring down upon the besiegers who might have forced their way across the drawbridge to the portcullis. "Fancy melting lead here to pour down upon men's heads! What wretches we must have been in the old days."

He altered his mind, though, directly, as he went back to the stairway.

"Perhaps we never did pour any down, for I don't think anybody ever did attack the castle."

Thinking he might as well go a little higher, he mounted the spiral instead of descending, the dry elm twigs brought in by the jackdaws which made the untenanted corners their home crackling again beneath his feet.

Passing out of the corner turret, which supported a stout, new flag-pole, he was now on the leaded roof of the great square tower, which frowned down upon the drawbridge and gazed over the outer gate-way, in whose tower old Jenkin Bray, the porter, dwelt, and whom Roy could now see sitting beside the modern iron gate sunning himself, his long white hair and beard glistening in the light.

There were openings for heavy guns in front here, and a broad, level, projecting parapet with a place where the defenders could kneel, and which looked like a broad seat at the first glance, while at its foot was a series of longish, narrow, funnel-shaped openings, over which the boy stood, gazing down through them at the entrance to the main gate-way, noting how thoroughly they commanded the front of where the portcullis would stand when dropped, and where any enemies attacking and trying to break through would be exposed to a terrible shower of molten lead, brought up from the furnace in the chamber below to pour down upon the besiegers, while those who assailed them were in perfect safety.

"Horrid!" muttered Roy; "but I don't know; the enemy should stop away and leave the people in the castle alone. But hot lead! Boiling water wouldn't seem so bad. But surely Master Pawson's friend is wrong; we can't be going to have war here in England. Well, if we do, there's nothing to bring them here."

Roy left the machicolations and knelt upon the broad stone seat-like place to stretch himself across the parapet, and look down, over the narrow patch of stone paving, down into the deep moat, whose waters were lit up by the sunshine, so that the boy could see the lily and other water-plant stems and clumps of reed mace; at the farther edge the great water-docks and plantains, with the pink-blossomed rush. But his attention was wholly riveted by the fish which swarmed in the sunny depths, and for a time he lay there upon his breast, kicking up his heels and studying the broad-backed carp, some of which old age had decked with patches of greyish mould. There were fat tench, too, walloping about among the lilies, and appearing to enjoy the pleasure of forcing their way in and out among the leaves and stems; while the carp sailed about in the open water, basking in the sunshine, and seemed to find their satisfaction in leaping bodily out of the water to fall back with a splash.

There were roach, too, in shoals, and what seemed remarkable was that they kept swimming close up to where a great pike of nearly three feet long lay motionless, close to a patch of weed.

"Must be asleep," thought Roy, "or not hungry, and they all know it, because he would soon snap up half a dozen of them."

Then, as he lay lazily watching the fish in the drowsy sunshine which had warmed the stones, the political troubles of the nation and the great cloud of war, with its lightnings, destruction, and death, were unseen. He was surrounded by peace in the happiest days of boyhood, and trouble seemed as if it could not exist. But the trumpet-blast had rung out the call to arms, and men were flocking to that standard and to this, and the flash and thunder of guns had begun.

But not there down to that sleepy, retired part of Devon. There was the castle built for defence, and existing now as Sir Granby Royland's happy country home, surrounded by its great estate with many tenants, while its heir was stretched out there in the sunshine upon his chest, kicking up his heels, and thinking at that moment that it would not be a bad amusement to bring up a very long line with a plummet at the end, to bait it, and then swing it to and fro till he could drop it right out where the great pike lay, ten or a dozen feet from the drawbridge.

"I will some day," said the boy, half aloud; "but it's too much trouble now."

He swung himself round and lay there, looking back over the top of the spacious building, on whose roof he was, right across the now floral old court-yard, and between the two angle towers, to the wide-spreading acres of the farms and woodlands which formed his father's estate.

The jackdaws flew about, and began to settle at the corners as he lay so still and languidly said to himself—

"Need to lie still; it wouldn't do to slip over backward. I shouldn't even go into the moat, for I should come down on those stones."

"Stupid to be in dangerous places," he said to himself directly after, and, rolling over, he let himself down upon the broad seat-like place, where he could lie and watch the prospect just as well.

"Rather stupid of me not to come up here oftener," he thought. "It's a capital place. I will ask father to let me have all this old empty tower to myself. What's that? A fight?"

For there was a sudden rush upward of jackdaws from where they had blackened the farthest corner tower to the left, and, looking in that direction as he lay, he saw the reason of the sudden whirr of wings and outburst of sharp, harsh cries, for there upon the leads, and holding on by the little turret which covered the door-way of the spiral staircase, stood Master Pawson.

"Feels like I do, I suppose," thought Roy, as the secretary cast his eyes round the old building, particularly watchful of the pleasaunce, but keeping right back by the outer crenelles as if not wishing to be seen.

At first Roy felt that the secretary saw him, and as his eyes roved on and he made no sign, the boy's hand went to his pocket in search of his handkerchief to wave to him. He did not withdraw it, but lay lazily watching while the secretary now turned his back and stood gazing right away.

"Never saw him do anything of that kind before," thought Roy. "What's he looking after? I shouldn't have thought he had ever been up there in his life."

Roy lay quite still, with his eyes half closed, and all at once the secretary drew out his white laced handkerchief, wiped his forehead three times with a good deal of flourish, and returned it, after which he slowly stepped into the turret opening and backed out of sight.

"Mind you don't slip," said Roy, tauntingly, but quite conscious of the fact that his words could not be heard. "Why, he has gone down like a bear—backward. I could run down those stairs as fast as I came up."

Perhaps it was the warm sunshine, perhaps it was from laziness, but, whatever the cause, Roy Royland went off fast asleep, and remained so for quite a couple of hours, when, starting up wonderingly, and not quite conscious of the reason why he was there, he looked about him, and finally over the great parapet, to see the secretary beyond the farther end of the drawbridge, talking in a very benign way to the old porter, who stood with bent head listening to his words.

"Why, it seems only a few moments ago that I saw him on the leads over his chamber staring out across country, and he must have been down since, and had a walk.—How time does go when you're snoozing," thought Roy, "and how stupid it is to go to sleep in the daytime! I won't do it again."

Chapter Four
The Use of a Sword

Several days passed away, but Lady Royland always put off sending in search of news, and seemed to be more cheerful, so that Roy soon forgot his anxiety in the many things he had to think about,—amusements, studies, and the like. But he had a few words with his father's old follower on the subject of the absence of news, one day, when Ben was busy, as usual, in the armoury.

"Not heard lately from the master, sir? Pish, that's nothing; soldiers have got their swords and pistols to think about, not their pens. Best soldiers I ever knew couldn't write at all. Enough for them to do to fight. You'll hear from him some day, and when you do, you'll know as he has been pretty busy putting the people straight,—more straight than some on 'em'll like to be, I know. Sarve 'em right; nobody's a right to fight agen the king.—Looks right, don't it?"

He held up an old sword which he had rubbed and polished till it flashed in the light.

"Splendid!" said Roy. "Is it sharp?"

"Sharp enough to take your head off at one sweep."

"Nonsense!" said the boy, laughing.

"Oh, it's true enough, Master Roy. Here, you stand all quite stiff and straight, and I'll show you."

"No, thank you, Ben. Suppose I try it on you."

"There you are, then," said the man; "but I must have one, too, for a guard."

He handed the boy the sword, and took up another waiting to be cleaned from galling rust, and, throwing himself on guard, he cried—

"Now then, cut!"

"No; too dangerous," said Roy.

"Not a bit, my lad, because you couldn't touch me."

"I could," said Roy, "where I liked."

"Try, then."

"Not with this sharp sword."

"Very well, then, take one of those; they've no more edge than a wooden one. It's time you did know how to use a sword, sir."

Ben exchanged his glittering blade, too, and once more stood on guard.

"I won't bother you now about how you ought to stand, sir," he said; "that'll come when I begin to give you some lessons. You go just as you like, and hit where you can."

"No, no," said the boy. "I don't want to hurt you, Ben."

"Won't hurt me, sir; more likely to hurt yourself. But do you know you're standing just as badly as you possibly could? and if I was your enemy, I could take off your head, either of your ears, or your legs, as easily as look at you."

Roy laughed, but he did not seem to believe the old soldier's assertion, and, giving his blunt sword a whirl through the air, he cried—

"Now, then, Ben; which leg shall I cut off?"

"Which you like, sir."

Roy made a feint at the right leg, and, quickly changing the direction of his weapon, struck with it softly at the old soldier's left.

"Tchah!" cried the old man, as blade met blade, his sword, in the most effortless way, being edge outward exactly where Roy struck. "Why, do you know, sir, if I'd been in arnest with you, that you would have been spitted like a cockchafer on a pin before you got your blade round to cut?"

"Not I," said the boy, contemptuously.

"Very well, sir; you'll see. Now, try again, and cut hard. Don't let your blade stop to get a bit of hay and a drop of water on the way, but give it me quick."

"But I don't want to hurt you, Ben."

"Well, I don't, either; and, what's more, I don't mean to let you."

"But I shall, I'm sure, if I strike hard."

"You think so, my lad; but do you know what a good sword is?"

"A sword."

"Yes, and a lot more. When a man can use it properly, it's a shield, and a breastplate, helmet, brasses, and everything else. Now, I'll just show you. Helmet, say. Now, you cut straight down at my head, just as if you were going to cut me in two pieces."

"Put on one of the old helmets, then."

"Tchah! I don't want any helmets. You cut."

"And suppose I hurt you?"

"S'pose you can't."

"Well, I don't want to," said Roy; "so look out."

"Right, sir; chop away."

Roy raised his sword slowly, and the old soldier dropped the point of his and began to laugh.

"That won't do, my lad; lift your blade as if you were going to bring it down again, not as if you meant to hang it up for an ornament on a peg."

"Oh, very well," said Roy. "Now, then, I'm going to cut at you sharp."

"Oh, are you, sir?" said Ben. "Now, if ever you're a soldier, and meet a man who means to kill you, shall you tell him you're going to cut at him sharply? because, if you do, you'll have his blade through you before you've half said it."

"You are precious fond of your banter," cried Roy, who was a little put out now. "Serve you right if I do hurt you. But this blade won't cut, will it?"

"Cut through the air if you move it sharp; that's about all, my lad."

"Then take that," cried the boy.

Clang—cling—clatter!

Roy stared, for his sword had come in contact with that of the old soldier, and then was twisted out of his grasp and went rattling along the floor, Ben going after it to fetch it back.

"Try again, sir."

Roy was on his mettle now, and, grasping the hilt more firmly, he essayed to deliver a few blows at his opponent's legs, sides, and arms. But Ben's sword was always there first, and held at such an angle that his weapon glided off violently, as if from his own strength in delivering the blow; and, try hard as he could, he could not get near enough to make one touch.

"Arms and head, my lad; sharp."

Better satisfied now that he would not hurt his adversary, Roy struck down at the near shoulder, but his sword glanced away. Then at the head, the legs, everywhere that seemed to offer for a blow, but always for his blade to glance off with a harsh grating sound.

"There, it's of no use; you can't get near me, my lad," said Ben, at last.

"Oh, yes, I can. I was afraid of hurting you. I shall hit hard as hard," cried Roy, who felt nettled. "But I don't want to hurt you. Let's have sticks."

"I'll get sticks directly, sir. You hit me first with the sword."

"Oh, very well; if you will have it, you shall," cried Roy, and, without giving any warning now, he delivered a horizontal blow at the old soldier's side; but it was turned off just as the dozen or so which followed were thrown aside, and then, with a quiet laugh, the old fellow said—

"Now, every time you hit at me, I could have run you through."

"No, you couldn't," said Roy, sharply.

"Well, we'll see, sir. Put that down, and use this; or, no, keep your sword; the hilt will protect your hand in case I come down upon it."

He took up a stout ash stick and threw himself on guard again, waiting for Roy's blow, which he turned off, but before the next could descend, the boy's aim was disordered by a sharp dig in the chest from the end of the ash stick; and so it was as he went on: before he could strike he always received a prod in the chest, ribs, arms, or shoulders.

"Oh, I say, Ben," he cried at last; "I didn't know you could use a stick like that."

"Suppose not, my lad; but I knew you couldn't use a sword like that. Now, I tell you what: you'd better come to me for an hour every morning before breakfast, and I'll begin to make such a man of you as your father would like to see when he comes back."

"Well, I will come, Ben," said the lad; "but my arm does not ache so much now, and I don't feel quite beaten. Let's have another try."

"Oh, I'll try all day with you, if you like, sir," said the old soldier; "only, suppose now you stand on guard and let me attack."

"With swords?" said Roy, blankly.

"No, no," said Ben, laughing; "I don't want to hurt you. We'll keep to sticks. Better still: I want you to get used to handling a sword, so I'll have the stick and you shall defend yourself with a blade."

"But that wouldn't be fair to you," cried Roy. "I might hurt you, while you couldn't hurt me."

"Couldn't I?" said the old fellow, drily. "I'm afraid I could, and more than you could me. Now, then, take that blade."

He took one from the wall, a handsome-looking sword, upon which the armourer who made it had bestowed a good deal of ingenious labour, carving the sides, and ornamenting the hilt with a couple of beautifully fluted representations in steel of the scallop shell, so placed that they formed as complete a protection to the hand of the user as that provided in the basket-hilted Scottish claymore.

"Find that too heavy for you, sir?"

"It is heavy," said Roy; "but one seems to be able to handle it easily."

"Yes, sir; you'll find that will move lightly. You see it's so well balanced by the hilt being made heavy. The blade comes up lightly, and, with a fair chance, I believe I could cut a man in two with it after a few touches on a grindstone."

"Ugh!" ejaculated Roy; "horrid!"

"Oh, I don't know, sir. Much more horrid if he cut you in two. It's of no use to be thin-skinned over fighting in earnest. Man's got to defend himself. Now, then, let's give you a word or two of advice to begin with. A good swordsman makes his blade move so sharply that you can hardly see it go through the air. You must make it fly about like lightning. Now then, ready?"

"Yes; but you won't mind if I hurt you?"

"Don't you be afraid of doing that, sir. If you hurt me, it'll serve me right for being such a bungler. *En garde!*"

Roy threw himself into position, and the old soldier attacked him very slowly, cutting at his neck on either side, then down straight at his head, next at his arms and legs; and in every case, though in a bungling way, Roy interposed his blade after the fashion shown by his adversary.

Then the old fellow drew back and rested the point of his ash stick upon his toe, while Roy panted a little, and smiled with satisfaction.

"Come," he said; "I wasn't so bad there."

"Oh, no, you weren't so bad there, because you showed that you'd got some idea of what a sword's for; but when you're ready we'll begin again. May as well have something to think about till to-morrow morning. First man you fight with won't stop to ask whether you're ready, you know."

"I suppose not; but wait a minute."

"Hour, if you like, sir; but your arms'll soon get hard. Seems a pity, though, that they're not harder now. I often asked the master to let me teach you how to use a sword."

"Yes, I know; but my mother always objected. She doesn't like swords. I do."

"Of course you do, sir. It's a lad's nature to like one. Ready?"

"Yes," cried Roy, standing on his guard; "but look out this time, Ben, because I mean you to have something."

"That's right, sir; but mind this: I'm not going to let my stick travel like a snail after a cabbage-leaf this time. I'm going to cut as I should with a sword, only I'm going to hit as if you were made of glass, so as not to break you. Now!"

The old soldier's eyes flashed as he threw one foot forward, Roy doing the same; but it was his newly polished sword that flashed as he prepared to guard the cuts, taking care, or meaning to take care, to hold his blade at such an angle that the stick would glance off. The encounter ended in a few seconds. *Whizz, whirr, pat, pat, pat,* and the elastic ash sapling came down smartly upon the boy's arms, legs, sides, shoulders, and finished off with a rap on the head, with the result that Roy angrily threw the sword jangling upon the floor, and stood rubbing his arms and sides viciously.

"You said you were going to hit at me as if I were made of glass," cried the boy.

"So I did. Don't mean to say those taps hurt you?"

"Hurt? They sting horribly."

"Why, those cuts would hardly have killed flies, sir. But why didn't you guard?"

"Guard? I did guard," cried Roy, angrily, as he rubbed away; "but you were so quick."

"Oh, I can cut quicker than that, sir. You see I got in before you did every time. I'd cut, and was on my way to give another before you were ready for the first. Come, they don't tingle now, do they?"

"Tingle? Yes. Here, I want a stick. I'm not going to leave off without showing you how it does hurt."

"Better leave off now, sir," said the man, grinning.

"But I don't want to," cried Roy; and picking up the sword which he had handled with a feeling of pride, he took the other stick, and, crying "Ready!" attacked in his turn, striking hard and as swiftly as he could, but *crack, crack, crack*, wherever he struck, there was the defensive sapling; and at last, with his arm and shoulder aching, the boy lowered his point and stood panting, with his brow moist with beads of perspiration.

"Well done!" cried Ben. "Now that's something like a first lesson. Why, those last were twice as good as any you gave before."

"Yes," said Roy, proudly; "I thought I could make you feel. Some of those went home."

"Not one of them, my lad," said Ben, smiling; "you didn't touch me once."

"Not once?"

"No, sir; not once."

"Is that the truth, Ben?"

"Every word of it, sir. But never you mind that; you did fine; and if you'll come to me every morning, I'll make you so that in three months I shall have to look out for myself."

"I don't seem to have done any good at all," said Roy, pettishly.

"Not done no good, sir? Why, you've done wonders; you've taken all the conceit out of yourself, and learned in one lesson that you don't know anything whatever about a sword, except that it has a blade and a hilt and a scabbard. And all the time you'd been thinking that all you had to do was to chop and stab with it as easy as could be, and that there was nothing more to learn. Now didn't you?"

"Something like it," said Roy, who was now cooling down; "but, of course, I knew that you had to parry."

"But you didn't know how to, my lad; and look here, you haven't tried to thrust yet. Here, give me a sharp one now."

"No, I can't do any more," said Roy, sulkily. "I don't know how."

"That's a true word, sir; but you're going to try?"

"No, I'm not," said Roy, whom a sharp sting in one leg from the worst cut made a little vicious again.

"Come, come, come," said the old soldier, reproachfully. "That aren't like my master's son talking; that's like a foolish boy without anything in his head."

"Look here, Ben; don't you be insolent."

"Not I, Master Roy. I wouldn't be to you. Only I speak out because I'm proud of you, my lad, and I want to see you grow up into a man like your father. I tried hard not to hurt you, sir, but I suppose I did. But I can't say I'm sorry."

"Then you ought to be, for you cut at me like a brute."

The old soldier shook his head sadly.

"You don't mean that, Master Roy," he said; "and it's only because you're tingling a bit; that's all."

The man's words disarmed Roy, and the angry frown passed away, as he said, frankly—

"No, I don't mean it now, Ben. The places don't tingle so; but I say, there'll be black marks wherever you cut at me."

"Never mind, sir; they'll soon come white again, and you'll know next time that you've got to have your weapon ready to save yourself. Well, I dunno. I meant it right, but you've had enough of it. Some day Sir Granby'll let you go to a big fencing-master as never faced a bit o' steel drawn in anger in his life, and he'll put you on leather pads and things, and tap you soft like, and show you how to bow, s'loot, and cut capers like a Frenchman, and when he's done with you I could cut you up into mincemeat without you being able to give me a scratch."

"Get out!" cried Roy. "You don't think anything of the sort. What time shall I come to-morrow morning—six?"

"No, sir, no. Bed's very nice at six o'clock in the morning. You stop there, and then you won't be hurt."

"Five, then?" said Roy, sharply.

"Nay, sir; you wait for the big fencing-master."

"Five o'clock, I said," cried Roy.

The old soldier took the sword Roy had held, and fetching a piece of leather from a drawer began to polish off the finger-marks left upon the steel.

"I said five o'clock, Ben," cried the boy, very decisively.

"Nay, Master Roy, you give it up, sir. I'm too rough an old chap for you."

"Sorry I was so disagreeable, Ben," said the boy, offering his hand.

"Mean it, sir?"

"Why, of course, Ben."

The hand was eagerly seized, and, it being understood that the sword practice was to begin punctually at six next morning, they separated.

Chapter Five
Roy takes his next Lesson

The clock in the little turret which stood out over the gate-way facing Lady Royland's garden had not done striking six when Roy entered the armoury next morning, to find Ben hard at work fitting the interior of a light helmet with a small leather cap which was apparently well stuffed with wool.

"Morning, Ben," said the boy. "What's that for?"

"You, sir."

"To wear?"

"Of course. Just as well to take care of your face and head when you're handling swords. You can use it with the visor up or down, 'cording to what we're doing. You see, I want to learn you how to use a sword like a soldier, and not like a gentleman who never expects to see trouble."

"Ready?"

"Yes, sir, quite; and first thing 's morning we'll begin where we left off, and you shall try to learn that you don't know how to thrust. Nothing like finding out how bad you are. Then you can begin to see better what you have to learn."

"Very well," said Roy, eagerly. "You'll have to look out now then, Ben, for I mean to learn, and pretty quickly."

"Oh, yes; you'll learn quickly enough," said Ben, placing the helmet upon the table and taking the pair of sticks up from where he had placed them. "But say, Master Roy, I have been working here. Don't you think the place looks better?"

"I think my father would be proud of the armoury if he could see the weapons," said Roy, as he looked round. "Everything is splendid."

The old soldier smiled as he walked from suit to suit of armour, some of which were obsolete, and could only be looked upon as curiosities of the day; but, in addition, there were modern pieces of defensive armour, beautifully made, with carefully cleaned and inlaid headpieces of the newest kind, and of those the old soldier seemed to be especially proud. Then he led the way on to the stands of offensive weapons, which numbered quaint, massive swords of great age, battle-axes, and maces, and so on to modern weapons of the finest steel, with, guns, petronels, and horse-pistols of clumsy construction, but considered perfect then.

"Yes, sir, I'm proud of our weepuns," said Ben; "but I aren't a bit proud of the old castle, which seems to be going right away to ruin."

"That it isn't," cried Roy, indignantly. "It has been repaired and repaired, whenever it wanted doing up, again and again."

"Ah! you're thinking about roofs and tiles and plaster, my lad. I was thinking about the defences. Such a place as this used to be. Look at the gun-carriages,—haven't been painted for years, nor the guns cleaned."

"Well, mix up some paint and brush it on," said Roy, "and clean up the guns. They can't be rusty, because they're brass."

"Well, not brass exactly, sir," said the man, thoughtfully. "It's more of a mixtur' like; but to a man like me, sir, it's heart-breaking."

"What! to see them turn green and like bronze?"

"Oh, I don't mind that so much, sir; it's seeing of 'em come down so much, like. Why, there's them there big guns as stands in the court-yard behind the breastwork."

"Garden, Ben."

"Well, garden, sir. Why, there's actooally ivy and other 'nockshus weeds growing all over 'em."

"Well, it looks peaceful and nice."

"Bah! A gun can't look peaceful and nice. But that aren't the worst of it, sir. I was along by 'em a bit ago, and, if you'll believe me, when I put my hand in one, if there warn't a sharp, hissing noise!"

"A snake? Got in there?"

"Snake, sir? No! I wouldn't ha' minded a snake; but there's no snakes here."

"There was one, Ben, for I brought it up out of the woods, and kept it in a box for months, till it got away. Then that's where it is."

"Nay. It were no snake, sir. It were one of them little blue and yaller tomtit chaps as lays such lots o' eggs. I fetches a stick, and I was going to shove it in and twist it in the hay and stuff o' the nest and draw it out."

"But you didn't?"

"No, sir, I didn't; for I says to myself, if Sir Granby and her ladyship like the place to go to ruin, they may let it; and if the two little birds—there was a cock and hen—didn't bring up twelve of the rummiest little, tiny young uns I ever did see. There they was, all a-sitting in a row along the gun, and it seemed to me so comic for 'em to be there that I bust out a-laughing quite loud."

"And they all flew away?"

"Nay, sir, they didn't; they stopped there a-twittering. But if that gun had been loaded, and I'd touched it off with a fire-stick, it would have warmed their toes, eh? But would you clean up the old guns?"

"I don't see why you shouldn't, Ben. They're valuable."

"Vallerble? I should think they are, sir. And, do you know, I will; for who knows what might happen? They tell me down in the village that there's trouble uppards, and people gets talking agen the king. Ah! I'd talk 'em if I had my way, and make some of 'em squirm.—Yes, I will tidy things up a bit. Startle some on 'em if we was to fire off a gun or two over the village."

"They'd burst, Ben. Haven't been fired for a hundred years, I should say. Those brass guns were made in Queen Elizabeth's time."

"Oh, they wouldn't burst, sir; I shouldn't be afraid of that.—But this is not learning to thrust, is it?"

"No. Come on," cried Roy, and he took one of the stout ash rods. "Here, hadn't I better put on this helmet?"

"Not yet, sir. You can practise thrusting without that. Now then, here I am, sir. All ready for you on my guard. Now, thrust."

Ben dropped into an easy position, with his legs a little bent, one foot advanced, his left hand behind him, and his stick held diagonally across his breast.

Roy imitated him, dropping into the same position.

"Where shall I stab you?" he cried.

"Just wherever you like, sir,—if you can."

The boy made a quick dart forward with his stick, and it passed by his teacher, who parried with the slightest movement of his wrist.

"I said thrust, sir."

"Well, I did thrust."

"That wasn't a thrust, sir; that was only a poke. It wouldn't have gone through a man's coat, let alone his skin. Now, again!"

The boy made another push forward with his stick, which was also parried.

"Nay, that won't do, my lad; so let's get to something better. Now, I'm going to thrust at you right in the chest. Enemies don't tell you where they're going to hit you, but I'm going to tell you. Now, look out!"

Roy prepared to guard the thrust, but the point of the old man's stick struck him sharply in the chest, and he winced a little, but smiled.

"Now, sir, you do that, but harder."

Roy obeyed, but failed dismally.

"Of course," said Ben. "Now that's because you didn't try the right way, sir. Don't poke at a man, but throw your arm right back till you get your hand level with your shoulder, and sword and arm just in a line. Then thrust right out, and let your body follow your arm,—then you get some strength into it. Now, once more."

Roy followed his teacher's instructions.

"Better—ever so much, sir. Now again—good; again—good. You'll soon do it. Now, can't you see what a lot of weight you get into a thrust like that? One of your pokes would have done nothing. One like that last would have sent your blade through a man. Now again."

Roy was now fully upon his mettle, and he tried hard to acquire some portion of the old soldier's skill, till his arm ached, and Ben cried "Halt!" and began to chat about the old-fashioned armour.

"Lots of it was too clumsy, sir. Strong men were regularly loaded down; and I've thought for a long time that all a man wants is a steel cap and steel gloves. All the rest he ought to be able to do with his sword."

"But you can't ward off bullets with a sword, Ben," said Roy.

"No, sir; nor you can't ward 'em off with armour. They find out the jyntes, if they don't go through."

"Would that suit of half-armour be much too big for me, Ben?" said Roy, pausing before a bronzed ornamental set of defensive weapons, which had evidently been the work of some Italian artist.

"No, sir, I shouldn't think it would. You see that was made for a small man, and you're a big lad. If you were to put that on, and used a bit o' stuffing here and there, you wouldn't be so much amiss. It's in fine condition, too, with its leather lining, and that's all as lissome and good as when it was first made."

"I should like to try that on some day, Ben," said the boy, eagerly examining the handsome suit.

"Well, I don't see why not, sir. You'd look fine in that. Wants three or four white ostrich feathers in the little gilt holder of the helmet. White uns would look well with that dark armour. Looks just like copper, don't it?"

"How long would it take to put it on?" said Roy.

"Hour, sir; and you'd want some high buff boots to wear with it."

"An hour?" said Roy. "There wouldn't be time before breakfast."

"No, sir. But I tell you what—I've only cleaned and polished and iled the straps. If you feels as if you'd like to put it on, I'll go over it well, and see to the buckles and studs: shall I?"

"Yes, do, Ben."

"That I will, sir. And I say, if, when you're ready, I was to saddle one of the horses proper, and you was to mount and her ladyship see you, she'd be sorry as ever she wanted you to be a statesman."

Roy shook his head dubiously.

"Oh, but she would, sir. Man looks grand in his armour and feathers."

"But I'm only a boy," said Roy, sadly.

"Who's to know that when you're in armour and your visor down, sir? A suit of armour like that, and you on a grand horse, would make a man of you. It's fine, and no mistake."

"But you were sneering at armour a little while ago, Ben," said Roy.

"For fighting in, sir, but not for show. You see, there's something about armour and feathers and flags that gets hold of people, and a soldier's a man who likes to look well. I'm an old un now, but I wouldn't say no to a good new uniform, with a bit o' colour in it; but if you want me to fight, I don't want to be all plates and things like a lobster, and not able to move. I want to be free to use my arms. Right enough for show, sir, and make a regiment look handsome; but fighting's like gardening,—want to take your coat off when you go to work."

"But you will get that armour ready, Ben?"

"Course I will, sir. On'y too glad to see you take a liking to a bit o' armour and a sword. Now, then, what do you say to beginning again?"

"I'm ready," said Roy, but with a longing look at the armour.

"Then you shall just put that helmet on, and have the visor down. You won't be able to see so well, but it will save your face from an accidental cut."

He placed the helmet on the boy's head, adjusted the cheek straps, and drew back.

"Find it heavy, sir?"

"Rather! Feels as if it would topple off as soon as I begin to move."

"But it won't, sir. The leather cap inside will stop that. Now, then, if you please, we'll begin. I'm going to cut at you slowly and softly, and you've got to guard yourself, and then turn off. I shall be very slow, but after a bit I shall cut like lightning, and before I've done I shan't be no more able to hit you than you're able now to hit me."

Roy said nothing, and the man began cutting at him to right and to left, upward from the same direction and downward, as if bent upon cleaving his shoulders; and for every cut Ben showed him how to make the proper guard, holding his weapon so that the stroke should glance off, and laying especial weight upon the necessity for catching the blow aimed upon the *forte* of the blade toward the hilt, and not upon the *faible* near the point.

Then came the turn of the head, and the horizontal and down right cuts were, after further instruction, received so that they, too, glanced off. Roy gaining more and more confidence at every stroke. But that helmet was an utter nuisance, and half buried the wearer.

"I'm beginning to think you're right, Ben, about the armour," said the lad, at last.

"Yes, 'tis a bit awkward, sir; but you'll get used to it. If you can defend yourself well with that on, why, of course, you can without. Now, then, suppose, for a change, you have a cut at me."

"Why, what tomfoolery is this?" said a highly-pitched voice; and Roy tried to snatch off his helmet as he caught sight of the secretary standing in the door-way looking on.

But the helmet would not come off easily, and, after a tug or two, Roy was fain to turn to the old soldier.

"Here," he said, hastily, "unfasten this, Ben, quick!"

"Yes, sir; but I don't see as you've any call to be in such a hurry. You've a right to learn to use a sword if you like. Only the strap fastened over this stud, and there you are."

Red-faced and annoyed, Roy faced the secretary, who had walked slowly into the armoury, to stand looking about him with a sneer of contempt upon his lip.

"Only practising a little sword-play, sir," said the boy, as soon as his head was relieved.

"Sword-play! Is there no other kind of play a boy like you can take to? What do you want with sword-play?"

"My father's a soldier," said Roy.

"Yes; but you are not going to be a fighting man, sir; and, behindhand as you are with your studies, I think you might try a little more to do your instructor credit, and not waste time with one of the servants in such a barbaric pursuit as this. Lady Royland is waiting breakfast. You had better come at once."

Feeling humbled and abashed before the old soldier, Roy followed the secretary without a word, and they entered the breakfast-room together, Lady Royland looking up pale and disturbed, and, upon seeing her son's face, exclaiming—

"Why, Roy, how hot and tired you look! Have you been running?"

The secretary laughed contemptuously.

"No, mother; practising fencing with Ben."

"Oh, Roy!" cried his mother, reproachfully; "what can you want with fencing? My dear boy, pray think more of your books."

Master Pawson gave the lad a peculiar look, and Roy felt as if he should like to kick out under the table so viciously that the sneering smile might give place to a contraction expressing pain.

But Roy did not speak, and the breakfast went on.

Chapter Six
Ben Martlet feels Rusty

"Come to me in half an hour, Roy," said Master Pawson, as they rose from the table, the boy hurrying away to the armoury to find Ben busy as ever, and engaged now in seeing to the straps and fittings of the Italian suit of bronzed steel.

"Thought I'd do it, sir," he said, "in case you ever asked for it; but I s'pose it's all over with your learning to be a man now."

"Indeed it is not," said Roy, sharply. "I'm sure my father would not object to my learning fencing."

"Sword-play, sir."

"Very well—sword-play," said Roy, pettishly; "so long as I do not neglect any studies I have to go through with Master Pawson."

"And I s'pose you've been a-neglecting of 'em, sir, eh?" said the old man, drily.

"That I've not. Perhaps I have not got on so well as I ought, but that's because I'm stupid, I suppose."

"Nay, nay, nay! That won't do, Master Roy. There's lots o' things I can do as you can't; but that's because you've never learnt."

"Master Pawson's cross because I don't do what he wants."

"Why, what does he want you to do, sir?"

"Learn to play the big fiddle."

"What!" cried the man, indignantly. "Then don't you do it, my lad."

"I don't mean to," said Roy; "and I don't want to hurt my mother's feelings; and so I won't make a lot of show over learning sword-play with you, but I shall go on with it, Ben, and you shall take the swords or sticks down in the hollow in the wood, and I'll meet you there every morning at six."

"Mean it, sir?"

"Yes, of course; and now I must be off. I was to be with Master Pawson in half an hour."

"Off you go, then, my lad. Always keep to your time."

Roy ran off, and was going straight to Master Pawson's room in the corner tower, but on the way he met Lady Royland, who took his arm and walked with him out into the square garden.

"Why, mother, you've been crying," said the boy, tenderly.

"Can you see that, my dear?"

"Yes; what is the matter? I know, though. You're fretting about not hearing from father."

"Well, is it not enough to make me fret, my boy?" she said, reproachfully.

"Of course! And I'm so thoughtless."

"Yes, Roy," said Lady Royland, with a sad smile; "I am afraid you are."

"I try not to be, mother; I do indeed," cried Roy; "but tell me—is there anything fresh? Yes; you've had some bad news! Then you've heard from father."

"No, my boy, no; the bad news comes through Master Pawson. He has heard again from his friends in London."

"Look here, mother," cried the boy, hotly, "I want to know why he should get letters easily, and we get none."

Lady Royland sighed.

"Father must be too busy to write."

"I am afraid so, my dear."

"But what is the bad news he has told you this morning?"

They were close up to the foot of the corner tower as Roy asked this question; and, as Lady Royland replied, a few notes of some air being played upon the violoncello high up came floating down to their ears.

"He tells me that there is no doubt about a terrible revolution having broken out, my boy; that the Parliament is raising an army to fight against the king, and that his friends feel sure that his majesty's cause is lost."

"Then he doesn't know anything about it, mother," cried the boy, indignantly. "The king has too many brave officers like father who will fight for him, and take care that his cause is not lost. Oh, I say, hark to that!"

"That" was another strain floating down to them.

"Yes," said Lady Royland, sadly; "it is Master Pawson playing. He is waiting for you, Roy."

"Yes, playing," said the boy, hotly. "It makes me think of what I read with him one day about that Roman emperor—what was his name?—playing while Rome was burning. But don't you fret, mother; London won't be burnt while father's there."

"You do not realise what it may mean, my boy."

"Oh, yes, I think I do, mother; but you don't think fairly. You are too anxious. But there! I must go up to him now."

"Yes, go, my boy; and you will not cause me any more anxiety than you can help?"

"Why, of course I won't, mother. But if it is going to be a war, don't you think I ought to learn all I can about being a soldier?"

"Roy! No, no!" cried Lady Royland, wildly. "Do I not suffer enough on your father's account?"

"There, I won't say any more, mother dear," said Roy, clinging to her arm; "and now I'll confess something."

"You have something to confess?" said Lady Royland, excitedly, as she stopped where they were, just beneath the corner tower, and quite unconscious of the fact that a head was cautiously thrust out of one of the upper windows and then drawn back, so that only the tip of an ear and a few curls were left visible. "Then, tell me quickly, Roy; you have been keeping back some news."

"No, no, mother, not a bit; just as if I would when I know how anxious you are! It was only this. Old Ben is always grumbling about the place going to ruin, as he calls it, and I told him, to please him, that he might clean up some of the big guns."

"But you should not have done this, my dear."

"No; I'll tell him not to, mother. And I'd made an arrangement with him to meet him every morning out in the primrose dell to practise sword-cutting. I was going to-morrow morning, but I won't go now."

Lady Royland pressed her lips to the boy's forehead, and smiled in his face.

"Thank you, my dear," she said, softly. "Recollect you are everything to me now! And I want your help and comfort now I am so terribly alone. Master Pawson is profuse in his offers of assistance to relieve me of the management here, but I want that assistance to come from my son."

"Of course!" said Roy, haughtily. "He's only the secretary, and if any one is to take father's place, it ought to be me."

"Yes; and you shall, Roy, my dear. You are very young, but now this trouble has come upon us, you must try to be a man and my counsellor so that when your father returns—"

She ceased speaking, and Roy pressed her hands encouragingly as he saw her lips trembling and that she had turned ghastly white.

"When your father returns," she said, now firmly, "we must let him see that we have managed everything well."

"Then why not, as it's war time, let Ben do what he wanted, and we'll put the place in a regular state of defence?"

"No, no, no, my dear," said Lady Royland, with a shudder. "Why should you give our peaceful happy home even the faintest semblance of war, when it can by no possibility come into this calm, quiet, retired nook. No, my boy, not that, please."

"Very well, mother. Then I'll go riding round to see the tenants, and look after the things at home just as you wish me to. Will that do?"

Lady Royland smiled, and then pressed her son's arm.

"Go up now, then, to Master Pawson's room," she said; "and recollect that one of the things I wish you to do is to be more studious than you would be if your father were at home."

Roy nodded and hurried up into the corridor, thinking to himself that Master Pawson would not like his being so much in his mother's confidence.

"Then he'll have to dislike it. He has been a bit too forward lately, speaking to the servants as if he were master here. I heard him quite bully poor old Jenk one day. But, of course, I don't want to quarrel with him."

Roy ascended the staircase and entered the room, to find the secretary bending over a big volume in the Greek character; and, as he looked up smiling, the boy felt that his tutor was about the least quarrelsome-looking personage he had ever seen.

"Rather a long half-hour, Roy, is it not?" he said.

"Yes, sir; I'm very sorry. My mother met me as I was coming across the garden, and talked to me, and I could not leave her in such trouble."

"Trouble? Trouble?" said the secretary, raising his eyebrows.

"Of course, sir, about the bad news you told her this morning."

"Indeed! And did Lady Royland confide in you?"

"Why, of course!" said Roy, quickly.

"Oh, yes,—of course! Her ladyship would do what is for the best. Well, let us to our reading. We have lost half an hour, and I am going to make it a little shorter this morning, for I thought of going across as far as the vicarage."

"To see Master Meldew, sir?"

"Yes; of course. He has not been here lately. Now, then, where we left off,—it was about the Punic War, was it not?"

"Yes, sir; but don't let's have anything about war this morning."

"Very well," said the secretary; "let it be something about peace."

It was something about peace, but what Roy did not know half an hour later, for his head was in a whirl, and his reading became quite mechanical. For there was the trouble his mother was in, her wishes as to his conduct, and his secret interview with Ben, to keep on buzzing in his brain, so that it was with a sigh of relief that he heard the secretary's command to close his book, and he gazed at him wonderingly, asking himself whether the words were sarcastic, for Master Pawson said—

"I compliment you, Roy; you have done remarkably well, and been very attentive this morning. By the way, if her ladyship makes any remark about my absence, you can say that you expect Master Meldew has asked me to stay and partake of dinner with him."

"Yes, sir."

"Not unless she asks," continued the secretary. "In all probability she will not notice my absence."

Roy descended with his books; then felt that he should like to be alone and think, and to this end he made his way to the gloomy old guard-room on the right of the great gate-way, ran up the winding stair, and soon reached the roof, where he lay down on the breastwork over the machicolations, and had not been there long before he heard steps, and, looking over, saw Master Pawson cross the drawbridge and go out of the farther gate-way, watching him unseen till he turned off by the pathway leading through the village and entering the main road.

Then it occurred to Roy that, as he had an unpleasant communication to make, he could not do better than get it over at once. So he descended, and began to search for the old soldier; but it was some time before he could find him out.

Yet it seemed to be quite soon enough, for the old fellow looked very grim and sour as he listened to the communication.

"Very well, Master Roy," he said; "the mistress is master now, and it's your dooty to obey her; but it do seem like playing at fast and loose with a man. There, I've got no more to say, —only that I was beginning to feel a bit bright and chirpy; but now I'm all going back'ard again, and feel as rusty as everything else about the place."

"I'm very sorry, Ben, for I really did want to learn," said Roy, apologetically.

"Yes, sir, I s'pose you did; and this here's a world o' trouble, and the longer you lives in it the more you finds out as you can't do what you like, so you grins and bears it; but the grinning's about the hardest part o' the job. You're 'bliged to bear it, but you aren't 'bliged to grin; and, when the grins do come, you never has a looking-glass afore you, but you allus feels as if you never looked so ugly afore in your life."

"But you'll have to help me in other things, Ben."

"Shall I, sir? Don't seem to me as there's anything else as I can help you over."

"Oh, but there is, —while the war keeps my father away."

"War, sir? Nonsense! You don't call a bit of a riot got up by some ragged Jacks war."

"No; but this is getting to be a very serious affair, according to what Master Pawson told my mother this morning."

"Master Pawson, sir! Why, what does he know about it?"

"A good deal, it seems. Some friends of his in London send him news, and they said it is going to be a terrible civil war."

"And me not up there with Sir Granby!" groaned the man. "Oh, dear! oh, dear! it's a wicked, rusty old world!"

"But I've promised to help my mother all I can, Ben, and you must promise to help me."

"Of course, sir; that you know. But say, sir, war breaking out, and we all rusted up like this! We ought to be ready for anything."

"So I thought, Ben; but my mother says there's not likely to be trouble in this out-of-the-way place."

"Then bless my dear lady's innocence! says Ben Martlet, and that's me, sir. Why, you never knows where a spark may drop and the fire begin to run."

"No, Ben."

"And if this is sure to be such a peaceful spot, why did the old Roylands build the castle and make a moat and drawbridge, and all the rest of it? They didn't mean the moat for nothing else, sir, but carp, tench, and eels."

"And pike, Ben."

"No, sir. They thought of very different kind of pikes, sir, I can tell you,—same as they I've got on the walls yonder in sheaves. But there; her ladyship gives the word to you, and you gives it to me, and I shouldn't be worth calling a soldier if I didn't do as I was ordered, and directly, too, and—Hark!"

The old soldier held up his hand.

"Horses!" cried Roy, excitedly. "Why, who's coming here?"

Chapter Seven
News from the War

Roy and the old soldier hurried to a slit which gave on the road, and the latter began to breathe hard with excitement as his eyes rested upon three dusty-looking horsemen, well-mounted, and from whose round-topped, spiked steel caps the sun flashed from time to time.

"Why, they're dragoons!" cried the old fellow, excitedly. "Enemies, perhaps, and we're without a drawbridge as'll pull up. Here, quick, take a sword, Master Roy. Here's mine. Let's make a show. They won't know but what there's dozens of us."

Roy followed the old soldier's commands, and, buckling on the sword, hurried with him down to the outer gate, just as the venerable old retainer slammed it to with a heavy, jarring sound, and challenged the horsemen, whom he could hardly see, to halt.

"Well done, old man!" muttered Ben. "The right stuff, Master Roy, though he is ninety-four."

"What is it?" cried Roy, as he reached the gate, where the men were dismounting and patting their weary troop-horses.

"Despatches for Lady Royland," said one, who seemed to be the leader. "Are you Master Roy, Sir Granby's son?"

"Yes. Have you come from my father?"

"Yes, sir, and made all the haste we could; but we've left two brave lads on the road."

"What! their horses broke down?"

"No, sir," said the man, significantly; "but they did."

He took off his cap as he spoke, and displayed a bandage round his forehead.

"My mate there's got his shoulder ploughed, too, by a bullet."

"Open the gates, Jenks," cried Roy.

"One moment, sir," whispered Ben. "Get the despatches and see if they're in your father's writing."

"Right," whispered back Roy. "Here!—your despatches."

"No, sir," said the man, firmly. "That's what they asked who barred the way. Sir Granby's orders were to place 'em in his lady's hands."

"Quite right," said Roy. "But show them to me and let me see my father's hand and seal."

"Yes, that's right enough, sir," said the man. "We might be enemies;" and he unstrapped a wallet slung from his right shoulder, took out a great letter tied with silk and sealed, and held it out, first on one side, then upon the other, for the boy to see.

"Yes," cried Roy, eagerly, "that's my father's writing, and it is his seal. Open the gate, Jenkin, and let them in. Why, my lads, you look worn-out."

"Not quite, sir; but we've had a rough time of it. The country's full of crop-ears, and we've had our work cut out to get here safe."

"Full of what?" said Roy, staring, as the troopers led in their horses, and he walked beside the man who bore the despatches.

"Crop-ears, sir,—Parliamentary men."

"Is it so bad as that?"

"Bad? Yes, sir."

"But my father—how is he?"

"Well and hearty when he sent us off, sir."

"Come quickly then," cried Roy, hurrying the men along to the great drawbridge, over which the horses' hoofs began to rattle loudly. But they had not gone half-way across the moat before there was the rustle of a dress in front, and, looking ghastly pale and her eyes wild with excitement, Lady Royland came hurrying to meet them.

Roy sprang to her, crying—

"Letters from father, and he is quite well!"

He caught his mother in his arms, for her eyes closed and she reeled and would have fallen; but the next minute she had recovered her composure, and held out her hand for the packet the trooper had taken from his wallet.

"Thank you," she said, smiling. "Martlet, take these poor tired fellows into the hall at once, and see that they have every attention. Set some one to feed their horses."

"Thank you, my lady," said the man, with rough courtesy, as he took off his steel cap.

"Ah, you are wounded," cried Lady Royland, with a look of horror.

"Only a scratch, my lady. My comrade here is worse than I."

"Your wounds shall be seen to at once."

"If I might speak, my lady, a place to sit down for an hour or two, and something to eat and drink, would do us more good than a doctor. We haven't had a good meal since we rode away from Whitehall and along the western road a week ago."

"Eight days and a harf, comrad'," growled one of his companions.

"Is it? Well, I haven't kept count."

"See to them at once, Martlet," said Lady Royland; and the horses were led off, while, clinging to her son's arm, the anxious wife and mother hurried into the library, threw herself into a chair, tore open the great letter, and began, wild-eyed and excited, to read, while Roy walked up and down the room with his eyes fixed longingly upon the despatch till he could bear it no longer.

"Oh, mother!" he cried, "do, do, do pray give me a little bit of the news."

"My poor boy! yes. How selfish of me. Roy, dear, there is something terribly wrong! Your dear father says he has been half-mad with anxiety, for he has sent letter after letter, and has had no news from us. So at last he determined to send his own messengers, and despatched five men to guard this letter to us—but I saw only three."

"No," said Roy, solemnly; "the roads are in the hands of the enemy, mother, and two of the poor fellows were killed on the way. Two of these three are wounded."

"Yes, yes! Horrible! I could not have thought matters were so bad as this."

"But father is quite well?"

"Yes, yes, my dear; but he says the king's state is getting desperate, and that he will have to take the field at once. But the letters I sent—that he sent, my boy?"

"They must have all fallen into the enemy's hands, mother. How bad everything must be! But pray, pray, go on. What does he say?"

Lady Royland read on in silence for a few moments, and, as she read, the pallor in her face gave way to a warm flush of excitement, while Roy, in spite of his eagerness to hear more, could not help wondering at the firmness and decision his mother displayed, an aspect which was supported by her words as she turned to her son.

"Roy," she cried, "I was obliged to read first, but you shall know everything. While we have been here in peace, it seems that a terrible revolution has broken out, and your father says that it will only be by desperate efforts on the part of his friends that the king's position can be preserved. He says that these efforts will be made, and that the king shall be saved."

"Hurrah!" shouted the boy, wildly. "God save the king!"

"God save the king!" murmured Lady Royland, softly, with her eyes closed; and her words sounded like a prayerful echo of her son's utterance.

There was a pause for a few moments, and then Lady Royland went on.

"Your father says that we lie right out of the track of the trouble here, and that he prays that nothing may disturb us; but as the country grows more unsettled with the war, evil men will arise everywhere, ready to treat the laws of the country with contempt, and that it is our duty in his absence to be prepared."

"Prepared! Yes, mother," cried Roy, excitedly; and he flung himself upon his knees, rested his elbows on his mother's lap, and seized her hands. "Go on, go on!"

"He says that you have grown a great fellow now, and that the time has come for you to play the man, and fill his place in helping me in every way possible."

"Father says that, mother?" cried the boy, flushing scarlet.

"Yes; and that he looks to you to be my counsellor, and, with the help of his faithful old servant Martlet, to do everything you can to put the place in a state of defence."

"Why, mother," said Roy, "old Ben will go mad with delight."

Lady Royland suppressed a sigh, and went on firmly.

"He bids me use my discretion to decide whom among the tenants and people of the village I can—we can—trust, Roy, and to call upon them to be ready, in case of an emergency, to come in here and help to protect the place and their own belongings; but to be very careful whom I do trust, for an enemy within the gates is a terrible danger."

"Yes, of course," cried Roy, whose head seemed once more in a whirl.

"He goes on to say that there may not be the slightest necessity for all this, but the very fact of our being prepared will overawe people who might be likely to prove disaffected, and will keep wandering bands of marauders at a distance."

"Of course—yes; I see," cried Roy, eagerly. "Yes, mother, I'll go to work at once."

"You will do nothing foolish, I know, my boy," said the mother, laying one hand upon his head and gazing proudly in his eyes.

"Nothing if I can help it," he cried; "and I'll consult you in everything, but—but—"

"Yes, my boy, speak out."

"I don't want to hurt your feelings, dear, and yet if I speak of a sword or a gun—"

Lady Royland shivered slightly, but she drew a long, deep breath, and raised herself up proudly.

"Roy," she said, "that was in times of peace, before this terrible emergency had arisen. As a woman, I shrink from bloodshed and everything that suggests it. It has been my constant dread that you, my boy, should follow your father's profession. 'My boy a soldier!' I said, as I lay sleepless of a night, and I felt that I could not bear the thought. But Heaven's will be done, my son. The time has come when my weak, womanly fears must be crushed down, and I must fulfil my duty as your dear father's wife. We cannot question his wisdom. A terrible crisis has come upon our land, and we must protect ourselves and those who will look to us for help. Then, too, your father calls upon us to try to save his estate here from pillage and the ruthless wrecking of wicked men. Roy, my boy, I hope I shall not be such a weak woman now, but your help and strengthener, as you will be mine. You will not hurt my feelings, dear, in what you do. You see," she continued, smiling, as she laid her hand upon the hilt of the sword the lad had so hastily buckled on, "I do not wince and shudder now. Fate has decided upon your career, Roy, young as you are, and I know that my son's sword, like his father's, will never be drawn unless it is to protect the weak and maintain the right."

"Never, mother," cried the boy, enthusiastically; and as Lady Royland tried to raise him, he sprang to his feet. "Oh," he cried, "I wish I were not such a boy!"

"I do not," said his mother, smiling. "You are young, and I am only a woman, but our cause will make us strong, Roy. There," she continued, embracing him lovingly, "the time has come to act. You will consult with Martlet what to do about the defences at once, while I write back to your father. When do you think the men will be fit to go back?"

"They'd go to-night, mother; they seem to be just the fellows; but their horses want two or three days' rest."

"Roy!"

"Yes, mother. It's a long journey, and they'll have to go by out-of-the-way roads to avoid attack."

"But we have horses."

"Yes, mother, but they would sooner trust their own."

Lady Royland bowed her head.

"The letters must go back by them," she said, "and they must start at the earliest minute they can. But there is another thing. It is right that Master Pawson should be taken into our counsels."

"Master Pawson, mother?"

"Yes, my boy. He is your father's trusted servant, and I must not slight any friends. Go and ask him to come here."

"Can't," said Roy, shortly. "He went out this morning, and said he didn't think he would be back to dinner."

"Indeed!"

"Gone over to see the vicar."

"Gone to Mr Meldew," said Lady Royland, whose face looked very grave. "Then it must be deferred till his return. Now, Roy, what will you do first?"

"See to the gates, mother, and that no one goes out or comes in without leave."

"Quite right, Captain Roy," said Lady Royland, smiling.

The boy looked at her wonderingly.

"My heart is more at rest, dear," she said, gently, "and that aching anxiety is at an end. Roy, we know the worst, and we must act for the best."

Chapter Eight
Ben means Business

With his blood seeming to effervesce in his veins from the excitement he felt, Roy placed the writing-materials in front of his mother and then hurried out, crossed the drawbridge, and made for the little gate tower, where, upon hearing steps, the old retainer came out, bent of head and stooping, with one ear raised.

"Master Roy's step," he said; and as the boy came closer: "Yes, it's you, sir; just like your father's step, sir, only younger. What's the news, Master Roy?"

"Bad, Jenk,—civil war has broken out. Father is well and with his regiment, but there is great trouble in the land. I'm going to put the castle in a state of defence. Shut the gate again and keep it close. No one is to come in or out without an order from my mother or from me."

"That's right, Master Roy, sir; that's right," piped the retainer. "I'll just buckle on my sword at once. She's as sharp and bright as ever she was. Nobody shall go by. So there's to be a bit of a war, is there?"

"Yes, I'm afraid so, Jenk."

"Don't say afraid so, Master Roy; sounds as if you would be skeart, and your father's son couldn't be that. But nobody goes by here without your orders, sir, or my lady's, and so I tell 'em. I'm getting on a bit in years, and I can't see quite as well as I should do, not like I used; but it's the sperrit as does it, Master Roy."

"So it is, Jenk; and you've got plenty in you, haven't you?"

"Ay, ay, ay, Master Roy," quavered the old man, "plenty. Up at the house there they get talking about me as if I was so very old; but I'll let some of 'em see. Why, I want five year o' being a hundred yet, and look at what they used to be in the Scripter. I'll keep the gate fast, sir—I did this morning, didn't I, when they three dragoons come up?"

"Yes, capitally, Jenk—but I must go. I'm busy."

"That's right, sir—you go. Don't you be uneasy about the gate, sir. I'll see to that."

"Yes," said Roy to himself, "it is the spirit that does it. Now I wonder whether I've got spirit enough to do all the work before me!"

He hurried back over the drawbridge, and glanced down into the clear moat where he could see the great pike lying, but he did not stop to think about catching it, for he hurried on to the servants' hall, drawing himself up as he felt the importance of his position, and upon entering, the three troopers, who were seated at a good substantial meal, all rose and saluted their colonel's son.

"Got all you want, men?" said Roy, startling himself by his decisive way of speaking.

"Yes, sir; plenty, sir," said the man who bore the despatch. "Master Martlet saw to that."

"That's right. Now, look here, of course we want you and your horses to have a good rest, but when do you think you'll be ready to take a despatch back?"

"Take a despatch back, sir?" said the man, staring. "We're not to take anything back."

"Yes; a letter to my father."

"No, sir. Colonel Sir Granby Royland's, orders were that we were to stop here and to help take care of the castle."

"Were those my father's commands?" cried Roy, eagerly.

"Yes, sir, to all three of us—all five of us, it were, and I'm sorry I couldn't bring the other two with me; but I did my best, didn't I, lads?"

"Ay, corporal," chorused the others.

"Oh, that's capital!" cried Roy, eagerly. "It relieves me of a good deal of anxiety. But my father—he'll expect a letter back."

"No, sir; he said there was no knowing where he would be with the regiment, and we were to stay here till he sent orders for us to rejoin."

"Where is Martlet?" asked Roy then.

"Said something about an armoury," replied the corporal.

Roy hurried off, and in a few minutes found the old soldier busy with a bottle of oil and a goose feather, applying the oil to the mechanism of a row of firelocks.

"Oh, here you are, Ben," cried Roy, excitedly. "News for you, man."

"Ay, ay, sir, I've heard," said the old soldier, sadly. "More rust."

"Yes, for you to keep off. My father's orders are that the castle is to be put in a state of defence directly."

Down went the bottle on the floor, and the oil began to trickle out.

"But—but," stammered the old fellow, "what does her ladyship say?"

"That she trusts to my father's faithful old follower to work with me, and do everything possible for the defence of the place. Hurrah, Ben! God save the king!"

"Hurrah! God save the king!" roared Ben; and running to the wall he snatched a sword from where it hung, drew it, and waved it round his head. "Hah! Master Roy, you've made me feel ten years younger with those few words."

"Have I, Ben? Why, somehow all this has made me feel ten years older."

"Then you've got a bit off me that I had to spare, Master Roy, and good luck to you with it. Then," he continued, after listening with eager attention to Roy's rendering of his father's orders, "we must go to work at once, sir."

"Yes; at once, Ben."

"Then the first thing is to order the gate to be kept shut, and that no one goes out or in unless he has a pass from her ladyship or from you."

"Done, Ben. I have been to old Jenk, and he has shut the gate, and buckled on his old sword."

"Hah! hum! yes," said the old soldier, rubbing one of his ears; "that sounds very nice, Master Roy, but," he continued, with a look of perplexity, "it doesn't mean much, now, does it?"

"I don't understand you."

"Why, sir, I mean this: that if any one came up to the gate and wanted to come in—'Give the pass,' says Jenk. 'Haven't got one,' says whoever it is. 'Can't pass, then,' says Jenk, and then—"

"Well, yes, and then?" said Roy. "Why, sir, if he took a good deep breath, and then gave a puff, he'd blow poor old Jenk into the moat. He's a good old boy, and I don't want to hurt his feelings, but we can't leave things at the gate like that."

"But it would break his heart to be told he is—he—"

"Too rusty to go on, sir," said Ben, grimly. "But it would break her ladyship's heart if we didn't do our duty, and we shan't be doing that if we leave our outwork in the hands of poor old Jenk."

"What's to be done?"

"I know, sir. Tell him the gate's very important, and that he must have two men with him, and let him suppose they're under his command."

"That's it, capital!" cried Roy. "Then we must place two men there with him at once."

"Ye-e-es, sir," said Ben, drily. "But who are we to place there—ourselves?"

Roy looked hard at Ben, and Ben looked hard at Roy.

"You see, sir, we've got the castle and the weepuns, but we've no garrison. That's the first thing to see to. Why, when those three troopers have gone back with their despatch, we shall have as good as nobody."

"But they're not going back, Ben. Father's orders are that they're to stay."

"Three trained soldiers, sir, to start with!" cried Ben. "Me four, and you five. Why, that's just like five seeds out of which we can grow a little army."

"Then there are the men-servants."

"Well, sir, they're more used to washing cups and cleaning knives, and plate, and horses; but we shall have to lick 'em into shape. Let's see, there's the three men indoors, the groom, and coachman, that makes five more."

"And the two gardeners."

"Of course, sir! Why, they'll make the best of 'em all. Twelve of us."

"And Master Pawson, thirteen."

"P'ff! him!" cried Ben, with a look of contempt. "What's he going to do? Read to the sentries, sir, to keep 'em from going to sleep?"

"Oh, he'll be of some use, Ben. We mustn't despise any one."

"Right, sir; we mustn't: so as soon as he comes back—he's gone over to Parson Meldew's—"

"Yes, I know."

"You tell him to get to his books and read all he can about sword and pike wounds, and how to take a bullet out of a man when he gets hit. Then he can cut up bandages, and get ready knives and scissors and thread and big needles."

"Do you mean in case of wounds, Ben?"

"Why, of course, sir."

"But do you think it likely that we shall have some—"

"Rather queer sort of siege if we don't have some damage done, sir. Well, that settles about Master Pawson. Now, what next?"

"The men at the farm, Ben."

"Yes, sir; we ought to get about ten or a dozen. They're good stout lads. We must have them up at once and do a bit of drilling. They needn't stay here yet, but they can be got in order and ready to come in at a moment's notice. Next?"

"All the tenants must be seen, Ben. They'll all come too, and drill ready for service if wanted."

"And that means about another twenty, I suppose, sir."

"Yes, or more, Ben."

"If they're staunch, sir."

"Ah, but they would be. My father's own tenants!"

"I dunno, sir. If times are going to be like we hear, you'll find people pretty ready to go over to the strongest side."

"Oh, nonsense! There isn't a man round here who wouldn't shout for the king."

"Quite right, sir," said Ben. "I believe that."

"Then why do you throw out such nasty hints?"

"'Cause I've got my doubts, sir. Lots on 'em'll shout for the king, but if it comes to the pinch and things are going wrong, I want to know how many will fight for the king."

"Every true man, Ben."

"Azackly, sir; but, you see, there's a orful lot o' liars in the world. But we shall see."

"Well, we've got to keep the castle, Ben."

"We have, sir, and keep it we will, till everybody's about wounded or dead, and the enemy comes swarming and cheering in, and then they shan't have it."

"Why, they'll have got it, Ben," said Roy, laughing, but rather uncomfortably, for the man's words as to the future did not sound pleasant.

"Ay, and I shall take it away from 'em, sir; for if the worst comes to the worst, I shall have made all my plans before, and I'll do a bit o' Guy Fawkesing."

"What do you mean?"

"Why, I should ha' thought you'd ha' understood that, sir."

"Of course I do; but how could you blow up the castle?"

"By laying a train to the powder-magazine, knocking the heads out of a couple o' kegs, and then up it goes."

"Powder—magazine—kegs?" cried Roy. "Why, we haven't one, and I wanted to talk to you about getting some. How's it to be done?"

"By going to your father's lib'ry, sir, and opening the little drawer as he keeps locked up in the big oak table. There's the keys there."

"Yes, of the wine-cellars, Ben; but no—Oh, absurd!"

"Is it, my lad? I think not. Think it's likely as your grandfather and his father would have had swords and pikes and armour, and big guns and little guns, and not had no powder to load 'em with?"

"Well, it doesn't sound likely, Ben; but I'm sure we have none here."

"Well, sir, begging your pardon for contradicting my master, I'm sure as we have."

"Down in the cellars?"

"Down in one of 'em, sir."

"But I never knew."

"Perhaps not, sir; but I've been down there with your father, and I don't suppose it's a thing he'd talk about. Anyhow, there it is, shut up behind three doors, and I'll be bound to say dry as a bone. It's very old, but good enough, may be. All the same, though, Master Roy, the sooner we try what it's like the better, and if you'll take my advice you'll have one of the big guns loaded and fired with a good round charge. That'll try the gun, scale it out, and give 'em a hint for miles round that, though Sir Granby's gone to the wars, his son's at home, and his dame too, and that they don't mean to stand any nonsense from a set o' crop-eared rascals. That'll do more good, Master Roy, than a deal o' talking, and be less trouble."

"We must do it at once, Ben," said Roy, decidedly.

"The first thing, sir; and, by the way, as we're going to begin to get our garrison together, it'll be as well to make a little show. If I was you, I'd put on a pair of buff boots, wear a sword and a sash always, and I don't say put on a lot of armour, but if you'll let me, I'll take the gorget off that suit of Italian armour, and you can wear that."

"But it will look so—" said Roy, flushing.

"Yes, sir; but we've got to look so," said the old soldier, decidedly. "It makes people respect you; and if you'll be good enough to give me my orders, I'll take to a buff coat and steel cap at once."

"Very well, do so," said Roy. "But I will not promise to make any show myself."

"But you must, sir, please, for her ladyship's sake. Look here, Master Roy, you'll be calling the tenants and labourers together, and you'll have to make them a speech."

"Shall I?" said Roy, nervously.

"Why, of course, sir, telling 'em what their duty is, and calling upon 'em to fight for their king, their country, and their homes. Yes, that's it, sir; that's just what you've got to say."

"Well, Ben, if I must, I must."

"Then must it is, sir; but if they come here to the castle, and you're like you are now, they'll be only half warmed up, and say that Master Roy can talk, and some of 'em'll sneer and snigger; but if you come out when they're all here, looking like your father's son in a cavalier hat and feathers, with the gorget on, and the king's colours for a sash, ay, and buff boots and spurs—"

"Oh, no, not spurs when I'm walking," protested Roy.

"Yes, sir, spurs,—a big pair with gilt rowels, as'll *clink-clink* with every step you take; they'll set up a cheer, and swear to fight for you, when you've done, to the death. And look here, Master Roy, when you've done speaking, you just wave your hat, and chuck it up in the air, as if fine felts and ostridge feathers weren't nothing to you, who called upon 'em all to fight for the king."

Roy drew a deep sigh, for his follower's words had nearly made him breathless.

"We shall see," he sighed.

"Yes, sir, we shall see," cried Ben. "So now, if you please, sir, I won't wait to be getting into my buff jerkin now, but I'll take your orders for what we're to do first."

"Yes, Ben; what ought we to do first?"

"Well, sir, it's you as know. You said something about strengthening the guard at the gate."

"Oh, but I say, Ben, that was you said so."

"Only as your mouthpiece, sir."

"But it sounds silly to talk about strengthening the guard at the gate when we've only got old Jenk, and no regular sentry to put there."

"Never you mind about how it sounds, sir, so long as it's sense," cried Ben, striking his fist into his left palm. "We've got to make our garrison and our sentries out of the raw stuff, and the sooner we begin to sound silly now the better. It won't be silly for any one who comes and finds a staunch man there, who would sooner send a musketoon bullet through him than let him pass."

"No, Ben, it will not, certainly. Whom shall I send?"

"Well, sir, if I was you, I'd do it as I meant to go on. You give me my orders, and I'll go and enlist Sam Rogers in the stable at once, bring him here fierce-like into the armoury; put him on a buff coat, buckle on a sword, and give him his bandoleer and firelock, and march him down with sword drawn to relieve guard with old Jenk."

"But he'll be cleaning the troopers' horses, and begin to laugh."

"Sam Rogers, sir? Not him. He'll come like a lamb; and when I marches him down to the gate, he'll go out like a lion, holding his head up with the steel cap on, and be hoping that all the servant-girls and the cook are watching him. Don't you be afraid of him laughing. All I'm afraid of is, that while he's so fresh he'll be playing up some games with his firelock, and mocking poor old Jenk."

"Pray, warn him, then."

"You trust me, sir. Then, when that's done, perhaps you'll give the orders to find quarters for our new men, and tell 'em that they're to rest till to-morrow by your orders; and after that there's the drawbridge and portcullis."

"Yes; what about them?"

"Why, sir, you know how they've been for years. You must have 'em seen to at once; and, if I was you, I'd have the portcullis seen to first, and the little sally-port door in the corner of the tower. We shall want half a dozen men. I'm a bit afraid of the old bars and rollers, but we shall see."

"Order the men to come, then, when you've done, and let us see, and get everything right as soon as possible."

Ben saluted in military fashion, and marched off to the hall, where Roy heard him speak in a cheering, authoritative voice to the new-comers, and then came out to march across to the stables, which were in the basement of the east side of the castle, with their entrance between the building and the court; but the gate-way that had opened into the court-yard had been partly closed up when that was turned into a flower-garden, and the archway was now covered with ivy.

Roy went up to one of the corridors beneath the ramparts, and watched, out of curiosity, to see how the groom would take his new orders.

He was not long kept in suspense, for the sturdy young fellow came out talking eagerly with Ben and turning down his sleeves. Then they went inside, through the great gate-way to the armoury, and in an incredibly short space of time came out together, the groom in steel jockey-shaped cap with a spike on the top, buff coat, sword, and bandoleer, and shouldering the clumsy firelock of the period.

As they reached the archway, Ben stopped short, drew his sword, said a few words in a sharp tone, and marched off, with Sam Rogers keeping step; while a muttering of voices told of how strangely matters had turned out according to old Ben's prophecy, for, on turning to see what it meant, Roy saw down through one of the narrow windows that the whole of the household had turned out to do likewise. But there was no giggling and laughing, for the women seemed to be impressed, and the men-servants were shaking their heads and talking together earnestly about the evil times that had come.

Another sound made Roy turn sharply in the other direction to see his mother approaching.

"Then you have begun, my son," she said, gravely.

"Yes, mother. The sentry was set, after a long talk with Martlet."

"You need not speak in that apologetic tone, my boy," said Lady Royland, quietly. "I see the necessity, and I am sure you are doing well. Now, come and tell me more of your plans."

She led the way to the library, and as they entered Roy glanced towards the big oak table standing at one end; his eyes fixed themselves upon the small drawer, and he seemed to see a rusty old key lying there, one whose wards were shaping themselves plainly before his eyes, as he told of his arrangements with the old soldier.

"Yes, you have begun well, Roy," said Lady Royland at last. "And what Martlet says is quite true."

"But you would not dress up as he advises, mother?" protested Roy, rather bashfully.

"Dress up? No, my boy; but I would put on such things as a cavalier and an officer would wear under such circumstances,—a gorget, sword, boots, hat and feathers, and the king's colours as a scarf. Why, Roy, your father would wear those in addition to his scarlet coat."

"Yes, mother; but he is a soldier."

"So are you now, Roy," said the dame, proudly. "And so must every man be who loves his king and country. Martlet is quite right, and I shall prepare your scarf and feathers with my own hands."

"Why, mother," cried the boy, wonderingly, "how you have changed since even a short time ago."

"So has our position, Roy, my son," she said, firmly. "Who's there?"

The butler entered.

"Benjamin Martlet would be glad, my lady, if Master Roy would come and give him his instructions, and, if you please, my lady, he wishes me to help."

"And you will, I am sure, Grey?"

"Oh, yes, my lady," said the man, eagerly; "but I was afraid your ladyship might be wanting something, and no one to answer the bell."

"I want my servants, Grey, to help me to protect their master's interests while he is forced to be away in the service of the king. Can I count upon that help?"

"Yes, my lady, to a man," cried the old servant, eagerly.

"I thought so," said Lady Royland, smiling proudly. "You will go, then, Roy, and see what Martlet is to do."

Roy was already at the door, and five minutes later he was standing in the gate-way with every man employed about the place, the three troopers being fast asleep, exhausted by their long journey down from town.

Chapter Nine
Portcullis and Bridge

As Roy appeared, there was a low buzz of voices, and directly after the butler cried, "Three cheers for the young master!" with a hearty result.

Just then Ben came close up to say, confidentially—

"I made it all comfortable with poor old Jenk, sir."

"That's right; and Sam Rogers?"

"Proud's a dog with two tails, sir. Now, sir, if you'll give the orders, we'll go up and see what can be done about making the place safe, and I'm afraid we're going to have a job."

Roy felt a slight sensation of shrinking, but he mastered it, and calling to the men to follow him, he turned in by the low arched door-way, and ascended to the first chamber of the gate tower, to pause where the great iron grating hung before him in its stone grooves formed in the wall, and with its spikes descending through the slit on the floor, below which the stone paving of the entrance could be seen.

To make sure of its not descending by any accident of the chains giving, three massive pieces of squared oak had been thrust through as many of the openings at the bottom, so that the portcullis rested upon them as these crossed the long narrow slit through which it descended, and a little examination showed that if the chains were tightened by turning the two capstans by means of the bars, and the chains drawn a little over the great wheels fixed in the ceiling, it would be easy enough to withdraw the three supports and let the grating down.

"Chains look terribly rusty," said Roy. "Think they'll bear it, Ben?"

"They're rusty, sir, and a good deal eaten away; but they used to put good work into these sort o' things, because if they hadn't, they'd have come down and killed some one. Shall we try?"

"Yes; no one can be hurt if a watch is kept below. Go down, one of you, and see that no one passes under."

One of the men ran down, the old capstan-bars were taken from the corners, and two men on each side inserted them into the holes, and waited for the order to tighten the chains round the rollers.

"Ready? All together!" cried Roy; and the men pulled the bars towards them with a will, the chains tightened, the pulleys creaked and groaned, and the grating rose an inch or two, sufficient for the pieces of oak crossing the narrow slit to have been drawn out, when *crack—crack—*two of the bars the men handled snapped short off, and their holders fell, while the portcullis sank back to its old place with a heavy jar.

"Hundred years, perhaps, since they've been used," said Roy. "Any one hurt?"

"No, sir," said the men, laughing in spite of a bruise or two; and the bars being examined, it was found that the tough oak of which they were composed was completely honeycombed by worms, and powdered away to dust.

"First job, then, sir, to make new bars," said Ben, promptly.

"Yes; we'll have the carpenters in from the village directly, Ben. With these pulleys well greased, I suppose this will work."

"Ay, sir, no doubt about that; it's the drawbridge I'm afraid of," said Ben.

"Let's go up and see, then."

Roy led the way again, and the men followed into the dark chamber above, where the old furnace stood, and in the corners on either side of the narrow window, with its hollowed-out notches for firing or using crossbows from, were two great round chimney-like constructions built in the stone, up and down which huge weights, which depended from massive chains and passed over great rollers, had formerly been used to glide.

Ben shook his head as he put his hand upon one of the weights, which were formed of so many discs of cast lead, through the centre of which the great chain passed, a solid bar of iron being driven through a link below to keep them from sliding off.

The weights hung about breast-high; and at the slight pressure of the man's hand began to swing to and fro in the stone place open to the chamber, but closed below where they ran down in the wall at the sides of the gate-way.

"Well, these must have been worked by hand, Ben," said Roy. "Men must have stood here and run them down. Two of you go to the other side, and all press down together, but stand ready to jump back in case anything breaks. I don't see how you can be hurt if you do."

"No, sir; no one can't be hurt, for the weights will only go down these holes with a bang."

"Try, then. Now, all together—pull!"

The men tugged and strained, but there was no sign of yielding, and Ben shook his head.

"Rollers must be rusted, sir, and stick."

But upon his climbing up to examine them, it proved that these had not been made to turn, only for the chains to slide over them, as the grooves worn in the iron showed.

"Nothing to stop 'em here, sir," said the man.

"Then it must be set fast at the end of the bridge," said Roy; and, descending with the men, they crossed the moat and found the bridge completely wedged and fixed in the opening of stone which embraced the end.

Picks and crowbars were fetched, the stones and sand scraped out, and when the place was cleared they reascended to the furnace-chamber, when, upon another trial being made, it was found that the weights so accurately balanced the bridge that with very little exertion the chains came screeching and groaning over the iron rollers, and the men gave a cheer as the end rose up and up till it was drawn very nearly up to the face of the tower.

Ben rubbed his ear and grinned with satisfaction.

"Come, sir," he said, "we can make ourselves pretty safe that way; but I'm afraid the moat's so filled up that a man can wade across."

"That he can't," cried one of the gardeners. "I've plumbed it all over, and there aren't a place less nor seven or eight feet deep, without counting the mud."

"Then you've been fishing!" thought Roy, but he did not say so, only gave orders for the bridge to be lowered again, and sent a man for a supply of grease to well lubricate the rollers and chains.

Down went the bridge, in a most unmusical way, and as soon as it was in its place once more, a man was sent across for the village carpenter to come with his tools, there being plenty of good seasoned oak-wood stored up in the buildings.

Then a consultation ensued. They had the means of cutting themselves off from the outer world, and in a short time the portcullis would add to the strength of their defences.

"What's next, Ben?" said Roy.

"I'm a-thinking, sir. We've done a lot already, but there's so much more to do that things get a bit jumbled like in my head. We've got to get our garrison, and then there's two very important things—wittles and water!"

"The well supplies that last," said Roy; "and if we were running short, we could use the water from the moat for everything but food."

"Yes, sir, that's good. Cart must go to the mill, and bring all the corn and flour that can be got. Then we must have some beasts and sheep from the farm."

"That's bad," said Roy, "because they'll want feeding."

"Have to be driven out every morning, sir, till we're besieged. Must have some cows in too, so that if we are beset we can be independent. But first of all, sir, we ought to see to the powder and the guns. But you and me must see to the powder ourselves. We shall want some help over the guns, and I'm thinking as you'd best make that carpenter stay. The wheels are off one or two of the gun-carriages, and there's no rammers or sponges; and I shouldn't wonder if the carriages as I painted over and pitched are only so many worm-eaten shells."

"Well, all these things will have to be got over by degrees, Ben. We have done the first great things towards making the castle safe, and an enemy need not know how unprepared we are."

"I don't know so much about being safe, sir."

"What, not with the drawbridge up?"

"No, sir," said Ben, in a low tone. "But suppose you sends the men to dinner now, and orders 'em to meet in a hour's time in the court-yard—oh dear, oh dear! that's all garden now."

"You can make room for the men to meet without disturbing the garden," said Roy, sharply.

"Very well, sir; you're master. Will you give your orders?"

Roy gave them promptly, and the men walked away.

"Now, then," said Roy, "what did you mean about the place not being safe? With the bridge up, they could only cross to us by rafts or boats, and then they couldn't get in."

"Well, sir, it's like this. I've heard tell, though I'd forgotten all about it till just now, as there's a sort o' passage goes out from the dungeons under the nor'-west tower over to the little ruins on the hill over yonder."

"Impossible! Why, it would have to be half a mile long, Ben."

"All that, sir."

"But it couldn't go under the moat. It would be full of water."

"Nay, not if it was made tight, sir."

"But what makes you say that? You've never seen the passage?"

"No, sir, I've never been down, but your father once said something about it. It was a long time before that tower was done up and made right for Master Pawson. I don't recollect much about it, but I suppose it must be there."

"That's another thing to see to, then," said Roy. "Because, if it does exist, and the enemy heard of it, he might come in and surprise us. I know; we'll find it, and block it up."

"Nay, I wouldn't do that, sir. It might be that we should have to go away, and it isn't a bad thing to have a way out in case of danger."

"Not likely to do that, Ben," said Roy, haughtily. "We are going to hold the place."

"Yes, sir, as long as we can; but we can't do impossibilities. Now, sir, will you go and have your bit o' dinner, while I have mine?"

"Oh, I don't feel as if I could eat, Ben; I'm too full of excitement."

"More reason why you should go and have your dinner, sir. Man can't fight without he eats and drinks."

"Nor a boy, neither—eh, Ben?"

"That's so, sir; only I wouldn't be talking before the men about being only a boy. You leave them to say it if they like. But they won't; they'll judge you by what you do, sir; and if you act like a man, they'll look at you as being the one in command of them, and behave like it."

"Very well, I'll go to dinner, and in an hour meet you here."

"Fifty minutes, sir. It's a good ten minutes since the men went in."

Roy joined his mother, feeling, as he said, too full of excitement to eat; but he found the meal ready, with one of the maids in attendance, and everything so calm and quiet, that, as they sat chatting, it seemed as if all this excitement were as unsubstantial as the distant rumours of war; while, when the meal was at an end, his mother's words tended to lend some of her calm to his excited brain.

"I have been hearing of all that you have done, Roy," she said. "It is excellent; but do not hurry. I cannot afford to have you ill."

That was a fresh idea, and the consequences of such a trouble too horrible to be contemplated; but it made Roy determine to take things more coolly, and in this spirit he went to where the servants were assembled in the gate-way, and joined his trusty lieutenant, who had just drawn them up in line.

Chapter Ten
Roy visits the Powder-Magazine

"Now, Ben, what next?"

"The thing I've been thinking, sir, is that, little as it be, we must make the most of our garrison. It's war time now, and if you'll give the order I'll march the men to the armoury and serve out the weepuns and clothes."

Roy nodded, gave the word for the men to march, counter-ordered it, at a hint from Ben, and then, telling them to face right, put himself at their head, and marched them to the long, low room at once.

Ben began to serve out the buff jerkins and steel caps.

"Can't stop for no trying on now," he said; "you must do as we used in the army,—change about till you get them as fits you."

This done, the firelocks and bandoleers followed, and, lastly, to each man a belt and sword.

And all the time the old soldier handed every article to the recipient with a grave dignity and a solemnity of manner which seemed to say, "I am giving treasures to you that I part from with the greatest regret," and he finished with—

"Now, my lads, look here: it's a great honour to bear arms in the service of your king, and if you're carrying Sir Granby Royland's arms you're carrying the king's, so take care of 'em. A good soldier wouldn't have a speck of rust on his helmet or his sword; they're as bright as I can make 'em now, and as sharp, so mind they're always so. Now go to your new quarters and put 'em on—proper, mind; and your master, the captain here, will have a parade in an hour's time."

The men went off, leaving Roy wondering at the calmness with which he stood by listening while old Ben talked to the men and kept on referring to him as "your master."

Ben now turned to him. "What do you say, sir?" he said. "Don't you think we had better go down and see if all's right in the powder-magazine?"

"But it's in the cellar, Ben, and you'd want a light."

"Hardly fair, sir, to call it the cellar. I believe it's one of the old dungeons where they used to shut people up in the good old times."

"That would be darker still, Ben. How are we to see?"

"Have to feel, sir; for I don't fancy taking down a lantern. Once we get there and the place open, we can go round and tell with our hands how many kegs there are on the shelves, and then if we bring one out and try it, and it turns out all right, we shall know we're safe."

"Very well: it isn't a nice job; but, if it has to be done, we'd better get it over."

"As you say, sir, it aren't a nice job; but, if we're very careful, I don't see as we can come to much harm; so, if you'll get the keys, sir, we'll go at once."

Roy nodded, and went in without a word, to find his mother seated in the library writing.

"What is it, my boy?" she said. "What do you want?"

Roy hesitated for a moment, and then said, rather huskily, "The keys. Ben and I are going down into the magazine."

Lady Royland looked at him in a wondering way.

"The magazine? Do you mean the store-room?"

"No; the powder-magazine."

She started now, and looked anxious.

"I had almost forgotten its existence, Roy. But is it necessary? It may be dangerous to go into such a place."

"We shall take care, mother, and have no light. It is necessary, Ben says, for we must be provided with gunpowder, and he wants to try whether it is good, because it must be very old."

"Very old, my boy. Probably older than your grandfather's day. I hardly like you to go upon such an errand."

"But if I'm to be captain, mother, and look after the place, I can't go back and tell Ben that. It would look so weak."

"Yes, yes, of course," said Lady Royland, making an effort to be calm and firm. "But you will be very careful, Roy."

"You may trust me, mother," he said; and she drew the keys, with a sigh, from the drawer in the old table, and handed them to her son, who took them and returned to his lieutenant.

"Here they are, Ben," said Roy, quietly. "Ready?"

"Yes, sir, I'm ready. I want to be satisfied about that powder, because it means so much to us, for I'm sure I don't know how we could get any more in times like these. You might send an order to London or one of the places in Kent where they make it, but I should never expect to see it come down here. Well, we won't waste time; so come along."

Taking off his sword, and signing to Roy to do the same, he led the way to the flight of spiral steps in the base of the south-east tower, but, instead of going up, followed it down to where there was a low arched door on their left and an opening on their right.

"Long time since any one's been in that old dungeon, Master Roy. Hundred years, I dare say. Maybe we shall be putting some one in, one of these days!"

"In there? Whom? What for?"

"Prisoners, sir, for fighting against the king." The old fellow laughed, and went along through the opening on their right, which proved to be an arched passage very dimly lit by a series of little pipe-like holes sloping inward through the outer wall of the castle and opening about a foot above the moat. On their aft were doors of a row of cellars built beneath the old court-yard; and as Ben walked onward he said—

"Who'd think as there were green grass and flower-beds up above them, Master Roy? But we do see changes in this life. Halt! here we are."

He stopped at the end of the passage, where there was a massive oak door-way facing them beneath a curious old Norman arch, and, after trying hard with three different keys, the rusty wards of the old lock allowed one to turn, and the door was pushed wide open, creaking back against the wall.

"Rather dark, sir," said Ben. "Get on a deal better with a candle; but it wouldn't do."

Roy peered in, and, as his eyes grew more accustomed to the obscurity, he made out that he was gazing into a small stone chamber; but there was no sign of chest or keg, or door leading onward.

"Why, the place is empty, Ben," said the boy, with a sigh of relief.

"We don't know that yet, sir, because we haven't seen it," said Ben, quietly. "This is only the way to the magazine. People in the old days knew what dangerous tackle it was, and took care of it according. But it's going to be a dark job, and no mistake."

The old soldier stepped in, and, stooping down in the middle of the blank stone chamber, took hold of a large copper ring and drew up one side of a heavy flagstone, which turned silently upon copper pivots, and this flag he laid back till it was supported by the ring.

"Looks darker down there, sir," said Ben, as Roy stood beside him and they tried to pierce the gloom, but only for the latter to make out the dim outline of a stone step or two.

"You've been down here before, of course?" whispered Roy, as if the place impressed him.

"Yes, sir; once. There's a door at the bottom, and that's the magazine. It will be all feeling, sir. Will you go back while I try and get a keg?"

"No," said Roy, firmly, but with an intense desire to say yes. "I shall stay while you go down. There can be no danger if you have no light."

"Unless the rusty key strikes a light, sir."

"Oh, that's impossible," whispered Roy.

"I suppose I'd better pull off my boots before I go down; it'll perhaps be safer."

He seated himself on the floor and pulled them off, Roy standing up, leaning against the wall, and doing the same.

"What's that for?" said Ben.

"Coming with you. I want to know what the place is like."

"Oh, there's no need for two of us to go, sir. One's enough."

Roy said nothing, but followed the old fellow down eight stone steps, and then they stood together against a door, which felt to the touch to be very strongly made of stone, while, after a little searching about for a keyhole, Ben said, with a grunt—

"Forgot! There aren't no key to this. It's fastened with these two wooden bars."

"I thought they were part of the door, Ben," said Roy, in the same suppressed tone.

"So did I, sir, at first. I ought to have remembered, and I think I do now. Yes! that's the way; they turn on pins in the middle like wooden buttons, and you turns one up and the other down out of the notches they fit in, and then push the door, which has stone hinges."

As he spoke, Ben turned the two great wooden bars, and then pressed upon the door.

"Hope the stones won't strike a light, sir," said Ben, in a low growl.

Roy felt as if a hand had suddenly compressed his heart, and he peered wildly through the door-way, half expecting to see a tiny spark or two, as a dull, grating sound arose; but the only sparks the door made were those glittering in his own eyes, and he drew a deeper, harder breath as the door ceased to move.

"Now, we've got to be careful, or we shall be hitting against one another, sir! Let me see: there's one step down, and then you're in a place like a dairy, with two sets of stone shelves,—one just above the floor, to keep it out of the damp; the other just about as high as a man's breast,—and there's kegs of powder piled-up on them all. You stand still, and I'll go in."

"No; let me," said Roy, though why he said this puzzled the boy himself, when the exciting minutes had passed.

"Well, sir, you're master, and if you'd rather, of course you can. But I don't mind going if you like."

"I'll go," said Roy, huskily, and, stretching out his hands in the now profound darkness, he felt for and touched the side of the entrance, then made a step forward to place his stockinged foot down upon the cold stone floor, which struck up like ice. Bringing forward his second foot, he reached out for the side of the vault, and found the place just as his companion had described, for his hands came in contact with small wooden barrels, neatly piled one upon the other on a great stone shelf, beneath which was another shelf laden in a similar way.

"Feel anything, sir?" said Ben, from the entrance.

"Yes: barrels, numbers of them," said Roy, huskily, his voice sounding a mere whisper in the darkness. "They go on—yes, to here. It is only a small vault."

"Yes, sir, but big enough. Try the other side now."

Three steps took Roy there, and his hands touched barrels again piled-up in the same way, and he whispered his experience.

"That's it, sir; just what I thought. But what we want to know now is, are they full? Would you mind lifting one, or shall I come and do it?"

Roy shuddered a little, but he did not shrink. Stretching out his hands, he took a careful hold of one of the kegs, raised it to find it fairly heavy, and then replaced it.

"Try another, sir."

Roy felt less compunction in lifting the second, and this being replaced, he began to sound others with his knuckles, to find that they all gave forth the same dull dead note.

"That's all we want to know down here, Master Roy," said the old soldier at last; "and now I think we'd better get back and take a couple of the little kegs with us. I'd take one from each side, sir. You pass 'em to me and I'll carry 'em up safely. It wouldn't do to drop one in case it should go off."

These words, lightly spoken, made Roy thrill as he lifted down one of the kegs, getting his fingers tightly fitted to the ends, and then stood there in the black darkness, afraid to stir for fear he should strike his elbow against anything and jerk the keg to the floor.

"Got him, sir?"

"Yes," said Roy, hoarsely. "Whereabouts are you?"

"Here, just at the door, sir; I haven't moved," was the reply.

"Reach out your hands, then, and take hold very carefully. Tell me when you've got it tight."

"Tight hold," said Ben, the next moment.

"Sure?"

"Yes, sir; let it go, and I'll carry it up."

Roy quitted his hold of the keg unwillingly, and his heart beat violently as he listened to the soft *pat, pat*, of his companion's feet, and thought of the consequences of a fall. Possibly one vivid flash and the whole place destroyed; and yet for years they had all been living so close to this terribly destructive power.

"If Ben should drop that keg!"

But Ben only set it down quietly a short distance from the top of the steps and descended.

"T'other one, sir, please," he said; and Roy placed this in the man's hands with the same shrinking feeling of reluctance.

It was carried up, and Roy stepped out, drawing the door after him, and after a few trials managing to close the two bars which secured the place.

"Don't want no help there, sir?"

"No; I have done it," was the reply; and Roy ascended the steps and waited for his companion to close the stone trap.

"Not a bad hole this to shut any one up in if we ever wanted to get rid of him, eh? He'd have to shout pretty hard to make any one hear."

"Don't talk; let's get away from the dreadful place," said Roy, whose face was wet with perspiration. "Can you carry both kegs?"

"Half a dozen if you'd range 'em, sir," replied Ben.

"Then I'll fasten the doors after us; and, mind this, the magazine must always be most carefully locked up."

"You trust me for that, sir!" replied Ben. "I know too well what powder can do to try any tricks or trust anybody with it but myself. Why, do you know, sir, what would happen if I gave a fellow like Tom Rogers a keg to carry?"

"No; how can I tell?" said Roy, shortly.

"Well, I can, sir: he'd set it up on end, sit upon it, and take out a flint and steel to light his pipe as like as not."

"Don't talk any more, please, Ben," said the boy as he proceeded to lock one of the doors.

"No, sir; I only did it so as to keep you from thinking about what we've been doing. I suppose one would get used to it, but it does seem to me rather ugly work even to an old soldier."

"Where are we to put these two kegs?" said Roy.

"In the big closet in the armoury, sir," replied Ben. "Don't you fidget about them; they shall be all right, for that's my part of the place, and nobody goes in there without my leave."

"It's impossible to help feeling a little uncomfortable about them, Ben, but I know you'll take care."

"I just think I will, sir. I'm very particular about no harm coming to Sergeant Benjamin Martlet; and as to doing anything that might mean risks for my lady—but there, I needn't say nothing about that. You can come and see me put 'em away."

Roy insisted upon carrying one of the kegs, in spite of the old soldier's opposition, not to relieve him of the load, but as a lesson to himself in the art of getting used to the dangerous composition. In addition, it had occurred to him that he should have to be present when the barrels were opened, and the gun or guns fired to test their utility and strength after lying by for so many years. Roy had never even heard a big gun fired, and he told himself that it would not do for him to display the slightest dread before the men.

Consequently he hid his nervousness, and helped to deposit the kegs in the great cupboard which contained Ben's tools and cleaning apparatus.

"There!" said that individual, "as soon as we've had our parade, and dismissed the troops, we'll see to that powder, and find out what it's like."

He thrust the key into his pocket, buckled on his sword again, and, drawing himself up, asked the "captain" to lead the way to the entrance gate.

Chapter Eleven
Master Pawson gives his Opinions

"You're quite turning everything into military style, Ben," said Roy, as they left the armoury.

"Yes, sir; nothing like it. Keep the men up to the mark."

"But isn't it comic to speak of the people as the troops?"

"No, sir; not a bit. Troops are troops whether there's many or few. It's serious work is fighting, and, with due respect to you, sir, there's nothing comic in treating our new levies as if they were seasoned men."

All the same, though, Roy felt that he could not agree with his companion, when they reached the great gate-way, now, for the time being, made the parade ground. To his eyes the aspect of the place was decidedly comic, and his first impulse upon seeing the familiar figures of butler, footman, grooms, and gardeners, looking stiff and awkward in their heavy buff coats, creased and angular for want of use, was to burst out laughing.

But he did not even smile, for he could see that the men were glancing at him consciously, and he knew that any such display of mirth at their personal appearance would have had a most disastrous effect. As it was, he behaved very wisely, for when Ben shouted out an order for them to fall into line, Roy advanced to the men at once with a few encouraging remarks.

"The accoutrements and things have been lying by so long," he said, "that they must be very uncomfortable and stiff."

"Yes, sir, they really are," said the butler, shaking his head. "You feel as if you can't move in them; and my steel cap is terribly heavy."

"You'll find them grow more easy to wear after a bit," said Roy, at a venture. "I see you are pretty well fitted, and—What's that, Ben?"

For voices came from the gate-way beyond the drawbridge, a hundred yards from where they were standing.

"I'll see, sir," said Ben, importantly, as he drew himself to the salute. "Beg pardon, sir," he added in a low tone; "be better now if you'd make everything soldierly and speak to me as sergeant. Don't see why my old rank shouldn't tell now, and it will help me with the three troopers, for one of 'em's a corporal."

Roy nodded, and directly after followed his sergeant, for he began to have an inkling of what was going on.

As he crossed the drawbridge, it was in time to hear Master Pawson say, in his high-pitched voice and in a tone of anger that was quite new —

"Oh, there you are, Martlet! What is the meaning of all this folly? Rogers dressed up, and telling me I can't come in without an order from her ladyship."

"Quite right, sir," said Ben, steadily; "only he didn't know he was to let in any one belonging to the place."

"But what does it mean? I've been out since morning, and I return to find the gate locked, and a man playing at being a sentry. Why, Roy, my dear boy, surely this is not some bad joke of yours?"

"Unfasten the gate, Rogers, and let Master Pawson in," said Roy, with his face turning scarlet; and, seeing his look of confusion, the secretary continued —

"Oh, I see; it is playing at soldiers. And gracious me! who are those under the gate-way? Surely troops have not arrived in my absence. My dear Roy, surely her ladyship does not countenance this? It is too absurd."

Annoyance made the boy feel indignant, and he knew that those near him expected him to speak on their behalf.

"It is not absurd, Master Pawson," he replied, sharply. "The castle is being placed under military rule now, and will be put in a state of defence as soon as possible."

"That's so!" growled Ben, whose face was black as a thunder-cloud.

Master Pawson gave him a quick look, but he did not speak to him, but to Roy.

"A state of defence!" he said, in a tone of raillery; "what nonsense! and pray, why?"

"On account of the troubled times, sir."

"Troubled times! What troubled times?"

"Surely you know, sir, who have been bringing my mother news of the revolution."

Master Pawson's eyes opened a little more widely, for he was astonished. The boy addressing him seemed no longer the quiet, sport-loving pupil who came up into the tower to read with him and listen patiently while he played on his violoncello, but one who had suddenly been transformed.

"Ah, you mean the tidings of those people who object to some of the king's orders? But really that has nothing to do with us out here in this quiet, retired place. And you are making it an excuse for all this folly? For shame, Roy! Dressing up the servants, and putting on a sword! Go and take it off, boy, and do not make yourself ridiculous."

Ben glanced at his young master, whose face was redder than ever, and waited impatiently for him to speak, while Master Pawson turned towards his pupil smilingly, extending one hand to lay upon his shoulder, the other to lay hold of his sword.

"There is nothing absurd or nonsensical about it, Master Pawson," he said, firmly. "As I have told you, the castle will be put in a state of defence."

"You mean repair, my dear boy," said the secretary, mockingly.

"Yes, repair if you will, as to the weak parts, sir. And as to playing at soldiers, we may look a little awkward at first, as we are not used to our weapons and arms; but that will soon pass off, and you will have to join us, and do your best."

"That's so!" growled Ben, whose face began to lighten up a little as Roy spoke out so firmly.

Master Pawson turned upon the old soldier with his eyebrows raised in a look of surprise.

"My good man," he said, "will you please to recollect your position here."

Ben saluted, and drew himself up as stiff as a pike.

"Nonsense, my dear boy!" continued Master Pawson; "this is all foolish vanity, and I am sure that, when you have thought it over coolly, you will see that it is childish for you, a boy, to imagine that you can do any good by making this silly display. Why, you must have been reading some old book of chivalry and warlike adventure. If you only knew how ridiculous you look with that long sword buckled on, you would soon take it off. You look almost as absurd as Rogers here; I thought some scarecrow had been stuck up by the gate."

"Yes, sir; that's right," growled Ben. "Scarecrows who were going to scare off all the crows as try to peck at his majesty the king."

"Silence, Martlet!" cried Roy, sharply. "It is not your place to speak to Master Pawson like that."

"I should think not," said the secretary, with his face flushing slightly.

"Beg pardon, sir, a slip: not mutiny," said Ben.

"No, but insolence on the part of a menial," cried Master Pawson; "and if it is repeated, I shall ask Lady Royland to dismiss you, sir, at once."

"And my mother would refuse to dismiss so old and faithful a servant," said Roy, warmly.

The secretary looked at the boy wonderingly again, and his eyes darkened; but he smiled the next moment.

"Come, come, Roy!" he said. "Pray leave off this nonsense, and have the gate left open. Send the men back to their work. You will thank me for giving you this advice to-morrow."

"No, Master Pawson, I shall not," said Roy, firmly. "The gate will be kept locked; no one will be allowed to pass without the word, and to-night the drawbridge will be raised; by to-morrow, I dare say, we shall be able to lower the portcullis."

"Are you mad, my boy?"

"I hope not, sir."

"Do you mean to tell me that you will not listen to my advice?"

"Yes, sir; I cannot."

"Then, my good lad, I must be severe. I have tried gentle means. As your tutor, in whose charge you have been left by your father, I command you to give up all this silly mummery. You have something better to do than to waste time over such childish tricks. Go to your room, and stay there for a while before you come to mine with an apology. Quick! At once!"

He stood, looking very important, as he gave a quick stamp and pointed towards the castle.

"You, Jenkin, go and put that sword away! Rogers and Martlet, go back to your work at once!"

"Stop!" said Roy, firmly, as the men looked at him for help. "Keep as you are. Master Pawson is my tutor, but he has no right to give you any orders.—I must ask you, sir, to go to your room, and not to interfere with what is going on around."

"Hah!" ejaculated Ben, expelling a tremendous pent-up breath, and he turned and winked at Rogers and Jenk, though the poor old gate-keeper could not see.

"The boy is mad," cried Master Pawson, flushing angrily now. "This is beyond bearing. An act of rebellion. Once more, sir, will you obey me?"

"Obey you, Master Pawson? In my studies, yes. Over the business of the castle, no!"

"I am striving to save you from being ridiculed by the whole district, sir, and I appeal to you not to force me to have you humbled by going in to complain to Lady Royland."

"You will not humble me, sir, by going in to complain to my mother, for she endorses everything I have done."

"Her ladyship does!" cried Master Pawson, looking quite aghast.

"Of course. All this is by my father's orders."

"Absurd, boy! Your father has given no such orders."

"Indeed!" said Roy, flushing angrily at the contradiction. "You have not been at home, sir, or you would have seen his messengers, three troopers, ride up this morning, from his regiment, who will stay to help us strengthen the place. There they are! I hope you don't think they look ridiculous in their uniforms."

For, as he was speaking, the three men, rested now and refreshed, had marched from the servants' hall to where the new recruits were drawn up, and stood there waiting for their captain to return.

For a few moments Master Pawson's face dropped, and he stared in his utter astonishment.

But he recovered himself quickly, and said, with a smile—

"Of course I did not know of this, my dear boy, especially as it all was while I have been away. As your father has given the orders in his letter,—and I am very glad that your mother has heard at last,—of course there is nothing to be done, unless her ladyship can be brought to see how unnecessary it all is, and likely to cause trouble and misconstruction among the neighbours. I am sure that if Sir Granby could be here now, he would see that it was needless. Whatever troubles may arise, nothing can disturb us in this secluded spot. There, I will go now to attend to my reading. When you have done playing at soldiers," he added, with a slightly mocking emphasis upon the "playing," "perhaps you will join me, Roy. You will get tired of handling swords too large for your hand, but of studies you can never weary. *Au revoir*. I am sorry we had this little misunderstanding."

He patted Roy on the shoulder and walked on across the drawbridge, as if not perceiving that his pupil followed him; and as he drew near the servants, ranged rather awkwardly in their fresh habiliments, he smiled in a way which made every man shrink and feel far more uncomfortable than he had been made by his stiff buff coat. But as he passed the three troopers,— fine, manly-looking, seasoned fellows, who wore their uniforms as if to the manner born, and who drew themselves up and saluted him, evidently looking upon him as one of the important personages of the house,—he ceased to smile, and went on to his study in the north-west tower, looking very serious and much disturbed in mind.

Chapter Twelve
Guns and no Powder?

Very little more was done with the men that day, for, in spite of Roy's spirited behaviour, he felt afterwards that Master Pawson had cast a damp upon the proceedings. Still, he knew that something must be done to counteract that sneering smile distributed among the men by the tutor; and upon his return to the rank he walked to and fro, and expressed his satisfaction at the promptitude they had displayed, and, after ordering them to assemble at nine the next morning, he dismissed them. For the messenger had returned with the village carpenter, who took one of the old capstan-bars for a pattern, and undertook to have half a dozen new ones of the strongest oak made by the next morning.

Then there was the greasing of the drawbridge chains and rollers to see to, and, when this was successfully done, Roy found to his satisfaction that the men could raise or lower it with, if not ease, at all events without much difficulty.

To the boy's great delight, he found that the three troopers dropped into their places in the most easy manner, obeying his every order with alacrity and displaying all the readiness of well-drilled men. They began by assisting at once with the cleaning and easing of the drawbridge chains, one of them, after stripping off his coat, gorget, and cap, climbing the supports to apply the lubricant to the rollers from outside, where they needed it most; and when, that evening, Ben suggested that one of the guns standing in the pleasaunce should be examined, they made the servants stare by the deft way in which they helped him to handle the ponderous mass of metal, hitching on ropes and dragging it out from where it had lain half-covered with ivy to where it was now planted, so that it could be made to sweep the road-way approaching the bridge; the other one in the garden being afterwards treated in the same way.

"Well, yes, sir, they're pretty heavy," said the corporal, in answer to a compliment passed by Roy upon the ease with which the work had been done; "but it isn't all strength that does it. It's knack—the way of handling a thing and all putting your muscle into it together."

"Ay, that's it," said Ben. "That's what you see in a good charge. If it's delivered in a scattering sort o' way it may do good, but the chance is it won't. But if the men ride on shoulder to shoulder and knee to knee, and then give point altogether—"

"Yes, as Sir Granby Royland's regiment can," said the corporal, proudly.

"Ay, and always did," cried Ben, excitedly. "It takes something to stand against 'em."

There was a dead silence then, and Roy's heart beat fast, for the war spirit was getting hold of him tightly, for his eyes flashed, and his eagerness to go on with the preparations grew stronger every hour.

"Now, about these guns, sergeant?" he said.

Ben's eyes twinkled as his rank was mentioned, and he gave his young master a grateful look.

"Well, sir," he said, "they've been fast asleep in that garden all these years, with enough ivy over 'em to keep 'em warm in winter and the sun off 'em in summer; but, now they've been woke up, I believe they'll bark as loudly and bite as well as any dogs of their size. If they'd been cast iron, I should have been for putting a very light charge in 'em and standing a good way off when they were fired, but, seeing as they're regular good brass guns and not a bit worn, all they want is a good cleaning up, and then they'll be fit to do their work like—like—well, sir, like guns. What do you say, corporal?"

"I say they're a fine and sound pair o' guns, sergeant, as'll do their work. We should like a night's rest first, but in the morning my two lads and me will give 'em a good scour up, and you won't know 'em again."

"Right! If the captain says yes, you shall; but I want to be with you—I'm armourer here."

"Oh, of course, sergeant," said the trooper. "Don't you think we want to take your place."

"I don't, my lad," said the old soldier, warmly; "and I'm only too glad to have three comrades out of the reg'lars to stand by me and help me to lick the recruits into shape."

"Thank ye, sergeant," said the man. "We four can soon do that. They're the right stuff, and only want a bit o' training." Then, turning and saluting Roy respectfully, he went on: "Sir Granby give us all a talking-to, sir, and said he'd picked us out because we—I mean t'others—was the handiest fellows he knew in the regiment, and he hoped we'd do our best to get things in a good state of defence. And, of course, sir, we shall."

The great, manly fellow spoke with a simple modesty that made Ben's eyes sparkle, and he nodded his head and remained silent when the man had ended, but gave vent to his satisfaction by bringing his hand down heavily upon the trooper's shoulder.

"We'll see to the other guns now then," said Roy.

"Yes, sir," said Ben, promptly. "Forward there to the sou'-east tower."

The three men marched off at once in the direction pointed out, and Ben stopped back for a moment or two to whisper to Roy, in a quick, vexed manner—

"Don't go on saying we'll do this next, or we'll do that next, sir, as if you was asking a favour of us. You're captain and castellan, as they calls him. You're governor and everything, and you've got to order us to do things sharp, short, and strong."

"But I don't want to bully you all, Ben," cried Roy.

"Nobody wants you to, sir. You can't be bullying a man when you're ordering him sharply to do what's right. Of course, if you ask us in your civil way to do a thing, we shall do it, but aren't correct."

"I'll try differently, Ben."

"Sergeant, sir!"

"Ser-*geant*," said Roy. "But it's all so new yet, I can't quite realise it. And, of course, I'm so young to be ordering big men about."

"You've the right to do it, sir, and that's everything. Now, just suppose the enemy was in front playing up ruination and destruction, and your father was going to charge 'em with his regiment of tough dragoons, do you think he'd say, 'Now, my men, I want you to—or I'd like you to attack those rapscallions yonder'? Not he. He'd just say a word to the trumpeter, there'd be a note or two blown, and away we'd go at a walk; another blast, and we should trot; then another, and away we should be at 'em like a whirlwind, and scatter 'em like leaves. You must learn to order us, sir, sharply. Mind, sir, it's *must*!"

"Very well," said Roy.

"Don't you be afraid, sir; let us have your order sharp, whatever it is, and we'll do it."

"Then don't stand chattering there, sir!" cried Roy, fiercely. "Can't you see those three men are waiting for you at the bottom of the tower? Forward!"

"Ck!"

It was an unspeakable ejaculation which came from the old soldier's throat as he turned sharply and marched off to the men, chuckling to himself and shaking his shoulders as he went.

"He'll do," he muttered; and then aloud, "Up with you, my lads!"

Ben followed the men, and Roy came last, and, as he entered the door-way, he thought of the journey down to the powder-magazine, and felt a little shame at his nervousness.

Then up and up past the two floors and on towards the roof. As he reached the door-way leading out on to the battlements, he stood in the gloomy interior, and looked along the roof of the untenanted portion towards the north-west tower, wondering what Master Pawson was doing.

He was not left in doubt, for he could just see the secretary standing back from one of the narrow windows scanning the tower he was in, evidently having seen them enter, and watching to see what they were about to do.

A bit of boyishness entered into Roy just then, brought about by the business he was upon and the work he had been engaged in.

"I should like to startle him," he said to himself, as he gave his mischievous thought play. "One might load and train one of the guns, and fire the blank charge aimed just over his head. It would startle him."

The thought passed away directly, and he went up to the roof, where the four men were together upon the platform examining the two guns facing the embrasures.

These were not quite so big as the two standing now beneath the gate-way, but, for the date, they were of a pretty good size, and having the wood-work of the mounting in excellent condition.

"Well, how do they look?" Roy asked.

"Better than I thought, sir. They'll do. Only want a good cleaning. If you think a charge or two ought to be fired, sir, as was talked about, shall it be with one of these?"

"If—yes; fire them both," said Roy; and then he felt astonished at the fact that what he had imagined in mischief was really to be carried out.

"Next order, sir?" said Ben, gazing in his captain's face.

"See to the other guns on the north-east and south-west towers."

"Yes, sir. What's to be done with the two as was slung down when Master Pawson's rooms was furnished?"

"Sling them up again," cried Roy, promptly. "It is necessary now."

Ben gave his leg a slap and looked his satisfaction.

"Wouldn't like the two big guns hoisted over the gate-way, sir, I s'pose?"

"No, certainly not," cried Roy; "they will be of more value to sweep the approach of the castle. I'll have them kept there. Plenty of room to fire on each side of the drawbridge if it's up, and the muzzles would run through the square openings in the portcullis."

Old Ben stared at him round eyed, and shook his head; then he chuckled softly, and, muttering to himself his former words, "He'll do," he led the men to the south-west tower, upon whose platform three brass guns were mounted, and then to the north-east, where there were three more.

Twelve guns in all for the defence of the castle; but the question was, would the ammunition be of any use? Balls there were in abundance, for, in addition to piles standing pyramidally at the foot of each tower, half-covered now by flowers and shrubs, there were similar piles close to the carriage of each gun. But the vital force of the gun, the energy that should set the ball whizzing through the air, was the question, and to prove this, Ben asked for an order, and then walked with his young captain to the armoury, where he opened the great closet. One of the kegs was brought out and set down upon the broad oak table.

"I've been thinking, sir, that perhaps it would be best to fire the big guns under the gate-way to-night."

"Why?" asked Roy.

"Because we know their carriages are right, and I'm a bit doubtful about those upon the tower."

"Very well; try the powder in those."

"Yes, I hope I shall," said Ben; "but I'm a bit scared, sir."

"What! about the danger of opening the keg?"

"Tchah! no, sir. I can open that safely enough. It only means loosening the two hoops at the end, and then the heading will slip out. I mean this— the barrels have been down there no one knows how long, and what I want to know is, will it be powder after all?"

"Not powder after all!" cried Roy in astonishment, as his active mind began to question what liquor it could be there that was stored up so carefully as if it were a treasure indeed.

"I'm afraid it won't be, sir—very much afraid."

"Then what do you think it is?"

"Solid blocks o' stony stuff, sir, I should say."

"But they don't put stony stuff in kegs like these."

"No, sir, powder; but perhaps it has got damp with time and hardened so as it won't be of any use."

"Not if it's dried and ground up again."

"Don't know, sir; can't say; but we'll soon see." There was no hesitation shown. Ben tapped the two top hoops a little, and they soon grew loose and were worked up the staves; the top one withdrawn, and the next brought up into its place, having the wooden disc which formed the head free to be lifted out.

"I thought so, sir," said Ben with a sigh, as he looked in. "Just solid black, and nothing else."

He thumped the top of the contents with his knuckles, and then tapping the lower hoops they glided down and the staves fell apart, leaving a black block standing upon the table.

"Oh, this is bad luck, sir! horribly bad luck!" groaned Ben. "We shall have to get some powder from somewhere, Plymouth or—yes, Bristol's the most likely place."

"Fetch out the other keg, and open that, Ben," said Roy. "To be sure, sir," said Ben, and he turned to the closet and bore the second keg to the table. "If this is all right," he went on, "there's some hope for us, because we may find some more; but if it has gone bad from both sides it's all over with us: we can only stand well on the towers and throw stones down at whoever comes."

Ben's fingers were as busy as his tongue, and in a few minutes he had the head out of the second keg, looked in, and tapped it with his knuckles.

"Just the same, sir, just the same."

"Look here, Ben! I'll have one of these blocks chopped up, and then ground up fine, and we'll try it with a musket."

"Good, sir! that's the right thing to do; but after being wet once, I'm afraid it'll fizz off now like a firework."

"You don't know till you've tried, man. Now, let's see: get an axe, sergeant."

"If I might ask your pardon, captain, axes aren't the proper thing to break up a block of gunpowder. I should say a beetle or a mall was the thing."

"Well, get a mallet, then," said Roy; and the old man went to his tools used for repairing the armour, carpentering, or any other odd jobs, and brought out a mallet, with which he was about to strike a tremendous blow in the middle of the block, when Roy checked him.

"No, no!" he cried; "give it to me. I'll knock a piece off the top edge."

Ben handed the mallet respectfully enough, but he shook his head as if he did not consider that handling mallets was correct for the castellan of the place; while raising the implement not without some shade of doubt as to whether an explosion might follow the blow, but reassuring himself as he remembered that the mallet was only wood, Roy brought it down on the top with a sharp rap, and then started back in dismay, for a piece like a fragment of black potsherd fell upon the table with a bang, and a stream of fine grains came flowing out of the great hole he had made, covering the hardened piece and running on like black sand.

"Hurrah!" shouted Ben, excitedly; "they're all right, sir. Just formed a cake outside, and the inside's all safe and good. Twelve good brass guns, and plenty of powder. We're ready for all the enemies the king has got in this part of the world. Now we'll see for a couple of cartridges for the guns."

He fetched a couple of small bags, which he filled with the powder, and then, after putting back the unbroken keg-shaped block, as carefully cleared all the loose powder from the table, and placed that and the shape from which it had come in the oak closet, which he locked.

"Powder's powder, sir; so one has to take care," he said. "Now for a touch port-fire, and we'll try what sort of stuff it is."

Ben gave Roy a knowing look, and then from a drawer in the table he took a piece of prepared oakum such as was used for lowering into the pan of a freshly primed gun, stepped to a case in which were some old rammers, and declared himself ready to start, but hesitated and went to his tool-drawer again, out of which he routed a long thin spike.

"Now I think we're ready, sir," he said, and they went out to where the men were waiting, and prepared to load the two guns under the gate tower.

"These are only makeshifts," said Ben, apologetically, as he indicated his rough cartridges; "but they'll do to clear out the guns," and he set them down in the door-way leading into the old guard-room.

Then the long thin pin was tried in the touch-holes of both guns, and after a good deal of poking and drilling the orifices were cleared. Meanwhile, one of the troopers took the rammer Ben had brought out, inserted it at the muzzle, and found that it would only go in half-way. So a ragged stick was fetched, run in, twisted round and round, and withdrawn, dragging after it a wad of horsehair, cotton, hay, and feathers, while a succession of trials brought out more and more, the twisting round having a cleansing effect upon the bore of the gun as well.

"Ah!" said Ben, solemnly, "them tomtits have had the guns all to themselves for a fine time. I shall have to make some tompions to keep them out."

Quite a heap of nest-building material was drawn out of the two guns, the first obtained being evidently of that season, while farther in it was old and decayed to a mere mouldy powder that might have been carried in by the industrious little birds a score of years before.

At last all was declared clear. The bags of powder were thrust in, a wad of the cleanest hay from the heap followed, and one of the troopers rammed the charges home, with the result that the powder rose well in the touch-holes, and nothing remained to be done but to insert the lightly twisted pieces of touch-string and apply a light.

"Better way than doing it with a red-hot poker, as some of us might like to stand back till the guns are proved," said the old soldier, grimly. "One of you take that there to the kitchen and get a light," he said, "to do for a port-fire."

He handed a piece of the prepared oakum to one of the men, who ran off with it, and directly after Roy stepped back quickly and hurried into the house.

Ben said nothing, but he glanced after the boy with a fierce look, pursing up his lips, and then muttering to himself, his expression indicating the most profound disgust.

Meanwhile, Roy ran into the private apartments of the castle, and made his way to the library; but Lady Royland was not there.

Uttering an ejaculation full of impatience, the boy hurried into the withdrawing-room, where he had better fortune, for he found his mother waiting there as if she expected him.

"You, my dear?" she said. "I was waiting here to see Master Pawson; he sent me a message to ask if I would see him on matters of importance. Do you know what he wishes to say?"

"Well, I almost think I do, mother," replied the boy.

"Then you have come to meet him?"

"No," said the boy; "I didn't know he had sent. I came to warn you not to be alarmed, for we are just going to fire."

Boom!

A report like thunder made the casements rattle as if they were being dashed in. This was followed by an echoing roar, and then came a yelling cry as of some one in agony.

"Oh, my boy, what has happened?" cried Lady Royland, starting from her chair, clapping her hands to her ears, and then sinking back palpitating in the nearest chair. "Run and see; something terrible must have occurred."

Roy had already dashed to the door, and he ran out and along to the great gate-way, where his mother's words seemed to be verified, for, on reaching the spot where the gun which had been fired had run back a short distance, there was the knot of men half hidden by the smoke that was slowly rising, and in front of them, just below the portcullis, lay, apparently lifeless, the figure of Master Pawson, face downward upon the flags.

"What have you done, Ben?" cried the boy.

"Done? I never done it," growled the man, fiercely. "You runned away; so I put the light to the gun myself, and then we all stood and waited, till all at wunst Master Pawson comes round the corner like. I dunno how he come there; and off goes the gun and down goes he."

Roy was already upon one knee, turning the secretary over on his back and examining him for the terrible injury he felt must have been received. But as Roy was proceeding to open his collar, he opened his eyes, sprang up into a sitting position, and then began to abuse the boy fiercely.

"You did it on purpose," he cried; "and it's a mercy it did not kill me."

"Then you are not killed?" said Roy, dryly.

"No; but I might have been. It was a cowardly thing to do."

"Ay, it were, Master Roy!" whispered Ben, turning upon him. "I thought you'd ha' had heart enough to ha' stood by us."

"What do you mean?" cried Roy, rising angrily.

"Oh, you know, sir; sets such a bad example to the men."

"I don't understand you; nor you neither, Master Pawson."

"It's disgraceful; and Lady Royland shall put a stop to such monkey tricks."

"Powder-monkey tricks," growled Ben.

"Why, you don't think I fired that gun on purpose, sir?"

"No, I don't think so," cried Master Pawson, in his high-pitched, scolding tone; "I am quite sure, sir; and it is disgraceful."

"But I wasn't here!"

"You were there. I saw you with the men, pretending to clean the gun, while I was yonder watching the sunset and waiting for an answer to a message I had sent in to your mother, sir, when, as you saw me come round the corner, you fired."

"I did not, sir; for I was not there."

"Ay, that's true enough, sir," said Ben, bitterly; "he warn't here."

"I don't believe it," cried Master Pawson, angrily, and his voice sounded like that of some angry woman. "It was a trick; and all this nonsense shall be put a stop to."

"You can believe it or not, sir," said Roy, growing calmer as the secretary waxed more angry.

"I shall speak to Lady Royland at once."

"Do, sir. She is waiting to see you; she was telling me so when the gun went off."

"Gun went off! And what business has a gun to go off here in this place?" cried the secretary, as he stood, now feeling himself all over and brushing the dust from off his velvet coat.

"Only got the wind of the gun, sir," said the corporal, quietly.

"I was not speaking to you, my good man," cried the secretary.

"Bad plan to stand nigh the muzzle of a big gun when she's going to be fired," growled Ben, in a sententious voice, and the secretary turned upon him sharply.

"And you, sir," he cried; "how dare you let a boy play such antics? Do you know I heard the shot go by my face."

"Nay, sir; that I'll say you didn't," growled Ben.

"But I say I did, sir, with a fierce rush."

"One of the tomtits' eggs, perhaps, sergeant," said Roy, dryly. "I know I caught sight of one or two when the nest was rammed in."

The men all burst out laughing, and Master Pawson grew preternaturally calm.

"Was that meant as an insult, Master Roy?" he said, turning towards him and speaking slowly, with his eyes half shut and an unpleasant, sneering smile upon his lips.

"No, sir; as a joke," replied Roy, gravely.

"I thank you; but keep your jokes for the servants; try them upon the menials. Recollect that I am a gentleman, placed in authority over you by Sir Granby Royland as tutor and master, and, as I am in authority over you, I am in authority over all here. Have the goodness to recollect that."

He turned upon his heel and walked away, with the back of his doublet covered with scraps of hay from the tomtits' nest, and Roy's first inclination was to run after him to begin brushing him down.

"But he'll only think I want to insult him again," said the boy to himself. "I wish I hadn't said anything about the tomtits' eggs, though."

"Shall I run after him, sir, and ask if I shall give him a brush down?" whispered Ben.

"No; let him find it out. One of the maids will tell him, I dare say."

"But you should ha' stopped by us when the gun was fired, Master Roy," protested Ben. "I see them three chaps wink at each other, as much as to say, 'He won't stand fire,' and it hurt me, sir, and seemed to be undoing all I did afore. I didn't think it of you."

"I should like to kick you for thinking me such a coward," cried Roy, fiercely, for his encounter with the secretary had set his temper on edge. "How dare you! You had no business to fire till I came back. I did not want my mother to hear the report without some warning. — Here, corporal, give me that light."

The man stepped up with it, and Roy took it out of his hand.

"Going to fire this one, sir?" said Ben, eagerly.

"Of course. Stand aside!" And Roy applied the sparkling port-fire to the bit of prepared oakum standing out of the touch-hole, with the result that it, too, began to sparkle and fume.

"There," he said; "I hope Master Pawson won't come back and be frightened by this one."

He had hardly uttered the words when the secretary reappeared.

"Where are all the servants?" he cried, angrily. "I want some one to come and brush my clothes."

"Stand aside!" shouted Ben. "She'll run right back."

But the secretary did not understand what was meant, and turned haughtily upon the speaker, totally unconscious of the fact that he was exactly behind the breech of the piece, whose recoil might have produced fatal results.

It was no time for uttering warnings, and Roy knew it. He glanced once at the tiny sparkling going on at the touch-hole of the gun, and sprang right at the secretary, driving him backward and falling heavily with him to the ground.

It was none too soon, for the gun went off with a tremendous roar, leaping up from the paving and running back on its low wheels right over the spot where the secretary had just stood.

"Guns is guns, and always was," said Ben, very grimly; "and them as has to do with 'em wants to know all their little ways. I have know'd a man's arm took off by the recoil, and, if you don't take care, their breeches is as dangerous to them as fires 'em as is their muzzles."

"Hurt, sir?" cried Roy, offering his hand after gaining his own feet, ready to help the tutor to rise.

Master Pawson made no reply, neither did he take the extended hand, but rose and walked away limping, going right down through the pleasaunce so as to reach his own room without having to pass through the corridor.

"Bit rusty, I s'pose, sir," said Ben, quietly.

"I am afraid so, Ben," was the reply. "But I don't think there's much doubt about the powder."

"Doubt, sir; why, it's stronger than they makes now, or else it has got riper and better for keeping. We're all right there."

"Yes, capital! but that report rings in my ears still."

"Ay, sir, a brass gun can ring as well as roar; but you won't mind it after a few times."

"I don't feel to mind it now," said Roy, coolly.

"Not you, sir," whispered the old fellow. "And I beg your pardon, Master Roy, and you've done me, and yourself too, a lot of good. It would ha' been horrid for the men to think you was scared. I never thought of frightening my lady with the row. Tell the lads to sponge the guns out with a bit o' rag, and then we'll run 'em back to their places again."

Roy gave the order, and then had the sentry changed at the gate, after which there was another duty to have performed,—that of raising the drawbridge.

"No fear of any one forgetting and walking into the moat at night, is there, Ben?"

"Well, no, sir; I think not," said the old soldier, seriously. "You see, the bridge shuts up all the middle when it's raised, and that makes it sure, while at those sides nobody could tumble in without trying to; so I don't see no fear of that. Shall we haul her up, sir?"

"Yes." And giving the order, as soon as the guns were in place, he led the way up into the furnace-chamber, where two men seized each chain, and the ponderous structure slowly rose as the huge weights descended the stone-work tubes in which they hung, the difficulty of hoisting the bridge proving to be much lighter than at the former trial.

"Come, sir, that's safe. You won't set sentries to-night?"

"No, of course not," said Roy; "that will be unnecessary till there is news of some enemy being near."

Chapter Thirteen
The Coming of Recruits

The next morning the carpenter was there with the capstan bars soon after the bridge was lowered; and upon these being tried, after the capstans and pulleys had been well greased, the portcullis was lowered and raised several times with the greatest facility, each time becoming more easy to move, while old Ben's eyes glistened, and he worked as if all these preparations for the defence of the place, with the possible shedding of blood and loss of life, had suddenly added a delightful zest to his existence.

But he was not alone in this, for Roy found a strange exhilaration in his new position. There was something so novel in everything, and try how he would, it was hard to keep down a feeling of vanity, especially when he came upon his mother busily preparing a scarf for him to wear.

"For me?" he said. "Oh, mother! it's too fine."

"Not at all," she said, quietly. "Your men will like to see their leader look striking."

"Ah, well," he replied, "I can't wear it while there is so much dirty work to do."

"That will be done by the men. Roy, my boy, you must rise to your position, and give orders more for things to be done."

"That's what old Ben says, and I am trying; but it's hard work while everything is so new, and—"

"And what?"

"It seems as if Master—Oh, no; it's too paltry to be talked about."

"Tell me what it is, and I will be the judge."

"Well, you know how poor Master Pawson was upset with the firing?"

"Yes; and he ought to be very grateful to you for saving his life. Has he not thanked you?"

"No; unless looking sneeringly at everything I do is thanking me. That makes it seem so hard to put on a showy thing like that. He'll only laugh at it."

"Master Pawson is not behaving well," said Lady Royland, coldly. "He actually had the impertinence to speak to me last night about the preparations, and objected to the men being taken from their work."

"Said it was absurd?"

"Yes; those were his words, Roy, and I was compelled to silence him. He told me he was sure that if Sir Granby knew how utterly unlikely it was for any of the disaffected people to come into this neighbourhood he would immediately cancel the orders, and, under the circumstances, he could not refrain from advising me to act according to his advice."

"And what was his advice, mother?"

"To put a stop to the foolish preparations, which could only bring ridicule upon all here."

"He said something of the kind to me; more than I told you."

"Why did you not tell me all?"

"Because it seemed so paltry."

"Nothing is too paltry when we have so much at stake, Roy."

"And was that the end of it?"

"No, my boy; he made me indignant by his presumption, and I told him to remember who he was."

"What did he say to that?"

"Begged my pardon humbly, and said that perhaps I was right, and that he would do everything he could to help me in this painful situation. I am glad he has spoken out and forced me to be plain. Now he will keep his place."

"Yes, he will now," said Roy. "I know what he felt; of course he was annoyed at my taking the lead, after his going out leaving me only his pupil, and coming back to find me seeming to do exactly as I pleased. But I must go, mother, for there is such a lot to do. Don't ask me to begin wearing silk and gold and feathers yet, though, please."

Lady Royland smiled proudly as she kissed her son, and Roy hurried back to his lieutenant, who was anxiously expecting him.

"Farmer Raynes has come over, sir, to see you. Wanted to know what the guns were fired for."

"Where is he?"

"Yonder, sir, watching the corporal drill the men."

Roy went to the gate-way, where the trooper was busy at work drilling the men in the use of their firelocks, adding to his verbal instructions the examples of the two soldiers who came with him, these falling in just in front, and executing every order in the carriage of the piece, loading and firing, so that the servants could more easily understand.

"Morning, Master Roy," said the farmer, stepping out of the guard-room door-way. "Heard the guns last night, and couldn't make out where the noise come from. Found out this morning, though, and run over. Mean fighting, then, if they come here?"

"Certainly," said Roy. "My father sent word for us to be prepared. I was going to send for you this morning. I want your men and you to come in, and be ready in case you are wanted."

"Parson Meldew came and had a long talk with me day before yesterday, sir, and he told me that whatever I did I was to stay peacefully at home, mind my crops, and not interfere at all. But if I did, I was not to side with the king."

"He dared to tell you that?" cried Roy.

"Not quite in those words, sir, but he meant it."

"Oh, if he wasn't a clerk, I'd say something," cried Roy; "but what did you say?"

"Nothing, sir; I only laughed."

"And do you mean to stay at home and do what he told you?"

"Of course, sir, unless there's some fighting comes on, and then I suppose we shall have to begin."

"Against the king?"

"I'm going to fight for my good old landlord, Master Roy, the best man I know. He always stood my friend in hard times, and if he sends word I am to, why, here I be with ten stout fellows, only you'll have to drill us all, same as you're doing with these here, unless pitchforks and flails will do; we can handle them."

"Shake hands, Master Raynes," cried Roy; "I want you and the men to come and drill every day in the mornings, and I want you to bring us in as much wheat, oats, and flour as we can store up. You must buy when you have not plenty, for we must be ready in case we are attacked."

"What do you say to me going round and buying up all the ham and bacon and salt pork I can get, sir?"

"Yes, certainly," cried Roy. "My mother will supply the money."

"Oh, that's all right enough, sir," said the farmer. "But of course you don't want us to come and live in the place until there's real trouble."

"Certainly not. Give half your time to getting ready for troubles, and the other half to the farm."

"I see, sir. Ah, morning, Master Pawson. Wild times these."

"Terrible, Master Raynes, terrible," said the secretary, coming up. "Are you going to be drilled too?"

Roy glanced sharply round, but the secretary spoke earnestly, and with no suggestion of a sneer.

"Yes, sir, me and my men must come and support my landlord, spite of all that Parson Meldew may say."

"Does he object?"

"Yes, sir; and pretty strongly, too. If I was him, I don't think I should say quite so much, for he may be hearing of it again."

"But I hope all we hear is but exaggerated rumour, Master Raynes, for everybody's sake. If it were half so bad as you all say, I don't know what would happen."

"Ah well, sir, nothing shall happen here if me and my lads can prevent it. There, I won't waste time. The lads shall be over here in a couple of hours, Master Roy, and I'll be getting off to market."

The farmer went away, and Roy felt comparatively happy with his tutor, for Master Pawson seemed to have put aside the petty feeling of annoyance, and to wish to let the trouble over the firing be quite forgotten, so careful was he about avoiding any allusion to the guns.

"I can't help," he said, smiling; "only to look on. I was never meant for a fighting man. What a change, though, you seem to be producing, Roy."

This was sufficient to make Roy, with his natural boyish frankness, begin talking freely about his plans, for he was growing enthusiastic, and he even began to ask the secretary's opinion about two or three minor matters.

"Oh, don't ask me," said his companion, laughing, and with an air of protest; "you might just as well expect me to begin wearing armour. No. You must do all the defending if trouble does come, and I beg you will give particular orders to your men-at-arms to take the greatest care of the secretary, for you must not have him hurt. I suppose, then, that there will be no more studies for the present?"

"No, not for the present," said Roy, rather importantly; "I have so much to do."

"Very well, man o' war; the man o' peace will go back to his music and his books, but if you want me to do anything that I can do, send for me at once."

Master Pawson put his hands behind him and walked thoughtfully through the garden towards the door-way leading to the ramparts, and from thence to the north-west tower, by the green grass and flowers seeming to him a more attractive way than through the long corridor and past the occupied rooms; while Roy made for the armoury, which seemed to be his study now. Ben was there, busy, and he looked up and nodded. "Master Pawson's soon settled down then, sir?" he said.

"Oh, yes, Ben; he's good-tempered enough now."

"Good job for him, sir. Can't have quarrelling in a garrison. I began to think he was going to mutiny outright, and if he'd shown his teeth any more, I suppose I should have had to remind him that there were some deep, dark dungeons underground as a first dose, and the stone gallows up at the far corner of the ramparts for the very worst cases."

"But do you think that stone bar thing was ever used for executing people?"

"Sure of it, sir; and there's the opening underneath leading down to that square patch beneath the walls."

"But it may have been to hoist food or other things up during a siege."

"Ah, it may have been, sir," said Ben, grimly; "but I don't quite see why they should have chosen to make it just over the bit of a patch of ground between the walls and the moat where you couldn't get the forage to without a boat, and when there were a gate-way and bridge. 'Sides, too, why should they pick the old burying-place of the castle?"

"But that was not the old burying-place, surely, Ben?"

"You ask Dick Grey, gardener, what he found when her ladyship wanted the ivy planted there to cover that bit o' wall. It was full of 'em."

Roy shuddered.

"That's so, sir. I expect in the old fighting days they used to bury 'em there; and as it's just under that there gallows, why, of course, it was used for traitors or spies as well. That reminds me, sir, as a lot of that ivy ought to be cut away. We don't want any one to make a ladder of it for getting into the place."

"Leave it for the present. It could be torn down in an hour if there was any need."

"Ay, sir, that's the way you take it over such things. That there garden ought to be turned into a drilling-ground; you know it ought."

"If there does come any need for it, the garden can go," said Roy, "but not until the very last."

"That's right, sir. Only, if we're besieged, it will have to go. Now, let me see—that makes nine buff coats, and one more's ten, for Farmer Raynes's lot. Ought to give the farmer something a bit smarter, oughtn't I, as he'll expect to be a sergeant, won't he?"

"He'll like to be over his men."

"But, you see, he's a big one, and there's a buff coat would suit him exact. I'll tell you what, sir, if he has the same as the others, and a scarf, and a feather in his cap, he'll be satisfied."

"I should say so, Ben."

"Then scarf and feather it shall be, sir. I'll have all their arms and things ready for to-night; then they can have 'em in the morning when they come, and it'll put all them straw-whopping fellows in a good temper, and make 'em easy to drill. I want to pick out so many fellows for the big guns that we must have some more in soon. But it's better to go gently. Saves a lot of confusion."

"What's the next thing to do, Ben?"

"Everything, sir. Powder-bags to fill. Stores to get in. We must have a new flag. Place cleared out for garrison quarters. Something done to the two old guard-rooms on each side of the gate. We've months of work to do, sir, try how we may, but we're going to do it, Master Roy, and—Oh," continued the old fellow, pausing for a few moments in his task of taking down belts and swords to lay one on each buff coat below the steel caps just set out ready, "there's that other thing I wanted to talk to you about."

"What other thing, Ben?"

"I was up atop of the great tower this morning."

"I know. I saw you there."

"I was looking at the furnace and thinking that must be touched up a bit, and a good supply of wood and charcoal carried to it. There is plenty of lead at the foot of the north-east tower."

"Ugh! We don't want to do any of those barbarous things, Ben; they're too horrible. Fancy pouring molten lead down on people's heads."

"We don't want to pour no molten lead down on people's heads, sir," protested the old soldier. "All we says to 'em is, we've got a whole lot of hot silver soup up here, and we shall pour it down on you if you come hanging about our place, and trying to get in. Let 'em stop away, and then they won't be hurt."

"But it's too horrible, Ben. I will not have that got ready."

"Very well, sir. I don't know that it much matters, for they've got to cross the moat first, and I don't think we'll let 'em do that. The only way the enemy will get in here will be through traitors in the camp."

"And we shall not have any of them, Ben."

"Hope not, sir."

"So if we are to fight, let it be in a fair, manly, chivalrous way."

"Yes, sir, and hang all spies and traitors."

"Don't let's imagine that such people are possible," said Roy. "But was that what you wanted to talk about, sergeant?"

"No, captain, it wasn't. I got thinking this morning, as I was looking round for weak points in our defences, that there's the old tale about that there underground passage; the little chapel on the hill made me think of it first."

"But do you believe it's possible, Ben?"

"Not knowing, sir, can't say. But I tell you what I do say: there's nothing like taking care. Don't do to leave a hole in a sand-bag if it's ever so small. So as soon as we've got a little more ship-shape and our garrison beginning to grow, let's you and me get a lantern some night, and have a good look to see if there is such a rat's hole."

"Of course; yes."

"Keep it quiet, sir, except to her ladyship. There may be such a place, for in the good old times there were a great many curious doings, and it would be a fine one to have a way in and out when the enemy thought they'd got people shut up closely, and was going to starve 'em out; and them able to bring in more men, and sacks of corn, and pigs and ducks and geese and chickens, and laughing at the enemy all the time."

"We must see, Ben; and I want you, as soon as the farmer's party are settling down, to go and try about more men."

"I say, sir, aren't it strange as none of the gentry hasn't been over?"

"Too soon, perhaps, Ben."

"Perhaps so, sir; but I can't help fancying everybody about here don't think quite the same as we do."

"Not on the king's side? Oh, nonsense!"

"Hope it is, sir," said the old fellow, thoughtfully inspecting and drawing one of the swords; "but there, we shall see. Bad for some of 'em if they are agen us, or I'm much mistook."

Chapter Fourteen
Master Pawson shows his Colours

As the time glided on, no further communication arrived from Sir Granby, and Lady Royland and her son began to realise more and more that they were shut off in a part of England where the king's friends were few and far between, while those who remained true felt themselves so outnumbered by their neighbours that they dared not display their principles.

Letters had been sent round by Lady Royland to several of the gentry residing at different places, asking for help if it were needed, and at the same time offering the castle as a sanctuary and rallying-point.

One answer which was received will suffice to show the general feeling of the district.

The letter was brought in while Lady Royland and her son were seated at breakfast, and the servant-maid stated that it had been left with old Jenkin, at the gate, by a messenger the old man did not know, but who said that there was no reply needed.

A letter was sufficient to throw Roy's mother into a state of agitation, eager as she was for news from her lord, and she eagerly tore it open, read it with a sigh, and passed it on to her son.

Roy took it as eagerly and began reading it aloud.

It was very brief, and was written in a peculiar hand that was not familiar.

"Take counsel with yourself as to what you are doing. A great change is coming over the country, for the king's cause is undoubtedly lost. Many who respect the old family of Royland, and would help if they dared, feel that it is unwise to fly in the face of the new power, and to go in opposition to the people, who in all directions are declaring against the king. All who respect Dame Royland join in advising her to cease the show of resistance she is making, and to settle down quietly, ready to accept the fresh position, for resistance must mean destruction. Pause before it is too late.—From an old friend."

"Well," said Lady Royland, as her son read the letter through twice, "what do you think of that, Roy?"

"That the man who wrote it must be a coward."

"It explains why we have not had more offers of help, my boy. I have felt for days past that there must be something very wrong. We are, it seems, becoming isolated in an enemy's country, and so as to secure our safety, I am advised to lay down my arms, and turn over my allegiance to the new government, whatever it may be. That is what the letter advises."

"Yes, but who wrote it?" cried Roy.

"It is evidently written by one person acting for others, and explains why my letters to gentlemen who I should have thought would have been ready to help me have remained unanswered."

"Then we are to have no more help?"

"None, save that which we have secured from the village, and of course from the tenants on our estate. What do you think, Roy? If I resist, we shall, from our weakness, in all probability be beaten, and the new government will confiscate your father's property here; while, if we settle down to an ignoble peace—"

"They'll perhaps seize upon the estate all the same."

"Then you would resist, my boy?" said Lady Royland, watching her son's face closely.

"Resist, mother?" he cried, indignantly; "why, of course. After what father said, it is our duty to shut ourselves up here, hoist the king's flag, and show the cowards who sent that letter that we're going to fight as long as there's a tower left in the old place."

"Then you would advise me to go against everything that is said in that letter?"

"Pah!" cried the boy, with a look of disgust. "I wonder you can ask me such a question, mother."

Roy had risen from the table, and with his face scarlet was walking up and down the room.

"I asked you because I wanted to see what your real feelings were, my boy," said Lady Royland, going to him to lay her hands on his shoulder and look proudly in his face. "Roy, my boy, if I followed the advice of that contemptible time-serving letter, I should feel that I was proving false to the brave men who have gathered round us at my call, to my husband, and my king; lastly, my boy, to you. Give up? You know how I shuddered at the thought of war; how it was my prayer that you should not follow your father's career; but when duty called, Roy, I cast all my fears behind, and stood forward ready to do or die. No, Roy! not while we have a shot left to fire, a strong hand to raise! Let those who will seek for safety in this base submission to the rebel powers: we will show them that a woman and a boy can be faithful to the end. That for the letter and its cowardly advice," she cried, tearing it disdainfully to pieces. "We have but one thought here, Roy, and the old walls shall echo it as long as the stones will stand—God save the king!"

Roy leaped upon one of the chairs, drew his sword and waved it round his head, roaring out, with all his might, "God save the king!" And directly after there was a hurried step at the door, which was thrown open, and the electric excitement in the lad's breast was discharged as if he had received a touch from a rod.

For the maid-servant appeared, looked at him in astonishment, and said, "Did you call, Master Roy?"

The boy got down, and sheathed his sword, babbling out something, and his mother smilingly said—

"No; you were not called."

"I beg pardon, my lady," said the woman, and she retired.

"Oh, I say, mother!" faltered Roy; "how stupid I must have seemed!"

"I did not think so," said Lady Royland, smiling.

"But it looked as if I were acting."

"Go on acting so, then, my son," said his mother, proudly; "we need not study what people think."

"Here's Master Pawson," whispered Roy, quickly. "Go back to your chair, mother."

Roy went to his own, and Lady Royland slowly followed his example, as the secretary, after passing the window, entered the room.

"I beg pardon," he said, "for being so late. Good-morning, Lady Royland; good-morning, Roy. I slept so dreadfully soundly."

"You need not apologise, Master Pawson," said the lady, gravely; and she noted that his quick eyes had rested upon the fragments of the torn-up letter scattered about the room, where she had tossed them contemptuously. "You are looking at the letter I received this morning."

"A letter?" he cried, eagerly; "from Sir Granby?"

"No," said Lady Royland, with a sigh which she could not restrain; "it is from close at hand—from some of our neighbours. I wish I had kept it for you to see."

"Not bad news, I hope," he said, looking pale.

"Yes; very bad news," said Lady Royland. "I have been waiting for days—it is right that you should know—hoping to get promises of help from the different friends we have round, but till now the answer to my appeal has been silence. This morning they gave me their reason for not replying."

"May I ask from whom you have heard?"

"I cannot tell you," said Lady Royland; "the letter is signed 'a friend,' and it advocates total surrender to the rebellious power of which we hear so much."

"But you will not surrender, Lady Royland?"

"Surrender? No!" cried Roy. "Never!"

"That is right," said the secretary, flushing a little.

"No; I shall not surrender," said Lady Royland, firmly; "but as it means that we are becoming isolated, and are doomed to stand alone, I feel it my duty to speak plainly to you, Master Pawson."

He turned very pale again, and his eyes glanced restlessly from one to the other.

"I hope—I trust," he faltered, "that I have not done anything more to incur your displeasure, Lady Royland."

"No, Master Pawson, nothing; on the other hand, I have to thank you for the brave way in which for some days past you have mastered your dislike to the proceedings here, and helped my son to advance my objects."

"I—I have only tried to do my duty," he said, flushing again.

"Still, I cannot disguise from myself, Master Pawson, that dangers are gathering around us fast, and that it is my duty to relieve you of a position which must be growing intolerable."

"I—I do not understand your ladyship," he said, looking at her wonderingly.

"Let me explain, then. I feel that I have no right, Master Pawson, to keep you here. I think, then, that while there is the opportunity, and before you are compromised in any way, you should sever your connection here and go."

"Ah! I see what your ladyship means now," he said, drawing a deep breath as if of relief, and looking firmly in Roy's searching eyes. "Go away before any one of importance comes and makes a demand for the surrender of the castle."

"That is what I do mean."

"Yes, exactly," said the secretary, thoughtfully; "and when the troubles are over, and the king has chastised all these insolent people who have risen against him, and, lastly, when I meet Sir Granby Royland, and he asks me why I deserted his wife and son in their emergency, what can I say?"

Lady Royland was silent for a few moments, and her eyes rested in a softened manner upon the secretary's face.

"Say," she said at last, and her voice sounded a little husky, "that it was my wish that you should go, for I did not desire that any one but I should be compromised."

"Thank you, Lady Royland," said the secretary, quietly; and as he spoke, Roy felt his dislike to the man increasing moment by moment up to a certain point. "And, of course," he said, "I must require money for travelling and to make my way back to London."

"That you shall be properly supplied with, of course, Master Pawson."

"Thank you again, Lady Royland," he said, as he went on calmly with his breakfast; "it is very good of you, and when I require it, I will ask."

"Better that it should be done at once, sir," Lady Royland said, firmly, "and that you should go."

"And leave you and Master Roy here to your fate!"

"We can protect ourselves, sir."

"You must forgive me for being so slow over my breakfast, Master Roy," said the secretary, smiling in the lad's disgust-filled face. "I see you are impatient to go, but I am talking so much."

"Oh, eat a good breakfast," said Roy, now he was thus appealed to, "for the last —"

"Oh, no! not by a great many," said Master Pawson, smiling. "I like the dear old castle far too well, and I hope to have many a long year of happy days in it. It is very good of you, Lady Royland; but I hope I can do my duty to Sir Granby like a man. You judge me by what I said at the beginning of these preparations. I thought then that I was right. I did not believe we should be interfered with here; but I see now that I was wrong, and I am ready to help you heart and soul. Do you think I could go away at a time like this? Why, I should never forgive myself—never. It is impossible, Lady Royland; now isn't it, Roy? I'm not a fighting man; nature never meant me for anything but music and books, but I'm not such a contemptible coward as all that. When the enemy comes and begins firing, I may be induced to go somewhere that I think *is* safe; but go away? No, I could never hold up my head again."

"Master Pawson," cried Roy, excitedly, springing from his seat, "do you mean this?"

"Mean it, Roy?" said the secretary. "Why, of course. I promised Sir Granby to do my duty by his dame and his son, and according to the best of my powers. I'm going to do it, and—Well, that's a very nice raised pie."

"Here, I want to beg your pardon, Master Pawson, for all kinds of unpleasant thoughts about you," cried Roy, going round to the secretary and holding out his hand, which the other took and held.

"Do you?" he said, laughing. "Oh, no, there's no need. Boys generally quarrel mentally with their teachers just out of want of knowledge. I know. You've called me old Pawson many a time—now, haven't you?—and said I was fat and soft and stupid, eh?"

The lad did not answer, but looked scarlet.

"That's all right, Roy. I'm old enough to understand a little about human nature. Don't you think I mind what a boy says or does in a fit of spleen. We shall understand one another better as time goes on."

Then turning to Lady Royland, who stood there flushed and with her eyes humid, he said, with grave respect, "I thank you, madam. It is only what I should have expected from one of your good, considerate nature, and I shall never forget it.—There, Roy," he said, "I am going back to my room, and shall always be there when you want me. I stay there because I fear to be in the way, but I'll come and do anything you wish if I can be useful. But, please," he added, with a comical look of appeal, "don't ask me to buckle on a sword, to come and fight, nor yet to fire guns. I should be sure to shut my eyes when I pulled the trigger, and waste the charge. Good-morning; I'm sorry I was so late."

He made as if to go, but paused as Lady Royland took a step or two forward and held out her hand, which he took and kissed respectfully.

"Thank you, Master Pawson," she said, with her voice low from emotion; "you have made everything seem brighter to us than it has looked for days. I feel now that the world is not so cowardly and cruel as this letter makes out that it was. I thank you. Sir Granby shall know of your noble conduct, and—"

"No, no! please don't say any more now," cried the secretary, hurriedly; and he hastened to quit the room.

"I am glad," cried Roy, as the door was closed.

"Glad!" exclaimed Lady Royland; "and I am sorry, Roy, that we should have been so ready to misjudge."

Chapter Fifteen
Ben Martlet proposes a Search

The coming in of Farmer Raynes and his ten men had a capital effect upon the people round. It was an example which soon bore fruit. After the first two or three attendances at the castle, they marched there together, with the farmer by them, in thorough military fashion, and were followed by the people from the village, who would have gladly come across the moat had not the gate been clanged-to by the sentry of the day on duty, and then they had to content themselves with standing gazing across at the drilling and martial exercises which went on. The firing of the big guns—for all were tried in turn so as to see that they were serviceable—was a grand portion of the entertainment, and, in spite of secret adverse influences at work, the tenants on the estate soon began to present themselves for enrolment in the little body, eager to a man to don the castle uniform and bear arms; while the fact that the officer in command was a mere boy sent the lads of the neighbourhood half-mad. In fact, day after day they came in pairs to offer themselves for enlistment, but only to go disappointed away; those who showed the most surprise at the refusal to accept their services being the very young.

"Why, bless my heart!" Farmer Raynes would say, with his broad, deep chuckle, "it would be like putting a 'stinguisher on a rush-light to stick a steel cap on some of those boys' heads. You'd be putting them out, Ben Martlet."

"Ay," said the old fellow, showing his teeth; "but a few would be useful to go down the guns with a brush to clean them out. But there, I'm not going to laugh at the boys. Shows a good sperrit, Master Raynes, that I wish more of the older folk would follow."

"Ay, so do I," said the farmer, frowning; "but they're some of 'em ashamed and some afraid. Parson Meldew has a lot to do with it; and do you know why?"

"Nay, not I; perhaps it's because her ladyship has been such a good friend to him."

"Like enough. That sort's always the worst. He has such a poor living that it's my belief he's glad of the chance of a change. He thinks he must be the better for it if it does come. I never much liked him; old parson was the man. Why, if he'd been alive, he'd ha' been up here every day talking to the lads, and encouraging them to get on as well as they could to fight for church and state like good men and true. But you'll have six more here to-day, good strong fellows from Marlow Mill."

"Eh? You don't mean that?"

"Oh, yes, I do," said the farmer. "I was over there with the wagon last night to get that load o' flour that I brought in this morning, and I give them all a talking-to about how things are, and my lads showing up so in their coats and steel caps. It's of no use to bully 'em into coming. They want coaxing, not driving. I hadn't been talking to 'em long, 'fore they did exactly what I wanted, asking questions, and I answered 'em so that they wanted to know about sword-play, and loading and firing the big guns; and then they wanted to know whether there were buff coats and steel caps for all as liked to come and drill. When I told 'em there was, lo and behold! they all found out that they wanted to do a bit of soldiering, and they'll be over soon."

Farmer Raynes was quite right, for soon after, six sturdy young fellows came slouching up in a sheepish way to stand watching the drilling with open mouths, laughing and nudging one another as they recognised old acquaintances, and were apparently ready to joke and sneer. That passed off, however, in a few minutes, as they saw the goodly figure cut by the farmer's men, and Raynes himself, no longer in the rough, flour-soiled attire, as they had seen him when fetching the meal-bags over-night, but a fine, bluff, gallant-looking fellow now, in buff coat, breastplate, headpiece, and glittering steel cap which flashed in the sunshine as he marched half a dozen armed men into the gate-way, then through the guard-room and up to the ramparts, along which they were seen to have to go through a certain amount of practice with the big guns.

Within an hour the martial ardour that was glowing in the would-be recruits' breasts was red-hot, and they asked leave to pass over the bridge.

The sentry shook his head, but sent a messenger across to state the men's business, and they stood waiting, doubly impressed now, till the man returned with the order that they were to wait. This they did till, a few minutes later, sharp words of command were heard in the gate-way; and then, closely followed by Roy, gallant in bearing and in his Italian half-armour, gold and white scarf, gauntlets, and feathered felt hat, Sergeant Martlet came with the three troopers at a smart, elastic march across the drawbridge, which rattled and quivered to their tread, till they reached the outer gate, where, at the word of command, they were halted, and stood at attention.

Roy was on his mettle; his eyes glistening at the sight of the six awkward-looking fellows, knowing as he did what a change a few days in the hands of Ben and the troopers would effect; but he was growing strong enough now to begin adopting the policy of making it a favour to admit men to his chosen band. So he ruffled up like a young game-cock, to stand there glittering in the bright sunshine, with one gauntleted hand resting upon his hip, the other pressing down the hilt of his long sword.

"Want to see me, my lads?" he said.

There was a general whispering among the men as to who should speak, and at last one of them was shouldered forward with, "Go on, Sam; you say it."

Sam, the most sheepish of all, being thus thrust into prominence, wiped his mouth with the back of his hand, took off his hat, made an awkward bow, and thus delivered himself, with a smile:

"Morning, sir. You know me, Master Roy?"

"Eh? Oh, yes; Sam Donny, from the mill. What is it, my lad?"

"Only, sir, as me and my mates want to come and take sarvice here to fight for the king."

"Eh? You? Well, I don't know, my lad; we only want good men and true here, who will learn their duty, and do it."

"Oh, that's just what we are, sir," said the man, smoothing down his hair; "not one on us as'd go to sleep o' nights when the wind's blowing."

"Ah, but I don't want fellows to grind corn. I want men who will be ready to fight,—yes, and like men."

"Well, sir, ask all on 'em. I can fight, and lick any of the lot here. Oh, I can fight, and so can they."

"Hum—ha," said Roy, marching slowly round them, while the men drew themselves up and seemed to grow a couple of inches taller each under the inspection of the young captain. "What do you think, sergeant?" he continued; "think you can make artillerymen of 'em?"

Ben saluted, and took a few steps forward to march up and down the party, slapping their chests, feeling their arms, and pounding them heavily.

"Got some bone and muscle in 'em, sir," he said, respectfully, as his report. "Might try if they mean it."

"Take them across then to the armoury, measure them, and their names can be enrolled."

The men drew deep breaths of relief, and then grew nervous, for there was a short command or two given, a couple of the troopers stepped to their head, Ben and the corporal came up behind, and the little group of sturdy fellows was marched across into the guard-room, and afterwards into the armoury, to stand gaping at the weapons of war.

"Did I do that right?" said Roy, afterwards.

"Right, sir. The very thing. Those sort judge by what they see. They came to us half ready to laugh, but they soon saw how serious it all was; and they'll go away back to the mill to-night, and I'll be bound to say, Master Roy, if you followed 'em, you'd find they'd got a dozen other fellows about 'em, talking to 'em and boasting and bragging about how grand everything is, and showing 'em their uniforms and steel caps. This has about done it. You'll see we shall get as many men as we want now."

"But I felt all the time as if I were acting," said Roy.

"What? Look here, Master Roy, don't you go and say such a thing as that again. You weren't acting, and so I tell you; only doing your duty to your king and country, and your father and mother into the bargain. You can't do fighting without a bit of show along with it to brighten it up. You ask a man whether he'd like to wear a feather in his cap, and a bit o' scarlet and gold on his back, he'll laugh at you and say that such things are only for women. But don't you believe him, my lad; he won't own it, but he likes it all the same."

Ben was right. For the next week men from the village and the surrounding farms came up to the castle looking very serious and important, to be enrolled for its defence; and at the end of a fortnight there were fifty defenders, of whom fully forty looked as if they could be depended upon, while the rest would serve to make a show.

Meanwhile, Farmer Raynes attended the drilling and gun practice every morning with his men, the whole gathering rapidly picking up the rudiments of the military art under their four good teachers; while at noon all, save about a fourth, went back to their peaceful vocations, but ready at the arranged-for signal of two guns fired from the castle to hurry back, every man to his post, to stay in garrison continuously, instead of doing so one day in four.

Farmer Raynes devoted the rest of his time to going round and gathering stores, — provender and forage of every kind that would be necessary, — and his wagons seemed to be always coming or going across the drawbridge; while vaults and chambers in the castle which had remained unused for generations were now packed as store-rooms and granaries.

"Never mind the farm, Master Roy," said the bluff fellow, one day; "it isn't quite going backward."

"But the crops?" said Master Pawson, anxiously, for he was present.

"Well, Master Pawson, they won't be so good as they should be, of course, but they'll grow whether I'm there or no, and Sir Granby won't mind. He's a rich gentleman with a beautiful estate."

"Yes, yes," said Master Pawson; "it is a beautiful estate."

He looked quickly from the farmer to Roy, and back, as if he thought he had said too much.

"Ay, sir, it is a fine estate, and he's a lucky man who holds it. He won't mind a few things going wrong, so long as we take care to save it from some of the crop-eared rascals who'll be on the lookout to try and take possession. I'll be bound to say that there's some of 'em smelling about already, and making up their minds to make a grab at it if the king's crown goes down."

"Surely — surely not, Master Raynes," cried the secretary.

"That's what I think, sir. There's them here wouldn't be above taking possession of a pig, or a sack of my oats or barley; and there's bigger rogues who like bigger things, and would give their ears to get Sir Granby's fine estate. You mark my words, Master Roy; you'll see."

Roy did mark those words, thinking deeply of them during the following busy month, by which time the castle was in a fine state of defence, its little garrison of twelve or fourteen men, who kept watch and ward in regular military style, being relieved every day; while at the first bad news of danger, Roy was ready to summon his whole force from farm and mill, hoist the drawbridge, drop the portcullis, and with his stores of provisions set any beleaguering force at defiance, whether large or small.

"There, sir," said Ben one morning, "I begin to feel now as if I could breathe. There's a lot as wants doing yet, and I should dearly like to do away with that garden as spoils the court-yard, so as I could have a proper march round; but they won't come and catch us quite asleep."

"No, Ben; you've done splendidly. It's wonderful to see what smart fellows you have made of the men."

"Ay, and don't they know it too, sir?" said Ben, chuckling. "See the way they all marched past her ladyship this morning? There wasn't a man as didn't *feel* as if he was twice as big as he was a month or two ago. And see those big lads looking on?"

"Yes; there were forty or fifty across the moat."

"Ay, looking on as hungry as could be. Look here, Master Roy, I'm thinking a deal of getting say forty of 'em together—picked ones—as soon as I've more time, and knocking them into shape."

"I think it would be wise, Ben. They'd do well to work the guns."

"They would, sir; but we'll see. Any more news?"

"No, Ben; only rumours."

"Master Pawson heard anything?"

"No, not for a long time past. But look here, Ben, we have got the place in good order now, yet nothing has been done to see if there is any truth in the story about the secret passage leading into the old chapel."

Ben gave his head a punch.

"No, sir; and yet I think of it every night just before I go off to sleep. It ought to be done, for it's of no use to keep polishing up a pot that's got a big hole somewhere in the bottom."

"Of course it is not," said Roy. "Look here; when will you begin to search?"

"Let's hit while the iron's hot; sir, eh? You and I will go round and visit all the sentinels to-night, and then, as we shall have a lantern, we'll begin."

"Where?"

"Down under the north-west tower, sir."

"And ask Master Pawson to go with us?"

"Nay, sir; we'll keep it all to ourselves."

"But he will hear us about the steps, and opening and shutting doors."

"But he mustn't, sir. I'll oil all the locks and the keys I have, and we must smuggle our light under a big cloak. No, sir, we don't want Master Pawson with us; let him study his chirurgery and sewing of cuts, and stopping up bullet-holes. That'll do for him. This is a job for the castellan and his head-sergeant, sir; and, if you'll take my advice, that's the order for the night."

"Very well, Ben; that is the order for the night."

"One word, sir. How is my lady getting on with the flag? That old one is so tender like, I'm afraid it'll blow to pieces first time it's hoisted."

"Getting on splendidly."

"Big as the old one, sir?"

"Half as big again, Ben."

"That'll do, sir. I believe in a big flag. It gives the men courage, and bullies the enemy. Now I really do begin to feel as if I could breathe."

Chapter Sixteen
The Passage that is too Secret

"Going, Roy?" said Lady Royland to her son, as he rose from his seat in the library that night about an hour after Master Pawson had gone to his room, retiring early on the plea of a bad headache.

"Yes, mother; I'm going my rounds."

Lady Royland sighed.

"It seems very hard on you, my boy—all this work and watching."

"Oh, I don't mind," said the lad, smiling; "I've got used to it already. It makes everything go so regularly, and I feel sure that I have done everything to make the place safe."

"But it is hard upon the sentries, who, but for this, would be peacefully sleeping in their beds."

"Do us all good, mother. Good-night."

There was an affectionate embrace, and Roy went to his room, buckled on his sword, put on his helmet, threw a large cloak over his shoulders, and then went down to the guard-room door in the great lower gate-way, to be challenged at once, and forced to give the word.

A faint light shone out from the open door upon the military figure on duty, and Roy recognised in him one of the men from the mill, completely transformed from the heavy plodding fellow who had come in to take service.

But the challenge had brought out the old sergeant, also in a cloak, although it was a hot night, and within it he swung a lighted lantern.

The drawbridge was up and the portcullis down, making the entrance look black and strange, and shutting off the outer gate, from which the day guard was withdrawn, though this had not been accomplished without trouble and persuasion, for old Jenkin had protested.

"Like giving up the whole castle to the enemy, Master Roy," he said, with a full sense of the importance of his little square tower, and quite ignoring the fact that in the event of trouble he would be entirely cut off from his fellows if the drawbridge was raised.

But the old man gave in.

"Sodger's dooty is to 'bey orders," he said; and with the full understanding that he was to go back to his gate in the morning, he came into the guard-room to sleep on a bench every night.

"How is old Jenk?" said Roy.

"Fast asleep in his reg'lar place," replied Ben, and he led the way back into the gloomy stone guard-room, where he held up the lantern over the venerable old fellow's face, and Roy looked at him thoughtfully.

"Seems hard to understand it, Master Roy, don't it?" said Ben; "but if we lives, you and me'll grow to be as old as that. I expect to find some morning as he's gone off too fast ever to wake up again."

"Poor old fellow!" said Roy, laying his gloved band gently on the grey head. "How fond he always was of getting me to his room when I could only just toddle, and taking me to the moat to throw bread to the carp."

"Fished you out one day, didn't he, Master Roy!"

"To be sure, yes; I had almost forgotten that. I had escaped from the nurse and tumbled in."

"Ah! he's been a fine old fellow," said Ben. "I used to think he was a great worry sticking out for doing this and doing that, when he wasn't a bit of good and only in the way; but somehow, Master Roy, I began to feel that some day I might be just as old and stupid and no more use, and that made me fancy something else."

"What was that, Ben?" said Roy, for the old soldier had paused.

"Well, sir, I began to think that I was growing into a vain old fool after all, or else I should have seen that old Jenk was perhaps of more use here than I am. Can't you see, Master Roy?"

"I can't see what you mean, Ben."

"Why, that old chap's about the finest sample of a reg'lar soldier that these young fellows can have. I believe if the enemy did come, that old man would draw the sword that shakes in his weak old hand, and march right away to meet 'em as bravely as the best here."

"I'm sure he would, Ben," said Roy, warmly.

"Then he's one of our best men still, sir. Come on—I mean give the order, sir, and let's go our rounds."

Then, in the silence of the dark night, Roy led the way to the winding stair, and mounted silently to the ramparts, closely followed by Ben with the blinded lantern, and on reaching the top, they walked on to the left to the south-west tower; but before they could reach it a firm voice challenged them from the top. Then after giving the pass they went on through the tower and out onto the western ramparts, turning now to where the north-west tower loomed up all in darkness.

"Master Pawson's abed, sir," whispered Ben.

"Yes; not well," was the reply, in the same low tone.

But there was no challenge from here, and Roy walked silently in at the arched door-way, passed the secretary's door, and mounted the stair to severely admonish the sentry who was not keenly on the alert.

"Don't let him off easy, Master Roy," whispered Ben; "we might have been an enemy, sir, for aught he could tell."

This was spoken with the sergeant's lips to his young master's ear, and a few moments later Roy was at the top of the little turret, and stood there in the door-way ready to pounce upon the man whom he expected to find asleep.

But to his great satisfaction the sentry was well on the alert, for he was kneeling at one of the crenelles, reaching out as far as he could, and evidently watching something away to the north, while all was so still and dark that the movement of a fish or water-rat in the deep moat below sounded loud and strange.

Roy stepped out silently, crossed the narrow leads, and stood looking in the same direction as the sentinel; but he could make out nothing, and he was about to speak when the man, who had suddenly divined his presence, sprang up and clapped his hand to his sword.

"Stand!" he cried, hoarsely.

Roy gave the word, and Ben stepped out of the door-way to his side.

"Why, sir, you quite scared me," faltered the man; "I didn't hear you come."

"You should have heard," said Roy, sternly. "What were you watching there?"

"That's what I don't know, sir. I see a light out yonder somewheres about where them old stones is on the hill. And then I thought I heard talking, but that's quarter of an hour ago."

Both Roy and his companion had a good long look, but there was nothing to see or hear; and after admonishing the man to keep an eye upon the place, they descended and visited the sentries on the north-east and south-east towers, to find them well upon the *qui vive*.

After this they descended, and Ben led the way to the armoury, where he set the lantern on the table, took a spare candle from a box, and a bunch of keys from a drawer.

"May mean nothing, Master Roy; but I don't understand what light there could be up nigh the old chapel ruins, nor who could be talking there at this time of night."

"Not likely to be anything wrong, Ben, because if they had been enemies, they would not have shown a light."

"Signal perhaps, sir."

"Well, they wouldn't have talked aloud."

"Don't suppose they did, sir. Sound runs in a still, dark night like this. Well, anyways it seems to me as it's quite time we had a good look round to see if there's a hole anywhere in the bottom of the pot, so if you're ready, so am I. Only say the word."

"Forward!" cried Roy; and, going first with the lantern, Ben led the way along the corridor to the head of a flight of stone steps, down which they went to the underground passage, which with groined roof ran right along all four sides of the castle. The dark place seemed full of whispering echoes, as they went on past door after door leading into cellar and dungeon, all now turned into stores; for the great mass of provender brought in by Farmer Raynes's wagons had here been carefully packed away, the contents of each place being signified by a white, neatly painted number, duly recorded in a book where the account of what number so-and-so indicated was carefully written in Master Pawson's best hand, since he had eagerly undertaken the duties of clerk.

At each corner of the castle basement, the passage expanded into a circular crypt with a huge stone pillar, many feet in diameter, in the middle, from which radiated massive arches to rest on eight smaller pillars. This radial series of arches supported one of the towers, and, after passing the one to the north-east, Ben led on with his lantern along the passage running to the tower at the north-west corner, the dim light casting strange shadows behind, which seemed to be moving in pursuit of the two silent figures, urged on by the whispering echoes of their steps.

The pavement was smooth and perfectly dry, as were the massive stone walls; and as they went on, Roy fell into a musing fit, and thought of what a strongly built place Royland castle was, and how in times of emergency, if a garrison were hard pressed and had to yield rampart and tower to a powerful enemy, they would still have these passages and crypts as a place of refuge from which, if a bold defence were made, it would be impossible to dislodge them.

Apparently mind does influence mind under certain circumstances, for, just as Roy had arrived at this point, Ben stopped short and turned.

"Look here, Master Roy," he said, "you ought, now we're getting in pretty good order, to do two things."

"Yes; what are they?"

"Have that there stone gallows on the ramparts put a bit in order. It wants a few stones and some mortar."

"Why should I have that put in order?" said Roy, shortly.

"Case you want to hang any traitors, sir, for giving notice to the enemy of what we're doing, or trying to open the gates to 'em."

"I shall never want to hang any traitors," said Roy, sternly.

"I don't s'pose you will, sir; but it's just as well to let people see that you could if you wanted to. Might keep us from having any."

"I will not let the garrison see that I could have any such mistrust of the men who have come bravely up to help to protect my father's property."

"Well, Master Roy, that sounds handsome, and I like the idea of it: it's cheering-like to a man who tries to do his best. But all people don't think same as we do, and whenever we hear of a castle being attacked and defended, there were always people outside trying to make traitors of those who were in, and temptation's a nasty, cunning, 'sinuating sort of a thing. But you're castellan, and you ought to do as you please."

"I will, Ben, over that, at all events. Fancy what my mother would think if I were to be making preparations for such a horror."

"Hum! yes, sir. What would she think? That's a queer thing, Master Roy, isn't it, what a deal mothers have to do with how a man does, whether he's a boy or whether he's growed up?"

"Why, of course they have. It is natural."

"Yes, sir; I suppose it is," said the old soldier, as he went on. "You wouldn't think it, perhaps, of such a rough 'un as me, and at my time o' life, but I never quite get my old woman out of my head."

"I don't see how any one could ever forget his mother," said Roy, flushing a little.

"He can't, sir," said Ben, sharply; "what she taught him and said always sticks to the worst of us. The pity of it is, that we get stoopid and ashamed of it all—nay, not all, for it comes back, and does a lot of good sometimes, and—pst!—pst!—if we talk so loud we shall be waking Master Pawson. But I say, Master Roy, it won't do, really. Look at that now!"

They were close to the circular crypt beneath the north-west tower, and Ben was holding up his lantern towards the curve of the arches on his left.

"Roots! coming through between the stones."

"Yes, sir, that's it. Only the trees her ladyship had planted, and that's the beginning of pulling this corner of the castle down. There's nothing like roots for that job. Cannon-balls'll do it, and pretty quickly too; but give a tree time, and it'll shake stone away from stone, and let the water come in, and then the frost freezes it, and soon it's all over with the strongest tower ever made. Do 'ee now ask her to have 'em cut down, and the roots burned."

"I'm not going to ask anything of the sort, Ben," said Roy, shortly. "Now about this passage. You think it must run somewhere from here."

"Yes, sir," replied the old soldier, as he stood now under one of the arches of the crypt and raised his lantern to open a door. "There, now we can see a bit better. If there is such a place, it starts, I suppose, from somewhere here."

He walked slowly round the place, holding the lantern into the recesses, eight of which appeared between the pillars surrounding that in the centre.

"But there's plenty of room here for storing sacks or anything else, and you can have doors made to those two that haven't got any, if you like."

Roy walked into one of these recesses—cellar-like places of horse-shoe curve, going in a dozen feet, and then ending in a flat wall.

"Which way am I looking here, Ben?" said Roy.

"Out'ards, sir; you're standing about level with the bottom of the moat, or pretty nigh thereabouts. You're—yes—that's where you are, just at the nor'-west corner, and the moat turns there."

"Then the places on each side here face the moat, one to the north, the other to the west."

"Well, not exactly, sir, but nearly."

"Then the secret passage can't begin at the end of either of these, and been built up."

"I dunno, sir. Folk in the past as had to do with them passages did all they could to make 'em cunning."

"But they couldn't have made a passage through the moat."

"Of course not, sir; it must have gone under it."

"Then it couldn't have started from here."

"Why not, sir?" said Ben, with a low laugh; "what's to prevent there being another dungeon like this on the other side of the wall there, one with a trap-door in it leading down ever so many steps into another place, and the passage begin ten or twenty foot deeper."

"Something like the powder-magazine is made?"

"That's it, sir. We're in the lower part of a big round tower, and we know there's those floors above us one on top of the other, and we don't know that the old Roylands who built this place mayn't have dug down and down before they started it, and made one, two, or three floors below where we stand."

"What? Dug right down? Impossible!"

"They dug down that time as deep into the old stone to make the big well, sir."

"Of course; then it is possible."

"Possible, sir? Oh yes; look at the secret passages there are in some old walls, made just in the thickness, and doors leading into 'em just where you wouldn't expect 'em to be. Up a chimney, perhaps, or a side of a window. I heered tell of one as was quite a narrow door, just big enough for a man to pass through, and you didn't walk into it, because it wasn't upright; but you got into it by crawling through a square hole with a thin stone door which fell back after you were through. Then you stood up, and could go half round the old house it was in."

"Well," said Roy, "if there is such a passage, we must find it; but if it has been built up, we might have to pull half the place down."

"Yes, sir; but first of all, we'll have a good look in these cellars, for it mayn't have been built up, and we may find it easily enough. Begin then, and let's try."

Ben trimmed the candle with his forefinger and thumb, making the flame brighter, and then holding the light close to the flat face of the wall, they examined stone after stone; but as far as they could make out, they had not been tampered with since the day the masons concluded their task.

Then the curved walls right and left were examined quickly, as they were little likely to contain a concealed opening; lastly, the flags on the floor, and, finally, Ben drew his sword and softly tapped each in turn.

But not one gave forth a hollow sound. Everything was solid, even the walls at the back.

"Let's try the other open one, sir," said Ben, and they continued their investigations in this place, which was precisely similar to the first, and yielded the same results.

Then the keys of the great bunch Ben carried were tried on one fast-closed door of oak, studded with square nails much corroded by rust, but it was not until the last key had been thrust in that with a harsh creaking the bolt of the ponderous lock shot back; and then it required the united efforts of both to get the door to turn upon the rusty hinges.

Here they were met by precisely the same appearances, and the search was made, and ended by sounding with the sword pommel.

"No, sir; there's nothing here."

"I'm afraid not," said Roy; "everything sounds solid."

"Ay, sir, and solid it is."

"But if you tap so hard, Master Pawson will hear you," whispered Roy, as the old soldier tried the floor again.

"Maybe not, sir; but if he do, he do. Let's hope now he's fast asleep; you see, he's three floors higher up."

"But knocking sounds travel a long distance, Ben, and I'd rather he did not know."

"Me too, sir. Well, this is only three. Let's try the others."

"I hope you are not going to have so much work with the finding of the key," said Roy; "it hinders us so."

"Plenty of time before morning, sir," replied Ben, coolly; and after relocking the heavy low door, he tried the key he had just withdrawn upon the next door, and, to the surprise of both, it yielded easily, and was thrown open.

Again the same clean, swept-out place, with plenty of grey cobwebs; but that was all.

Upon sounding the stones, however, at the back, they fancied that they detected a suggestion of hollowness, still not enough to make Roy determine to have the wall torn down.

This place was locked and the next tried, the only satisfactory part of the business being that the key before used evidently opened all the locks in the basement of this tower; and so it proved, as one after the other the dungeons or cellars were tried with the same unsatisfactory results, for none of the eight afforded the slightest trace of the clew they sought.

At last, pretty well tired out and covered with cobwebs, they stood in the crypt while Ben lit a fresh candle, the first having burned down into the socket, with the wick swimming in molten fat, and Roy said, with a yawn—

"I wonder whether there is a passage after all, or whether it is some old woman's tale."

"Nay, sir, there is," said the old soldier, solemnly. "Your father said there was, and he must have known."

"Well, then, where is the door?" said Roy, peevishly.

"Ah! that's what we've got to find out, sir. You're tired now, and no wonder. So let's try another night. You're not going to give a thing up because you didn't do it the first time."

"I hope not," said Roy, with another yawn; "but I am a bit tired now. I say, Ben, though, think it's in one of the places we've filled up with stores?"

"I hope not, sir; that would be making too hard a job of it."

"Stop a moment," cried Roy, brightening up; "I have it."

"You know where it is, sir?" cried Ben, eagerly.

"Not this end," said Roy, laughing, "but the other."

"What, in the old ruins? Of course."

"Well, why not go and find that, and then trace it down to here. It would be the easiest way."

"There is something in that, sir, certainly," said the old soldier, thoughtfully; "ever been there, sir?"

"Once, blackberrying; but of course I never saw anything; only a rabbit or two."

"Then if we can't find it here after a good try or two, sir, we'll have a walk over there some evening, though I don't feel to like the idea of leaving the place, specially as all the gentry seem so unfriendly. Not a soul, you see, has been to see her ladyship. Looks bad, Master Roy, and as if there was more going on than we know of round about us."

"Ah, well, never mind that," said Roy; "let's get back out of this chilly, echoing place. I'm fagged."

"We'll go back this way, sir," said Ben; and he went on first with the lantern, till he came to one of the flights of stone steps leading up to the ground level.

"Let's go on here, Ben," said Roy; and, upon their reaching the corridor above, the boy looked back along it towards where the stairs went up into the corner tower, beneath which they had been so busy.

"Wonder whether Master Pawson heard us, Ben."

"Can't say, sir. I should fancy not, or he'd have been on the stir to know what was the matter."

"Mightn't have cared to stir in the dark, Ben. I say, I should like to know. Look here, he went off early to bed, because he said he was unwell. I'll go and ask how he is. That's a good excuse for seeing."

"Well, so it is, sir," said Ben, rubbing his ear; "and if he did hear anything, he'd be pretty sure to speak."

"Of course. Then I will go. Come and light me." Roy hurried along back with Ben following and casting the boy's shadow before him, till they reached the arched door-way, where they went up the few stone steps in the spiral staircase, reached the oaken door leading into the apartments, felt for the latch, raised it, and gave it a loud click; but the door did not yield to the boy's pressure, and he tried it again, and then gave it a shake. "Why, he has locked himself in, Ben!"

"Has he, sir? Didn't want to be 'sturbed, maybe."

"Perhaps he was frightened by the noise we made, and then fastened himself in," said Roy, with a laugh.

Ben chuckled at the idea.

"Well, sir, not the first time we've frightened him, eh?"

"Hush! I want to let him know who it is now knocking," said Roy; "it is startling to be woke up in the middle of the night. Master Pawson—Master Pawson!" he said, gently; and he tapped lightly with his fingers.

But there was no reply, and Roy tapped and called again, but still without result.

"He's too fast asleep to hear you, sir."

"Well, he ought to bear that," said Roy, giving the door a good rattle, and then tapping loudly.

"One would think so, sir; but he don't seem to have his ears very wide open, or else he's too much scared to stir."

"Master Pawson! Master Pawson!" cried Roy, loudly now; and he once more rattled the door. "How are you?"

"Fast as a church, sir," said Ben; "and I wouldn't rattle no more, because you'll be having the sentry up atop after us. Better go and speak to him, or he'll be raising the guard."

Ben went up on the winding stair, and spoke to the sentry, who challenged him as he reached the top, and was much relieved on hearing his sergeant's voice.

"Didn't know what to make of it," he said; "and I should have fired, only my piece wouldn't go off."

"Well, let this be a lesson to you, my lad, to keep your firelock in order."

"Yes, sergeant; I will in future."

"We might have been the enemy coming. See any more of that light, or hear any more noise over yonder?"

"No, nothing."

"Not heard nothing from Master Pawson, I suppose?"

"Not since he came up and spoke to me before he went to bed. Said his head was queer or something—spoke mighty pleasant, and that he was sorry for me who had to watch all night."

"Well?"

"That was all; only I said I was sorry for him having such a bad head."

Ben went down to where Roy was waiting in the secretary's door-way.

"Can't wake him, Ben. Come along; I am tired now."

"Feel as if an hour's sleep wouldn't do me much harm, sir," said the old soldier; and they went on along the corridor, whose windows looked out upon the pleasaunce. "Master Pawson's in the right of it. Once a man's well asleep, it's a woundy, tiresome thing to be wakened up. Good-night, sir."

"Good-morning, you mean, Ben," said Roy, laughing.

"Oh, I calls it all night till the sun's up again, sir. You and me'll have to try the old ruins, I s'pose, though I don't expect we shall find anything there."

Roy went straight to his room, half undressed, and threw himself upon the bed, to begin dreaming directly that he had discovered the entrance to the secret passage at the other end, but it was so blocked up with stones and tree-roots that there was no way in, and would not be until he had persuaded his mother to do away with the garden, cut down the trees, and turn the place back into a regular court-yard such as old Ben wished.

Chapter Seventeen
Farmer Raynes brings News

It was the loud blast of a trumpet which roused Roy from his slumbers to find that it was a gloriously clear morning, and that the call was bringing the little garrison together for the early parade.

The trumpeter was the youngest of the three men from his father's regiment, and consequently the call rang out in the true martial style, echoing through the garden court, and sounding exhilarating to the boy as he sprang off his bed and began to dress.

It roused the jackdaws, too, from their resting-places, and sent them sailing about in the clear sunny air, their black forms reflected from the moat, and their sharp, petulant cries sounding like protests against this disturbance.

For they had had a hard time of it lately. Under Ben's superintendence every loop-hole had been cleared, every collection of nesting ruins carefully removed, and they had no other married quarters but the holes in the walls, half-shaded by the green pellitory which rooted and flourished in company with the moss, that acted as sponges to retain enough moisture for its sustenance.

Roy was not long in dressing, buckling on his sword, and hurrying down to the tiny parade ground, for in his character of castellan he liked to be present every morning when the men who were to relieve the garrison assembled at the gate-way, across the moat, and waited for permission to march in.

All this was rigorously carried out in true military style by the old sergeant's management; and as Roy descended, it was to find the little garrison drawn up fully armed under Ben's command, he and the three troopers forming the regular staff who never left the castle.

Ben looked as fresh as if he had not made a night's rest out of two hours on a form in the guard-room; and giving the word as Roy appeared, there was the twinkling and glittering of headpiece and weapon as the men presented arms, and then stood again at attention as it was carried out some two hundred and fifty years ago.

Then a short inspection by the castellan followed, orders were given, and four men marched to the door-way, tramped up the staircase, and a few minutes later the ponderous drawbridge began to descend, till it spanned the moat; and at a word the men fresh from their homes marched across, to halt by the portcullis, which then began to rise slowly, the capstans creaking and cracking, till the row of spikes alone was visible as they hung like iron stalactites overhead.

Another sharp order rang out, and the new-comers filed into the guard-room, from whence came the clashing of metal and the buzzing of voices as the men assumed their arms and came out one by one to fall in opposite to those whose places they were to take, and who would, in a few minutes, go into the guard-room to deposit their arms in the racks, and then be free till their short term of service recommenced, but of course ready to hurry to the castle at the first summons should a necessity arise.

Everything went on according to the regular routine; the fresh men were all drawn up now, armed, the order given, and the relieved tramped into the guard-room and soon began to straggle out again, eager to troop over to a kind of buttery-hatch by the great kitchen, where a mug of milk and a hunch of bread for a refresher would be waiting for distribution, by Lady Royland's orders, for every man.

All this went on then as usual, and the old warder Jenkin had just come tottering out of the guard-room, to go and take up his customary post at the gate, the trumpeter had raised his instrument to his lips to blow a blast, and the new-comers were ready to march off to their several duties of mounting guard, drilling at the guns, and cleaning accoutrements, when there was the sound of hoofs rapidly beating the road across the moat, and directly after a figure, mounted upon a heavy cart-horse, came into sight, thundering along at full gallop. At the first glimpse it seemed as if the horse had run away with his bareheaded rider; but directly after it became plain that, though only riding saddleless, and with no rein but a halter, the big man was urging the horse forward with all his might.

"Why, it must mean news!" said Roy, excitedly, as he advanced towards the drawbridge.

"Ay, there's something wrong, sir," said Ben, gravely. "That we shall soon hear."

The armed men stood fast on one side, and those disarmed in a group on the other, waiting excitedly to see what this new thing meant.

"It's Farmer Raynes!" cried Roy.

"Ay, sir, that's who it be. He was coming with a wainload of oats this morning, and he wants help, for he has broken down, I should say."

The next minute the rider dashed up to the far gate, but did not draw rein, for he sent his horse thundering across the drawbridge before he checked the panting beast with a loud "*woho!*" and then threw himself off.

"What's the matter, Master Raynes?" cried Roy.

"They're here, sir," whispered the bluff farmer, excitedly. "I'd got a wagon loaded with oats last night, and was taking 'em from Dendry Town to the farm ready for bringing on here i' morning, when at a turn of the lane I come upon a troop of horse who surrounded the wagon at once, and a couple of 'em led me, whip and all, up to their officer, a lank-looking, yellow-faced fellow, who was sitting on his horse just under a tree.

"'Where are you taking that grain?' says he.

"'On the king's service,' says I. 'To Royland Castle.'

"His yellow wrinkly face grinned all over, and he turned and gave orders to an officer by him; and then I knew I'd made a mistake. For they were all well-mounted, and in a regular trooper's uniform, and I thought I'd happened upon one of the king's regiments, instead of which they were a pack of Roundhead rabble; and I had to drive the team back with the oats to their headquarters at Dendry Town. There they made me open a sack to feed their horses; and after that I was told I was a prisoner, and that my wagon and team was taken for the use of the state."

"Dendry Town—ten miles away," said Roy, thoughtfully.

"Many on 'em?" said Ben, sourly.

"There was about fifty as took me," said the farmer; "and I should say there were seven or eight hundred in the town swarming all over the place."

"But how did you get away, Raynes?"

"Left it till this morning, sir, when I was feeding my horses, after emptying a couple of sacks for theirs. Waited till there was a chance, and then I jumped on old Ball here, who can go like fun when he gets warm, and galloped off. They shot at me, and I heard the bullets whistle, and then about a dozen came in pursuit, galloping after me till we got within sight of the towers; and then they drew back, and here I am. I thought you ought to know somehow that the enemy was so near."

"Then they're not a mere rabble of men?"

"Not they, sir. Reg'lar soldiers, and they've got big guns in the market-place. Quite a little army."

"Thank you, Raynes," said Roy, gravely. "It was very good and brave of you to bring the news like this. Halt there, men. Take your arms again. We shall perhaps have some work to do." Then briefly giving his orders, which had long enough before been arranged between him and Ben, the latter led one little party to the south-west tower, and the corporal took another to the north-west, while Roy himself mounted with a party into the gate tower, where at his word of command the portcullis dropped with a loud clang, and directly after the drawbridge began to rise till it was back in the position it always occupied by night.

This part of the business of preparation for unwelcome visitors being accomplished, Roy mounted to the leads, where he placed a sentry to keep a good lookout, and then turned to see if his men were ready.

They stood in a group on each tower waiting, Ben and the corporal swinging a port-fire from time to time to keep it well in a glow; and then standing on the breastwork above the machicolations, Roy looked out as far as he could see in search of enemies, where, however, all looked beautiful and at peace.

But it could be no false alarm. The time for action had come; and, turning to the right, he waved his hands, turned to the left, and did likewise; and directly after a puff of grey smoke darted out from the top of each tower, followed by two rapidly succeeding peals like thunder, which echoed through the castle, making the jackdaws fly out of their resting-places to wheel round, crying vociferously.

"Now," said Roy to himself, "the staff is ready. It's time to raise the king's flag."

But the flag was still in Lady Royland's hands, and the boy descended to cross to her private apartments and fetch it away.

But half-way across the pleasaunce he encountered Master Pawson, looking wild-eyed, pale, and strange.

"What is the matter?" he cried. "What is that firing for?"

"The enemy are near, Master Pawson," said Roy, quietly; "and I suppose that before long they will pay us a visit."

"But the guns—why were the guns fired?"

"As a signal, of course, for our men to gather, and for such of the village people as like to take refuge here. I thought you knew."

"I? No. I did not know. But the people will not come," said the secretary, with undue excitement; and he now looked very pale indeed.

"It will be rather hard, though, if they do not, after all this drilling and teaching."

"Oh! those men may," said the secretary, hastily. "I meant the people from the village."

"Well, we shall see," said Roy.

"But what makes you say that the enemy are near?" said the secretary, giving him a searching look.

"The messenger who brought the news. Farmer Raynes."

"Farmer Raynes?"

"Yes; he was taken and escaped."

At that moment Ben came up with a grim look of satisfaction upon his countenance.

"Morning, sir," he said to the secretary. "You see the enemy have found us out. Ready for them?"

"I? What do you mean?"

"Ready to doctor some of us as gets our heads and legs knocked off by cannon-balls. I beg pardon, Master Roy, sir, her ladyship's a-signalling to you yonder. What does she say to the enemy coming?"

"My mother!" said Roy, excitedly, as he caught sight of her at one of the corridor windows. "I have not seen her yet."

Chapter Eighteen
Royland Castle after its Growl

Lady Royland received the news calmly enough, and was the first to allude to the flag, which she said would be, though unfinished, suitable enough to hoist whenever her son thought it right to do so.

"The sooner, then, the better, I should say, mother," cried Roy. "Let them see it waving when they come near."

"By all means, my boy. I am glad to find that you have everything in so good a state of preparation. The guns startled me a little, but I expected to hear them some time. Do you think the men will prove true and come in?"

"True, mother? Yes, of course."

A few minutes later Roy came out with the silken flag hanging in folds across his arm like a cloak, and hurried to where Ben and the three troopers were busy loading the two guns, run out now into the gate-way so as to command the road from each side of the raised bridge.

The men were all armed, and a look of excitement was in every face, notably in that of Farmer Raynes, who was fidgeting about and looking anxious.

Roy handed the flag to Ben, who took it proudly, and nodded his satisfaction.

"You'll come up and be there at the hoisting, sir?" he said.

"Of course. Yes—what is it?"

"Master Pawson, sir," whispered the old soldier, with a laugh; "we managed to wake him up at last."

Roy smiled and went to where the farmer stood, watching him anxiously, and finally making a sign to him to come.

"Want to speak to me, Master Raynes?" he said.

"Yes, sir; I'm in agonies about my men. They'll be coming along soon and falling into a trap, for some of those troopers will be hanging about the road."

"Yes, this is serious," said Roy, who grasped the difficulties of the reinforcements he hoped soon to receive.

Ben was called into counsel, and his suggestion was that the guns on the four towers should be manned ready to cover the advance of the friends, and keep back the enemy.

"Mounted men's orders are to keep clear of cannon-shot all they can, sir; and now, if you please, I should like you to arm all the people necessary, while I see to the ammunition."

This order was carried out, and the flag taken up into the furnace-chamber, just below where the new flag-staff with halyard had been erected against the staircase turret.

In a very short time all was ready, so far as so small a force was available, and four men kept ready in the chamber prepared to lower the bridge as soon as any friends approached, when it was to be kept down till the coming of strangers rendered it necessary that it should be raised again.

Ten minutes had not elapsed before a shout from the north-east tower was heard, and Roy turned in the direction pointed out by one of the men, to see a little party of four men who, in obedience to the signal, were advancing at a trot from the direction of the village.

The bridge was lowered, the portcullis raised, and, as the men came hurrying across, they were received with a hearty cheer from the tiny garrison.

The bridge being down and the portcullis raised, the state of preparation was deemed sufficient to warrant their remaining so, as no enemy was in sight; but the precaution was taken of having the port-fires ready and each gun in the gate-way manned so as to sweep the approach.

Another shout announced fresh arrivals, men coming up in twos and threes, every arrival sending a thrill of satisfaction through the young castellan's breast as he felt his strength increase, till only two parties were not accounted for,—six men from the mill and the ten from the farm.

"A terrible loss they would be, Ben," said Roy, as he swept the country from the highest point of the tower, and without effect. "Raynes wants to go in search of them."

"Then don't let him, sir. We can't spare him. Mightn't be able to come back. Wait a bit; they've all got some distance to come. Give 'em time."

"But they might have been here by now."

"Ay, they might, sir," said Ben, drily.

"Ha! you think they are afraid, now it comes to the pinch."

"Nay, sir, not yet. They may have a good way round to go 'scape the enemy, for I dare say they're beginning to occupy the roads. I'm most anxious about the farm lads, for they're nighest to where the enemy are.— Hi! there! Look! look!"

Ben had turned his head in a different direction to that in which the men from the mill might have been expected to come; and there, altogether, running in a group, six figures could be seen evidently making for the castle, while a party of a dozen horsemen suddenly rode into sight from behind a copse about a quarter of a mile away, and cantered across as if to head the men off.

"Now, sir, quick! Tell 'em yonder to make ready and wait. The corporal's there, and he'll know what to do."

Roy shouted the orders to the south-west tower, and the trooper-corporal answered loudly, and they saw him blow his port-fire.

"Now, sir, wait a bit, till they get nigher. That's it. Now, fire!"

The race had been growing exciting, for the horsemen were increasing their pace as they came on with their weapons glittering in the sun, and it was plain enough that the runners must be cut off and taken prisoners, when just at the right moment Roy's order rang out. There was a white puff from the tower, a heavy boom, the ball went whistling just over the heads of the horsemen, and a shout of triumphant derision arose from the towers, as, moved by the same spirit, the little troop wheeled round and went off at full gallop to get out of gunshot.

"Another shot, men!"

"Nay, sir, certainly not. That's the young soldier speaking. What for? You might bowl over a horse or two, but what good would that do? You've done what you wanted, and sent 'em to the right-about, saved six of our lads, and at the same time showed those fellows that we're on the lookout and don't mean to stand any nonsense. That's enough for one bullet, sir, eh?"

"Splendid! my lads," cried Roy, who leaned over the battlements, waving his hand to the panting and nearly exhausted men from the mill, who came at a steady trot now across the bridge, cheered loudly by all who could see them.

Roy's next thought was to go and tell Lady Royland all about the incident; but he felt that he must live up to his position, and be busy there in sight of his men; so, after watching the enemy's horse till quite out of sight, he bade Ben keep a sharp lookout, and descended to hear the report of the party who had just come in.

He found them in the guard-room, scarlet with exertion, and still panting from their long race, but evidently in high glee, Sam Donny, their spokesman, the young man who was put first to the front when they came to him, being full of their adventures,—how the troopers had passed the mill three times that morning, and stopped twice to demand corn for their steeds and water, their leader watching the miller's men curiously as if suspicious of them.

"But they went off at last, sir. Let's see: they come agen, though, twice after we'd heard the guns, and that kep' us back. Last of all, I says to t'others, 'Now for it, lads, or young Captin Roy'll be thinking we're feared to come.' They says, 'That's so,' and off we starts; but we hadn't gone far 'fore we finds they're on the road, and we had to run back and make for Water Lane. Hadn't gone far 'long Water Lane, when we finds a couple of 'em there. Back we goes again, and creeps along aside one of the fields, and there they was again, and dozens of 'em on the watch, as if some one had told 'em we was likely to come over here. Then we all goes back to the mill and talks it over, and some on us says as we'd better stop till night; but I says, 'Nay! They'll think we're all cowards, and get shooting at us if we comes in the dark,' and at last we said we'd go two miles round by the common. And so we did, sir, crawling on our stummicks in and out among the furze bushes, and every now and then seeing the sun shine on one of their caps as they rode here and there.

"Last of all, sir, they seemed to have gone away, and I lifts up my head and looks about. 'All clear, mates!' I says, and up we gets, keeping as far off as we could, so as to work round. 'We've done 'em this time,' I says, as we went on, and we was coming along splendid, till Bob Herries happens to look back, and, 'Run, lads,' he says; 'here they come arter us!' I was for hiding, sir, but there was no chance, so we all run our best, with the castle here seeming a long way off; but we got nigher and nigher, and so did they; and they'd ha' cut us off if it hadn't been for that gun—though we all thought the next shot might hit us."

"You did bravely, my lads," cried Roy. "But tell me, what about the men from the farm?"

"What! aren't they here, sir?" said the man.

"No; we've seen nothing of them."

"Well, I am glad, then, that we aren't the last," said the man, with a grin of satisfaction; but his face was serious directly. "I don't quite mean that, sir. I mean I'm sorry they're not here. Then some of those fellows must have took them. But what I want to know is, how could they tell we was a-coming to the castle?"

"They must have noticed that you all had a military bearing, my lad. You are all very different to what you were when you came to join."

A look of pride beamed in the man's face and was reflected in those of his companions, but he spoke out directly.

"Well, we have tried to get to be soldiers, sir, hard; haven't us, mates?"

"Ay!" was growled in chorus.

"Yes, you have done well," cried Roy, "and I'm heartily glad to see you safely here."

Chapter Nineteen
The Young Castellan speaks out

The day passed anxiously on, and it was getting well towards sunset, but there was no sign of the farm men, neither did the enemy appear in sight. Farmer Raynes appealed to Roy again and again for permission to go in search of his people; but, anxious as the young castellan was for news, he could not risk losing one of the strongest and most dependable men he had.

"They may get here yet, Master Raynes," he said; "and I'd give anything to see them; but I'd rather lose the swords of all ten than lose yours."

"Mean that, Master Roy?" said the bluff farmer, looking at him searchingly.

"Mean it? Of course!"

"Thank ye, sir. Then I'll stop; but I feel as if I'd failed you at a pinch by only coming alone."

"Then don't think so again," said Roy, "but help me all you can with the men, for I'm afraid we are going to have a hard fight to save the place."

"Oh, we'll save it, sir. Don't you fear about that," said Raynes; and he went away to join Ben and talk about the chances of the party reaching the castle.

In the guard-room the matter was also eagerly discussed; for the help of ten sturdy lads was badly needed, as all knew. Sam Donny, who was rather inflated by the success which had attended him and his companions that day, gave it as his opinion that the labourers had been taken prisoners solely because they had not thought to go down and crawl as he and his companions had that day.

Roy had hurriedly snatched a couple of meals, and tried to cheer his mother about their prospects, but to his surprise, he found that she was ready to try and console him about the loss of ten good strong men.

"But do you think they have thought better of it, and are afraid to come in?" said Master Pawson at their hurried dinner.

"No, I do not," said Roy. "I will not insult the poor fellows by thinking they could be such curs."

"Quite right, Roy," said the secretary, eagerly. "I was wrong. I'm afraid I understand books better than I do men. Yes; they must have been taken prisoners, I'm afraid."

The evening meal had just been commenced when there was a shout from one of the towers.

Roy hurried out, full of hope that the ten men had been descried; but he was soon undeceived, for on mounting to his favourite post of observation it was to see that a long line of horseman was approaching from the direction of Dendry Town, the orange sunlight making their arms glitter as they came gently on, spreading out to a great length, till at last Ben gave it as his opinion that there were at least five hundred men.

Hardly had he come to this conclusion when another body of men was descried approaching from the east, and in the face of this danger the drawbridge was raised, the portcullis lowered, and a trumpet-call summoned the men to the guns.

"They mean it then to-night, Ben," said Roy, whose heart now beat fast, and he turned to the old soldier, who, with a grim look of pride in his face, was affixing the silken flag to the rope, ready for hauling up when the enemy drew near.

Before Ben could reply, to Roy's surprise, Lady Royland came up the spiral stairs, and stepped out upon the leads, followed by Master Pawson, who looked sallow of aspect, but perfectly calm.

"You here, mother?"

"Yes, my boy; and why should I not be? I am visiting all the towers to thank the men for their brave conduct in coming here for our defence. How many do you muster now?"

"Thirty-six only," replied Roy.

"Well, thirty-six brave men are better than five hundred cowards.— How many men do you think there are coming against us, Martlet?"

"Seven or eight hundred, my lady."

"And will they attack this evening?"

"No, my lady; they don't come to attack strongholds with mounted men. They're coming to call upon us to throw open the gates and surrender the place; and this is the answer, I think, my lady, is it not?" and he pointed to the flag.

"Yes, Martlet," said Lady Royland, flushing; "that is our answer to such an insolent demand."

She turned and left the tower, attended by Master Pawson, and Roy remained there watching the long line of mounted men approaching with their arms glittering in the light. "Seven or eight hundred," he said, half aloud, "against thirty-six."

"Haven't counted the guns, Master Roy, nor the moat, nor the towers, nor all the other strong things we have. Pah! what's a regiment of horse against a place like this? But they know, and they're only coming to bully us, sir."

"I hope you are right, Ben," said the lad, seriously; and he waited for the approach of the men till they were halted about a couple of hundred yards away from the tower on which he stood, forming up in squadrons; and after a time an officer, bearing a little white flag, advanced, followed at a short distance by a couple of troopers. Roy's heart beat fast, for he felt that a crucial time had come.

"You'll have to go down, Master Roy; and we must lower the bridge for you to go out and meet him and hear what he has to say."

"Must I, Ben?"

"Of course, sir; and, if you give the order, the corporal and I will come behind you as your guard."

"And suppose, when the bridge is down, the others make a rush?"

"Flag o' truce, sir. But if they did, our guns would sweep 'em away."

"And what about us, Ben?"

"Well, sir," said the old fellow, drily, "we should be swep' away too."

"I say, Ben!"

"Yes, sir, sounds nasty; but soldiers has to take their chance o' that sort o' thing, and look at the honour and glory of it all. Ready, sir?"

"Yes," said Roy, in a husky voice; and a minute later he stood with the two martial-looking figures behind, and the drawbridge slowly descended in front. The two guns were manned, a small guard of three was behind each, and the port-fires sparkled and shot tiny little flashes of fire as if eager to burst out into flame.

Just then, as Roy was watching the heads of the three mounted men coming slowly forward, and, as the end of the bridge sank, seeing their chests, the horses' heads, and finally their legs come into sight, Ben leaned towards him, and said, in a whisper—

"They don't know how young you are, sir. Let 'em hear my dear old colonel speaking with your lips."

"Yes," said Roy, huskily; "but what am I to say, Ben?"

"You don't want no telling, sir. Advance now."

The officer had halted his men about fifty yards from the outer gate, and rode forward a few paces before drawing rein and waiting for some action on the part of those he had come to see; and he looked rather surprised as they stepped forward now, crossed the bridge, and advanced to meet him. For he had not anticipated to find such careful preparations, nor to see the personage who came to meet him in so perfect a military trim, and supported by a couple of soldiers whose bearing was regular to a degree.

The officer was a grim, stern, hard-looking, middle-aged man, and his garb and breastplate were of the commonest and plainest description. He seemed to glance with something like contempt at the elegantly fluted and embossed armour the boy was wearing, and, above all, at the gay sash Lady Royland's loving hands had fastened across his breast. But his attention was keen as he scanned the soldierly bearing of Ben and the corporal, and a feeling of envy filled his breast as he compared them with his own rough following. Perhaps he would not have thought so much if he had seen the rest of the garrison, but they were too distant.

Roy saluted the officer, and drew a deep breath as he tried to string up his nerves till they were stretched like a bow. For Ben's words had gone home, and he felt fully how big a part he had to play.

The officer saluted in response in a quick, abrupt manner, and said shortly:

"I come from the general commanding the army here in the west, to demand that you give up peaceable possession of this castle, once the property of the rebel, Sir Granby Royland, who is now in arms against the Parliament of England."

Roy gave a start at the word "rebel," and felt the hot blood rise to his cheeks. That insult acted like a spur. The nervous trepidation had gone, for there was no room for it alongside of the anger which flashed through him. Ben was right: the boy knew what to say. It was there ready, and only wanted bringing out.

"Look here, sir!" he cried, sharply; "you come here under a flag of truce to deliver a message, but that does not warrant insolence."

"Insolence?" said the officer, sternly.

"Yes. I hold no parley with a man who dares to call my father, King Charles's faithful servant, a rebel."

"Then go back, boy, and send your mother to make the arrangement for handing over the keys of the castle," said the officer, with a smile of contempt, "for I suppose the Dame Royland is here."

"Lady Royland is here, sir; and I, her son, tell you to inform your rebel general that we here recognise no authority but that of his majesty the king, and that we consider it a piece of insolent braggadocio for him to send such a demand."

"Indeed!" said the officer, laughing. "Well crowed, young game-cock!"

"Yes," muttered Ben; "and you mind his spurs."

"Have you anything more to say?" cried Roy.

"Yes; a good deal, my boy, and I will not notice your young, hot-blooded words. You have allowed your men to perform an act this morning that may mean serious consequences for you."

"I do not understand your meaning, sir."

"Yes, you do, boy," said the officer, sternly. "You allowed your men to fire upon a picket of our cavalry."

"Of course. You allowed your cavalry, as you term them, to try and ride down six unarmed men on their way to the castle, and I gave orders for them to be stopped, and they were stopped."

"I have no time to argue these things with you, sir. I have only this to say: if you give up the keys to me at once, your people can disperse unharmed to their homes, and Dame Royland and her son can depart with such personal effects as she desires, to go wherever she pleases, and an escort will be provided for her protection."

"And, if she declines this offer, sir, as my father's steward of his estates and possessions?"

"Your father has neither estate nor possessions now, my boy; he is a proclaimed rebel. If this kindly offer is refused, and you are both so weak and vain as to resist, the place will be battered down and left in ruins, while the sufferings and slaughter of your people will be at your door. Now, sir, briefly, what message am I to take back to the commanding officer?"

"God save the king!" cried Roy, warmly.

"That is no answer, sir—only the vain cry of an enthusiastic, misled boy. What am I to say to the general in chief?"

"That Lady Royland will hold Royland Castle in the king's name as long as one stone stands upon another, and she has a brave following to fight."

The officer raised his hand in salute, turned his horse and rode back, while Roy stood there with his heart throbbing as he watched the three figures depart, and wondered whether it was really he who had spoken, or all this scene in the deepening evening were part of a feverish dream.

He was brought back to the present by the deep gruff voice of Ben.

"There, sir," he said, with a look of pride at the boy in whose training he had had so large a share, "I knew you could."

At the same moment Roy glanced at the corporal, who smiled and saluted him proudly.

"I only wish, sir," he said, "that the colonel had been here."

Roy turned to recross the bridge, feeling as if, in spite of all, this was part of a dream, when something on high began to flutter over the great gate tower, and glancing up, it was to see there in front, gazing down at them as she leaned forward in one of the embrasures, Lady Royland.

"What is it to be, Roy?" she cried, as he came closer. "Peace or war?"

"War!" he replied, sternly; and the sound seemed to be whispered in many tones through the great archway as the portcullis fell with its heavy clang and the drawbridge began to rise.

Chapter Twenty
War to the Knife

War to the knife without a doubt, for in the gathering gloom of the evening, as Roy went up to the top of the north-west tower, followed by Master Pawson, it was to see that mounted men were in a goodly body making a complete circuit of the castle, roughly marking out a line about half a mile in diameter, and at every hundred yards or so a couple of troopers were halted, and retained their posts.

"Shutting us in, Master Pawson," said Roy, after watching the manoeuvre for some time.

"Ah!" said the secretary, with a sigh; "they will patrol the country all round now, and stop communications with the outside."

"Yes," said Roy, frowning; "and I suppose I must give up all hope of the men from the farm getting in."

"Ah, yes! they are prisoners before this. So your poor father is looked upon as a rebel now."

"Stop, Master Pawson," said Roy, hotly; "these words must not be spoken here."

"I only meant them as the opinion of the other party, who presume to say the estate is confiscated."

"My father acknowledges no other party. Confiscated! Why, this place has belonged to the Roylands from the days of the Plantagenets, Master Pawson. Let these people come and take it if they can."

"Ah, yes! that's brave and true, Roy, brave and true. Then you do mean to fight?"

"Yes, and you too," cried the boy. "You want to save my father's estate."

"Oh, yes, I want to save the estate," said the secretary, eagerly.

"Then do everything you can," cried Roy. "Yes, they will soon have formed a ring round the castle now! Well, let them keep their distance, for I shall give orders for the garrison to fire at any one who attempts to approach."

"And how long do you hope to be able to hold out?"

"As long as it is necessary," said Roy, proudly; "till my father comes with his men, and scatters all these people away."

"To be sure, yes," said the secretary. "How proud he will be of you, Roy, when he knows all."

Roy hurried down to join his lieutenant, whom he found humming a tune in the armoury, busy over some preparations by the light of a lamp.

"You don't seem in very bad spirits, Ben," he said. "Bad spirits! What about, sir? Why, it's like the good old time when your father and I were young. Not so young as you, though! Well, sir, we've been thinking over our plans. They won't do anything yet—only shut us in. They're going to wait for more men and more artillery."

"But we must be well on the watch against surprise, Ben."

"Why, of course, sir! You'll have your watch on the towers. And you've seen how they've got a ring of patrols round us?"

"Yes, I watched them. So we may give up all hope of getting those ten of Raynes's."

"I'm afraid so. It's a bad job, sir, as the corporal was saying just now, for we'd trained them into being our best gunners."

"A terrible loss."

"Well, not so very terrible, sir, because we must train up some more. Oh! we can keep the enemy outside the moat and enjoy ourselves while they're starving without a roof to cover them. But I want to say a serious thing or two, sir."

"I know, Ben; you want to say that my mother's garden must go."

"That's one thing, sir."

"Well, take what ground you want, and we'll put it straight when we've sent the Parliament to the right-about."

"Oh, you'll make a good general, sir; and this trouble's a blessing in disguise to save you from being wasted on books, and becoming a sort of Master Pawson. And that brings me to the other things."

"Well, what are those?"

"Just you tell me plain, as a soldier—which you are now—what you set down as the strongest bits of the castle?"

"Why, the towers, of course!"

"That's right, sir. Very well, then, they must be well manned."

"As well as we can man them."

"That's it, sir; and we must have elbow-room."

"Of course!"

"Then will you speak to my lady, and ask her to give Master Pawson a couple of rooms in the private part somewhere, or one room ought to be enough now, for I want those two chambers of his badly?"

"He won't like that, Ben," said Roy, quickly.

"I s'pose not, sir; and there'll be a lot of things none of us will like, but we've got to put up with them. If you'll see about that at once, I shall be glad."

"Is it very necessary, Ben?"

"You know best about that, sir."

"Yes, it is very necessary, Ben," said Roy; and he hurried off to talk the matter over with his mother, visiting the ramparts on his way.

He found Lady Royland busy writing, and she looked up with a smile.

"I am keeping a diary of all that has taken place since we began the defence. But tell me first—Raynes's men—are we to give them up?"

"I'm afraid so, mother. They have not failed us, but have been taken prisoners."

"This is a sad blow, Roy, but we must make up for it by working together.—But what is it? You have not come to chat about nothings."

"No, mother," said the boy, seriously. "I have come to say that the pleasaunce must go. Ben Martlet says he cannot do without it now."

"I have been expecting this, my boy. It has always been a dear delight to me, but it is a pleasure for peace; and when the happy days come back, I shall want the whole garrison to restore it to me again."

"Then I was right in telling Ben to take what he wanted?"

"Of course, my boy.—Something else?"

"Yes, mother—another bit of self-sacrifice. Martlet and I both feel that we must have the north-west tower.—Ah, Master Pawson, you there?"

"Yes. I knocked twice, and I thought you said 'Come in.'"

"Then you heard what I said just now."

"I heard you mention the western tower. Have you been telling her ladyship of what we saw this evening?"

"No. What did you see?" cried Lady Royland, quickly.

"The enemy has completely surrounded us with sentinels."

"Ah! they would, of course."

"It was not that, Master Pawson—but this; I was about telling my mother that, for the purposes of defence, Martlet and I feel that we must have the north-west tower."

"But you have it; the guns are there."

"The top only," said Roy. "The chambers below are required for the men who work the guns, for ammunition, and other purposes."

Master Pawson looked at him in blank horror.

"My mother will see that you have comfortable rooms or a room somewhere here. I will give up mine to you if you like."

"Oh! I could not take that," said the secretary, quickly. "But surely this is not necessary."

"Yes; it is absolutely necessary. Besides, that tower will certainly be battered by the enemy's guns, and it will not be safe for you."

"I wish you would not persist in looking upon me as such a coward, Roy; it is not fair. I was never meant for a soldier, but surely a man may be a man of peace and yet not a coward."

"No, no; I do not look upon you as a coward," said Roy, hastily. "It is really because that will be a dangerous spot, and the rooms must be strongly occupied."

"But, as I said, you have the guns at the top. Really, I must protest; I am so much attached to those little rooms. Surely you can let me stay. I do not mind the firing. I will not go near the windows."

"You do not grasp the fact that these angle towers are our greatest protection," said Roy, firmly. "I am sorry to give you all the trouble and annoyance, but we must have the chambers below. The one you use for a sleeping-room is absolutely necessary for the powder."

"Indeed, Lady Royland, they could manage without," protested the secretary, warmly. "It would be a dreadful inconvenience to me to give them up. There are the books and my papers. Oh, it is really impossible."

"You forget, Master Pawson, that we all have to make sacrifices now, and that we shall have to make more and greater ones yet, before this unhappy trouble is at an end."

"Yes, yes, I know, Lady Royland, and I am ready to do anything to assist you," cried the secretary, excitedly.

"Then give up your rooms like a man," said Roy, "and without making so much fuss."

Master Pawson darted an angry look at the boy and then turned to his mother.

"You know, Lady Royland, how I have thrown myself heart and soul into the defence since I have found it necessary. You bade me go, but I would not. Duty said stay, and I risked my life in doing so; but as a favour, I beg that you will not let me be ousted from my two poor little rooms to gratify the whim of a very obstinate old soldier, who would turn your pleasaunce into a drill-ground."

"I have given up my garden because it is wanted, Master Pawson," said Lady Royland, coldly.

"To gratify a good soldier, I know, but a man who would have everything turned into a fighting place."

"It is not fair of you, sir," said Roy, speaking very firmly. "This is no whim on the part of Martlet. Now that we are coming to using the guns, the men must have a place of shelter beneath the platform, and one where the powder may lie ready for handing up. We must have your sleeping-room."

"Take it then," cried the secretary. "I give it up; but spare me my little sitting-room."

"We want that too," said Roy. "We may have wounded men."

"Then bring them in there, and I'll help to dress their wounds; but I must keep that."

"Surely you can manage without depriving Master Pawson of that place, Roy," said Lady Royland.

"Thank you, thank you, Lady Royland.—Yes, you hear that, Roy. You can—you must—you shall spare me that poor place. It is so small."

"And suppose we have an accident, and the powder bestowed in your chamber above is blown up?"

"Well, I shall have died doing my duty," said the secretary, with humility.

"Wouldn't it be doing your duty more to try and avoid danger, so as to be useful to us all?" said Roy; and his mother's eyes flashed with pleasure, while the secretary started to hear such utterances from the mere boy he despised.

"Perhaps so," he said, with a faint laugh; "but really, Roy, you will not be so hard upon me as to refuse that favour. Do not make me think that now you are castellan, you are becoming a tyrant."

"There is no fear of my son becoming a tyrant, Master Pawson," said Lady Royland, smiling, and with something suggesting contempt for the speaker in her tones. — "Roy, dear, I think you might manage to let the lower room remain as it is for Master Pawson's use, if the upper floor is given up to the men. He could have the room next to yours for a bedchamber."

"Oh, that would not be necessary," said the secretary, eagerly. "The one room is all I want — it can be my bedchamber too."

"I hardly know what to say, mother," said the boy, gravely. — "Well, then, Master Pawson, keep your study; but we must have the upper room at once, and if you are annoyed by the going to and fro of the men on the staircase, you must not blame me."

"My dear boy," he cried, with effusion, "pray do not think me so unreasonable. I am most grateful to you, Lady Royland, and to you too, Roy. I shall never forget this kindness. I will go and see to the new arrangement at once. Can I have two servants to help to move down the few things I shall want?"

"You can have two of the garrison, Master Pawson," replied Roy, smiling; "they all consider themselves to be soldiers now."

"Thank you, thank you," he cried, in a voice which sounded as if it were choked by emotion, and he hastily left the room.

"I wish he would not be so dreadfully smooth," said Roy, petulantly. "I want to like Master Pawson, but somehow he always makes me feel cross."

"He is rather too fond of thanking one for every little favour; but it is his manner, dear, and he has certainly been doing his best to help us in this time of need."

"Yes," said Roy; "and we should have thought bad enough of him if he had gone and left us in the lurch. There, mother, I must go and see Ben Martlet and tell him what has been arranged. He will not like it, though; but he will have two things out of three."

"You must not give up too much to Martlet, my boy," said Lady Royland, retaining her son's hand as he rose to go. "He is a faithful old servant, and will fight for us to the death; but remember that you are governor of the castle."

"He makes me remember it, mother," cried Roy, merrily. "Don't you be afraid of his being presuming, for he will not do a thing without I give the order. There, good-bye."

"Good-bye? You will be back soon."

"No," replied Roy; "I must be on the battlements all night, visiting posts and helping to keep watch. You forget that the enemy surround us now."

"Alas! no, Roy. I know it only too well. Come back in an hour's time— you will want some refreshment. I will see that it is ready, and I hope by then you will find things so quiet that you can take a few hours' rest."

"We shall see, mother," said Roy, kissing her affectionately. "How brave you have grown!"

She shook her head sadly as she clung to him for a few moments; and, as soon as the door had closed, and his steps died away on the oaken floor of the corridor, she sank in a chair sobbing as if her heart would break.

Chapter Twenty One
A Grand Surprise

Roy had to go the whole round of the ramparts that night before he found Ben, who had always been visiting the parts he reached a few minutes before. But he came upon him at length, just at the door-way of the south-east tower, where it opened upon the southern rampart between that place and the great gate-way.

"Ladyship says I'm to have the garden to turn back to a proper court-yard?" said Ben, after hearing his master's report.

"Yes."

"And Master Pawson is turning out of his chamber, but he is to keep the lower place?"

"Yes; that is the arrangement, Ben; and you can have the upper chamber for use at once."

"Well, that's a good thing for the men who'll be up there, sir; but what does Master Pawson want with that lower room? I meant to have three firelock men there."

"Be content with what you can have, Ben. My mother did not want to be too hard upon Master Pawson."

"No, sir; she wouldn't be. But you've come all round the ramparts?"

"Yes."

"Kep' looking out of course, sir? What did you hear?"

"I? Nothing."

"Then you didn't try."

"Yes, I did; twice on each rampart. There was nothing to hear."

Ben chuckled.

"Ears aren't so sharp for night-work as they will be, sir, before you've done. I heard them on the move every time I stopped."

"What! the enemy?"

"Yes, sir; they're padrolling the place round and round. You listen."

Roy reached over the battlement, and gazed across the black moat, trying to pierce the transparent darkness of the dull soft night. The dew that was refreshing the herbage and flowers of field, common, and copse sent up a deliciously moist scent, and every now and then came the call of a moorhen paddling about in the moat, the soft piping and croaking of the frogs, and the distant *hoo-hoo-hoo-hoo!* of an owl, but he could make out nothing else, and said so.

"No; they're pretty quiet now, sir; don't hear nothing myself.—Yes; there!"

"Yes, I heard that," said Roy; "it was a horse champing his bit; and there again, that must have been the jingle of a spur."

"Right, sir, right. You'll hear plenty of that sort of thing if you keep on listening. There, hear that?"

"Yes, plainly. A horse stumbled and plunged to save itself."

"Enough to make it," said Ben, gruffly; "going to sleep, and him on it jigged the spurs into its flanks to rouse it up. There, you can hear 'em on the move again, going to and fro."

"Yes, quite plainly," whispered Roy; "why, they must have come in much nearer."

"No, sir. Everything's so quiet that the sounds seem close. They won't come in nigher for fear of a shot."

"But they must know we could not see them."

"Not yet, sir; but the moon'll be up in a couple of hours, and they know it'll rise before long, and won't run any risks after what they've seen of my gunners—I mean your—sir. Ah! it's a bad job about those ten poor lads. They would have been able to shoot. Master Raynes is in a fine taking about 'em."

"Can't be helped, Ben; we must do our best without them."

"Ay, sir, we must, even if it's bad."

They remained silent for a few minutes, gazing outward, hearing the jingle of harness, and the soft trampling of hoofs, all of which sounded wonderfully near.

The pause was broken by Ben, who whispered suddenly:

"You're right, Master Roy, after all; they are coming in a bit closer and no mistake. Mind coming round with me?"

"No. What are you going to do?"

"Have a word with the lads all round to be on the lookout. I don't want to make a noise, and get blazing away powder and shot for nothing; but they must be taught their distance, sir."

"With the cannon?"

"No; I think a few firelock shots might do it to-night, sir; and that wouldn't be so wasteful. Do our boys good too. They haven't fired their pieces yet in earnest."

Roy's heart began to beat a little faster, for this was exciting; and silently passing on with his lieutenant, post after post was visited, the men challenging, receiving the word, and then a sharp warning to be on the alert; while, after this, Ben and Roy passed on to listen again and again.

"Yes, sir," whispered the former; "there's no mistake they're a good hundred yards closer in. I almost fancied I could see one of 'em moving against that lighter bit of sky."

"I can, Ben," whispered Roy. "There, just to the left of where the ruins must lie—between it and the tower we just passed. Stay, though; why didn't we go up and see how they're getting on with clearing Master Pawson's chamber? There is a light up there."

"'Cause we've got something more serious on the way, sir."

"Halt! stand, or I fire!" came from the top of the north-west tower, and Roy was about to call out—

"Don't, you idiot; we gave you the word just now," when a voice from beyond the moat uttered a low "Whist!"

"Stand, or I fire!"

"If you do, Dick Davis, I'll punch your head, as sure as you stand there," came from across the moat. "Can't you see we're friends?"

"Give the word."

"Stop! Who's there?" cried Roy.

"That you, sir? Please speak to Dick Davis, or he'll be shooting somebody with that gun of hisn."

"Is that Brian Wiggins?"

"Yes, sir, and the rest on us, sir. But pst! The enemy's close behind."

"Quick! round to the bridge!"

"No, sir; there's a whole lot of 'em come close in. They nearly had us an hour ago, and we've had a fine job to creep through all in a line one arter t'other."

"Hist! cease talking," whispered Roy, "or you'll be heard."

The warning came too late, for an order delivered in a low tone a short distance away was followed by a tramping as if a line of horses was approaching cautiously.

"How many of you can swim? Now, as many as can, come across."

But no one stirred, and the trampling came on.

"Do you hear?" said Roy, in an angry whisper; "are you afraid?"

"Fear'd to leave our comrades as can't swim, sir," said the man who had first spoken.

"What's to be done," exclaimed Roy, excitedly.

But there was no response, for he was standing there upon the rampart alone.

The boy was in an agony of doubt and dread, for the right thing to do in such an emergency would not come to his inexperienced brain. He divined that Ben had gone for assistance, but he felt that before he could be back, the brave fellows who were trying to come to their aid would be surrounded by the enemy and taken prisoners.

To add to his horror and excitement, he plainly heard from the enemy's line the word given to dismount. This was followed by the jingle of accoutrements as the men sprang from their horses, and a loud bang—evidently of a steel headpiece falling to the ground.

To speak to the unarmed men from the farm was to obtain an answer and proclaim their whereabouts to the enemy; so Roy was baffled there; and, at his wit's end, he was about to order them to make their way to the bridge, when the man on the tower above challenged again:

"Stand, or I fire!"

"Draw swords! Forward, quick!" came from out of the darkness.

The sharp rattle and noise told that the party must be large, and like a call just then a horse uttered a tremendous neigh.

Involuntarily, at the first order from beyond the moat, Roy had half drawn his own sword, but thrust it angrily back as he realised his impotence, and reached forward to try and make out what was going on below him; for there was a loud splashing noise in the water as if the men were lowering themselves into the moat, the reeds and rushes crackled and whispered, and there was a panting sound and a low ejaculation or two.

"Now, every one his man," said some one, sharply.

Bang, bang! and a couple of flashes of light from the top of the tower just above Roy's head; and as the splashing went on, there was a loud trampling of feet.

"On with you!" roared the same voice. "They'll be an hour loading, and it's too dark to hit."

At that moment, from some distance along the rampart to the right, came flash after flash, and the reports of ten or a dozen muskets, followed by the rush of feet; and Ben's voice said, in a low stern tone—

"Steady, steady! No hurry. Reload!"

There was the rustling and rattling of bandoleer and ramrod, and the twinkling of sparks of light, as the reloading went on; while from the angry orders being given, some distance back in the darkness, it was evident that the volley had sent the enemy off in a scare, which was made worse by the plunging, snorting, and galloping of horses which had evidently dashed off, escaping from the men who held their reins.

"How many are you above there?" cried Roy.

"Three, sir."

"Only two fired."

"No. My piece wouldn't go."

"Are you reloaded?"

"Yes, sir."

"Be ready."

"They're coming on again, sir. He's rallied 'em," growled Ben; "but we shall be ready for 'em when they come."

Meanwhile, the sound of splashing and swimming came up from the moat, accompanied by a good many spluttering and choking noises, and now heads were dimly made out approaching the bank of the moat below.

"How many are there of you across?" said Roy.

"Eight of us, sir," came up in a panting voice; "we're going back for the other two."

"Who are—how many?"

"Four on us, sir," said one man; "they're hiding in the reeds. Can't swim."

"Can you bring them across?"

"Yes, sir. We did bring three as couldn't take a stroke, and they're down here half drowned."

"That's a loy," said a gruff voice; "I aren't: on'y full o' water."

The men lowered themselves into the moat again, and began to swim back, but just as they were nearly across, there came the thudding sound of horses passing along at a trot, and a rush of men towards the edge of the moat.

"Fire!" shouted Roy; and over the swimmers' heads a ragged volley tore, the flashes cutting the darkness, and once more, in spite of angry curses and yelled-out orders, horse and man were driven to the right-about, all save about a dozen, who came right on to the edge of the moat.

"Surrender!" roared a voice, as there was a quick splashing among the reeds below the bank. Then a shot was fired from a pistol, followed by another; but the men summoned to surrender had done so to their comrades, who whispered to them to trust themselves to their strong arms, two of the swimmers taking a non-swimmer between them, and bringing him across in safety to the rest, crouching upon the narrow strip of bank beneath the walls.

Another volley sent the attacking party back into the darkness, and a brief colloquy took place.

"All safe?" cried Roy.

"Yes, sir, and as wet as wet," came up in answer.

"Fall in, then, and quick march for the sally-port," cried Roy; and the men tramped round by the north-west tower, along beneath the western rampart, turned the southern corner, and were admitted by the little sally-port beside the portcullis, where, bedraggled as they were, they received a tremendous hand-shaking and a roar of cheers.

In half an hour the missing men were in dry clothes, ready to recount their adventures. The enemy had retired to a distance to continue their night patrol of the place; while the men upon the ramparts were reduced to the regular watch, and those off duty were being addressed by Ben, who sarcastically lectured them upon what he called their modesty.

"When the captain gives the order to fire," he said, "you're all to pull trigger together, and every man not to let his comrade fire first for good manners."

But here Roy interposed.

"No more to-night, sergeant," he said, firmly. "We are all fresh to our work. But I thank you all for the brave and manly way in which you have shown what you can do. This has been a grand night's work: your ten comrades safely brought in, and the enemy sent to the right-about. The sergeant has been finding fault, but he is as proud of you all as I am. Come, Martlet, what do you say?"

"Might ha' done better, captain," replied the old fellow, gruffly. "But it warn't so bad. Wait a few days, though, and we'll show you something better than that.—What do you say, lads?"

The answer was a hearty cheer, which was repeated, and was still echoing through the place, when Roy, thrilling still with the excitement of the past hour, made his way towards his mother's room to fully set her mind at rest with his last good news.

Chapter Twenty Two
But All's Well

Lady Royland was surrounded by the trembling women of the household, who, scared by the firing, had sought her to find comfort and relief.

"What! the ten men safely brought in!" she cried, as her son hastened to tell his tidings. "And no one hurt?"

"No one on our side, mother," said Roy, meaningly; "I cannot answer for those across the moat."

"Our ten poor fellows here in safety," cried Lady Royland, once again. "Oh, Roy, my boy, this is good news indeed! But you must be faint and exhausted. Come in the dining-room. I have something ready for you.— There, you have nothing to fear now," she said, addressing the women; "but one of you had better go and tell Master Pawson that we are ready to sup."

The women went out, some of them still trembling and hysterical, and all white and scared of aspect.

As soon as the door was closed, Lady Royland caught her son's hand.

"Eight of us women," she said, with a forced laugh: "eight, and of no use whatever; only ready to huddle together like so many sheep scared by some little dog; when, if we were men, we could be of so much help. There, come along; you look quite white. You are doing too much. For my sake, take care."

Roy nodded and smiled, and followed his mother into the dining-room, where with loving care she had prepared everything for him, and made it attractive and tempting, so that it should be a relief to the harsh realities of the warlike preparations with which the boy was now mixed up.

"You must eat a good supper, Roy, and then go and have a long night's rest."

"Impossible, mother," he said, faintly; "must go and visit the men's posts from time to time."

"No," said Lady Royland, firmly, as she unbuckled her son's sword-belt, and laid it and the heavy weapon upon a couch.

There was a tap at the door directly after, and one of the maids came back.

"If you please, my lady, I've been knocking ever so long at Master Pawson's door, and he doesn't answer. We think he has gone to bed."

"Surely not. He must be in the upper chamber arranging about the things being removed."

"No, my lady; that was all done a long time ago. It was finished before the fighting began, for he wouldn't have nothing but his bed and washstand brought down. The men had to take most of the other things right down in the black cellar place underneath, so as to clear the chamber."

"But did you ask the men on guard if they had seen him?"

"Yes, my lady; they say he shut himself up in his room."

"That will do. Never mind," said Lady Royland, dismissing the maid.— "Now, Roy, I am going to keep you company, and—oh, my boy! what is it? Ah! You are hurt!"

She flew to his side, and with trembling hands began to tear open his doublet, but he checked her.

"No, no, mother, I am not—indeed!"

"Then what is it? You are white and trembling, and your forehead is all wet."

"Yes, it has come over like this," he faltered, "all since the fight and getting the men in through the sally-port."

"But you must have been hurt without knowing it."

"No, no," he moaned, as he sank back in the chair, and covered his face with his hands.

"Roy, my boy, speak out. Tell me. What is the matter?"

"I didn't mean to speak a word, mother," he groaned; "but I can't keep it back."

"Yes; speak, speak," she said, tenderly, as she sank upon her knees by his side, and drew his head to her breast.

"Ah!" he sighed, restfully, as he flung his arms about her neck. "I can speak now. I should have fought it all back; but when I came in here, and saw all those frightened women, and you spoke as you did about being so helpless, it was too much for me."

"Oh, nonsense!" she cried, soothingly. "Why should their—our—foolish weakness affect you, my own brave boy?"

"No, no, mother," he cried; "don't—don't speak like that. You hurt me more."

"Hurt you?" she said, in surprise.

"Yes, yes," he cried, excitedly. "You don't know; but you must know—you shall know. I'm not brave. I'm a miserable coward."

"Roy! Shame upon you!" cried Lady Royland, reproachfully.

"Yes, shame upon me," said the lad, bitterly; "but I can't help it. I have tried so hard; but I feel such a poor weak boy—a mere impostor, trying to lord it over all these men."

"Indeed!" said Lady Royland, gravely. "Yes? Go on."

"I know they must see through me, from Ben down to the youngest farm hand. They're very good and kind and obedient because I'm your son; but they, big strong fellows as they are, must laugh at me in their sleeves."

"Ah! you feel that?" said Lady Royland.

"Yes, I feel what a poor, girlish, weak thing I am, and that all this is too much for me. Mother, if it were not for you and for very shame, I believe I should run away."

"Go on, Roy," sand Lady Royland; and her sweet, deep voice seemed to draw the most hidden thoughts of his breast to his lips.

"Yes, I must go on," he cried, excitedly. "I hid it all when I went to face that officer, who saw through me in spite of my bragging words, and laughed; and in the wild excitement of listening to-night to the troopers closing us in and trying to capture those poor fellows, I did not feel anything like fear; but now it is all over and they are safe, I am—I am—oh, mother! it is madness—it is absurd for me, such a mere boy, to go on pretending to command here, with all this awful responsibility of the fighting that must come soon. I know that I can't bear it—that I must break down—that I have broken down. I can't go on with it; I'm far too young. Only a boy, you see, and I feel now more like a girl, for I believe I could lie down and cry at the thought of the wounds and death and horrors to come. Oh, mother, mother! I'm only a poor pitiful coward after all."

"God send our poor distressed country a hundred thousand of such poor pitiful cowards to uphold the right," said Lady Royland, softly, as she drew her son more tightly to her swelling breast. "Hush, hush, my boy! it is your mother speaks. There, rest here as you used to rest when you were the tiny little fellow whose newly opened eyes began to know me, whose pink hands felt upward to touch my face. You a coward! Why, my darling, can you not understand?"

"Yes, I understand," he groaned, as he clung to her, "that it is my own dear mother trying to speak comfort to me in my degradation and shame. Mother, mother! I would not have believed I was such a pitiful cur as this."

"No," she said, softly; "I am speaking truth. You do not understand that after the work and care of all this terrible time of preparation, ending in the great demands made upon you to-day, the strain has been greater than your young nature can bear. Bend the finest sword too far, Roy, and it will break. You are overdone—worn-out. It is not as you think."

"Ah! it is you who do not know, mother," he said, bitterly. "I am not fit to lead."

"Indeed! you think so?" she said, pressing her lips to his wet, cold brow. "You say this because you look forward with horror to the bloodshed to come."

"Yes; it is dreadful. I was so helpless to-night, and I shall be losing men through my ignorance."

"Helpless to-night? But you beat the enemy off."

"No, no—Ben Martlet's doing from beginning to end."

"Perhaps. The work of an old trained man of war, who has ridden to the fight a score of times with your father, and now your brave father's son's right-hand—a man who worships you, and who told me only to-day, with the tears in his eyes, how proud he was of that gallant boy—of you."

"Ben said that—of me?"

"Yes, my boy; and do you think with all his experience he cannot read you through and through?"

"No, mother, he can't—he can't," said the lad, despondently; "no one can know me as I do."

"Poor child!" she said, fondly, as she caressed him; "what a piece of vanity is this! A boy of seventeen thinking he knows himself by heart. Out upon you, Roy, for a conceited coxcomb! Why, we all know you better than you know yourself; and surely I ought to be the best judge of what you are."

"No," said Roy, angrily; "you only spoil me."

"Indeed! then I shall go on, and still spoil you in this same way, and keep you the coward that you are."

"Mother!" he cried, reproachfully; "and with all this terrible responsibility rising like a dense black cloud before my eyes."

"Yes, Roy, because it is night now, and black night too, in your weary brain. Ah! my boy, and to how many in this world is it the same black night. But the hours glide on, the day dawns, and the glorious sun rises again to pierce the thick cloud of darkness, and brighten the gloomy places of the earth. Just as hope and youth and your natural vigour will chase away your black cloud, after the brain has been fallow for a few hours, and you have had your rest."

"No, no, no," he groaned; "you cannot tell."

"I can tell you, Roy," she said, softly; "and I can tell you, too, that your father is just such another coward as his son."

"My father!" cried Roy, springing to his feet, flushed and excited. "My father is the bravest, truest man who ever served the king."

"Amen to that, my boy!" said Lady Royland, proudly; "but do you think, Roy, that our bravest soldiers, our greatest warriors, have been men made of iron—cruel, heartless beings, without a thought of the terrible responsibilities of their positions, without a care for the sufferings of the men they lead? I believe it never has been so, and never will. Come, my darling," she continued, clinging to his hands, and drawing herself to her feet—"come here for a little while. There," she said, softly, taking the sword from the couch; "your blade is resting for a while; why should not you? Yes: I wish it; lie right down—for a little while—before we sup. Ah, that is better!"

Utterly exhausted now, Roy yielded to her loving hands, and sank back upon the soft couch with a weary sigh; while, as he stretched himself out, she knelt by his side, and tenderly wiped his brow before passing her hands over his face, laying his long hair back over the pillow, and at every touch seeming to bring calm to the weary throbbing brain.

After a few minutes he began to mutter incoherently, and Lady Royland leaned back to reach a feather-fan from a side-table, and then softly wafted the air to and fro till the words began to grow more broken, and at last ceased, as the boy uttered a low, weary sigh, his breath grew more regular, and he sank into the deep heavy sleep of exhausted nature.

Then the fan dropped from Lady Royland's hand, and she rose to cross the room softly, and with a line draw up the casement of the narrow slit of a window which looked down upon the moat, for the night wind came fresher there than from the main windows looking upon the garden court.

Softly returning, she bent down, and with the lightest of fingers untied the collar of her son's doublet and linen shirt, before bending lower, with her long curls drooping round his face, till she could kiss his brow, no longer dank and chilly, but softly, naturally warm.

This before sinking upon her knees to watch by his side for the remainder of the night; and as she knelt her lips parted to murmur—

"God save the king—my husband—and our own brave boy!"

A moment later, as if it were an answer to her prayer, a voice, softened by the distance, was heard from the ramparts somewhere above uttering the familiar reply to a challenge—

"All's well!"

Chapter Twenty Three
Roy gets over his Fit

The dawn came, and Lady Royland still knelt by the couch where her son slept heavily. She did not stir till the sun rose, and then she rose softly to go to the narrow slit in the massive wall, reach as far as she could into the deep splay, and gaze out.

She sighed, for far-away in the distance she could see mounted men with the sun flashing from their armour.

She turned back, for she had learned all she wished to know—the enemy was still there; and, wondering what that day might bring forth, she went and sat down now by her son's head to watch him as he slept.

The time crept on with the sounds of the awakening household mingled with the clangour of the morning calls and the tramp of armed men floating in through the window; but the watcher did not stir till the door was opened, and a couple of the maids appeared, to start back in affright, after a wondering glance at the untouched meal upon the table, for Lady Royland rose quickly with a gesture to them to be silent.

They crept away, and she followed to the door.

"Prepare the breakfast in the library," she said, and then returned to her seat.

The clock chimed and struck again and again, but Roy did not wake; and at last one of the maids came and tapped very softly.

"Breakfast is quite ready, my lady," she whispered.

"I am not coming till my son wakes," replied Lady Royland. "Ask Master Pawson not to wait."

"He's not down yet, my lady," said the woman.

"Very well: ask him not to wait when he does come. The gentlemen are weary after the troubles of a very anxious night."

The woman went away, and Lady Royland returned to her seat, to bend over her son again as he lay there breathing evenly, still plunged in his deep sleep; and then at its stated intervals, the clock in the gate-way chimed, and chimed, and struck, and struck again, to mark off the second hour before there was another tap at the door, and the maid announced in a whisper that Sergeant Martlet was asking for Captain Roy.

"Send him here," said her ladyship, "and bid him come in gently."

"Yes, my lady," said the woman; "and, if you please, my lady, Master Pawson has just come down, and is having his breakfast."

"Very good," said Lady Royland, coldly, and the maid retired.

Five minutes later, the old soldier, fully armed, came softly to the door, was admitted, and stood upon the thick carpet, saluting his lady. She pointed to the couch, and a grim smile of satisfaction crossed the soldier's deeply-lined face.

"He was quite worn-out and exhausted," said Lady Royland, in a whisper, as she crossed to where Ben stood,—"too faint and troubled with the cares and anxieties of this weary business even to eat."

"But he has slept, my lady?" whispered Ben.

"Ever since."

"Let him sleep, then, till he wakes, and he'll be right enough again."

"I hope so; but he was very low and despondent last night. He feels the responsibility of his position so much."

"Course he does, my lady. That's his breed. His father always did. Used to make as much fuss over one of us as went down or got a wound as if we'd been his own children. But you let him sleep, my lady; he'll be like a new man when he gets up. He's a wonder, my lady; that he is."

"He was afraid that the men were disposed to smile at him because he is so young."

"I should just like to ketch one on 'em a-doing it," growled Ben. "But it aren't true, my lady," he continued, excitedly. "They smiles when he comes up, o' course, but it's because he seems to do 'em good, and they can't help it, they're so pleased to see him. Why, if you'll believe me, my lady, from Sir Granby's corporal o' dragoons down to Isaiah Wiggens, as got nigh upon drowned being pulled across the moat last night, my lady—"

"Oh, how horrible!"

"Horrid? Not it, my lady—begging your pardon. Sarve him right! Great big hulking lubberly chap like that, and not able to swim!"

"But is he ill this morning?"

"Not he, my lady. He was so roasted in the guard-room after, that he got up at daylight and went into the moat again 's morning to begin to larn."

"But tell me, what news?"

"They're all padrolling us, my lady, same as they were last night. They got the oats from Farmer Raynes, and they think they're going to starve us by stopping everything else from coming in; but we can afford to laugh at 'em for about three months; and at the end of that time, if Sir Granby don't come and raise the siege, I've got an idee for trapping enough meat for the men."

"Indeed!"

"Yes, my lady," said Ben, with a grin. "Only to lower the drawbridge and hyste the portcullis, to let a whole court-yard-full ride in. Then drop the grating behind 'em, and they're trapped. After that we can make 'em lay down their arms, turn 'em out, and keep their horses. They'll do to feed the men. I've eaten horse, and Sir Granby too, at a pinch, and it aren't so bad; but o' course I'd rather have beef."

"Then there is nothing to fear for the present?"

"Aren't nothing to fear at all, past, present, or futur', my lady, so don't you be uncomfortable. And as for Master Roy, he needn't go thinking no nonsense o' that sort about the men, for they just worship him, all of 'em, and that's the honest truth."

"I believe it, Martlet. Have you breakfasted this morning?"

"Had a chunk o' bread and a mug o' milk, my lady."

"That is not enough for a busy man like you are. Sit down to that table, and eat."

"What, here, my lady! Oh, no, I couldn't presume!"

"Hush! Do not speak so loud," said Lady Royland, smiling. "These are not times for standing upon ceremony, Martlet. We women cannot fight; but we can help in other ways, above all in attending to our brave defenders, and seeing that they have all that is necessary. And if the worst comes to the worst, and—"

"Yes; I know what your ladyship means," said the old soldier, for Lady Royland had paused, "and to be plain, the men have been talking a bit about that same, and what they were to do if they were hurt and no doctor here. I said—"

It was the sergeant's turn to be silent now, and he stopped as if the words would not come.

"And what did you say?"

"Well, my lady, I took the liberty of saying that your ladyship was training up the women, and that when one of us was lucky enough to get wounded in the service of his king and country, he'd be carried into one of the big rooms o' the east side, as would be turned into a hospital, and there tied up and put to bed, and souped and jellied and pastied, and made so much of, that he'd be sorry for the poor comrades who were only working the guns and doing the fighting."

"You were quite right, Martlet," said Lady Royland. "Tell the men that the wounded shall each be treated as if he were my own son."

"Begging your ladyship's pardon, that's just what I did tell 'em, only I put a few flourishes to it, and I won't say it again, because it may make 'em rash and wanting to get wounded for the sake of being carried into the snug quarters, and—"

"Sit down, Martlet, and eat," said Lady Royland, pushing a chair towards the table.

"With your ladyship's permission, I'd rather cut off a bit o' something, and go and sit on one of the guns to eat it, and look out too. I should enjoy it better."

"Do as you wish," said Lady Royland. "There, take that fowl and loaf."

"Thank you kindly, my lady, and—Morning, Master Roy, sir. Had a good sleep?"

For at that moment Roy sprang from the couch and looked excitedly round.   •

"What is it?" he cried. "What's the matter? Morning! Surely I have not—"

"Yes, Roy, soundly and well, all night. Come, you must be ready for breakfast."

"Yes, yes, mother," cried the boy, impatiently.—"But tell me, Ben—Oh, you ought not to have let me sleep all night. Here, what has happened?"

"Nothing at all, sir, or I should have sent for you," said the old soldier, who had taken out a handkerchief, given it a shake, and spread it upon the carpet, placed in it the roast chicken and loaf, sprinkled all liberally with salt, and now proceeded to tie the ends of the handkerchief across, to make a bundle. "They're a-padrolling round and round, just as they have been all night, and keeping well out of gunshot. Wouldn't like me to send a ball hopping along the ground to try the range, would you, sir?"

"No, not unless they attack," said Roy, quickly.

"Thought you wouldn't, sir, when I spoke.—Thank ye for this snack, my lady. I'll go back now to the ramparts.—P'raps you'll jyne me there, Master Roy, when you've had your breakfast. All's well, sir; and them ten farmers are ready to stand on their heads with joy at getting through the enemy's ranks."

"Ah! how was it?"

"Only kept back by the sentries watching 'em; so they all went home as if they'd done work, and agreed to crawl to our place after dark, and creep to the gates."

"But no one was hurt?"

"No, sir; nothing worse happened to 'em than a wetting in the moat, and that don't count, because they were well wet before with crawling through the grass and damp ditches. See you in 'bout an hour's time then, sir?"

Roy nodded shortly, and the man left the room with his bundle; while Roy, uneasy still in mind, turned to his mother, who embraced him tenderly.

"You will not be long, Roy, my dear?" she said. "I want my breakfast, too."

"But surely, mother, you have not been sitting up all night while I slept?"

"Indeed, yes," she said, merrily. "And many a time before last night, when you were a tiny thing and could not sleep. Last night you could, peacefully and well, to awake this morning strong mentally and bodily, to do your duty like my brave son."

Roy winced; but there was something in his mother's look which told him that his words of the past night were as if uttered only to himself, and that the subject of their conversation must be buried in the past.

"You will not be long?" said Lady Royland, as she went to the door.

"No, mother; not above ten minutes. Quite enough for a soldier's toilet," he said, cheerily. And she nodded and went off; while he hurried to his own room, and after plunging his face in the fresh cold water felt such a healthy glow coming through his veins, that he was ready to wonder at the previous night's depression.

"What a glorious morning!" he muttered. "Couldn't have been well last night.—Hope my mother didn't think me stupid.—What a shame to let her sit up there all night!—Why, how hungry I do feel!—And only to think of our getting those fellows in quite safe after all.—Ha, ha, ha! how mad the enemy must have felt."

Roy was standing before a mirror combing his wet locks as he burst out into a hearty laugh, full of enjoyment; but he checked it directly, and stood staring at himself in wonder as the thoughts of the past night intruded, and he remained for a few moments puzzled to account for the change that a long rest had wrought in him.

The next minute he was hurrying with his sword and belt under his arm to the breakfast-room, where he found his mother waiting, and Master Pawson, who looked very pale, in conversation with her.

"Good-morning, Roy," he said. "I congratulate you upon the accession to the strength of the garrison. The men are all in the highest spirits, and full of praise of the gallant way in which you drove the enemy back."

"Then I shall have to undeceive them, Master Pawson," replied Roy, as he joined his mother at the table. "It was in the dark, and they could not see. All Ben Martlet's doing from beginning to end."

"I'm afraid you are too modest," said the secretary, smiling, as Roy began his breakfast with a splendid appetite. "And tell me," he continued, anxiously—"I ought not to ask, perhaps, but I take such interest in the proceedings—you will not listen to any proposals for surrender, even on good terms, which may come from the enemy?"

"What capital ham, mother," said Roy. Then turning to the secretary: "I wouldn't have listened to any proposals for surrender without those ten men, Master Pawson. When all the guns are disabled and the powder done, and nearly everybody wounded, I won't surrender; for you'll put on a helmet and back-piece then, and come and help the maids throw down stones upon their heads, and—yes, we shall have to use the machicolations then; but it shall be hot water for the enemy, not hot lead. The women can manage the boiling water better than the metal. Surrender! Bah! I say, sit down and have some more breakfast. I'm too busy to talk."

"Ah! what a spirit you have," cried the secretary, with a look of admiration in the lad's face. "But you are right. No surrender upon any terms; and if you talk much more like this, Roy, you will inspire me. I, too, shall want to fight, or at least help to load the guns."

"I hope you won't," thought Roy; "for I'd a great deal rather you would stop away."

Ten minutes later he was buckling on his sword, without a trace of the last night's emotion visible on his countenance.

"I'll go down to the great gate," said the secretary. "You will join me there?"

"Yes, directly. But I say, Master Pawson, I hope you managed to make shift at your new bedroom."

"Don't mention it. I shall be all right.—For the present, Lady Royland!" And the secretary left the room.

"No surrender, Roy, my boy."

"No, mother; and—and—last night, I—"

"Was tired out, and no wonder. No—hush! Not another word. Some day when all is at peace once more, I will reopen the subject in your father's presence. Till then, it is our mutual confidence. There, go and show yourself to the men, and see how they will greet you on this bonnie, sunny day."

The boy hurried out with burning cheeks, and they seemed to scorch as he found his mother's flower-beds trampled down, and the whole strength of the garrison on parade; for the moment he appeared, discipline seemed to be at an end, swords and muskets, adorned with steel caps, were waving in the air, while the flag flew out bravely from the great tower overhead, as if fluttered by the wind of the great hearty cheer which arose as he marched to the front, saluting as he went.

"Ah!" he sighed to himself, as his blood seemed to effervesce, and a thrill ran through his nerves, "who could be a coward at a time like this?"

Chapter Twenty Four
Ben Martlet is very full of Doubts

That day matters remained unchanged, save that only about a fourth of the enemy were visible, there being mounted men stationed at intervals upon the higher portions of the country round the castle, where they could command a view of all the approaches; but towards evening these men were relieved, and strong bodies appeared, but not for purposes of attack, merely to draw in and take up stations at closer distances before recommencing what Ben called "padrolling." Meanwhile, drilling went on busily, and the arrangements were advanced for the proper service of the guns.

A quiet, uninterrupted night succeeded, Roy having arranged with Ben to divide the post-visiting with him and the corporal, who was now looked upon as the third officer in command.

Roy saw but little of Master Pawson that evening. The secretary had been very busy about the place all the day, and, making the excuse of weariness after vainly trying to keep his eyes open, he retired early.

Two more days passed in the same way, valuable days to the garrison, which went on with gun and sword practice from morn till night, and rapidly approached a condition in which they would be able to give a good account of themselves before the enemy.

On the afternoon of the fourth day, it was evident that a change was taking place, for the head of a column of infantry became visible, probably the men for whom the officer in command had been waiting.

Roy hurried to the top of the gate tower with Ben, and the secretary followed, and was the first to point out that behind the regiment of infantry, horses were visible—led horses; and no one was surprised, when the infantry opened out a little, to see that four heavy guns were being laboriously dragged along the rough country lane, a road-way ill fitted to bear the pressure of the wheels with their burden.

"They mean business now," said Roy, who felt as if something was compressing his heart.

"Oy, sir," said Ben, coolly; "they'll knock up an earthwork before morning, and set the guns in a position for battering the gate-way."

"But you will not surrender, Roy?" said the secretary, excitedly.

"Not I," said Roy. "I told you so before."

"Not him, sir," said old Ben. "Let 'em batter. Them guns won't be heavy enough to hurt the tower and walls more than to send chips of stone flying."

"What about the drawbridge, Ben?"

"Oh, they can't hurt that, sir, because you'll give orders to lower that down and hoist the portculley."

"Rather tempting for them to make a rush, Ben."

"Tchah, sir! We shall be keeping a good watch, and up and down bridge and portcullis would be, long before they could get up to 'em. I s'pose, sir, you'll make sure that old Jenks doesn't go across to his gate-house."

"Of course."

"And I s'pose, sir, you'll have the two big guns hoisted up on to the great tower now: we could easily dismount 'em and do that. They'll be handier up there now, and very awkward for them as works the guns in their earthwork."

"Yes, I shall order that to be done at once," said Roy, with a comical look at his Mentor—one which Ben refused to see.

"And then, sir," he continued, "there's that there earthwork as'll stop half the shot they send in through the gate-way, and send a lot of 'em flying right up over the towers."

"What earthwork?"

"Well, sir, that one as you're going to start as soon as it's getting dark. Ground's pretty soft for working, and we've got plenty of timber. I s'pose you'll reg'larly fill up Jenks's gate-way, and leave quite a deep ditch behind it on our side."

"Why not on their side, Ben?" said Roy, sharply.

"Why, of course, sir; I seemed to fancy this side; but t'other's better, and all the earth we throw out of the ditch goes on the front and top in a slope, eh?"

"Yes, of course; and turns the balls upward."

"Not many on 'em will go up, sir. Ground'll be too soft. They'll just plump in there and stop; and so much the better for Royland Towers."

As they watched attentively, they found that the horses were halted, and the guns drawn right in front of the castle gate, but at the distance of quite half a mile. There the men seemed to be bivouacking; and the smoke of several fires rose slowly in the air.

No more time was lost: the gunners were summoned, ropes got ready, some heavy beams were hoisted up to the platform of the gate tower, and, under the guidance of Ben and the corporal, a rough kind of crane was fitted up; and after the guns had been dismounted, the carriages were hoisted and placed in position behind the embrasures.

The heavier task was to come; but Ben and the three troopers seemed to master every difficulty, carefully securing the guns with ingenious knots of the ropes; and at last the word was given to hoist.

The hemp stretched and strained, and as the first gun rose a little from the ground, it seemed to Roy as if the strands must give way, and he ordered every one to stand well aside. Ben smiled.

"No fear of that, sir," he whispered. "Those are the toughest of hemp, those ropes, and as the length gets shorter, the strain grows less. Steady, my lads! a little at a time."

The hauling went on till the first gun was level with the top of the battlements, when there was a clever bit of management with a big wooden bar or two handled by the troopers on the roof, and the first gun was easily dropped right upon its carriage.

"One," said Roy, with a sigh of relief, for he was in constant dread of an accident.

"Ay, sir; and it will be two directly; and I wish it was three for the enemy's sake."

The second gun was hoisted, and mounted rapidly, thanks to the trained skill of the four regular soldiers; while the men from the mill who helped looked on with profound admiration, though they were pretty clever at moving stones.

Discipline was relaxed over this manual labour, with the consequence that Sam Donny's tongue began to run rather freely, a certain intimacy having existed in the past between Roy and the miller's man connected with the demand and supply of meal-worms for catching and feeding nightingales, which came about as far west as the castle and no farther.

"Beat us chaps to 'a done that, Master Roy," he said.

"Captain Roy," growled Ben.

"Ay. Forgetted," said the man. "T'other seems so nat'ral. Beat us chaps, Captain Roy. We'm as strong as them, but they've got a way a handling they brass guns as seems to come nat'ral to 'em like. But if they'll come to the mill, we'll show 'em something along o' flour-sacks, and the grinding-stones as'll make 'em stare. Every man to his trade."

"Well, you're a soldier now, Sam Donny, and you must learn to handle guns as well as you handle sacks of flour."

"We will, master—I mean cap'n. I should just like me and my mates to have the letting o' them guns down again. May we, sir?"

"No. Absurd."

"But we'd get 'em up again, sir."

"Wait till the enemy have gone," said Roy, "and then we'll see."

A portion of the afternoon was devoted to taking up the necessary ammunition and re-arranging the top platform they had to prepare for the guns; and just at dusk, after the sentinels had been doubled, a strong party stood in the gate-way, armed with shovel and pick, waiting for the bridge to be lowered. Another party had a number of beams; and, lastly, already drawn up, stood a guard prepared to watch over the safety of the workers, and hand them weapons for their defence, if, perchance, they were seen by the enemy, and an attempt made to rush in.

But no sign was given to warn the parliamentarians, and Roy and the secretary stood on the platform of the great gate-way, watching the enemy, till, in the dim light, a body of men marched to the front, halted a quarter of a mile from the gate; a large square was rapidly marked out with pegs, and then an order seemed to be given, for the party began at once to dig and throw up a breastwork, evidently for the shelter of their guns.

Master Pawson watched everything eagerly, and kept on pointing out what was going on, while Roy leaned upon one of the guns, saying, "I've been wondering whether these guns will carry as far as that work they are making—I mean so as to hit hard."

"They think they will not," said the secretary, "and have placed their battery just out of reach."

"How do you know?" said Roy, sharply.

"I—oh, of course, I don't know," said Master Pawson; "it is only what I judge from seeing them make their battery there."

"Oh, I see," said Roy, quietly. And he thought no more of the remark just then. He waited till the figures of the men digging grew more and more indistinct, and then quite invisible from where they stood; and he was just about to descend, when the sergeant joined them, to say, respectfully—

"We're all ready, sir, and I've got some more poles and planks out of the wood-house."

"Then we'll start at once," said Roy; "but I'll have these guns manned at once to cover our working-party."

Ben coughed.

"You don't think that's right?" said Roy, quickly.

"Well, sir, I wouldn't have presumed to interfere with my commanding officer's orders 'fore any one else. But—"

"Now don't talk nonsense, Ben," said Roy, warmly. "There's no one here but Master Pawson, who is as anxious about preserving the place as we are."

"Indeed, I am," said the secretary, earnestly.

"So don't let's have any of that silly ceremony. I wish you wouldn't pretend to believe I was so conceited."

"I don't, captain," said Ben, abruptly; "only want you to see when you're wrong."

"Then speak out at once. Now then; you don't think it worth while to man these guns now?"

"No, sir. If they hear us at work, and attack, we've got to retreat over the bridge fast as we can, and get it hoisted. Say you've got these guns manned and loaded, a shot or two might check the attacking party; but how in the dark are we to know when it is best to fire? How are we to take aim? And what's to prevent our hitting friends instead of enemies."

"Fire high, over their heads."

"That's wasting two good charges for the sake of making a noise. I don't think I'd trouble about them to-night, sir."

"No; you're right.—Eh, Master Pawson?" said Roy.

"I don't much understand these things," said the secretary; "but it sounds the more sensible idea. You're not offended by my speaking out?"

"*No*; but I soon shall be if you all treat me as if I thought of nothing but dressing up as a soldier, and wanting to have my own way over matters where I'm wrong. Come along, down."

Roy led the way down through the corner turret, Master Pawson following and Ben coming last; while, as they wound round the narrow spiral, the secretary turned his head to whisper—

"He'll make a splendid officer, Martlet."

The only reply he obtained was a very hog-like grunt; then Ben spoke to himself:

"I wish to goodness you were along o' the enemy, or anywhere but here; you're supposed to be a friend, but somehow I can't never feel as if you are one. My cantank'rousness, I s'pose. Not being a scholard like you, maybe. Anyhow, though, I'm more use just now than you are; not but what that's easy, for you aren't none at all."

By this time they were down in the gate-way once more, where the portcullis was raised as silently as possible in the darkness, the bridge lowered, and the heavily laden working-party, followed by their guard marched slowly and silently out; a second strong guard was posted at the far end of the bridge to cover the retreat if one should have to be made— these last being under the command of the corporal; and Master Pawson volunteered in a whisper to stay with the men. Roy acquiesced, feeling rather glad to be without his company.

Next a halt was called, and all listened as they gazed out in the darkness in the direction of the enemy. Then feeling how commanding a position the latter had in the possession of their horsemen to act as scouts, and who might approach very near unseen, and discover the plans of the night, Roy gave orders for the guard at the end of the bridge to advance two men, to station them as sentries at equal distances, to keep in touch with the working-party.

"Fiddler's right," growled Ben, to himself. "He will make a splendid officer one of these days."

The next minute the work was silently begun, the guard being thrown out in a half-moon formation in front of the outer gate-way which covered the bridge.

Ben's plans were very simple. He had the heaviest beams they had brought stretched across the gate-way, as high as they could reach overhead, and propped against the masonry on either side with shorter beams; then poles, planks, and fagots were stretched in a slope from the ground to the crossing timbers, so as to make a scarp; and, as soon as this was done, shovel and pick were set to work to dig a deep wide ditch, the earth from which was thrown up over the wood; while men on either side filled baskets and carried their loads to pile upon the slope as well.

It was roughly done work, but every shovelful added to the strength of the bank, which rapidly grew in thickness as the hours glided on, the workers being relieved from time to time to do duty as guards, while the guard took their turn at shovelling and filling.

There was no halting, the men having refreshments served out to them by Roy's forethought as they were relieved; and so the work went on till towards dawn, when a couple of men were strengthening the bank from behind with short pieces of wood wedged up against the crossbeams, as the weight of the earth began to make them bend.

"You'll have to set a party to work by daylight, filling up on this side, Master Roy," said Ben, quietly. "If we heap up earth and turf here, it will be the best support, and a regular trap for all their balls."

"I begin to fear that as soon as they begin to fire they will batter it all to pieces, Ben."

"Dessay they'll damage it a bit, sir; but if they do, we must mend it; and every night we work, we can get it stronger and more earthy. Nothing like soil to swallow balls. Of course it's no use as a defence, because the enemy could come round either end; but it'll do what's wanted, sir—stop the shot from hitting the bridge-chains and smashing through the grating. Hello! what's that?"

That was a challenge, followed by a shot, and the rush of feet as the sentries thrown out ran back. This was followed by the trampling of hoofs, and the shouting of orders, as a small body of horse made a dash at the working-party, sweeping by the gate, but only to be received by a scattered volley as they were dimly seen riding out of the black darkness and disappearing again. But not without coming to the closest of close quarters, for there was the clashing noise of swords striking against steel, and, in the brief time occupied by their passing, blows were returned amidst angry shouting, and several dull thuds told that the blows had taken effect on horse or man.

It was merely the work of moments, the charge having been delivered from the left by a party of mounted men who had evidently been reconnoitring along by the edge of the moat, and came up at a slow walk unheard by the sentries on the walls. Then, finding the working-party before them, they had charged and galloped clear.

Roy fully expected another attack, for which he was now well prepared, the workers having seized their weapons; but all was still, and he was arguing with himself as to whether it would not be as well to work on till daybreak, when a voice from out of the darkness said, faintly—

"Will some 'un come and lend me a hand?"

"Sam Donny!" cried Roy, and, in company with Ben, he ran forward for quite forty yards before they came upon the man lying prone upon the earth.

"Why, Sam!" cried Roy; "are you hurt?"

"Well, it's only a scratch, sir; but it do hurt, and it's a-bleeding like hooroar. One on 'em chopped at me with his sword. I'd only got a pick, you see; but I hit at him with that, and somehow it got stuck, and I was dragged ever so far before I had to let go. He's got the pick in his big saddle, I think. But I'll pay for it, sir, or get you a new one."

"Never mind the pick, Sam. Where are you hurt?"

"Oh, down here, on my right leg, sir. He made a big cut at me; but I'll know my gen'leman again. I'll have a sword next time and pay him back; and so I tell him." Ben was down upon his knees, busy with a scarf, binding the wound firmly, a faint suggestion of the coming day making his task easier; and, summoning help, a rough litter was formed of a plank, and the wounded man rapidly carried in over the bridge.

That brought the defensive operations to an end, for Roy withdrew his men into the castle, and the daylight showed their rough work, which pretty well secured the gate-way; but it also displayed the work of the enemy, who had constructed a well-shaped earthwork, out of whose embrasures peered a couple of big guns.

The rapidly increasing light, too, showed something more, for about a couple of hundred yards from the outworks, a horse, saddled and bridled, lay upon its side, quite dead; for the terrible stroke the miller's man had delivered with his pickaxe had struck into the horse's spine.

Chapter Twenty Five
Lady Royland turns Nurse

Roy was face to face with the first of the stern realities of war, as he hurried into the long chamber beneath the eastern rampart, which Lady Royland had set apart for the use of any of the men who might, she said, "turn ill."

Poor Sam Donny had fainted away before he reached the hospital-room, and upon Roy entering, eager to render assistance, it was to find himself forestalled by Lady Royland, who, with the old housekeeper, attended to the wounded man.

Lady Royland hurried to her son, as he appeared at the door.

"No," she said, firmly, "not now: leave this to us. It is our duty."

"But, mother, do you understand?" protested Roy.

"Better, perhaps, than any one here," she replied. "Go to your duties; but come by-and-by to see how the poor fellow is. It will cheer him."

Roy could not refuse to obey the order, and hurried back to meet Ben on the way to the sufferer's side.

"Not go in?" said the sergeant. "Her ladyship says so? Oh, very well— then of course it is all right."

"But I feel so anxious," said Roy; "my mother is not a chirurgeon."

"More aren't we, Master Roy; but she's what's just as good—a splendid nurse. So's old Grey's wife; so Sam Donny's in clover. I was being a bit anxious about him, for fear Master Pawson was doing the doctoring, and I'd rather trust myself."

"But the wound—the terrible wound?" cried Roy.

"Tchah! Nothing terrible about that, captain. Just a clean sword-cut. You've cut your finger many a time, haven't you?"

"Of course."

"Well, did you want a doctor? No; you had it tied up tightly, and left it alone. Then it grew together again!"

"Yes, yes, yes," cried Roy, impatiently. "But this was a terrible slash on the poor fellow's thigh. You saw how horribly it bled."

"Come, Master Roy, we're both soldiers, and we mustn't talk like this. I saw his leg bleed, and stopped it, but it wasn't horrible. Leg's only like a big finger, and a strong healthy chap soon grows together again. You mustn't take any notice of a few cuts. They're nothing. What we've got to mind is the cannon-balls. Now a wound from one of them is terrible, because you see they don't cut clean, but break bones and do all kinds of mischief. Well, we mustn't talk away here, but see to the men, and get ready for what's to come."

"Do you think they'll attack us to-day?"

"Yes, sir; and as soon as they've finished their two-gun battery. Now, by rights, we ought to go and destroy that work, and spike their guns; but they've got the advantage of us with all that horse, and if we tried they'd cut us up before we could get at it. Only chance is to try and do it at night, if we can't dismount the guns with ours."

A hasty breakfast was eaten, and then the sergeant went up to the newly mounted guns on the top of the square tower, where Roy promised to join him as soon as he had been to visit the wounded man.

"Tell him I mean to come as soon as I can, my lad," said Ben, "but it won't do him any good for me to come now. Wounded man's best left alone till he gets over his touch of fever. But tell him I'm sorry he's down, and that I shall very much miss my best gunner. It'll please him, and it's quite true."

Roy nodded, and in due time went to the hospital-room, where he tapped lightly, and the door was opened by the old housekeeper, who looked rather pale; but Lady Royland, who was seated by the wounded man's bedside, rose and came to her son.

"Yes," she said; "go and speak to him; but don't stay many minutes, for he must not talk much. A few words from you, though, will do him good."

Roy glanced towards the bed, which was close to one of the windows looking out on the court-yard garden, and he could see that the man was watching him intently.

"Go to him. I'll leave you and come back when I think you have been here long enough."

The door closed behind Lady Royland and her old assistant as Roy made for the couch, expecting to see a painful sight of agony and terror; but, as he approached, the man's countenance expanded into a broad grin.

"Don't be hard on a poor fellow, captain," he said, just as Roy was ready with a prepared speech about being sorry to see the man in so grievous a condition.

"Hard upon you, Sam! What for?"

"Sneaking out o' all the fun like this here! 'Taren't my fault, you know. I didn't want to stop in bed; but my lady says I must, and that she'll report me to you if I don't obey orders. I say, let me get up, sir. It's just foolishness me lying here."

"Foolishness! What! with that bad wound?"

"Bad, sir? Why, you don't call that bad. If he'd cut my head off, I'd ha' said it was."

"How?" cried Roy, unable to repress a smile.

"How, sir? Why—oh! o' course not. Didn't think o' that; I s'pose I couldn't then. But I say, Master Roy, sir—I mean cap'n, I'm just ashamed o' myself letting her ladyship wait on the likes o' me!"

"Why should you be, Sam? Haven't you been risking your life to defend us?"

"Me? No, sir, not as I knows on," said the man, staring.

"Well, I do know; and now you are not to talk."

"Oh, sir! If I'm to be here I must talk."

"You must not, Sam. There, I came to see how you were."

"Quite well, thank ye kindly, sir."

"You are not. You have a bad wound."

"But I aren't, Master Roy. It's on'y a bit cut; and I want to have a stick and come up on the tower in case we have to work that gun."

"If you want to help to work that gun again, Sam, you will have to lie still and let your wound heal."

"Master Roy!—I mean oh, cap'n—it's worse than the wound to hear that."

"We can't help it. Tell me, are you in much pain?"

"Oh, it hurts a bit, sir; but if I was busy I should forget that, and—"

Crash!—Boom!

A strange breaking sound, and the rattling of the windows as a heavy report followed directly after, and Roy sprang from the chair he had taken by the wounded man's couch.

"On'y hark, sir—that was my gun atop o' the gate tower begun firing, and me not there."

"Be patient, Sam," cried Roy, excitedly. "It was not one of our guns, but the enemy's, and the fight has begun in earnest. Good-bye, and lie still."

He was half across the room as he said this, and the door opened to admit Lady Royland, looking deadly pale.

"Roy, my boy," she cried, in a low, pained voice, as she caught his hands; "they are firing."

"Yes, mother; and so will we," cried the lad, excitedly.

"You—you will not expose yourself rashly," she whispered; "you will take care?"

"I'm going to try not to do anything foolish, mother," he said; "but I must be with the men."

She clung to him wildly, and her lips trembled as she tried to speak; but no words came, and Roy bent forward, kissed her, and tried to withdraw his hands, but they were too tightly held.

Boom! came another report following closely upon a peculiar whizzing sound, apparently over the open window.

"Another gun from the enemy, and we're doing nothing," said Roy, impatiently. "Mother, don't stop me; they will think I'm afraid. I must be with the men."

Lady Royland drew a deep breath, and her face became fixed and firm once more, though the pallor seemed intensified.

"Yes," she said, quickly, as she threw her arms about her son for a brief embrace; "you must be with your men, Roy. Go, and remember my prayers are with you always. Good-bye!"

"Just for a while," he cried. "You shall soon have news of how we are going on."

Chapter Twenty Six
Going under Fire

Roy ran out of the room, leaving the old housekeeper, who was waiting outside, to close the door, and dashed down the few stairs and out into the court-yard, where the greater part of their little force was drawn up on either side of the gate-way, looking very serious and troubled; but as soon as he appeared they burst into a cheer, to which Roy answered by waving his hand.

"The game has begun," he cried.

"Yes, sir," said one of the troopers, who with Farmer Raynes was in command of the men; "first shot struck the tower full, and splintered down some stone. Better mind how you cross the gate-way."

"Yes," said Roy, quickly; "I will." And he ran across to the door-way at the foot of the big spiral, reaching it just as a shot came whizzing overhead, and a heavy report followed.

"Third, and not one from us," muttered Roy, as he hurried up the stairway to reach the platform at the top, and found Ben Martlet and the troop-corporal from his father's regiment, each busy with one of the guns, arranging wedges under the breeches, and assisted by the men told off to work each piece, while two more now came to the turret door-way, bearing fresh charges ready when wanted.

Ben looked up and smiled grimly as Roy appeared, and the boy cried, excitedly—

"Three shots from them, and you doing nothing."

Rush!—Boom!

Roy ducked down his head, for the rushing noise seemed to be close over him; and as he raised it again, flushing with shame and glancing sharply round to see what impression his flinching had made on the men around, Ben said, quietly—

"Four, sir; and you see on'y one hit us; the earthwork has thrown all the others upward. That last one was nigh to a hundred foot overhead."

"A hundred feet! and I flinched," thought Roy. "But why don't you fire?" he cried, aloud.

"Thought I'd wait for you, sir, and that you'd like the first shot."

"Yes, of course," cried the boy, excitedly.

"And we haven't wasted time, sir; corp'ral and me's been pretty busy, getting what we thinks about the right depression of the muzzles, for you see we're a good height up here. I don't know that we shall be right, but we can soon get the range; and if you'll begin now, sir, I'd like you to try my gun first."

"Ready!" cried Roy, whose heart began to thump heavily.

"Like to take a squint along her, sir, first?" said Ben.

"No; I'll trust to your aim."

"Then, stand fast there!" cried Ben; and taking the port-fire from the man who held it, he presented it to the young castellan, who glanced at the earthwork, where he could see men busy, and a couple of squadrons of troopers drawn up some distance back on either side; and then, setting his teeth hard, he let the sparkling fuse fall softly on the touch-hole of the gun.

There was a flash, a great ball of smoke, the gun rushed backward, and the report seemed to stun Roy, whose ears rang, and a strange singing noise filled his head.

Ben said a few words, and leaned over the battlement, sheltering his eyes to watch the effect of the shot, as the smoke rose and began to spread. Then he turned and shouted something; but what it was Roy could not hear, neither could he catch a word that was uttered by the trooper-corporal, though the movement of his lips suggested that he was speaking.

"Can't hear you," shouted Roy, as loudly as he could; and the man smiled, and pointed to the port-fire and the second gun.

That was clear enough to understand; so Roy took a couple of steps towards the breech, and as the men stood drawn up in regular form on either side, he once more touched the priming.

Another flash, puff, and deafening roar, which he heard quite plainly; and oddly enough it seemed to have had the effect of restoring his ears to their customary state, for, in spite of the tremendous singing and cracking going on, he heard the order given to the men to stop the vents, sponge, and begin to reload.

"Just a shade more up," said Ben; "and yours wants a bit more than mine, corporal.—See where the shot hit, sir?"

"I? No," said Roy.

"Both on 'em just in front of their works, and covered 'em with earth and stones. They all bolted out. Look, they're coming back again, and they'll give us something directly."

"Yes," said the corporal, as the men went on loading; "and those shots have shown 'em what we can do. Look, sir."

"Why, they're drawing off those two troops of horse."

"Yes, sir," said the corporal; "and if Sir Granby Royland had been in command they'd never have been there."

"No," said Ben, with his lips pinched together; "we could have bowled over two or three of 'em with the guns, but I thought the captain would like to have a try at the earthwork first.—For they're not soldiers, Master Roy.— Are they, corporal?"

The trooper laughed.

"Just a mob of men scratched together, and put into jerkins and headpieces, and with swords stuck in their fisties. Why, there aren't many of 'em as can ride," continued Ben.

The thought occurred to Roy that his own garrison was composed of extremely raw material, but he said nothing, and Ben went grumbling on:

"I don't say but what they could be made into decent soldiers in time; but they don't seem to have anybody much over them."

Just then a couple of shots were fired by the enemy, one of which struck the tower with a tremendous crash, sending splinters of stone flying, and a tiny cloud of dust rose slowly. The other shot went whizzing overhead.

"I wouldn't get looking over the edge, Master Roy, sir," whispered Ben. "Some of those chips of stone might give you an ugly scratch. But that just shows what I say's right. They haven't got the right man there or he'd soon change things. You see they've brought up their guns with orders to batter down our drawbridge and smash the portcullis, thinking they'll make you surrender. Don't seem to come into their thick heads that if they did manage to smash the bridge, they'd be no nearer to us than before, because we should soon pile up a good breastwork, and pitch every man back into the moat who swam across. But, as I was going to say, they've got their orders to batter down the bridge, and they keep at it. We've been hit up here, but only by accident; they never fired straight at us. Now, if you were in command out there, sir, you'd do something different."

"I should fire straight up here, Ben, and try to silence these guns."

"Of course you would, sir; just as you're going to silence theirs."

"And the sooner the better, Ben. They're nearly ready again."

"Are they, sir? I can't see. My eyes are not so young as yours. Well, we're quite ready; and if you orders, we're going to give it 'em in earnest."

"Go on, then," said Roy, "and see if you can't stop their firing."

Ben smiled grimly, and bent down to regulate the aim he took, while the same was done with the other gun. The result was that the corporal's shot went right through the embrasure of the piece to the left, while Ben's went over.

As the smoke cleared away, a scene of confusion was visible; but the gun on the right was fired directly after, and the shot plunged into the bank of earth raised the previous night.

"Ah!" grumbled Ben; "you've got the best gun, my lad; there must be a twist in mine, for she throws high."

"Like to change?" said the corporal.

"No. I'm going to get used to mine and make her work better."

Shot after shot was fired from the gate tower, the men warming to their work, and the results were very varied; for, in spite of the care exercised and the rivalry between Ben and the corporal, the clumsily cast balls varied greatly in their courses, so that at the end of an hour's firing very little mischief was done on either side. The enemy had had their earthen parapet a good deal knocked about, and some men had been injured; but all the advantage they had obtained was the battering down of some scraps of stone, which lay about the front of the great gate-way.

"Soon clear that away with a broom," growled Ben; "but I'm a bit disappointed over these guns, captain. We ought from up here to have knocked theirs off the carriages by this time."

"We shall do it yet," said Roy; and during the next few shots he himself laid the guns, taking the most careful aim.

"As I said afore, your eyes are younger and better than mine, Master Roy, but you don't shoot any more true. — Hullo! what are they doing there?"

He looked earnestly at the battery, where the men seemed to be extra busy, and at a solid mass of troops marching on from some hundreds of yards behind, straight for the castle.

"They're never mad enough to come and deliver an assault; are they, corp'ral?" cried Ben, excitedly.

"Seems like it, sergeant."

Ben turned to Roy with an inquiring look, and he nodded.

"Do what you think best," he said.

What Ben thought best was to withdraw the great wedge which depressed the muzzle of his gun, the corporal doing the same; and then, after a careful aim-taking, both pieces roared out a salute to the coming infantry, which was marching forward in steady array.

The balls went skipping along after striking the ground a hundred yards or so beyond the enemy's battery, and, ricochetting, darted right for the solid moving mass of men. The effect was ludicrous, for in an instant they could be seen from the tower to be in a terrible state of confusion, breaking and running in all directions, and, as it were, melting away.

"First time they've ever faced cannon-ball," said Ben, with a smile. "I've seen better men than they after more training do the same. They won't do it next time, though."

As far as could be seen, few people were hurt; but the shots had their effect, for the men, as they were restored to something like order, were marched back behind a patch of woodland, and the duel between the two pairs of guns was recommenced with a couple of shots from the battery, both of which struck the tower high up.

"Aha!" cried Ben, with another of his grim smiles; "got tired, then."

"Does not seem like it, Ben," said Roy.

"Tired of plumping balls into our earthwork, and doing what they ought to have begun with.—Come, corporal, it's time we did better."

"Let's do it, then," said the man, sternly.

"Look here, Master Roy," said Ben, in a low tone; "they've just sent out two parties of horse to right and left, and it strikes me they're going to try something on the other side of us when they meet. Will you take a round of the ramparts, and see as all's right, and keep the lads on the lookout?"

"Let me fire these two shots first," said Roy.

He fired both guns, and there was a tremendous mass of earth sent flying; but that seemed to be the only mischief done; and then as Ben superintended the reloading, which began to be carried out now with a fair amount of speed, he said, in a low tone—

"Now, capt'n, will you take a look round? You ought to be everywhere at once now."

At that moment a shot just grazed one of the crenelles, and hurtled away close overhead, making the men wince, as it gave them a better idea of the enemy's powers than they had had before.

"Yes, that's why you want me to go, Ben," whispered Roy. "You think it is getting dangerous here. Thank you; I'll stay. I daresay the men are all right."

"Well, sir, I did think something of the kind; but it's real truth. You ought to be everywhere, and you must really give a look round and tell 'em to fire at any of the enemy who come too near, specially at the troops of horse; it'll teach 'em to keep their distance."

Another shot struck the tower, and the splinters of stone rattled down, making Roy hesitate to leave. But he felt that the old sergeant was right, and, descending to the ramparts, he visited the south-west tower, where the men in charge of the guns awaited orders to join in the fray. Then the north-west tower was reached, and here Roy encountered Master Pawson.

"I am glad you've come," he cried. "There's a strong body of horse gathering over at the foot of the hill to the north."

"Whereabouts?" said Roy, hurrying through. "Anywhere near the old ruins?"

"Ruins? ruins?" said the secretary, looking at him in a peculiar manner. "Ah, I see now: you mean those old stones on the top. No; they are on the level ground below. Hadn't we better fire?"

"As soon as they come within reach, send a ball at them. Let the gun be well elevated, so as to fire over their heads. We want to scare them off, and not to destroy."

As he spoke, Roy ascended with the secretary to the platform, and there, well within range, saw a strong squadron of horse approaching; while Roy's keen eyes detected a flash or two as of the sun from steel in amongst the trees at the foot of the hill.

"They have infantry there," he said. "And these horse must be coming to feel their way for them, and to see if we are prepared."

The men at the guns watched their young captain eagerly; and as soon as he gave orders for one of the guns to be used as he had directed, he was obeyed with an alacrity which showed how eager the people were to join in the fray commenced on the other side of the castle.

A shot soon went whizzing overhead, and caused a general movement among the horsemen; but they steadied again, and advanced. Upon a second shot being fired directly with the muzzle depressed, a little cloud of dust was seen to rise in front of the advancing squadron, which was suddenly thrown into confusion; and directly after the body of cavalry divided into two and began to retire, leaving an unfortunate horse struggling upon the ground; while after a close scrutiny Roy made out the fact that two men were riding upon one horse in the rear of the right-hand troop.

The men on the tower gave a loud cheer, trifling as their success had been, and were eager to fire again; but Roy was content to show the enemy that the defenders were well prepared let them advance where they would, for he knew that the slaying of a few men by a lucky shot would not have much influence on his success.

He stayed till the men had disappeared beyond the trees on the hill slope; and then, enjoining watchfulness, completed his visit to the other towers, descended to report how matters were progressing to his mother, who announced that her patient slept, and lastly hurried back to where the enemy were pounding away at the gate-way, and Ben and his men steadily replying.

"Hurt?" he cried excitedly, as he saw that one of the men had a rough bandage about his arm. "You had better go below at once."

"What! for that, sir?" said the man, staring; "it's only a scratch from a bit of stone."

The injury was very slight; but during Roy's absence the enemy had managed to send one shot so truly that it had struck the front corner of the embrasure of the corporal's gun, and splintered away a great piece of the stone, many fragments still lying about on the platform.

"Yes, sir; they're shooting better than we are, or their guns are more true. Our powder's good, old as it is; but it doesn't matter how carefully we aim, we can never tell to a foot or two where the shot will hit. They won't go where we want 'em."

"Well, theirs will not either, Ben," said Roy, "or they would have done more mischief to us than this."

"That's true, sir," grumbled the old soldier; "and after all said and done, I don't think much of big guns. If you could get 'em close up to the end of a ridgement, and the men would stand still, you could bowl a lot of 'em over like skittles; but there's a lot of waste going on with this sort of firing, and if it warn't for the show we make, and which keeps 'em off, we might as well sit down and smoke our pipes, and watch where the balls went that they send."

"But you must keep on, Ben. You may have a lucky shot yet."

"Oh, we aren't done so very badly since you went, sir! Soon as they'd done that bit o' damage to the top there, as'll cost Sir Granby a lot o' money to repair, the corporal sent 'em an answer which made 'em carry away four men to the rear."

"Killed?" said Roy, excitedly.

"Ah! that's more than we can say, sir. They didn't send us word. He's got the best gun, you see, sir; and I don't take so well to this sort of work. I want a good horse between my knees, and your father ahead of me to lead. Why, if he was here with his ridgement, he'd take us along like a big brush, and sweep this mob o' rebels off the country, as clean as one of the maids would do it with a broom. I say, sir; try your luck. The men like to see you have a shot or two. You boys are so lucky."

Roy tried and tried again as the day wore on, and the duel between tower and battery went on, but tried in vain. The men were relieved, and the fresh relay kept up a steady fire, shot for shot with the enemy; but nothing was done beyond knocking the earth up in all directions; while as fast as the face of the battery was injured, they could see spades and baskets at work, and the earth was replaced by more. A demonstration was made by the enemy on the sides of the castle, as if to try what was to be expected there; but a shot or two from the corner towers forced the horsemen to retire; and night was approaching fast when Ben and the corporal relieved the men who had been firing all the afternoon, and Roy was with them just as the old soldier took aim for his first shot.

"I've given her an extra charge of powder, sir," he said. "I'd ha' give her a double dose, on'y it would be a pity to burst her. Like to run your eye along before she's fired, sir?"

"No; you try this time, Ben."

As Roy spoke, there was a tremendous crash, followed by the report of the enemy's gun; and the rattling down of the splintered stone told how heavy the impact of the shot had been.

"More damage," growled Ben. "They're a-shooting ever so much better than us, corporal."

The next minute he applied the port-fire, and the gun sprang back, as a tremendous report followed.

"Made her kick quite savage, sir," said Ben, with a chuckle. "She says it's more powder than she likes."

He stepped to the embrasure as the smoke slowly rose, and gazed out at the enemy's battery.

"Come and look, Master Roy," he said, with a grim smile.—"I say, corporal, that's one to me."

The men raised a tremendous cheer, for plainly enough seen in the dim evening light, the interior of the battery was in confusion; and as the smoke quite cleared away, they saw that one of the guns was lying several feet back behind the shattered carriage, and at right angles to its former position.

"Give 'em yours now, my lad," growled Ben; and the corporal fired; but his shot went right over the battery and struck up the earth twenty yards behind.

"Depress the muzzle, man!" cried Roy.

"I did, sir, more than usual," said the corporal, rather sulkily.

"Yes, sir," said Ben; "he's a better gunner than me. Mine was on'y a bit o' luck, for I raised mine this time."

While the guns were being reloaded, Roy and his lieutenant watched the proceedings in the battery, waiting to withdraw when the enemy seemed to be about to fire.

But no further shot was sent roaring and whizzing against the tower, and, night falling, it soon became impossible to see what was going on.

Chapter Twenty Seven
A Startling Portent

That same night the proceedings at the earthwork were repeated under cover of a strong guard, the greater portion of the little garrison being engaged in repairing and strengthening the great earthen bank from the inner side; and this was carried out till dawn without the slightest interruption.

When the day broke, the reason for this was plain, for the enemy's battery had been carefully repaired; and just at sunrise a troop of horse was seen coming from the encampment of the main body of the force, half a mile away. As they came nearer, it was made out why they approached. For the troop was the escort of a couple of guns, each drawn by six horses; and an hour later a fresh embrasure was unmasked, and there were three guns ready to try and solve the problem unsolved on the previous day.

"Shall we hoist up another gun, Ben?" said Roy; but the old fellow shook his head.

"No, sir; I don't see any good in it. You know it's just a chance about hitting, and though they keep touching us, what good do they do? They may hammer away at the gate tower till they've half knocked it down, and it'll take 'em about a month to do it. And what better will they be then? They won't stand an inch nearer to getting in than they do to-day. Let 'em fire. You give 'em a shot now and then to tell 'em you're at home. Don't you waste more good ammunition than you can help."

Roy took his lieutenant's advice; and for a week the siege went on with the accompaniment of demonstrations of cavalry round the castle, and approaches by night, all of which kept the little garrison well on the alert, but did not advance the reduction of the stronghold in the least.

Sam Donny's wound progressed favourably; but the hospital-room was occupied as well by three more men, all suffering from cuts and contusions, caused by the flying chips of stones when a ball struck the edges of the crenelles.

The routine of the defenders was becoming monotonous, mounting guard, firing a little, and drilling a great deal; for Ben gave the men no rest in the way of practising them in the management of their weapons.

The result was that the condition of the garrison improved day by day, while Lady Royland grew more hopeful as she listened to her son's words.

"It can't last much longer, mother. Either they'll get tired of trying to drive us out, or some of the king's forces will come and relieve us."

Lady Royland shook her head the first time, but the second, Roy added—

"Look here, mother; the news is sure to reach London that we are being besieged. Then father will hear it; and do you suppose he will stand still? Either he will come himself, or see that help is sent."

Roy repeated his encouraging words one day at dinner, in the presence of the secretary, a full three weeks after the enemy had sat down before the castle, and Master Pawson laughed and rubbed his hands.

"They must give in," he said. "They'll never take the place."

"Never!" said Roy, triumphantly; "But I say, Master Pawson, I'm going to ask a favour of you."

"What is it?" said the secretary, eagerly.

"I want you to take a turn at the watch-keeping now and then."

"Keep watch?" said the secretary, staring.

"Yes, just now and then, so as to relieve a man and give the poor fellow a good sleep."

"Master Pawson will, I am sure," said Lady Royland, gravely. "He has said that he would do anything he could to help us in our time of need."

"Of course, Lady Royland, of course," he replied, hastily. "I only hesitated because I am so helpless—such a poor creature over matters like this."

"It doesn't want anything but to keep awake, and a sharp lookout. You ought to be able to do that, sir. You've had plenty of sleep lately, going to bed at nine, and sometimes at eight."

"Yes, I—I often go to bed very soon, Roy. My head seems to require a great deal of sleep. I suppose it's from studying so much. But I'll come and keep watch—after to-night. You will not want me to-night?"

"Why not to-night?"

"I don't feel prepared for it. My head is bad, and I fear that I should not be of much use. To-morrow night, if you want me, I will gladly come and take any duty you wish me to perform."

"Very well, Master Pawson," said Roy. "To-morrow night, then. I say, though," he added, merrily, "you had better come to the armoury with me."

Bang—bang! in rapid succession went the guns from the battery, followed a moment or two later by the third.

"That's right!" cried Roy. "Hammer away; only you might let us have our dinner in peace."

"Yes," said the secretary, with a forced laugh; "they might let her ladyship have her dinner in peace."

"Oh, mother!" cried Roy, "don't look so white and anxious. You ought to be used to the firing by now."

Lady Royland gave him a wistful look, and smiled faintly.

"They are only powdering down the stone; and I daresay the king will pay for it all being done up again."

"No doubt he will," said the secretary. "But you were saying something about the armoury. Shall I have to see to the men's weapons being served out?"

"No," said Roy, merrily. "I want you to select a helmet, breastplate, and back-piece to fit you, and a good sword."

"Oh, no, no!" said the secretary, quickly. "I am not a man of war."

"But you'll have to be, while you are on guard."

"Not like that. I might wear a good sharp sword; in fact, I did pick out one, and I have it in my room."

"Well done!" cried Roy, clapping his hands. "There, mother, who's ever going to think of surrendering when Master Pawson makes preparations like that.—I say, don't be too hard on the enemy, sir. Try and wound; don't cut off heads."

"Ah, you are making fun of me, Roy! But never mind. Don't you forget that by-and-by, when the fighting's over, I shall take my revenge."

"What—over lessons? Very well. I'm having a capital holiday from the old Latin."

The bent of the conversation turned, and the dinner ended in a very cheerful manner, for as time went on, Lady Royland could not help feeling hopeful. For want of the necessary war-material, the enemy seemed to be able to do no more in the way of a regular siege, and their efforts with the battery were becoming somewhat relaxed. No more men had been injured, and the sufferers in hospital were doing well. In fact, the general opinion in the castle was that before very long the enemy would, if they found they could not starve the defenders out, give up the attack, the castle being too hard a nut to crack.

That evening, while the firing was going on in a desultory way, Roy visited the hospital, meeting the secretary on the way.

"You've been to see the poor fellows?" said Roy, smiling.

"Yes—yes—they look white and ill. It is very sad, Roy. Such fine strong men, too. But what do you think of my going to read to them for an hour or two every day?"

"Not Latin?" said Roy, laughing.

"No, no, of course not. Something about the old wars."

"Capital!" cried Roy. "Do!"

"And I might take my viol over, and play to them a little."

"No, no; I say, don't do that," cried Roy.

"Eh? Why not? It would be so soothing."

"No; it wouldn't. Only make them miserable. They don't understand sarabands and corantos; and you can't play jigs."

"No," said the secretary, grandly, but with a peculiar look. "Perhaps they would not appreciate good music. And you are right; I do not understand jigs."

He nodded and crossed to the door-way leading up to his room, and Roy directly after encountered old Jenk.

"Hallo! where are you going?"

"Eh, eh? Master Roy? Oh, only up on to the platform to see the firing for a bit!"

"I say, don't you get shot."

"Me? Me? No, sir; they won't hit me. Look—look!" he cried, pointing upward. "Flag—ladyship's flag! Blows out bravely. See—we'll never surrender."

"Yes. Never surrender, Jenk. Too good soldiers for that."

"Ay, ay, ay!" cried the old man. "Too good soldiers for that. Brave boy! Your father's son. But you'll have my little gate-house built up again,

Master Roy, when they've gone, eh? They've knocked it about a deal. But old soldiers don't mind scars."

"Oh, yes; we'll have it put right when we've made the enemy run."

"Yes, yes, make 'em run, Master Roy; and I'll tell your father what a brave soldier Ben Martlet and I have made you."

The old man chuckled and went in at the door-way to mount the spiral stairs, while Roy turned and looked up at the flag, well blown out by the evening breeze.

"Poor old fellow! Helped to make me a soldier, has he? Well, it pleases him to think so."

The lad ran his eye along the side of the court-yard, sadly trampled now, and fancied he saw a head quickly withdrawn at one of the narrow windows of the north-west tower; but he was not sure, and it did not impress him then as he went on to the hospital-room, where the wounded men received him eagerly, Sam Donny being the most demonstrative, and ending by begging that he might be ordered on duty again.

"Another week at least, first," said Roy. "Only too glad to have you all back."

Roy stayed till it was dark, and he was descending to the court-yard when a loud shouting below took his attention, and upon running out he found a knot of men eagerly talking and looking up at the gate tower.

"What is it? What's wrong?" said the boy, excitedly.

"The flag, sir," cried Farmer Raynes. "Did you order it to be pulled down?"

"I? No!" cried Roy, excitedly. "I said it was to be kept up night and day. Who has dared to do this?"

Chapter Twenty Eight
By a Traitor's Hand

The last words were spoken as he hurried across to the door-way in the gate tower; and before he reached the platform at the top, he could hear Ben Martlet storming and shouting at the men, who were very silent; but from the noise of footsteps it was evident that they were running to and fro.

As Roy reached the top of the stairs, it was to find his exit on to the platform blocked by Ben and the corporal, the former being decked with the flag hanging over his shoulder like a mantle. They were evidently busy with the halyards at the little opening, down beside which the flag-pole butt was fixed in iron loops, and through which window the flag was hoisted and the halyards secured.

"What's the meaning of this?" cried Roy, breathlessly. "The enemy will think we have surrendered."

"Let 'em come, then, sir, and we'll show 'em we haven't," roared Ben, fiercely.

"But why was the flag hauled down?"

"Wasn't hauled down, sir. Come down with a run right on to the leads."

"What! Did the line break?"

"I wish it had broke, sir. You just look at that!" And he held out an end of the thin, strong hempen cord which ran through a pulley at the top of the pole, and to which the flag was always attached.

"Cut?" cried Roy.

"Yes, sir; cut. Some one has sawed through it with a sharp knife; and I want to know who it was."

"Some one up here on the platform?"

"No, sir; I'll answer for that," said the corporal.

"Some one then in the ammunition chamber?"

"Nay; I don't believe any one there would do it, sir," growled Ben, who was now busy splicing the line, which came swinging down by the window.

"How's that?" said Roy, eagerly.

"What—that rope, sir? One of the lads has swarmed up the flag-staff, and run it over the wheel again," cried Ben, who now re-attached the flag, well above the splice, and began to haul it up again, the folds gliding from his shoulder, and out of the window, to rise into sight from the platform, where the men greeted it with a hearty cheer.

"Ha!" ejaculated Ben, as the colours reached the top, and he fastened the line. "That don't look like surrendering, sir."

"No, Ben; but I want to know who dared to cut it. Who has been here?"

"No one but old Jenk, sir. He came and stopped some time, standing in the door-way, looking on and chattering to us a bit before he went down."

"Oh, but surely he wouldn't have done such a thing as that, Ben!"

"So I say, sir. If he did, it's quite time he was taken over to the church, and buried, for he must be out of his wits."

"Oh, impossible! He couldn't have done it. Are you sure it was cut?"

"Well, sir, you see the end."

"It must have been frayed by rubbing against the edge of the parapet."

"Didn't look like it sir; that's all that I can say."

"Has any one else been here?"

"Not as I know of, sir; but we've been too busy to see, keeping our faces to the enemy. I thought I heard some one run down."

"Well, it was an unfortunate accident, Ben; but you've soon repaired it," said Roy. And he stepped out on to the platform to look aloft at the flag, which was once more fluttering and flapping in the breeze; and then he stepped upon a stone to gaze over towards the enemy's battery to see if the lowering of the flag had had any effect there.

But all was quiet. They had evidently ceased firing for the evening, and the shades of night were descending so quickly, that the figures in the rear of the earthwork were beginning to look dim and indistinct. Away to the right, though, was a shadowy body which seemed to be moving along towards where the enemy's camp lay, behind the wooded patch of country;

and Roy was not long in coming to the conclusion that it was a troop of horse, returning from the neighbourhood of the battery.

He took a long sweep round, gazing hard at the beautiful wooded landscape, and the soft calm of the hour, with the sweet moist odours of evening which were wafted to him by the breeze, had a depressing effect. He found himself thinking of what a sad business it all was, that the peaceful district should become the scene of war and bloodshed — little enough of the latter; but who could tell how soon a terrible assault might be made upon the place, and their guns would have to be directed so as to mow down the advancing enemy like the hay fell before the mower's scythe.

Away to the west a bright planet was seen blinking in the dark grey sky, but that evening it did not seem to Roy like a star of hope; and when, a few minutes later, there came the faintly heard, mournful cry of an owl, he turned away to descend to the ramparts and walk round so as to visit, according to his custom, each tower in turn, where he was respectfully questioned by the men as to the lowering of the flag, and whether it had any meaning.

Roy laughed it off; but the fact of this incident impressing the men so strongly had a bad effect upon him, and he found himself forced to make an effort to fight it back before he joined his mother for the quiet hour or so he always spent with her before going on duty or retiring to rest.

But he was not to go straight to her; for on descending to the sadly trampled garden, he found the secretary slowly walking up and down the least-injured patch of grass, with his head bent, shoulders rounded, and his hands behind him, clasped together as if they were manacled.

He started sharply as Roy came near, actually wincing, and looking deadly pale.

"I wasn't going to hit you, Master Pawson," said Roy, with a smile.

"No, of course not; but all this firing has made me nervous. I am afraid I am not at all brave, Roy, and my head is so bad to-night, it makes me worse. I started just as if you were some enemy, and it sent a shock right through me."

"Better now?" said Roy, mockingly.

"Oh, yes, better now; but I'm very glad I do not go on duty to-night. I think I shall go to bed very soon, and sleep it off."

"Best thing; but you'll come with me to have some supper?"

"No, not to-night. Please make my excuses to my lady. It's a sad thing to be so weak of health, Roy. Sadder still to see this lovely garden spoiled by the trampling of armed men."

"Yes, it's a great pity," replied Roy; "but we'll soon set it straight again as soon as the enemy's sent to the right-about; and who would not sacrifice a few flowers for the sake of king and country?"

"Ah, who, indeed!" cried the secretary, with a slight flush coming into his cheeks. "Going?"

"Yes; I must join my mother now."

"And—er—are you on duty to-night?"

"Not till twelve o'clock," said Roy, frankly. "Then I have to go my rounds, and again at four. I hope the enemy will not disturb us."

"How can they?" said the secretary. "They cannot deliver an assault without rafts and ladders, or with boats; and we should see their preparations long before they could attack us."

"Yes, I suppose so," said Roy, thoughtfully. "The only thing I dread is a surprise."

"Surprise!" cried the secretary, starting violently. "Don't say that."

"Sorry I did say it," replied Roy, smiling; "for it made you jump as if you had been shot."

"Yes, Roy; sieges do not agree with me. But whatever made you say that?"

"Only because I think it possible, in spite of all our precautions, that the enemy might find a way to get into the place; that's all."

"What a horrible idea!" faltered the secretary.

"Well, I suppose it is," said Roy; "but don't let it keep you awake to-night, Master Pawson. Perhaps it is impossible."

"Impossible? Of course it is. There, good-night. I must go and lie down."

"And I am late in going to my mother," said Roy.

"Then good—good-night. Make your men keep the strictest of watches for all our sakes, my brave young castellan!"

"I will," said Roy; and each went his way.

"Now, if I didn't begin to know that Master Pawson really liked me, I should have thought he was sneering," said the lad to himself. "I'm always fancying people look down upon me because I'm such a mere boy. But he's trusty enough, as he has shown us. I wish he hadn't called me 'my brave young castellan,' though. It sounds so sugary and oily. Surprise—surprise?" he thought. "No, they couldn't surprise us, unless they got in by a secret passage; and if there were one, they would never find it out. If we couldn't, it isn't likely that strangers would. I wish Ben and I had had another big search. All this put it out of our heads. I'll ask mother if she thinks it possible there is one. No, I will not," he said to himself, as he reached the door. "It would frighten her into fits. She'd be too nervous to go to sleep, and want me to let all the men search the dungeons, and make them nervous, too. Bah! It's only an old woman's tale. I don't believe in such things."

He opened the door, to be welcomed by Lady Royland, who sprang from her chair, and proudly monopolised the task of taking off her son's helmet, cuirass, and back-piece, after unbuckling his sword.

"My duty, Roy," she said. "The one I was proud to perform for your father. Ah, my boy, if he were only here that I might assist him now! But no news, Roy; no news. It is cruel work."

"No news is good news, mother," cried Roy, cheerily. "Come and feed me, for I'm terribly hungry again."

An attractive meal was waiting; and to have seen mother and son soon after at the table, no one would have imagined that they were in a beleaguered castle with a strong body of the enemy close at hand.

Roy sat till the clock struck nine, and then rose.

"Then you will get no proper sleep to-night, my boy?" said Lady Royland, as she helped her son to resume his arms.

"Oh, yes; I shall lie down as I am, and jump up at twelve to take the round. I shall be back in my room in a quarter of an hour if the enemy is quiet, and sleep again till four, when I go my round again. I say, isn't it wonderful how one wakes at the right time when one has had a little practice."

"Roy, my boy, it is wearing you out. Let me go and see if the men are doing their duty to-night."

"What nonsense, mother!" cried the lad, merrily. "Just as if this was going to wear me out. To-morrow night old Ben will make the round, and I shall be snoring in my bed. There, good-night."

"Good-night, my darling," cried Lady Royland, pressing him to her breast.

"I say, what a hard-hearted creature I must feel with this on," said Roy, laughing merrily.

"I never notice the cuirass," said Lady Royland, embracing her son again. "I only feel my boy's warm, true heart beating against mine."

She followed him to the door, and he turned and kissed her again, and then hurried away, depressing his sword-hilt to keep the steel end of the scabbard from clinking on the pavement.

"Why did I do that?" said Roy to himself. "It was not as if—as if—Oh, what nonsense! It's the weather makes me feel low; and she feels low too. I was obliged to try and cheer her up."

He mounted to the battlements, whence he entered the room over the guard-chamber where, according to custom now, Ben was waiting with his lighted lantern, and wearing his long cloak, one side of which he threw over the light when he took it up.

"All well, Ben?"

"All's well, sir. Enemy as still as mice. I'm beginning to think that one of these mornings we shall get up and find they've gone without saying good-bye."

"Hope you're right, Ben. Ready?"

"Ready, sir."

"Then march."

They ascended to the top of the gate tower, where they were challenged, and then descended to the rampart to be challenged by the sentinel posted half-way between the towers, and again by the sentry on each tower in turn. It was everywhere the same. The men were well upon the lookout, and they had all the same report to give, that everything was still and nothing had been seen.

"You'll have Master Pawson on duty to-morrow night, so as to relieve one man, Ben," said Roy, as he completed his round.

"Won't relieve no man, sir," said Ben, sourly. "I shall want one to watch that chap to see that he don't do nothing foolish."

"Ah, you're prejudiced. But I say, Ben, suppose we were surprised, how long would it take us to man the walls?"

"Couldn't surprise us, sir," growled the old soldier. "First alarm, the men would be out of the rooms and up atop of the leads at the guns; and all the rest would make for the ramparts, ready to run to any spot that was attacked. We're all right, sir, 'cept one thing."

"What's that?" cried Roy, anxiously.

"Old Jenk is worrying me, sir. He's been wandering about the ramparts to-night in a curious, crazy way, speaking to nobody, and acting silly-like. I'm pretty sure it was him as cut that line and let down the flag."

"I'll talk to him to-morrow. Good-night till twelve, Ben. I'm tired, and shall be glad of my rest."

"Good-night till twelve, captain," said the old soldier; and Roy went to his room, took off helmet and sword-belt, and threw himself upon a couch, to forget all his low spirits and troubles in less than a minute, falling at once into a deep sleep, from which he started at the first chime of the tower clock.

The little lamp was burning dimly now on the mantelpiece, but it gave him light enough to buckle on his sword; and as he did so, the chiming and striking of the midnight hour went on in the midst of what seemed an unnatural silence, which impressed him. The next moment his helmet was on, and he stepped quickly out into the corridor, to find it full of armed men, four of whom dashed at him as his hand flew to his side, and he drew his sword.

It was a vain effort; his arms were roughly grasped, and the cry he tried to raise was smothered by a hand pressed upon his mouth; while, by the light of a lantern raised on high, he saw the figure of the secretary, who stepped forward and took the sword wrenched from his hand.

"Thanks, my brave young castellan," he said, mockingly. "We will take off your steel toys and gewgaws by-and-by. One word, though," he said, in a fierce whisper: "make the slightest sound, and you will be thrown into the moat. Be silent, and we will recollect that you are only a boy, and treat you as one."

For answer, Roy threw all his strength into one desperate effort, wrenched his head round so that it was clear of the hand pressed upon it, and shrieked out the one word—

"Judas!"

The word seemed to cut into the wretched traitor's brain; and, raising the boy's sword, he struck at him; but the blade glanced from the perfectly tempered helmet, and the next moment one who seemed to be an officer interposed.

"Prisoners are not treated like that, sir," he said, sternly. "Which way now?"

"This," said the secretary; and he led the way along the corridor, towards the door opening upon the court-yard.

Chapter Twenty Nine
A Dark Night's Deeds

At that moment, when Roy would have surrendered his life to have rung out an alarm, the signal of danger, treachery, and hopeless disaster rang out in the form of a shot from the battlements overhead, and this was followed by another and another. But as the prisoner was hurried into the open air, armed men seemed to be gliding out of the darkness on all sides, their source, as far as he could make out in those agitated moments, being the bases of the towers. Then, as the trumpet rang out, fighting began all around the castle at once, not from the outside, but from within. Men had evidently crept silently up to the four towers, and gathered there from the corridors to which they had been admitted; and at the sound of the trumpet, a simultaneous attack was made, which, coming from the unguarded rear, and in tremendous, constantly increasing force, could not fail of being successful.

Roy stood there in the midst of his mother's once pleasant garden, with the stars glinting over his head, and guarded by half-a-dozen troopers, listening to the clash of steel, and the firing going on all round where the little garrison made desperate efforts to maintain themselves. But they could not even grow stronger by joining, for the occupants of each tower were isolated and driven back as they tried to communicate with their officers, who, at the first alarm, tried to lead the men in the guard-room to the gathering point selected in case of emergency. Ben had just lit his lantern, expecting the coming of Roy at twelve, when the first shot came; and, shouting an alarm, he drew his sword to dash out, but only to be hurled back, the door-way of the guard-room being blocked by men; while, when the occupants of the chambers beneath the platforms of each tower tried to descend, they, too, in spite of desperate efforts, were driven upward by the constantly arriving enemies, who forced them on to the leads by the now useless guns.

Here, in each case, a desperate encounter went on, which Roy, with his blood running cold, was able to mentally picture, as he stood there listening to the wild shouts of the attacking party, the defiant cries of the garrison — the mere handfuls of men who tried to hold their own.

There was no more firing: all was being done with the keen-edged naked blade for a few minutes; and this was followed by a wild despairing cry from the gate tower, and directly after there was a dull, sickening crash which told that a man had been hurled from the parapet into the court-yard, where he lay never to move again.

The shock of this was succeeded by others nearly as terrible, as the struggle went on at the tops of the different towers; and cry after cry arose, followed by heavy splash after splash, which, Roy interpreted rightly, meant that the victors were driving the defenders over the battlements into the moat, to sink or swim for life as they could.

A mad feeling of rage and despair seized upon the boy as he heard all this, and he struggled desperately with his captors in his endeavours to escape, and try to aid the poor fellows fighting to the death in their vain efforts to defend the place.

Vain, too, were his efforts; for a couple of men held him while others wrenched his arms behind his back, and tearing off his gay scarf, bound his elbows so tightly together that he could not stir, but had to listen helplessly to the yells and despairing cries that arose towards the silent vault of heaven.

It seemed to Roy like an hour of horror, during which he was listening to what seemed to be the massacre of the men, every one of whom he looked upon as a friend. But it was only a matter of a few minutes at the most, before a shout rang out from the top of the gate tower, to be answered with a burst of wild "hurrahs" from the four corners, and the ramparts as well; for the clashing of swords, the yells of rage, and the sounds of fierce and desperate struggles going on had ceased.

Roy's despair was at its height; he knew that the castle was taken, and its defenders killed, hurled into the moat, or captive.

But the boy's sinking heart gave one leap, for he knew that the flickering fire of defence blazed up in one spot, and that was in the guard-room, where he calculated that there must be twelve or fourteen men, with Ben Martlet, Farmer Raynes, and the corporal.

He was nearly right to a man. There were, including their officers, twelve men penned up in the big stone chamber, where they had plenty of arms and ammunition. The others had their quarters in the five chambers in the towers, and were stationed as sentinels. All these had been accounted for, save the wounded men in hospital.

And as Roy listened to the hurrying tramp of feet, there was gathering silence on the ramparts, while around him, in the court-yard, hundreds of men were united and drawn up in line.

Then, in the darkness beneath the gate-way, Roy heard a commanding voice call upon the men in the guard-room to surrender.

"What?" came out clearly in a harsh, snarling voice, which Roy hardly knew as Ben's. "Do what?"

"Surrender, my man! The place is taken."

"Yes, by cowardly treachery, Ben," yelled Roy, desperately. "Don't give in. Fight to the last."

A man came hurrying up, and the secretary, fierce with passion, stood before him.

"If this boy dares to speak another word, ram a gag in his mouth.—No, not yet.—Here, bring him up to the gate."

Roy was half pushed and dragged to the great archway, and, as he reached it, the clock chimed the quarter after midnight.

"Now, general," cried Pawson, "we'll have them out. It's not worth while to waste good men's lives to tear a set of mad rats out of their hole."

"Well, get them out," said the same commanding voice, and in the officer a short distance from him, Roy recognised the one he had met with the flag of truce.

"Now, then, if you value your life," snarled Pawson in the boy's ear, "order those fools to come out before we blow them to pieces with a keg of powder. Do you hear? Come forward and speak!"

Roy felt a fierce desire to spit in the traitor's face, but he mastered himself and stepped forward.

"Ah, you've come to your senses, then," said Pawson. "Lucky for you, my popinjay. Now, then, tell them to surrender."

"Why?" said Roy, spitefully. "They don't know what it means."

"Speak!" cried Pawson; and he pricked the lad with the point of his sword.

Roy in those terrible moments had to fight hard to be dignified, as he felt he ought to be, before the enemy; but the desire was strong upon him, when he felt a slight prick in the side from the keen point of the sword, to turn round and kick his aggressor with all his might.

Then he spoke.

"Sergeant Martlet, corporal, Farmer Raynes, all of you, I'm a prisoner, and can't help myself. There are two or three hundred men here. Can you hear me?"

"Ay, ay, sir; go on," cried Ben.

"They bid me tell you to surrender. What do you say?"

"Let 'em come and make us. God save her ladyship and the king!"

"Hurrah!" came rolling back from nearly a dozen lusty throats, and was followed by a shout from Ben.

"Get back, Master Roy; we're going to fire."

"Then fire," cried Roy. "Never mind me now."

Another cheer followed this; and there was a rattling noise which Roy interpreted, for he knew that the men in the guard-room had seized the pikes from the rack, and that a bristling hedge of steel was being formed in the door-way.

Just then the officer in command stepped forward.

"Silence there!" he cried, in a loud clear voice. "Listen to me, my men. The castle is taken, and I have four hundred men here. You are the only defenders left.—Sergeant Martlet, I suppose you are an old soldier, and if so, you know this boy's words are madness. Enough men have perished, and I should be sorry to add your party to those who have made so brave a defence. Come, you have all done your duty, and your case is hopeless; surrender, and you shall suffer no harm."

"When my captain tells me—not before."

"Well spoken, and like a brave man," said the officer; and he turned to Roy.

"Now, captain," he said, and there was a touch of sarcasm in his voice, "you don't want those stout fellows shot down, or smothered like rats in their holes. Tell them to give up their arms and come out."

"To a set of cowards who attacked us as you did with the help of that treacherous dog!" cried Roy, passionately. "No!"

"Hurrah!" was shouted from the guard-room door and Farmer Raynes roared out:

"Well said, Master Roy; we'll beat 'em yet."

"Take that boy away," cried the officer; and Roy was dragged to one side, where he heard the speaker again bid the party surrender; but only received a shout of defiance in reply.

A few short, sharp orders followed; and Roy quivered with passion as he saw from the brightening sparks that a party of men who tramped forward were blowing the matches of their firelocks.

An order followed, and a ragged volley was fired in at the door, which was answered by a cheer, and directly after by half-a-dozen shots and some confusion among the attacking party, for two men staggered back and fell groaning upon the stones.

The officer stamped his foot.

"Pikes and swords," he cried; and in obedience to his orders a little column of a score of men dashed forward and tried to enter, thrusting in their pikes; and as many as could get to the door striving desperately, but only to be beaten back, and their discomfiture increased by a few more shots.

The attack was resumed with fresh men again and again, but the defenders fought desperately, and in every case the attacking party were driven back with several men badly wounded.

"Block the place up and starve them out," said Pawson.

"No," said the officer sternly. "The work must be done at once. Powder," he cried to a couple of men near him, and a party marched off.

After a short delay, during which Roy looked vainly round for the secretary, the latter appeared again with the men, one of whom bore a keg. To this a piece of fuse was attached ready for lighting, and the officer walked to Roy's side.

"Look here, youngster," he said. "I shall stand at nothing to complete the reduction of this nest. You see that keg of powder. If these men do not surrender at once, I shall treat them as desperate vermin and blast them out or bury them, with perhaps half the tower upon their heads. It rests with you whether I shall kill a dozen or so of brave men or spare them. Which is it to be?"

Roy was silent.

"Come," said the officer, "I want to be merciful now. You are Sir Granby Royland's son. He is a brave soldier, though mistaken in defending a tyrant. I tell you that when a cause is hopeless he would act as I ask you to do. Now you have well proved your courage, and you spoke before in the rage of defeat. Speak now as a brave officer who would not willingly sacrifice his men. What do you say?"

Roy said nothing, for his heart swelled with emotion, and the words would not come. The officer came closer, so that none other could hear.

"In God's name, boy," he whispered, "don't force me to do this brutal act; I ask you as the son of a brave soldier. Tell them to surrender now."

The way in which these words came to Roy's ear achieved that which no threats or insult would have done. It was an enemy speaking, but something told him that he was a brave soldier too; and without another word Roy stepped up to the door-way, from whence a mistaken shot might have laid him low.

The officer grasped this, and shouted loudly—

"Within there! Don't fire!"

It was only just in time, for half-a-dozen muskets were presented.

The next moment Roy's voice rang out clearly:

"Sergeant Martlet, corporal, Raynes, all of you, we have done our duty, and it is hopeless to fight longer. You are the only men left. To resist is to give all your lives for nothing. March out and throw down your arms."

A groan rose from within, and a figure came to the door-way.

"Don't say that, Master Roy," cried Ben, hoarsely. "Couldn't we do it if we held out?"

"No; they will blow the place up. The powder is waiting. I am your captain; I order you to surrender now."

"Master Roy! Master Roy!" cried the old soldier in a piteous voice; "it was no doing of mine. I was on the alert. Don't think it was any fault of mine."

"Fault of yours, Ben?" cried Roy. "No, nor mine neither."

"But how did they get in, sir?"

"By the secret passage that we could not find."

"But how? Where can it be?"

"I've been thinking, Ben. I don't know for certain; but it must open into Master Pawson's room."

"And he let 'em through?"

"Yes; filling the corridors silently with troops while I slept."

"The traitor! Then that was the signal, boy. Oh, my lad, my lad, why didn't I kill him when I thought it must be he? What about repairing the stone gallows now?"

"I—don't understand you."

"The lowering of the flag, sir—the lowering of the flag."

"Yes," said the officer, who had advanced to them unobserved in the gloom of the archway; "that was the signal, sergeant. You were betrayed from within. Step out now with your men, like the brave fellow you are. Give me your hand; and let me tell you that I don't believe I could have taken the place without."

"Am I to surrender, Master Roy?" said the old fellow, bitterly.

"Yes, Ben; it is all over now."

The hilt of a sword was thrust out as the old soldier held it to the officer by the blade.

"Shake hands with that, sir," he said, bitterly. "I'm a king's man still. — Forward!"

This to his brave companions; and as they marched slowly out and gave up their arms, a tremendous roar arose from all assembled in the court-yard.

It was no derisive cry, no jeer at the conquered, but a full-throated cheer of admiration for the brave little party, blood-stained, bandaged roughly, three of them hardly able to keep their feet; and Roy's heart once more swelled within him in spite of his despair, for he noticed in the gloom that the officer in command took off his helmet as the men marched by into the court; and then, as he replaced it, he said quietly to Roy —

"All this is not necessary, sir. — Quick, one of you; untie this gentleman's hands."

For the first time that night, Roy felt giddy and sick with pain. But he roused himself directly, for Master Pawson came up, and spoke quickly in a low voice to the officer, who replied coldly, and with a ring of contempt in all as he said, loudly —

"Of course, sir," he said, "in some things, by the terms of your bargain, you are master here of the place and the estate. All that the Parliament desires is the destruction of the castle as a stronghold; but as to the garrison, that is another thing. We shall hold the place for a time, and while I await further orders the prisoners will be my charge."

He turned to give some orders, and the secretary turned to Roy.

"Yes," he said, "I am master here now of everything; so go and take off all that tawdry rubbish. You will never make a soldier, and I shall tame down all this bullying haughtiness. You never thought my day would come when I was forced to put up with the insults and jeers of a miserable cub of a boy. But every man has his day. Your party has gone down at last, and mine is in power. Ah, you may pretend not to hear me, and that you treat everything I say with contempt! Judas, am I, because I saved bloodshed by a diplomatic stroke? Well, we shall see. You'll come cringing to me soon."

"When my father returns, and, if you have not already been hung for a traitor, he punishes you as you deserve. Shall I cringe to you, then?"

"Your father," said Pawson, mockingly. "Your proud swashbuckling father is dead,—killed as he deserved, with scores of his fighting bullies. You may look to me as your father now. Your mother and I thought it better to end this sham defence at once. Hah! does that sting you? I thought I should manage it at last. Yes, she thought with me. A fine, handsome woman still, Roy, and a clever one, though she did pet and spoil her idiotic cub of a son. But there, I forgive her, and we understand each other fully now. Ha, ha! I thought that would touch you home!"

Roy nearly staggered as he heard these words, and the next moment he would have flung himself at the traitor's throat; but just then a friendly hand was laid upon his shoulder, and the officer said—

"I have given orders for your wounded men to be seen by our doctor. Meanwhile, you had better come with me."

He passed his arm through Roy's, and turned his back on Pawson, marching the lad towards the private apartments of the castle; while the traitor stood gazing after them, stung as deeply as his victim now in turn.

Chapter Thirty
"And all through my Neglect"

Seeing how completely prostrated his companion seemed to be, the officer turned to him as they reached the entrance to the private apartments and said, quietly—

"Perhaps you will show me a room where I and my officers can have some refreshment. We are starving. You can tell your servants that they have nothing to fear. I will see that they are not insulted; and then perhaps you would prefer to be alone."

"Thank you," faltered Roy, speaking in a strange, dazed way, as if he were in a dream.

"Come, be a man, sir," said the officer, rather sternly. "It is the fortune of war. A young soldier must not lose heart because he finds he is a prisoner. There, meet me at breakfast-time, and you and I will have a chat together. But listen first before you go: do not attempt any foolish, reckless pranks in the way of trying to escape. I tell you honestly, the castle will be so guarded and watched that it would be madness.—By the way, where are Lady Royland's apartments?"

Roy pointed to a door.

"Tell her when you see her that there is nothing to fear. But Master Pawson told me that he would place guards over her."

Roy drew a deep breath but said nothing, merely contented himself with pointing out the dining-room and library to his conqueror. Then he stopped at his own door.

"Your room? Very well; take my advice, and have a few hours' sleep," said the officer, opening the door, entering, and looking round by the light of the dim lamp. "Where does that big window open upon?"

"The garden,—the court-yard."

"And that narrow slit?"

"Upon the moat."

"Hah! Good-night to you."

He strode out, and Roy stood where he had been left, with his head throbbing as if it would burst from the terrible thoughts that invaded it.

Directly after he heard the tramp of heavy feet, a few words delivered in an imperious tone, and there was the heavy *rap, rap* of a couple of musket butts upon the oaken floor, telling him that guards had been placed at his door. His despair now knew no bounds, for he had determined to go straight to his mother's chamber, and ask her if Master Pawson's words were true. Now all communication was cut off, for he was a prisoner.

But his agony had reached its greatest height, and in a short time he grew calmer; for light came into his darkened brain, and he told himself he was glad that he had not been able to go and insult his mother by asking such a question.

"It is horrible!" he said to himself; "and I must have been mad to think such a thing possible. Liar! traitor! wretch! How could I think there was the faintest truth in anything he said!"

Utterly exhausted, he took off his armour and laid it and his sword-belt and empty scabbard aside.

"Done with now," he said, bitterly; and he sank upon the couch to try and think whether he was to blame for not searching more for the passage leading out beyond the moat.

"But I did try, and try hard," he muttered. "No; I could not foresee that the man chosen by my father would betray us. It was my duty to trust him. It was not my fault."

Through the remainder of that night he sat there thinking. Now listening to the tramp of the sentries at his door and overhead upon the ramparts, starting from time to time as he heard them challenge, and the word passed on, till it died away; now thinking bitterly of the ease with which they had been beaten, and of the men who must have fallen in their defence. Then, from utter exhaustion, his eyes would close, and consciousness leave him for a few minutes as he sank back.

But he never thoroughly went to sleep, the act of sinking back making him start into wakefulness, bitter and angry with himself for these lapses, and in every case springing up to pace the room.

"Poor mother! What she must have suffered through it all, and I scarcely gave her a thought. That wretch must have locked her in her room or she would certainly have been seeing to the wounded."

The clock chimed and struck, and chimed and struck again, with Roy counting the long lingering hours as they went on, for he was longing for the day to appear, hopeless as the dawn would be. But he wanted to see the general, to beg that he might go to Lady Royland; and the time when he would meet him seemed as if it would never come.

But at last the faint light began to dawn through the window, and, hot and feverish, he threw it open, to look out across the court and over the eastern ramparts at the coming signs of day, which grew brighter and clearer till the sentinels upon the terrace-like place, and the crenellations, stood out of a purply black plainly marked against the sky.

There were at least twenty men marching to and fro where at the most he had had two; and he groaned in spirit for a time as he went over again the occurrences of the past night. But far on high the sky began to be dappled with orange and golden clouds, which increased in brightness till the whole east was one glory of light, bringing with it hope; while the soft cool breeze he drank in gave him fresh courage and the strength to act the part he had to play, — that of one too proud to be cast down, so that his men should speak of him ever after as his father's son.

"Better than being in one of the dungeons," he thought, as he indulged in a good bathe, and dressed himself simply; after which he carefully hung up his armour, with the helmet above, and longed for his sword that it might occupy its old place.

"Better be lying rusting in the moat than resting in such hands as his," he muttered.

After spending some time at the window gazing across the court at the windows of the long chamber used for the hospital, and at the opening to the stabling down below, he fell to wondering as to how the poor fellows who were wounded had passed the night; and this brought a shudder, and he ran across to the little slit in the thickness of the wall to open the tiny casement, and look down at the moat, peering to right and left with starting eyes in expectant dread of seeing some ghastly sign of the horrible struggle that had taken place upon the tower platforms. But the lilies floated peacefully enough, and displayed their great white cups, and the fish played about beneath the leaves, making rings in the smooth patches where they rose—rings which spread and spread till they slightly swayed the reeds and rushes at the edge.

But he saw no dead white face gazing up at the sunlit heavens, and, search the waters as he would, there was not a sign to send a shudder through his frame.

All at once there was the tramp of feet overhead, and he went back to the other window, where he stood and looked across, and on the eastern rampart saw the guard relieved, the sun burnishing the men's steel caps; and soon after, as he watched, wondering what the day would bring forth, he heard the sentries at his door relieved in turn.

This ended, the echoes of the place were awakened by the blast of a trumpet, and the boy stood looking in wonder at the strength of the force drawn up in the court, and saw fully half of them march towards the great gate-way. Then he heard the drawbridge lowered, and the heavy, hollow tramp of the men as they passed across. Soon after, the neighing of horses reached his ears, and then came the beating of hoofs on the bridge, raising echoes from the walls at the other end, as a troop rode in and were drawn up on either side—sturdy-looking fellows, who sat their horses well, as Roy was fain to grant in spite of Ben Martlet's disparaging remarks.

He was still watching the troopers and their horses, when he heard a movement outside his door as if the sentries had presented arms; and directly after the general strode into the room, with his stern, thoughtful countenance lighting up as he encountered Roy's frank, bold eyes.

"Good-morning," he said, holding out his hand.

Roy flushed, but made no movement to take it.

"As one gentleman to another, Roy Royland," he said, smiling. "We can be enemies again when we have fighting to do. Come, we can be friends now."

Roy felt drawn towards him, and he slowly raised his hand, which was firmly gripped and held for a few moments.

"Ah, that's better!—Well, prisoner, how have you slept?"

"I? Not at all," said Roy, bitterly.

"That is a pity, too," said the general. "You ought to have slept. You had no guilty conscience to keep you awake. You only had the knowledge of duty done."

"And what about the poor fellows who fell fighting for us? Would not that keep me awake?"

"Ah, yes!" said the general, laying his hand on Roy's shoulder. "That is right. Well, as far as I have ascertained, not a man failed to cross the moat after his plunge. There are some ugly wounds, no doubt, but the doctor tells me that my men have suffered worse than yours, and he does not anticipate that any of your brave fellows will even have to stay in bed."

"That is good news," said Roy in spite of himself, for he meant to be very stern and distant.

"Better than was given me, my boy. There, come along; breakfast is waiting."

Roy shrank back.

"I would rather have some bread and water here," he said.

"Indeed! But I'm not going to feed my prisoner upon bread and water. I find you have plenty here, and that plenty you shall share. Ah! I see you do not want to meet our friend Pawson."

Roy started violently, and changed colour.

"He will not be with us, sir. Master Pawson prefers to stay in his own chamber, and I am quite willing."

"My mother?" asked Roy, in agony.

"Keeps to her room, boy. Her women are with her, and she knows that you are safe."

"She knows that?" cried Roy.

"Well, yes. I am what you would call a brutal rebel and traitor to my king; but I have a wife who knows what anxiety is about her husband and her son during this cruel war, and I took the liberty of asking an interview last night, before going to rest, and telling Lady Royland how you had behaved."

"Thank you, General — General — "

"Hepburn, my lad," and he caught the hand the boy held out. "And let me tell you that you have a mother of whom any boy should be proud — your father a wife such as few men own. She passed the whole night tending the wounded and winning our doctor's esteem. But come; I am hungry, and so must you be too."

Roy followed him without a word, feeling that, prisoner though he was, the salutes of the sentinels they passed were full of respect; and when he reached the dining-room, in which about twenty officers were gathered waiting their general's presence to begin, they rose like one man, and pressed forward to shake him by the hand, making the boy flush with mingled shame and pride, for had he taken the castle instead of losing it, his reception could not have been more warm.

"Come," said the general, after their hasty meal was at an end, "you are my prisoner, but I will not ask you to make promises not to escape. You can go about the castle; the men will let you pass anywhere within the portcullis. You will like to visit your wounded men, of course."

"And the other prisoners?" said Roy.

"I am going to parade them now; so come with me and see."

The strong force pretty well filled the square court-yard, but left a vacant place in the middle into which the general strode; and then giving his orders, there was a pause, during which Roy's gaze turned involuntarily towards the little turret at the corner of the gate tower; but no flag fluttered there, and he felt a pang as he gazed at the tall pole with the halyard against it swayed by the wind.

But he had something else to take his attention directly as he glanced round the walls.

There, standing at the window of the north-west tower, was the upper part of the figure of Master Pawson, framed as it were in stone; and Roy turned away in disgust as a hearty cheer arose, and he saw it was to welcome the brave fellows, who marched from their prison of the night, bandaged, bruised, and sadly damaged in their personal appearance, but with heads erect and keeping step with Ben Martlet, who looked as if he were flushed with victory instead of labouring under defeat.

The men were drawn up in line in the middle of the narrow square, and as they caught sight of Roy just by the general, their military manners gave place to a touch of human nature, for Ben nodded eagerly to his young captain, and wounded and sound all waved steel cap or hand, Farmer Raynes the latter in a left-handed way, for his right was in a sling; and then all burst into a cheer.

Just then, behind the prisoners and over the heads of the line of mounted men, whose horses' hoofs were trampling the flower-beds, Roy caught sight of something white in the open hospital window, and his heart leaped as his mother waved her handkerchief to him, wafting away with it the last trace of the vile mist Master Pawson had raised around her by his assertion.

Roy eagerly responded to the salutation, and then had his attention taken up by the action of the general, who walked along the little line of prisoners, who, to a man, returned his stern scrutiny with a bold, defiant stare. Then turning to Ben, he said—

"How many of these are disciplined soldiers, sergeant?"

"All of 'em far as we could make 'em," replied Ben.

"Yes. But how many were in the Royalist army?"

"Three and me," said Ben.

"You three men, two paces to the rear," said the general, sharply; and the three troopers stepped back.

"Nay, nay!" shouted Farmer Raynes, angrily. "Share and share alike. We were all in it; and I say if you shoot them, shoot us, too;" and he stepped back, the others after a momentary hesitation following his example.

There was a murmur in the Parliamentary ranks as the men witnessed this little bit of heroism, and the general shouted his next order in a very peremptory way.

"Attention!" he cried, addressing the prisoners. "I do not shoot brave men in cold blood, only cowards and traitors."

"Then have that hound down from yon window, general," cried Ben, excitedly, pointing to where Master Pawson stood looking on, "and shoot him. Nay, it's insulting good soldiers to ask 'em to do it, sir. We've an old stone gallows here on the ramparts; have him hung."

A yell of execration burst from the prisoners, and the ex-secretary disappeared.

"Silence!" cried the general. "Attend there. You, sergeant, and you three men, will you take service under the Parliament, and keep your ranks with the promise of early promotion?"

"Shall I speak for you, comrades?" asked Ben.

"Yes," they cried together.

"Then not a man of us, sir. We're Sir Granby Royland's old troopers, and we say, God save the king!"

The general made a sign, and the four men were surrounded and marched to one side in the direction from whence they had been brought;

while at another sign, the rest of the prisoners, with Farmer Raynes at their head, closed up in line.

"What are you?" said the general, sternly, beginning with the sturdy tenant of the estate.

"Farmer."

"And you?"

"Butler."

And so all along the line, each man making his response in an independent, defiant tone.

"Will you come and serve the Parliament?" said the general. "I want strong, brave men."

He looked at Farmer Raynes as he spoke, but glanced afterwards at every man in turn.

"Then you must go and look for 'em somewhere else, squire. You won't find a man on Sir Granby Royland's estate."

A murmur from the rank showed how the rest acquiesced.

The general made a sign, and a squad of musketeers surrounded the men.

"Go back to your homes, my lads; but remember, if you are found in arms again, you will be shot. Escort these men beyond the moat."

Farmer Raynes turned sharply to Roy.

"Can't help ourselves, captain," he cried, loudly; "but shot or no, we're ready when you want us again.—Good-bye, Martlet, old comrade.—Take care of him, general, for he's as fine a soldier as ever stepped.—Now, my lads, three cheers for my lady, and then march."

The prisoners burst into a hearty roar, and were then escorted through the gate-way and over the drawbridge beyond the strong picket stationed by the earthwork. Here they cheered loudly again.

"Hallo! who are you?" said the general, sharply, as his eyes lit upon the flowing white hair and beard of the tottering old gate-keeper, who, fully armed, and with his head erect, took a few paces forward from where he had stood before unobserved.

"Sir Granby's oldest follower, and his father's afore him," said Jenk, in his feeble, quavering voice. "Do I go with Ben Martlet and t'others to the prison?"

"No," said the general, shortly; "stop and attend to your young master, and mind you don't get playing tricks with that sword."

"But I'm a soldier as has sarved—"

"Silence, Jenk!" said Roy, hastily stepping to his side. "You must not desert me; I'm quite alone now."

"Oh, very well, if it's like that, sir, I'll stop with you," quavered the old man; and he stepped stiffly behind his young master, unconscious of the smiles and whispers which arose.

Half an hour later the new garrison had settled down to its quarters; the three heavy guns from the battery had been brought in and planted in the gate-way to sweep the approach, and Royland Castle was transformed into a Parliamentary stronghold, protected by whose guns a little camp was formed just beyond the moat, and occupied by the cavalry of the force.

Ben and his three comrades were placed in a room opening on the court-yard, with leave to go anywhere about the quadrangle, with a sentry placed over them—hardly a necessity, for they were all suffering from wounds, of which, however, they made light when Roy went to them, setting him a capital example of keeping a good heart.

Then, finding himself fully at liberty to go where he pleased, the sentries saluting and letting him pass, Roy made for the hospital-room, longing for and yet dreading the interview, fearing as he did to witness his mother's despair.

To his surprise, as she eagerly caught his hands in hers, her face was wreathed in smiles, and she strove to comfort him.

"Defeated, Roy; but even your enemies honour you for your brave defence," she whispered.

"Ours, mother; not mine only," he said. And then, feeling that he could not even allude to the traitor who carefully kept out of his way, he went round to the men's beds with Lady Royland. The place was pretty full now, but in spite of serious wounds the room looked cheerful, and the men of both sides received them with smiles. There was only one sad face, and that was Sam Donny's, for he had taken to his bed again, "from weakness," Lady Royland said.

She passed on to the next bed, and Roy sat down by the poor fellow for a few minutes, to take his hand, gazing the while in his drawn and wrinkled face.

"I'm very, very sorry, Sam," Roy said, gently. "Come, you must try and get right again."

"Yes, captain," said the man loudly, with a groan. "I was to have been out in a few days if I hadn't turned worse. This doctor don't understand my case."

"What is it?" said Roy, anxiously. "Has your wound broken out again?"

"Nothing at all," whispered the man, with his eyes twinkling. "I'm nearly as right as you are, sir; and when you want me, here I am."

"What?"

"Hush! Don't look like that. I'm gammoning my lady, so as they shan't send me away like t'others. You've got a strong man here when you and Ben Martlet wants to make a fight for it again. Oh-h-h!"

He groaned as he saw one of the wounded Parliamentarians looking in their direction, and Roy rose hurriedly and joined his mother, feeling as if he were playing false.

They finished their round of the place, and then went out into the corridor to talk.

"Don't speak about our disaster, Roy," said Lady Royland, clinging to his hand. "We must bear it, and your father cannot blame us for our reverse. There, I shall be busy here, and we must be thankful that we have fallen into the hands of General Hepburn, whose kindness and consideration are far more than we could have expected. He has only one fault—he is an enemy."

"Then you don't blame me for feeling as if I half liked him, mother?"

"We can like the man, Roy, without liking his principles," said Lady Royland, calmly. "Come and see me as often as you can; I shall generally be here, but I suppose you can come to my room sometimes."

"I suppose so," said Roy. "I believe I am to keep mine."

"Yes; General Hepburn told me you should; but, Roy, you will be careful."

"What—about trying to retake the place?"

"It is impossible, my boy. But I did not mean that; I meant about encountering that man—no, he is not a man," she cried, with an angry flash of her eyes. "He has taken possession of the library and the state-room, for he made a bargain with our enemies that his reward for delivering up the place was to be that he should retain the estate afterwards."

"And they wanted the stronghold put down, and agreed," said Roy. "Yes; I pretty well know all, mother. Of course you have heard how he got the men in? All through my neglect?"

"Yes, Roy! No, Roy, there was no neglect! We could not know of that communication."

"I did; but I could not find it. Oh, how that villain did cheat—"

Roy got no further, for his mother's hand was laid upon his lips, and they parted directly after, her last words being:

"Don't think of it, Roy; our position is a happy one compared to his. Even the enemy look upon him with disgust."

"And I was ready for a few moments to believe all he said," thought Roy, as he returned to the court-yard with a strong desire now in his mind, one which grew minute by minute. He only waited for a favourable opportunity to make his request.

Chapter Thirty One
Old Jenk's Mind is Troubled

Two days passed before Roy was able to ask what he wanted. For during this interval General Hepburn seemed too much immersed in affairs to more than give him a friendly nod when they met at meals. Men were being constantly sent out with despatches, and others came. Then the cavalry regiment was always going and coming, "sweeping the country," Ben said, when Roy sat talking by the old soldier, who was more injured than he would own to, and spent most of his time on a stone seat in the sun.

"Tchah! not I, sir," he said, peevishly. "My lady's got her hands full enough. We chaps know how to manage with clean water, fresh bit o' linen, and keep quiet in the sunshine, and natur' does all the rest. We're getting on right enough.—Eh, comrades?"

"Couldn't be better," said the corporal. "Soon be ready to begin again, Master Roy, when you see your chance."

Words like these, and a hint or two again and again from the sick men in the hospital, could not fail to set ideas growing in Roy's brain; but everything was confused and misty yet, and the time went on. Poor old Jenk crept up to the four men, and always had the sunniest spot in the corner given to him, and here he would settle himself, nursing his sword in his lap, and go fast asleep.

"Yes, sir," said Ben, one day; "you see he's so very old. I believe after all he's a hundred, and it's a honour to him, I say. Mean to live to a hundred myself if I can. But see how he sleeps; I don't believe he's quite awake more than three hours a day, and I dessay he'll just come to an end some time in his sleep."

"Poor old fellow," said Roy, softly, as he laid his fresh young hand upon the gnarled and withered fingers that rested upon the sword across the old man's knees.

"Ah, he has been a good soldier in his day, Master Roy, but it's rum how he can't see that he's not a fine strong man now! Why, you might really nigh blow him over, and all the time he keeps on talking about what he's going to do to Master Fiddler as soon as he gets a chance."

"What! he doesn't threaten to attack him?"

"Don't threaten, sir?" said Ben with a chuckle. "But he just do; and then he's going to retake the castle singlehanded."

"But he mustn't have a sword; he'll be making some trouble."

"Well, if he makes an end to Master Pawson, sir, I think he may just lie down and die at once like a regular hero, for he'll have done the finest thing he ever did in his life."

"Oh, nonsense, Ben! You and all of you must mind the poor old fellow does nothing foolish."

Ben growled and shook his head, for his ideas were not at all in accordance with his young master's.

"You need not look so sour, Ben," Roy hastened to say. "Master Pawson will get his deserts some day."

"Yes, sir," said the old soldier, sourly; "his sort generally seem to in this precious world. His deserts seem to be your father's fine old property to wallow in, and get fatter and rounder-faced every day. He'd better not go and sit and read big books belonging to your father atop of either of the towers when I'm nigh, sir, for I'll pitch him off as sure as he plays the fiddle."

The men laughed.

"Oh, you may grin," said Ben, "but I mean it. You know, I s'pose, Master Roy, as they've emptied his room and carried everything into your father's library,—fiddle and all. Oh, how I should like to smash that caterwaulin' thing!"

"I did not know it, Ben," said Roy, thoughtfully. "I keep away from there as much as I can. But I say, Ben," he continued, smiling, as he laid his hand upon the old soldier's knee, "your wound is hurting you a good deal to-day."

"Awful, my lad, awful; it's getting better, but it feels as if a hungry dog was gnawing the bone."

"I thought so."

"Why, how did you know, my lad?" said Ben, innocently.

"Only by your manner. But look here," continued Roy, "I want very badly to see that place where the enemy got in."

"Ay, and so do I, sir. I've lain awake at nights with that place worrying me more than my big chop as ought to ha' been well by this time. I don't understand it yet, only I expect as he let 'em in. So he filled all the long underground passages with the men, and got 'em there ready to go up the towers when the signal was given? I daresay he give it with his miserable squeak of a pipe."

"I'm going to ask General Hepburn to let me see the place."

"And he won't let you, of course. You'll have to give the sentries something, and perhaps they may."

"No; I'm not going to do anything underhanded, Ben. I shall ask the general himself."

"Oh come, I like that, sir," said Ben, derisively. "He didn't do anything underhanded along with Fiddler Pawson, did he?"

"Wound shooting, Ben?" said Roy, drily.

The old soldier chuckled, and the boy rose and went straight to the general's snug quarters in a little place adjoining the dining-room to prefer his request.

Chapter Thirty Two
The Way in and the Way out

The sentries challenged Roy as he went along the corridors, and it made his heart ache for this to take place in his own old home; but as he was passed on directly, he drew himself up, went to the door, knocked, and the general's deep hard voice cried, "Come in."

General Hepburn was seated at a table writing, but he threw down his pen as he saw who it was, and smiled.

"What can I do for you, my restless prisoner?" he said.

"I want you to give me a pass for the sentries, so that I can go and examine the passage through which you brought your men that night, sir."

"Why? What for?"

"Out of curiosity. Isn't it natural, sir, that after being here all my life, and then tricked like that, I should want to know how it was done?"

"Yes," said the general, abruptly; and he took up his pen and wrote something upon a piece of paper, swept some pounce over it, shook it, and gave it to his petitioner. "You can go and see it."

"And take Sergeant Martlet with me, sir? He was my lieutenant and adviser."

The general snatched the paper back, wrote in a line, and once more handed it.

"Yes," he said; "but I must be strict, boy. You will have a sergeant's guard with you all the time."

"Of course," said Roy; "but I am not going to try and escape to-day."

"No," said the general, smiling, and taking up his pen again; "you are not going to try and escape to-day."

As Roy went away, the guard was being changed, and the place rang with the tramp of men, the officer on duty visiting the different posts and examining everything in the keenest way.

"Ah, they're doing it right enough, Master Roy," said Ben; and the lad started, for he had not heard the old sergeant's approach. "Taking a lesson?"

"I was watching them, Ben."

"Ah, and if they warn't enemies, and taken our place, I'd say the general was a thorough good soldier, and knew what he was about."

"You do think that, then?" said Roy, who was glad to hear his own ideas endorsed.

"Course I do, sir. I growled and grumbled because I'm sore; but it does one's heart good to see the fine discipline, and the way in which they work our guns. He didn't seem very clever at managing his horse, but I s'pose he was right, for sorry am I to say it, he's made the castle twice as strong as it was, and only by having his men in such order."

"Yes; everything goes like clockwork, Ben," said Roy, sadly.

"Better, sir; clocks get out of order; garrison like this don't. A man or two may go wrong, but there is always more to take their places. We did our best, and was very proud of it, sir; but it's one thing to have three trained soldiers for your garrison and to make it stronger out of such men as you can get together, and another thing to march in as many as you can make room for, and all well-drilled. There, it's of no use to grumble, sir; we did wonders.—So the general won't let you go and see the fox's hole?"

"Yes, he will, Ben. I have the pass here to present to the officers on duty."

"Why didn't you say so before?" cried Ben, sharply. "Come along, then, sir. I wouldn't go and say anything to them yonder, because they might feel a bit jealous."

Roy nodded, and followed by the old sergeant he walked straight to the guard-room, presented his paper, feeling all the while how strange it was to have to ask permission in his own old home. But he had no time for thought. The officer promptly called out a sergeant, and selected four men, and with them for guard, Roy and Ben led across the court to the entrance of the north-west tower.

Roy felt eager and yet depressed as they passed in, the sergeant leading and going up the spiral stairs to Master Pawson's old room, which was partly dismantled now, and the furniture left just sufficient to provide seats and a table for a dozen men who used it as a second guard-room.

"You don't know the way out and in by this passage, then, sir?" the sergeant said.

"No," replied Roy, who was examining the walls. "I have no idea where it is. Surely it can't be here?"

"Take a look round, sir; perhaps you'll make it out."

Roy did look round—an easy thing to do in a round chamber—but the door, the one large cupboard, the locker in the window, and a broad oaken panel over the mantelpiece were examined and in vain. The last took his attention the most, looking as if it might be a low door-way, and sounding hollow; but he could make nothing of it, and he fell to examining the wainscot in other parts and the floor boards.

"Better give it up, sir," said the sergeant, smiling. "I don't suppose any one would find it out unless it was by accident. Shall I show you now?"

"No," said Roy, who was on his mettle; and he examined the whole place again, beginning with the locker in the window, opening an oaken box-like contrivance in which lay a few of the soldiers' cloaks for which there was no room on the nails and hooks lately driven into the wall.

But after a quarter of an hour's keen search, Roy gave it up.

"I am wasting time," he said.

"Yes, sir," said the sergeant; "but, as children say at play, you were burning more than once."

Roy felt disposed to renew his quest, but he refrained, and the sergeant went to the casement window, and as Roy watched him, opened it till it stood at a certain angle, which allowed him to thrust down a pin and secure it—a simple enough thing to do, and apparently to keep the wind from blowing it to and fro.

"That unlocks the trap-door, sir," said the man. "If you open it more or less, it doesn't act. Look here."

He opened the lid of the locker, and turned a catch over it to keep it from shutting down again, then threw out the cloaks.

"Now pull up that end, sir."

Roy took hold of the panelled oaken side of the locker on his left, and to his astonishment the end of the coffer-like affair glided easily up, bringing with it one end of the oaken bottom; while the other end, turning upon a pivot on the middle, went down, laying open a square shaft going at a slope apparently into the thickness of the wall.

Roy uttered an ejaculation of wonder, while the sergeant struck a light, lit a lantern, got feet first into the locker, and let himself slide; and they saw him descend a dozen feet at an easy slope, stand upright, and hold the light for them to follow and stand by him in a narrow passage with an arched roof.

"Easy enough, when you know how," said the man.

"Ay, easy enough, when you know how," growled Ben, while Roy examined a short, stout ladder hanging from a couple of hooks by the arched ceiling.

"For going back?" he said.

"Yes, sir," was the reply, as the sergeant moved forward a few steps to allow his men to follow, which they did as if quite accustomed to the task.

The narrow passage ended at the top of a spiral staircase just wide enough to allow a man to pass along, and down this he went with a light, the others following, till they had descended to a great depth.

"Hundred steps," growled Ben, as they stood now in a square crypt-like chamber, with a pointed archway in the centre of the wall at one end.

"There you are, sir," said the sergeant, holding up the lantern, "cut right through the stone. It's as dry as tinder, though it does go straight under the moat. Isn't it strange that you didn't know of this?"

"Strange!" cried Ben, taking the answer out of his young master's lips; "why, I didn't know anything about it myself. I mean, where it was."

Roy was silent, for he was thinking of how easily the passage could have been blocked, or a few men have held it against a host.

"Want to go any farther, sir?" asked the sergeant.

"Farther? Yes!" cried Roy, excitedly. "I want to go right to the end."

"Long way, sir, and it's all alike. It comes out in the old ruined place at the top of that little hill."

"Yes, I suppose so," said Roy. "Lead on, please."

The sergeant went forward with the light, and Roy followed, whispering to his companion as they went along.

"Oh, Ben, if we had only found it out!"

"Ay, sir. If we had only found it out; but it wanted a man like Master Pawson."

"Why, Ben," cried Roy, who had a flash of inspiration; "he must have found out about it in one of those old books from the library, one of those which tell about the building of the castle."

"Why, o' course, sir!" growled Ben; "and you, with all those books to look at when you liked, and not find it out yourself."

"And I know the very book," cried Roy, "and have looked at the pictures in it scores of times. But, I remember now, I have not seen it since that wretch has been here."

They had to increase their pace, for the sergeant was striding along over the fairly level floor, which had doubtless been lately cleared, for the lantern showed where portions of the arched roof had shaled off, though much of it was in almost the same condition as when it was laboriously chipped away with the mason's hammers, whose marks were plainly enough to be seen.

"Seen one bit, we've seen all, Master Roy," said Ben at last in a disgusted tone; "but it don't want a trained soldier to take a castle if he's got a way in, made ready for him like this."

But they proceeded, and went right to the end, which was carefully masked in the ruin of the old chapel. But some time before they reached the other opening they were challenged, and Roy felt no surprise on finding a strong body of horse bivouacked in the ancient ruin.

On the way back to the castle Roy gleaned a few facts from the sergeant, which only, however, endorsed those already gathered,—to wit, that the ex-secretary had been holding communications with the enemy for some time before they came to terms, visiting the camp again and again at night, and eluding the vigilance of those who tried to follow him, dodging, as he always did, and then doubling back and reaching the ruins where they were not watched. It was not until General Hepburn had realised that it would be a very long and tedious task to reduce the castle, and only to be achieved at the cost of much bloodshed, that he, after communication with headquarters, came to Pawson's terms, and then the result was immediate.

Roy's first step on returning was to seek Lady Royland and tell her of his visit, at the same time asking her opinion about the book, which she remembered at once.

"Yes," she said, at last; "if ever we find that book again, we shall read the story of our ruin there."

Chapter Thirty Three
Roy hears the Simple Truth

A month had passed, and the prisoners knew nothing of what was going on in the outer world. Now and then rumours floated to Roy's ears through different channels of how matters progressed in the country, but they were rumours which, Lady Royland pointed out, could not be trustworthy. One day it would be that the king was carrying everything before him, and that the rebellion was nearly stamped out; while on another they heard that the Parliamentarians held the whole country, and the king hardly had a follower left.

The moat embraced the world of the prisoners during their captivity, and they knew what went on within its enclosure,—little else.

"We must wait patiently, Roy," said Lady Royland.

"Yes, mother," he replied, with a smile full of annoyance; "we must wait, but I can't do it patiently. In the old days I could fish and climb after the jackdaws' nests, and make excursions, and read; but I can't do any of those things now. I only seem able to think about escaping."

"Well, my boy," said Lady Royland, sadly—one day when Roy said this for perhaps the twentieth time, and she looked at him with a pained expression in her eyes—"I know how hard it must be for a young bird to beat its wings, shut in by a cage. Escape, then. You may be able to find your father. But at the least you will be free."

Roy thought of Pawson's words about his father's death, but mentally declared it was a lie like the other assertion, and burst out into a mocking laugh, which made his mother look at him wonderingly.

"Escape?" he said. "I say, mother, do you know I've often thought how easily I could get on to the ramparts, slide down a rope, and swim across the moat."

"Yes, I am sure you could," she said, eagerly, but with the pain in her eyes growing plainer. "Well, it would be bitter for me to part with you, but go."

Roy laughed outright once more.

"Why, you dear, darling, silly old mother!" he cried, flinging his arms about her neck, and kissing her; "just as if I could go away and leave you here. I should look a nice young cavalier when I met my father—shouldn't I?—and he asked where I had left you. No! I'm only grumbling like old Ben does about being shut up, though General Hepburn does treat us very well."

"Yes; no gentleman could behave to us with more consideration, my boy."

"But why doesn't father or the king, or some one of his officers, come and attack this place? All this time gone by, and the general here seems to hold the country for miles round, and all the gentry are friendly to him. Do you know Parson Meldew was here yesterday to see the beast?"

Lady Royland looked at him wonderingly.

"Well, I can't help calling him that. He is a beast, and he lives in a den. No one seems to associate with him. I believe he hates the general, but the general told me one day that Pawson was not good enough to hate."

"Don't mention his name in my presence," said Lady Royland, sternly.

The conversation came to an end, Roy walking off into the court-yard, a garden no longer, to see a squadron of horse drawn up before starting upon some reconnoissance.

They rode out to the sound of the trumpet; and as the horses' hoofs echoed on the lowered bridge, and mingled with their snorting and the jingle of the accoutrements, Roy felt his heart burn within him, and the longing to be free grew almost unbearable.

As the drawbridge was raised again, a grunt behind him made the boy turn sharply, to face the old sergeant, who had come up, his step unheard amidst the tramping of the horses as they passed over the planks.

"Sets one longing, sir, don't it?" said Ben.

"Ay, it does," said Roy, sighing.

"'Tick'larly at your age, sir. Why, I almost wish my wound hadn't got well. It did give me something to think about. If I go on with nothing to do much longer, they'll have to dig a hole to bury me."

"Nonsense, Ben!"

"No, it aren't nonsense, sir; for you see I always was a busy man. Now there's no armour to polish, no guns to look after, no powder-magazine to work at, and no one to drill. I'm just getting rusty, right through to the heart."

"But you've been weak and ill, Ben, and a rest does you good."

"No, it don't, sir. Does t'others good; and thanks to my lady and the doctor, every one's got well 'cept Sam Donny, whose leg is reg'lar twissen up like, and as if it would never come straight again. Seems queer, too, as a wound uppards should affect him so downards."

"Oh, he'll be right when the war's over."

"When it's over, sir? But when will that be?"

"Ah! I don't know, Ben," said Roy, with a sigh. "But there, don't fret. Take it easy for a bit, and grow strong."

"I am strong, sir. Strong as a horse—but do I look like the sort of man to take it easy? I've sat on that bench in the sun warming one side, and turning and warming the other side, till I've felt as if I hated myself. It aren't as if I could read. Begin to wish I could now, not as I ever knowed much good come out o' books."

"Why, Ben!"

"Ah, you may say 'Why, Ben!' sir, but look what books'll bring a man to! Look at that there Fiddler Pawson. Shuts hisself up even now, doing nothing but read, and only comes out o' nights, and goes prowling round the ramparts like an old black tom-cat. You can often hear the sentries challenging him."

"Oh, that's it, is it?" said Roy. "I've heard them challenge some one when I've been watching the stars."

"What business have you watching the stars o' nights, sir?" said Ben, sourly.

"Can't always sleep, Ben, for thinking."

"Humph!" growled the man. "Howsoever, sir, I do live in hopes."

"Yes; so do I."

"Ah, not same as me, sir. I lives in hopes o' one o' the sentries making a mistake some night."

"And shooting him, Ben?"

The sergeant winked, nodded, and rubbed his hands.

"Only wish they'd put me on duty, sir."

"You wouldn't shoot him, Ben, if they did."

"Then I'd save the powder and bullet, sir, and pitch him into the moat, same as the enemy did a lot of our chaps—all them as didn't jump—but they all got safe over, I suppose."

Roy began to walk up and down with his companion, passing the other prisoners from time to time on the wide bench in the corner; while old Jenk sat on the mossy stone steps at the foot of the sun-dial in the middle of the court, one arm nursing his sword upon his knees, the other embracing the lichen-covered pedestal against which he rested his head—no bad representation of old Father Time taking a nap.

"Wish I could sleep like he does," growled Ben. "Nothing to do. Won't let me help any way. Tried to have a go in the armoury, but that sergeant as went through the rat's hole with us grinned at me and turned me out. Pah! I hate him! He's reg'lar took my job out o' my hands."

"Patience, patience, Ben," said Roy.

"Don't believe there's any o' that stuff left in the castle, Master Roy. What do you think they're doing?"

"I don't know. What?"

"Got big stones and mortar down in the hole in three places, ready to build it up. Done it by now, perhaps."

"How do you know?"

"Sergeant told me. Grinned at me and said they didn't mean to have any one go out that way, nor yet come in at twelve o' clock at night."

"Indeed!" said Roy, to whom this news was troublous, interfering as it did with sundry misty notions in which he had indulged about retaking the castle, or all making their escape.

"Yes, sir; that general aren't a bit of a fool. Wouldn't be at all a bad officer, if he was on the right side. That other chap wouldn't be a bad sort o' sergeant either, if he knowed his duty to his king and country. But there's going to be a fight some day 'twix' him and me."

"Nonsense! While we are prisoners we must behave ourselves, Ben."

"Oh, must we, sir? What call's he got to get grinning at me? I'll make him grin the wrong side of his mouth if he don't look out."

"Yes; you are getting rusty, Ben," said Roy, merrily.

"Then why don't you make some plan, sir?" whispered the old sergeant in an earnest whisper. "Let's make a bold stroke for it, and retake the castle. Think of what your father would say if you did. Why, if the king was to hear of it, he'd be that pleased, he'd send for you to the palace and make a knight of you at once."

"Poor king!" said Roy, sadly. "Perhaps by this time he has no palace to call his own."

"And he won't have, unless some of us shows we've got the right stuff left in us."

At that moment they were passing the sun-dial, and old Jenk started into wakefulness, rose, shaded his eyes, and stared at Roy.

"That you, sir?"

"Yes, Jenk."

"So it be. How are you, Master Roy—how are you? I've been thinking a deal about you, sir. Don't you be downhearted; just wait a bit, and you'll see."

"See—see what, Jenk?"

The old man shook his head and smiled in a cunning fashion.

"You wait, sir, and you'll see," he said; and he sank down again, laid his head against the pedestal, and went off fast asleep.

"Yes, Master Roy, you'll see, and before many months have gone by," said Ben, solemnly. "Poor old Jenk! He's been a fine old soldier, and a true follower of the house of Royland."

"He has, Ben."

"And he's going to be the first prisoner set free."

He gave Roy a meaning look, and they separated, the lad to pass the other prisoners on the bench, and return their salutes as he went on to the private apartments and made his way to his own room, to sit down by the open window to try to think out some way of ending their captivity by turning the tables on the enemy.

The day was warm, the thinking hard, and at last his brain refused to work any longer at the task of trying to do an impossible thing, the result being that Roy suddenly opened his eyes after dreaming that some people were talking angrily in his room while he slept.

But as he lay back, staring, and seeing that the room was empty, a familiar and very stern voice came in through the window with these words, uttered in a perfectly unimpassioned voice, but one which suggested that against it there was no appeal:

"I have listened to all you had to say, Master Pawson, and all your complaints. Now, hear me: and you had better take my advice, with which I shall conclude. In the first place, in accordance with my instructions, I concluded that iniquitous bargain with you."

"Iniquitous, sir?" cried Pawson, in his highly-pitched voice, which now sounded quite a squeak.

"Yes, iniquitous. What else do you call it to sell your honour for the sake of gain? Iniquitous, treacherous; it is all that, but war made it a stern necessity that we should listen to your proposals. You kept to your terms; the new government will keep to its bargain. You will retain the castle and estate, but there was no question of time. I shall hold this place as a centre as long as we find it necessary. You can stay here or go till we have left. If you stay, take the advice I gave you. Go to your room, and stay there always, save when, like some unclean beast of prey, you come out to prowl at night. For, though your life is safe, I tell you that there is not a soldier in my force who does not look upon you with contempt. In future, sir, if you wish to make any communication to me, be good enough to write."

Roy would have shrunk away, so as not to listen, but these words filled the room in the silence of that afternoon, and the general's retiring steps were plainly heard, followed by a low hissing sound, as of some one expiring his pent-up breath.

Then a soft, cat-like step was heard, and Roy said to himself—

"It seems as if Master Pawson's punishment has begun."

Chapter Thirty Four
The Use of a Powder-Magazine

Roy found, as the time glided on in his monotonous life, that Ben's news was correct. General Hepburn was determined not to be surprised by any party of the Royalists who had learned from the fugitives that such a passage existed; and to make assurance doubly sure, he was about to build up the tunnel in three different places; but on second thoughts he did otherwise, setting his men to work to carry kegs of powder to some distance from the castle, placing them in a suitable position in the tunnel, and then, after making a fuse of several yards in length, having a tremendously strong wall built up across the place, leaving a hole just big enough for the fuse to pass through.

This was all done very quietly, Roy supposing that the men were merely building. Then a few days were allowed to pass for the cement to settle and harden before the fuse was fired.

The fact was known one morning at breakfast, when a terrific roar made Roy rush from the table and up to the ramparts, in full expectation of seeing a battery of guns just opening fire on the castle.

"Yes, it is," he panted to himself as he looked over towards the chapel hill, and saw the smoke rising from a mound of earth.

But in a few minutes he knew the truth from one of the officers who challenged him for coming there, and went back to breakfast with his appetite gone, for he felt that one of the means of escape was completely sealed up, and the night would never come when he could, with the help of his friends, lead Lady Royland through the passage on their way to liberty.

"And a good thing, too," he said bitterly to the old sergeant, for the grapes seemed to be very sour. "I don't want to escape. I wouldn't go if the way were open, and I'm sure my mother would not leave our own old home. Why, it would be like giving it all to Pawson, and I'll die before he shall have it in peace."

"'Ray, 'ray, 'ray, 'ray!" cried Ben, softly. "Can't shout it out as I should like to, Master Roy. That's the right sperit, sir. We won't never give up, come what may."

Old Jenk passed them just then, muttering to himself as he tottered by, and paying no heed when spoken to, while the various sentries treated him as a kind of amiable old madman, who was licenced to go about as he pleased, being perfectly harmless.

Another day passed, and Roy was walking up and down in his favourite part of the court-yard thinking of when he should ask General Hepburn for a written permission to go about on the ramparts, for the officer had spoken rather sharply to him after he had run up on the occasion of the blowing up of the tunnel.

But he did not ask the general, for the events that followed came one upon another so quickly that the matter passed out of his mind.

For all at once, just as Ben was coming slowly up to him, one of the sentinels shouted to the officer of the guard below, and word was passed to the general that a dragoon was galloping up along the road as fast as he could hurry his horse along.

A few minutes later, in the midst of a little excitement, the man drew rein at the outer gate-way, held up a packet in answer to a challenge, and as soon as the drawbridge was lowered, he dismounted and walked his horse over, for the poor beast was terribly distressed, and the rider appeared exhausted.

Roy stood eagerly watching, for this evidently meant something important, otherwise the messenger would not have nearly ridden his horse to death, the poor beast standing drooping in the middle of the court-yard; while the man, whose face was blackened with dust and sweat, and disfigured by a broad strip of plaster which extended from high up among the roots of his closely-cropped hair on the left temple down to his right eyebrow, leaned heavily on the sun-dial and asked for water.

The general read his despatch carefully twice, and then turned to the messenger to question him in a low voice, looking at him searchingly the while.

"Did General Braxley give you this despatch to bring?"

The man straightened himself up, but reeled and snatched at the sun-dial again from weakness.

"No, sir; to my comrade. We met a vedette of the enemy, and had to make a running fight for it till he went down, and I snatched up the despatch and came on."

"How far from here are the enemy?"

"About five-and-twenty miles, sir, I should say."

"In what direction?"

"Towards Exeter, sir. I did hear say that the king was with them."

"Hah! And how strong are they, do you suppose?"

"'Bout four hundred horsemen, I heard say, sir; but it was only what my comrade told me."

"Go into the guard-room and get some refreshment," said the general, after reading his despatch carefully again.

The man turned to go, and just then his horse fell heavily, the blood gushed from its nostrils as it gave a few convulsive struggles, and then lay dead.

The messenger went to its head, sank upon one knee, as Roy joined the group around, bent lower, kissed the poor animal's brow. Then he drew his sword, cut off a piece of its forelock, thrust it into his wallet, and amidst perfect silence, followed one of the men to the guard-room, hanging his head, while Roy longed to go and shake him by the hand.

The next moment the silence was broken by the loud blare of a trumpet, and a gun was fired from the gate tower.

Roy had directly after a specimen of the general's military capacity, for by the time the court was filling with armed men, one of the sentinels on the north-west tower announced the coming of the squadron of horse that had been camping by and in the ruined chapel; while, within half an hour, the troop in the castle rode out, each bearing a foot-soldier upon the crupper of his saddle,—the squadron without waiting to take on an equal number themselves. The general meanwhile sat upon his charger conversing in a low tone with the officer he was about to leave in command.

Just then, looking very weak and ill, the messenger came hurrying out of the guard-room, putting on his steel cap.

He waited till the general approached, and Roy was near enough to hear what was now said, the man speaking in a husky voice.

"Beg pardon, general; will you give orders for me to be supplied with a fresh horse?"

"What for?" said General Hepburn, turning on him sharply.

"To go with you and join my regiment."

"No; stay here. Captain Ramsay, if there is any ruse being practised, as soon as you hear that disaster come to nay party, place that man against the wall and have him shot."

The dragoon raised his hand to his cap in salute; and as soon as the general had ridden out, he staggered more than walked to where the dead horse lay, and took its head into his lap, to sit gazing sorrowfully into its reproachful-looking, glazing eyes.

"I'm a tough old chap, Master Roy," whispered Ben, "but my eyes are so watery I can hardly see; and if that orderly warn't an enemy, I'd just go and shake him by the fist."

Unconsciously the old sergeant had exactly expressed Roy's own feelings; but the next minute all show of weakness and sentiment had passed away. The trooper turned from the lookers-on, giving the horse's neck three or four pats, and then began to unbuckle headstall, and take off bridle and bit before unbuckling the girths, rising and taking hold of the saddle, giving it a sharp snatch to drag it free. But he had to put his heavily-booted foot against the horse's back, and tug several times before he could get the girths from beneath the heavy weight.

Then, throwing the saddle across his arm, and picking up the bridle, he turned to the nearest sentinel, asked a question, had the low archway pointed out which led into the basement used for stabling, and disappeared down the slope.

"Oh, my lad, my lad," said Ben, softly; "what a chance if we'd got anything ready!"

"What—to surprise?" said Roy, as he watched the portcullis re-descending, and saw the drawbridge begin to glide up directly after.

"That's it, sir. They're as weak as weak here now, with all them gone, and we're nine strong men, for Sam Donny could fight in spite of his twissen foot."

"There's nothing the matter with Sam's foot, Ben; it's all sham; I've known it from the first."

"What?—So much the better, then."

"So much the worse, because we can do nothing. They are still a hundred strong."

"Nay, sir—not above eighty."

"Ten to one, Ben. I'd do anything, but we have no arms."

"Take 'em from them, sir."

"Rash folly, Ben. I'm soldier enough now to know that it would be like throwing away your lives."

"Humph!" growled Ben; and the officer now in command came up and said, firmly—

"Now, Master Royland, I am sorry to seem harsh with you, but, saving at meal-times, when I shall be glad to see you, I must ask you to keep your chamber till General Hepburn returns, and hold no communication whatever with your fellow-prisoners."

"Very well, sir," said Roy, majestically.

"And you, sergeant, go to your fellows and keep with them. You can have an hour in the court-yard every day under guard. March!"

Ben saluted and went to where the corporal, Sam Donny, and the rest were seated on the stone bench in the sun, spoke to them, and they all rose and went through the door-way close at hand; while Roy bowed to the captain stiffly and went through to the private apartments, and thence to his own room, where he shut himself in, and soon after heard a sentry placed at his door, a piece of routine that had for some time been discontinued.

"How suspicious!" muttered Roy. "But no wonder! He doesn't mean to be caught napping. More didn't I, but I was. No chance of him having the same luck."

He went to the window, and the first thing he saw was the dead horse being dragged towards the gate-way, where it was left to wait till the bridge should be lowered again.

"Poor thing! How roughly they are using it!" he thought. "Can't feel, though, now."

Then his attention was taken up by seeing old Jenk with his white hair and beard streaming, as he tottered here and there in the sunshine, looking excited and without his weapon.

"Why, they've taken the sword away from the poor old fellow," thought Roy. "How absurd! It will make him half-mad, if it hasn't done so already."

But in a few moments the old man sat down on the pedestal of the sun-dial, and his head drooped on his breast.

Beyond him, just visible at the foot of the slope and outside the stables, Roy could see the Roundhead trooper, bareheaded and stripped to his breeches and shirt, rolling up his shirt-sleeves and beginning to clean his horse's harness. But something which seemed to be more important took the boy's attention the next moment, and that was the figure of Master Pawson upon the ramparts, walking up and down in the sunshine, this being the first time he had been visible by daylight since the general's stern words.

"Taking advantage of his being away," thought Roy; and he was about to shrink back to avoid being seen, but his pride forbade that, and he leaned out and amused himself by parting the thick growth of old ivy, and thinking how easily he could get down into the court if he liked.

"And that wretch could climb up while I'm asleep and kill me if he liked," he thought, with a slight shudder, which he laughed off the next moment as folly.

Dinner was announced in due time, and he was half-disposed not to go; but he joined the officers, and obtained permission from the captain to visit his mother's room to tea.

"Oh, yes," said that officer, quietly. "I do not wish to be too hard upon you, Royland, only I cannot have you conspiring with your men to retake the castle now we seem weak."

So Roy spent a pleasant evening with his mother, and in good time returned to his own room, heard the sentry placed outside, and then sat in the summer evening, trying to see the men stationed opposite, and upon the towers, from his open window.

It was a very dark night, hot and promising a thunderstorm, the air feeling so close that, when at last Roy retired, he left the large window wide open.

"No fear of Master Pawson playing any tricks," he said to himself with a laugh as he undressed and lay down, wondering whether the general was going to attack some place, being in perfect ignorance of everything but the fact that he had gone on some expedition.

He fell asleep directly, and lay breathing hard till, in the midst of an uneasy dream, he was awakened suddenly by feeling a hand pressed upon his mouth.

Like a flash through the darkness he saw everything: Master Pawson had climbed up to his window from the court, entered silently, and was about to strangle him as he lay.

But before he could attempt to resist, a pair of warm lips were pressed upon his brow, and then glided to his ear to whisper—

"Roy, my boy, not a sound! Don't speak! It is I—your father."

The lad's breast rose as a great sob of joy struggled to his lips, while his hands seized that upon his mouth, pressed it closer, kissed the palm, and were then passed round the neck of him who knelt by his bed.

They did not stay there a moment; for one began to feel the face, and the other was passed over the head.

No moustache and pointed beard, no long flowing curls, only stubble and short hair, and a long patch of plaster extending from the hair about the left temple to the right eyebrow.

Roy's mental eyes were opened; he saw it all now. At last! His gallant father had risked his life to come to them in the disguise of a Roundhead trooper, and the general must have been sent on a fool's errand so that the castle could be captured again.

Thump, thump, thump! went Roy's heart as these thoughts rushed through his brain. Then the lips at his ear said, and it sounded strangely incongruous—almost mocking:

"Go on snoring as you were, so that the sentry at your door may hear."

Roy obeyed, and imitated the real thing as well as he could.

"Your mother? If safe and well press my hand."

The pressure was given, and the whisper went on through the snoring.

"Roy, I have come at great risk through the accident of the capture of a messenger with a despatch. The general has gone where he was desired, but we have had time to take our men in another direction. To-night two hundred Cavaliers will have ridden in as near as they dare, and then one hundred and fifty will have dismounted and marched silently under cover of the darkness opposite the gates.—Snore, boy, snore!"

Roy had ceased his hard breathing, but his heart worked harder than ever, and he snored again; while Sir Granby went on:

"Tell me how many of our men you have here; where they are; whether the guard in the gate tower can be mastered while the bridge is lowered and the portcullis raised. Tell me everything you can, with your lips to my ear. My men must be waiting by now."

Roy went on snoring, for the sound of the sentry pacing to and fro came plainly through the door. But Sir Granby took up the hard breathing, and Roy placed his lips to his father's ear and whispered—

"Nine good brave fellows, but they are in the lower hall, and sentries are placed over them.—They are all unarmed.—Guard-chamber and turret-stair are carefully guarded.—At least ten men in the portcullis-room and furnace-chamber.—Impossible to get in that way!"

Sir Granby's lips were at his son's ear directly, and he said—

"I heard a legend when I was a boy, that there was a secret way into the castle, but it made no impression, and I never recalled it till I heard that the place was taken. Don't tell me that the enemy surprised you through that?"

"Must," whispered Roy; and anticipating that his father would suggest using the same means, he continued: "Can't use it now; all blown up. Is there no other way? Can't you scale the ramparts?"

"Impossible, boy. I must leave you, then. My life will be forfeit when the colonel returns, and it is too valuable to my king, my men, to you and your mother, to be thrown away."

"But how can you escape, father?"

"By reaching the ramparts and plunging into the moat. Good-bye, boy. Tell your mother I will return soon with as great a force as I can; for this place must be retaken. There—Heaven be with you! I dare not stay, for it may be hours before I can reach the ramparts."

"But is there no other way, father? A hundred and fifty men, and no way of getting them in!"

"Unless the drawbridge can be lowered and portcullis raised—none!"

A deep silence, only broken by the pacing of the sentry outside, and Roy dreaded now lest the change of men should take place, and the door be opened to see whether the prisoner was safe. He tried all he could to think out some plan, but every one seemed mad; and it was horrible to be so near success, and yet to fail.

"It is of no use, boy; we are wasting time," said Sir Granby, as Roy clung to him. "It would be mad to try any other way, and spilling precious blood. Good-bye!"

Roy tried to say the words in return, but they would not come; and, thoroughly unnerved in his despair, he clung to his father's neck till he felt himself repelled; and then the way of escape from their dilemma came.

In one instant a flash which vividly lit up the whole chamber darted in through the open window, and a deafening roar followed.

But it was not the breaking of the storm, for the next moment they realised that the magazine below the opposite range of buildings had been blown up, and the crumbling down of masonry, and the roar and crash of falling stones, endorsed the idea.

"Hah!" cried Sir Granby, excitedly; "then there is a way!" And hardly had the words passed his lips when a distant huzzaing was heard, and without a moment's hesitation he sprang to the window and lowered himself down.

Chapter Thirty Five
How the Castle came back to its Owner

Shrieks and cries for help mingled with the blast of a trumpet and the trampling of feet, as Roy hurried on his clothes, his first thought being not to follow his father, but to reach his mother's room, though, in the confusion of brain from which he suffered, he felt that he could explain nothing about the cause of the explosion. All he could think was that by some means the Cavaliers must have contrived to gain access to the powder-magazine. But how?

That was a mystery.

While he hurriedly dressed, he could hear orders being given, and the guns which had been brought in and planted beneath the gate-way being dragged into the middle of the court, and planted where they would command the terrible breach in the castle defences; for, by a flickering light, which was now rising, falling, and always gathering in intensity, Roy could see that a large portion of the eastern side of the building was blown down, leaving a tremendous gap. The stabling, corridor, hospital-room, and servants' and other adjacent chambers, were gone; and as he gazed across from his open window, the light suddenly blazed up, brightly illuminating the ruin, and showing the garrison busily preparing for their defence.

It was time; for, as Roy paused for a few moments, hesitating to leave the scene which fascinated him by its weird horror, the Royalists were crossing the half-filled-in moat, scrambling, wading, helping each other, and cheering madly. There was no formation; they were forced to come on straggling as they could, but a fierce enthusiasm filled their breasts, and they literally swarmed into the ruins, and climbed here and there among the flames and smoke.

Fully expecting to be stopped, Roy opened his door; but the sentry had been summoned with those from the towers and ramparts to defend the great gap, and Roy passed on to his mother's room, entered without stopping to knock, to see her surrounded by the women-servants at the window, their faces lit up by the flames rising brighter and brighter from the ruins.

Lady Royland did not hear her son enter, but turned and caught his hands as he ran to her.

"Roy!" she cried, wildly. "What does this mean?"

"Our turn at last, mother," he said, wild with excitement. "Look,—look at them, the Royalists; they've blown down that side, and father is there with two hundred Cavaliers!"

"Roy!" she cried, hysterically.

"Yes," continued the lad, as he forced himself to the front, and gazed out; "look, mother; nothing stops them. Hurrah! More and more, and—"

The roar of one of the guns from the middle of the court drowned his words, and there was another roar, but the effect was little. The guns were discharged point-blank at the storming party climbing on the ruins; but they were scattered like skirmishers, and the gun-fire did not check them in the least. To Roy it only seemed that they dashed in more furiously, swarming, by the light of the blazing ruins, like bees; and before the guns could be reloaded, the Cavaliers were upon the defenders of the place, and a desperate hand-to-hand fight commenced.

Roy turned excitedly to his mother.

"Stop here; keep the women with you, and don't go near the window; there may be firing;" and, even as he spoke, shots began to ring out.

"Stop! Where are you going?" cried Lady Royland, clinging to him.

"To release our men, and help my father," said Roy.

Lady Royland's hands fell to her sides, and the boy darted out of the room and along the corridor, full of the idea that had flashed into his brain.

Away to the end he ran unchallenged, turned to the right, and without meeting a soul, reached the north-east tower, listening to the shouting and clashing of swords in the court as the desperate fight went on, his way lit by the glare from the flames in spite of the dense, heavy smoke and the choking fumes of exploded gunpowder which rolled along the passage.

With his heart beating wildly for fear he should be too late, Roy dashed down the spiral staircase to the basement, and the next minute he reached the door of the lower hall, which formed the men's prison-chamber.

The sentries were gone, and he thrust back the bolts and turned the ponderous key.

"Ben! Corporal! Donny! All of you—quick!"

"Ay, ay, sir. You're only just in time, for we're most smothered. What does it all mean?"

"Don't talk! Follow me—guard-room. Enemy all in the court."

He led the way back, the men literally staggering after him, half suffocated as they had been by the fumes of the powder, the explosion having been so near their prison. But they revived moment by moment in the pure air, and growing excited by the sounds that reached them from the court-yard, they followed on along the lower passages till they reached the crypt of the south-west tower, passed on to the stairway at the base of the gate tower, and ascended unchallenged to the great gate-way, where Roy dashed into the untenanted guard-room, and the men rapidly armed themselves with weapons from the racks.

"Ready?" said Roy, in a whisper.

"Yes," came in a deep, excited growl.

"Back, then," cried Roy, "and we'll attack them in the rear."

He ranged his men in the shadow, the combatants being wildly engaged amid a blaze of light, which prevented the movements of Roy's little party being seen; and he was about to lead them back through the great corridor to where they could dash out suddenly and make their diversion in the rear, when Ben suddenly laid his hand upon the boy's arm, and ran to one of the narrow slits of windows in the guard-room.

"Trampling of horses," he whispered, as he peered out, the glow upward now lighting the other side of the moat. "General's men coming back, sir. Take us up into the portcullis-room, and we must defend that and keep it and the furnace-chamber to the death. They must not come in."

Roy grasped the position, knowing well enough that as soon as the defenders knew of the return of their friends, they would admit them, and the Cavaliers would suffer defeat.

Giving the word, he dashed up the spiral followed by his men, and as they stood ready to defend the place to the last, and keep bridge and portcullis as they were, he stepped up into the window and thrust out his head, to see dimly a body of about fifty horsemen, who galloped up to the edge of the moat.

"Halt!" shouted their leader. "No good: impossible. We must ride round, dismount, and join Royland through the breach. Forward!"

"Halt!" shrieked Roy with all his force in his cry, and then in a voice he did not know as his own, he yelled out, "Royland! Royland! God save the king!"

The effect was electrical. His words were answered by a loud "hurrah!"

Roy looked back from the window-splay.

"Friends!" he panted. "Ben, up with you, and lower the bridge;" and as the old sergeant sprang to the staircase, followed by five more, the others seized the capstan-bars and began to hoist the portcullis; while, sword in hand, Roy stood on the narrow stair, determined to die sooner than an enemy should pass.

But the next minute the bridge was down, with the defenders in ignorance of what was going on; the first knowledge they had of what was to come being given by the thunder of the horses' hoofs, and a deafening cheer as the Cavaliers dashed in.

That charge decided the fight, for in less than five minutes, in spite of the officer's desperate valour, the defenders broke and fled, to take refuge in corridor and chamber, from whence they could fire upon their enemies.

But, half-mad now with excitement, and flushed by the certainty of victory, the Cavaliers, headed by Sir Granby Royland, went in pursuit, chasing the Parliamentary party through the passages, never giving them time to combine, capturing knot after knot, and forcibly driving the rest below, where, feeling that all was over, their captain ended the carnage by offering to surrender. Then the triumphant Cavaliers gathered in the court-yard, waving hat and sword in the bright light of the burning building, and raising the echoes with their shouts.

It was about this time that Roy, followed by his little party, sought out his father, to find him at last, busy, like the careful soldier he was, stationing men at the towers, and then arranging for a proper defence of the great gap in the castle side, though temporarily it was now well defended by a line of flames that no man could pass.

Roy gazed in dismay at the blackened, blood-stained man, bleeding from two fresh wounds, and was ready to wonder whether this was the gallant, handsome cavalier who had left the castle to go on the king's service so short a time before.

"Ah! my brave, true boy!" cried Sir Granby, catching him by the shoulders; "old Martlet tells me how you led them to open a way for our friends. It was the work of a good soldier, Roy. You'll be a general yet. What do you say?" he continued, with a laugh; "as I am now? There, everything is safe for the present. Where is your mother? Am I fit to see her, though?"

Roy said nothing, but clung to the hand that grasped his; and a few minutes later Sir Granby was locked in his wife's arms.

By this time a strong party had been formed to attack the flames; and as there was an abundance of water from the moat, the day broke upon the quenching of the last burst of fire, and revealed a sad scene of desolation, the side of the castle on the east being one long hollow range of burnt-out buildings, saving the hospital-room, which had escaped, with a wide gap of tottering and piled-up ruins where the magazine had exploded, hurling great masses of stone into the court-yard and the moat.

The fire mastered, Sir Granby commenced forming a rough breastwork of the stones, using for the most part all that could be dragged from the moat, the Cavaliers wading in and working like labourers to strengthen the breach, which towards evening began to look strong with the rough platforms made for the enemy's three heavy guns. The work was so far completed none too soon, for just at dusk a body of men was seen approaching in the distance, and General Hepburn soon after appeared, to find that he had been outwitted in turn, and that a long siege would be necessary before he could hope to be master of the place again.

That long siege followed; and at last, weakened by loss of men and reduced from want of food, the Cavaliers were unable to combat the terrible assault delivered by the little army that had gradually been gathered about the walls, and the castle fell once more into the hands of the Parliamentarians, who were generous enough to treat the gallant defenders with the honours they deserved.

"But they would never have taken it, Roy," said Sir Granby, "if that gap had not been blown out. I'd give something to know how it occurred. Could it have been done by that villain Pawson out of despite?"

It was long before the truth was known, when, after years of exile with his wife and son, Sir Granby Royland returned to take possession of his ruined castle and estate. For the young king had ridden into London, and his father's defenders were being made welcome to their homes.

It happened during the excavating that went on, while the masons were at work digging out and cleaning all the stones which would be available for rebuilding the shattered side, that Sir Granby wrote a letter to Captain Roy Royland, the young officer in the body-guard of his majesty, King Charles the Second. The letter was full of congratulations to the young man on his promotion, and towards the end Sir Granby said —

"I have kept your mother away from the work going on, for I have been afraid that the digging would mean the turning over of plenty of sad mementoes of that terrible time; but, strangely enough, these discoveries have been confined to two. You remember how we wondered that Master Palgrave Pawson never showed himself again, to take possession of the place he schemed to win, and how often we wondered what became of poor old Jenk. Well, in one day, Roy, the men came upon the poor old man crouched up in a corner of the vault, close to the magazine. From what we could judge, the powder must have exerted its force upward, for several of the places where the stones were cleared out were almost uninjured, and this was especially so where they found old Jenk. The poor fellow must have been striking his blow against his master's enemies, for, when the stones were removed, he lay there with a lantern and a coil of slow-match beneath, showing what his object must have been in going down to the magazine. The other discovery was that of the remains of my scoundrel of a secretary. They came upon him crushed beneath the stones which fell upon the east rampart, where, perhaps you remember, there was a little shelter for the guard. Master Pawson must have been on the ramparts that night, and perished in the explosion.

"Come home soon, Roy, my lad; we want to see you again. They ought to give you leave of absence now, and by the time you get here, I hope to have the old garden restored, and looking something like itself once more. The building will, however, take another year.

"Roy, my boy, they bury soldiers, as you know, generally where they fall; and your mother and I thought that if poor old Jenk could have chosen his resting-place, it might have been where we laid him. As you remember, the old sun-dial in the middle of the court was levelled by the explosion. It has been restored to its place, and it is beneath the stones that your grandfather's faithful old servant lies at rest.

"Ben Martlet begs me to remember him to you, and says it will do his eyes good to see you again; and your mother, who writes to you as well, says you must come now. My wounds worry me a good deal at times, and I don't feel so young as I was; but there, as your mother says, what does it matter now we can rest in peace? for we live again in another, our own son—Roy."